ORPHANS ASCENDING

Written by Leon Webber.

Part one of a trilogy.

FIRST PRINTING, September 2024.
Harry Markos, Director.

Paperback: ISBN 978-1-916968-84-4
eBook: ISBN 978-1-916968-85-1

Book design by: Ian Sharman

www.markosia.com

First Edition

Little Rosa hadn't stopped thinking about the look in Henrietta's eyes as she watched her from the bedroom window. Her best friend had glanced up for a moment, her face all forlorn, before being herded with her parents into the back of the dirty green open top truck, to join the other sad faced people huddled together in the cold early morning light.

It was Saturday, the day when they always played out, but not today. Today Henrietta's eyes were wide and sorrowful. She was confused, uncertain, frightened about what was going to happen next. All Rosa had been able to do was stand at the window from the safety of her room as she witnessed Henrietta's mother and father trying to shield her from the evil faced men all dressed in green who prodded them like cattle with their big guns. Shoving them towards the truck along with the other families, one soldier had stepped into their path to stop them, tearing Henrietta away and lifting her up in his arms to the horror of her parents, their protests abruptly cut short by the swift intervention of two other soldiers who dragged them away and forced them into the vehicle. With a broad toothy smile, the soldier then passed her up teasingly to her terrified looking mother, arms outstretched, frantically snatching Henrietta into her bosom to the loud amusement of her captors.

It was then that Rosa heard a sound above the muffled commotion outside that she knew she would never be able to forget. It was a woman's shrill scream, but from where it came, she could not see. She pressed her face to the cold pane of glass, trying to pinpoint that sound, and then she saw them, more soldiers crowded around in a circle like children witnessing a playground fight, but she could not see the woman, she could only hear her pleading voice.

'Rosa, what are you doing?' Looking around, her stern faced mother stood in the doorway. "Come away from the window this instant," she commanded, already halfway across the room.

'But they're hurting her mama,' Rosa protested.

'Right now I said,' her mother insisted, taking her firmly by the arm.

'But can't you hear her, the woman outside?'

'I don't hear anything,' her mother lied, a strange panic rising in her voice.

'She's screaming, why is she screaming mama?'

'You're imagining things.'

'No I'm not, look,' Rosa protested, turning back to the window as the screaming continued below outside, but her mother did not look because she already knew what was happening, instead wrenching her away from the window, Rosa yelping with pain as her mother's grip on her arm tightened like a vice and she found herself being dragged across the room towards the door and downstairs to the cold damp larder at the rear of the house where she was ordered to sit still and keep quiet until she was told she could come out, her mother closing the door behind her hard with a decisive thud to serve as a final punctuation mark to end proceedings. Sat on the cold wooden stool Rosa stared at the wall, noticing that the shelves seemed much barer since the last time she had been shut in the naughty room. She normally drifted away during these hours of confinement where she would run away from home, but today she could only think of Henrietta and where she was being taken, perturbed that her best friend had never said anything to her the day before about going away when they had played snakes and ladders in her room.

When the door eventually opened and she saw her mama stood there, she noticed something was different in her expression from the last time she had been released from the naughty room.

That familiar forgiving smile was missing, instead her mama's expression was drawn and strained, like an elastic band about to snap. Without a word her mother simply turned and went back into the kitchen, Rosa standing up and following her, closing the larder door behind her. It was at this moment that Rosa, her obsession with learning the truth about her friend overriding everything else, made the mistake of speaking and worse, of asking the very question that her mama had for the last hour been secretly praying she would not as she took her anguish out on kneading the dough for a loaf with her strong hands. She had tried to prepare herself for the question, determined not to lose control, but an overwhelming panic brought on by the horrific events unfolding right on their doorstep over recent months had taken their toll and her nervous predisposition she knew was about to get the better of her.

'Mama?' Rosa asked, her mama's hand freezing in mid motion back at the kitchen table where she had returned to her kneading, deliberately stood with her back to the larder door so she wouldn't have to look at her daughter. Hearing Rosa speak, she kept that way, desperately hoping she would be able to keep her composure if she could avert eye contact, but her hands began to tremble uncontrollably, and she felt her breathing involuntarily quicken. She decided not to answer, pretending she hadn't heard as she forced her hands back to work on the dough.

'Mama, why did those men take Henrietta and the others away?' Time seemed to stand still for her mama as she heard those words, ringing in her ears like a deafening bell, and she felt her body go rigid, frozen to the spot, then suddenly without warning her legs collapsed underneath her and she dropped like a stone to the cold stone floor and curled up on her side in the foetal position.

'Mama?' Rosa cried out, terrified. Her mama looked up her with an expression that was incomprehensible, a mixture of terror and anger she had never seen before and then she heard an animal wailing sound from her mama's lips, like the wounded dog Rosa remembered she and her father had found when they had been hunting a few months back. As her mama's cries of anguish became louder, slurred words began to form.

'Get out, get out,' her mama was moaning over and over, but Rosa just stood there confused. Suddenly her mama's moans turned into a hysterical rant as she screamed those same words again and again, faster and faster, until a terrified Rosa panicked and raced out of the kitchen and upstairs, her mama's deafening shrill voice seeming to follow her. Reaching the sanctuary of her room, she slammed the door behind her and ran to her bed to seek refuge under her Barbie Doll duvet, pulling it over her head and pressing her hands over her ears to drown out her mama's voice. After a few minutes Rosa nervously took her hands away a little and listened, her own heavy breathing the only sound. There Rosa stayed, hidden under the duvet, fearful that she would hear her mama's footsteps coming up the stairs. Soon she lost track of time and her mind drifted away, the indelible image of Henrietta's parting look turning over and over in her mind.

It was the sound of the front door opening downstairs immediately followed by the familiar deep jovial voice of her papa that awakened her from her trance and she realized she had been in bed for hours. Pulling the duvet down over her face she listened, her papa's usual happy to be home from a long day at work tone having turned to low slow murmurs of concern, interspersed with replies from her mama, her voice subdued yet still threatening to erupt into hysteria again. Then the voices stopped, Rosa's breathing quickening as she anticipated the inevitable. Moments later the heavy footsteps started on the stairs, but to Rosa's utter relief they were slow, not purposeful and her breathing immediately slowed. Throwing the duvet aside she sat upright on the edge of her bed, her excited eyes transfixed on the door. She held her breath as her papa's footsteps stopped just outside the door for what seemed like an eternity, before it opened slowly, and his tall imposing form appeared. He was a big man, over six feet with broad shoulders, his long arms ending in large, weathered hands down by his side. He had a rugged complexion framed by a wide jawline, but there was a relaxed gentle kindness in his eyes and his posture, somewhat out of place with his burly physique.

Tonight however, Rosa could not help but notice there was a moment as they locked eyes and smiled at each other, that his expression faltered, his smile fading and his eyes narrowing into a sad frown, but then it was gone and her papa was back, all smiles and bright eyed. Then, without even knowing, she was running towards him across the room as he bent down to take her in his arms, and she felt the warmth of his strong embrace and the familiar way he always smelt of sweat and oily machinery after a long day in the factory.

They sat together on the bed side by side as always when he came home. He smiled at her with those kind reassuring eyes, instantly recognizing that familiar subdued look in hers, and waited patiently for her to speak, already knowing what she was going to ask.

'Papa, where have all the other people gone?' Rosa finally prompted in a concerned tone.

'They've gone on a special holiday,' came his reply, feigning surprise at her worried delivery.

'But nobody said anything about a holiday, not even Henrietta.'

'Well, that's because it was a surprise,' he countered excitedly, taking her hands in his.

'But there were men with guns all dressed in green and some of them were crowded around a woman, and she was screaming,' Rosa persisted.

'She wasn't screaming, she was shouting, they were just playing a game, that's all,' he lied, all too familiar with the sadistic pleasures that these troops saw as their right of passage.

'A game, what kind of game?' Rosa replied, her eyes lighting up.

'It's where they put you in the middle of a circle of people and you have to escape by pushing them out of the way,' he elaborated with a well-rehearsed deftness.

'That sounds like lots of fun, I want to play that game,' Rosa said, her excitement palpable.

'And you will, but you have to wait for Henrietta to come back from her holiday first, or she'll be upset that you didn't include her in the game, does that sound fair?' he persisted, looking into her disappointed eyes, anxious to bring the topic to a conclusion.

'I suppose so,' Rosa finally conceded defeatedly.

'Now give your papa another hug,' he begged, arms outstretched again. Flinging her arms around him she did not see his expression, his eyes filled with fear as he struggled to fight back the tears.

'Your mama and I love you very much, you must always remember that,' he said softly in her ear. Rosa had never heard her papa speak like that before, neither had she felt his embrace so tight and for so long, so tight in fact that she found herself struggling to breathe.

'Papa,' she gasped, his grip immediately loosening as he realized.

'I'm sorry, I didn't mean to hurt you,' he offered apologetically, kissing her on the forehead. 'Now come downstairs, your supper will be ready soon,' and with that he got to his feet and made for the door.

'Papa?' Rosa called out, just as he passed under the doorframe. He turned, forcing that patient smile of old.

'When will Henrietta be coming back?' she enquired optimistically, the question catching her papa off guard.

'Soon my little sweetheart, very soon,' he lied again, this time a sickening feeling of guilt rising up inside him as he spoke those words with as much sincerity as he could summon. 'Now don't be long, you know how your mama gets angry when you let your supper get cold,' he added, quickly turning away, praying there would be no more questions, at least for now.

'Will we be going on a holiday as well soon?' That question sent a shiver up his spine and for a long moment he was paralysed, unable to speak.

'Yes, I'm sure we will,' he replied, his voice emotionless, monotone, this time not turning around, certain she would know he was lying if she saw his face, and he had to fight his every instinct to keep from breaking down into tears there and then, realizing the morbid absurdity of those words even before they left his lips.

The atmosphere around the dinner table that evening was something Rosa had never experienced before. Her mama never spoke a word and seemed far away as she picked at her stew, her appetite clearly diminished. Rosa couldn't understand why she would not look at her, evading her daughter's gaze. At first Rosa thought she may still be angry from earlier, but her mama had never held out forgiving her for this long before. Her papa had noticed her mama's demeanour and as Rosa watched them exchanging silent glares across the table, she knew something was very wrong. Anticipating that Rosa was about to pipe up and undoubtably send her mama off the deep end for the second time that day, her papa asked her if she would like to go rabbit hunting with him that weekend, elaborating on the route they would take through the woods to the clearing overlooking the lake, where they could sit and eat their lunch. At this her mama's mood changed, glancing at Rosa reassuringly for the first time that evening, the faint suggestion of a forced smile as she touched her hand before willing herself to eat her stew.

They sat together watching television after dinner, warm in front of the wood burner, the orange flame reflected in the screen. Her parents were both thankful for the distraction that Rosa's favourite program created for her and as she sat snuggled between them glued to the screen she was blissfully unaware that they were both deep in thought, their eyes glazed over with worry, faces frozen like stone.

After the television show and the daily ritual of Rosa kicking up a fuss about having to go to bed so early, she gave her mama the usual goodnight kiss on the cheek, surprised to then find herself in her warm embrace, sure that this was her mama's way of letting her know that all was forgiven. As Rosa climbed the stairs, her papa assuring her he would be up to tuck her in, she noticed her mama was smiling at her, following her every step, but there was something not right about her expression, reminding her of the fixed frozen smiles that she saw on the shop dummies when her mama took her shopping in the clothes store.

When her papa came to her room to kiss her goodnight not long after, Rosa was under the sheets, her arms atop, clutching her teddy, eyes fixed on the ceiling, still thinking about that expression on her mama's face. Entering her room and seeing the way she looked at him as he approached, her papa instantly realized with a foreboding dread that she knew something was wrong and in those few steps between the door and her bed he tried to formulate some kind of explanation for his daughter, for the first time finding himself struggling with the challenge. Sitting on the edge of the bed he looked down at Rosa staring past him blankly into space, waiting for her to speak, buying himself more time. Eventually she looked directly at him, her face full of worry.

'Papa?' she said, pausing, the familiar preamble to a difficult question.

'Yes sweetheart?' he invited in as calm a voice as he could muster, dreading her next words.

'Why is mama sad?' Rosa asked with a frown.

'Your mama is just a little tired, that's all,' he replied, desperately hoping his answer would be enough to reassure her.

'But she was angry with me for looking out of the window at the people outside,' she persisted.

'Your mama wasn't angry at you, she was angry because they were making so much noise,' came his rational reply.

'But why did she shout at me?'

'It wasn't you she was shouting at, not really.'

'But I don't understand?'

'Sometimes people get tired and frustrated and they just don't know what to do, so they shout at the first person they see, but they don't mean it, not really.'

Rosa pondered those words, her papa searching her expression, praying that she would cease with her enquiry. After what seemed like an eternity, her eyes suddenly lit up as a mischievous notion came to her.

'Does that mean I can shout at anyone I want?' she exclaimed excitedly.

'No, it doesn't,' her papa laughed, mostly with relief. 'Now let's tuck you in with Thomas to keep you warm.'

Rosa lifted her teddy up so her papa could pull the sheets up over them both. He sat there looking down at her then for a long moment, his reassuring fatherly composure slipping for an instant.

'Please don't look sad papa.' Those words took him by surprise and he quickly forced a broad smile, his eyes beginning to well up.

'I'm not sad, I'm just a little tired like your mama that's all. Now it's high time that you went to sleep.'

'Alright papa, I'll go to sleep, but only if you and mama do as well.'

'Don't worry, we will.'

'Promise?'

'Promise, now go to sleep.' With that he kissed her on the forehead, lingering for longer than usual, before getting up to approach the door.

'Goodnight papa,' Rosa called out quietly as he reached for the bedroom light. He turned, putting on his bravest smile and praying it wouldn't be his last.

'Goodnight sweetheart.'

'Sleep tight, don't let the bed bugs bite,' Rosa chuckled.

'I won't.'

With that he flicked the switch, closing the door behind him, his footsteps fading as he descended the stairs. In the darkness Rosa closed her eyes and tried to sleep, but it wasn't more than a few moments before Henrietta's frightened face came to her again, silently calling out. Her mind drifted, visions of her best friend and her parents on holiday, playing in the sea on the coast, the other people from the truck around them, except that no one was smiling, the only laugher coming from the soldiers standing around.

With that image in her mind, she slipped away into a fitful sleep and dreamt that Henrietta was with her in the woods across the fields from their village. They were playing hide and seek, Henrietta playfully taunting her, her voice getting louder as she drew nearer to Rosa hiding in the hollow of a huge dead oak tree lying across a stream, its trunk as thick as she was tall. Then Rosa heard another voice crying out, a shrill echo from across the field that she instantly recognized. She found herself running across the field faster than she could comprehend, her feet barely touching the soil from which the brittle stumps of freshly harvested crop sprouted. In just a few moments she had reached the edge of the field, homing in on the source of that sound. It was coming from inside the familiar tall imposing barn of her homestead, one of the huge double doors partly open.

Not even conscious of sprinting to the door, Rosa found herself inside. Her papa was bailing hay at the far end of the dark cavernous barn, oblivious to the cries for help and the horrific spectacle being played out right in front of his eyes. The same men all dressed in green were stood in a circle laughing. It was the game that her papa had told her about, but glimpsing through the tiny gaps between them, Rosa suddenly felt her heart stop. Her mama was being held down, a few soldiers hungrily tearing her clothes from her body like savage wolves. Rosa could not understand why her papa could not see or hear what was happening, her mama calling his name over and over, louder and louder, until her voice was an exasperated cry.

Her mama turned her head, her eyes fixing on Rosa's as the first soldier lay down on top of her and her cries for mercy turned to high pitched screams. Rosa tried to run to her mama, but she could not move, her feet were stuck to the ground. She strained every muscle in her body to break free, desperately reaching out to try and stop the bad men, but it was no use.

A loud banging on the front door downstairs awakened Rosa from her nightmare and she salt bolt upright in bed, the ugly sound of raised male voices reaching her ears. She recognized her father's voice, calling out in a pleading tone as the other deeper voices shouted in a language she did not understand, the words all muddled up. The shouting got louder, reaching a crescendo as a cold rigidness gripped her body, but they were hurting her mama and papa and she had to help them. In the darkness of her room Rosa pushed back the duvet, her legs taking on a mind of their own as they swung off the edge of the bed and propelled her towards the closed bedroom door, her hand reaching up high, turning the handle to open it a fraction but freezing in mid motion as a loud bang startled her, her hand involuntarily dropping to her side. Her mama began shouting her papa's name over and over as the bad men laughed and Rosa couldn't understand why she could not hear his voice anymore. When her mama started screaming, that same shrill scream as she had just been hearing in her nightmare, Rosa knew what the men downstairs were doing to her. She tried to reach up with her hand to open the door again, but her arm was frozen at her side, just like her feet in the barn, and in that moment she prayed that she might still be in her nightmare. She would be safe if she just got back into bed, knowing that when she awoke it would all be over. Running back to her bed to scurry under the duvet, she pulled it over her head and pushed her hands as hard against her ears as she could, drowning out her mother's shrill cries, telling herself over and over that she would wake up any moment.

Then she heard a second bang, muffled by her hands but undeniably the same as the first. Against all her instincts, she forced herself to take her hands away from her ears. Her mother wasn't screaming anymore. A deafening silence rang in her ears and in that terrible moment the protective bubble of childhood innocence protecting Rosa abruptly burst around her, and she realized with a horrifying finality that she was not in her nightmare, but very much awake.

Hearing the thud of heavy boots coming up the stairs, Rosa began to sob as she buried her head in the pillow, the boots stopping right outside her door. Her panicked breathing was the only sound she could hear under her sheets as she trembled uncontrollably in the darkness. The door creaked open, and she heard the click of the old ceiling light switch. Biting down on her teddy's ear to stifle a scream as the boots approached and then stopped, Rosa sensed the weight of someone heavy sit on the bed and could not help letting out a muffled yelp as a hand tugged at the bedclothes above her head. She clung on for dear life in a futile attempt to stay hidden but the invisible force was too strong, pulling the duvet away, the cold air of the room making her hair stand up on end as she kept her face buried in the pillow, not wanting to see, but unable to escape the acrid stale sweat flooding her nostrils.

'It's alright little girl, you don't need to be afraid,' came a deep calm voice, much like her papa's when she used to wake up at night crying out. For an instant she saw his gentle face in her mind, before she realized with a chilling clarity that it couldn't be her papa because…

'Please don't hurt me,' she whimpered, trying to shrink away as a warm heavy rough hand stroked her hair.

'I'm not going to hurt you,' the voice replied in that same reassuring tone.

'What have you done to my mama and papa?' she begged.

'I haven't done anything to them,' came the quick reply, feigning surprise.

'But I could hear them screaming.'

'You were just having a bad dream, that's all. Your mama and papa are waiting downstairs for you.'

'No, it was real,' Rosa insisted.

'No, no, young lady, it was just a bad dream. I used to have bad dreams too just like you, when I was your age.'

'You did?'

'Yes, all the time.'

'What were they about?'

'It was always the same dream. I would be asleep in my bed and I would hear my mama and papa downstairs shouting and screaming, but when I woke up everything was so quiet and I would get out of bed and go downstairs, and guess what?'

'What?'

'They would be sat in front of the fire watching TV, like always.' The voice paused for a moment to let the comforting image sink in.

'Now why don't you show me how pretty you are?'

Slowly Rosa turned her head from the pillow, opening her eyes to see a shaven head, huge ebony expressionless eyes and a broad fixed toothy grin from ear to ear. She shrank away with a shudder as she noticed his familiar green army jacket.

'What's wrong?' the grinning mouth asked, surprised.

'You're wearing green, just like the bad men,' Rosa gasped.|

'What bad men?' came the quick but practised calm reply.

'The bad men from my nightmare.'

'But that was just a nightmare, remember?

Rosa frowned, thinking. Then it all came back to her. Her papa had said about the men dressed in green taking her best friend away with the other people on a holiday.

'Are you the same as the men I saw taking the people away?' she enquired, not comprehending the reason for the momentary falter in that toothy grin.

'Yes, but.'

'That's alright, my papa said they were taking them away on a holiday,' she interrupted excitedly.

'That's right, and that's where we are taking you and your mama and papa.'

'Are you, really?' she almost shouted with delight.

'Yes we are, but first you have to tell me your name.'

'No, you first,' she teased.

'But that's not fair, it's against the rules.'

'I'm not telling,' she persisted indignantly.

'But why?' he replied, feigning a hurt expression.

'First you have to tell me why you all wear green?'

'Because we want to look like the big, tall trees.'

'But that's silly,' Rosa chuckled.

'Is it, why?'

'Because the trees are much bigger than you.'

'But green keeps me warm, here give me your hand, I'll show you.'

'No,' she blurted playfully.

'Give me your hand and I'll tell you my name.'

'Promise?'

'I promise.'

Rosa's eyes narrowed for a moment as she pondered. Then she held out her hand, the enormous digits of her visitor clasping hers with a gentle but firm grip and guiding it towards him to touch the rough fabric of his jacket, the heat still permeating through from his not long distant physical activities bringing a smile to her face.

'You see, green keeps me warm.'

Rosa chuckled again before pulling her hand away as he relaxed his grip.

'Now you have to tell me your name,' she commanded.

'Alright, you win, my name is Vladimir.'

'I have an uncle called Vladimir,' she replied enthusiastically.

'And do you love your uncle Vladimir?' came his quick response, keen to capitalize on this opportunity to win her trust.

'Yes, he brings me lots of sweets.'

'Does he bring you chocolate?'

'Chocolate's my favourite.'

'Is it?'

'Yes.'

'Well guess what?'

'What,' she replied excitedly, her eyes following his other hand as it unfasted a breast pocket on his jacket.

'What do you think I've got in here?'

'Tell me,' she shouted.

'Not until you tell me your name,' he teased, Rosa screwing her face up before her hand shot out to try and take her reward, only to find Vladimir's hand guarding the hidden treasure. He waved a finger at her, tutting.

'Please, let me have it,' she begged.

'Not until you tell me your name.'

'Please.'

'Name first.'

She fell silent for a moment.

'It's Rosa,' she finally said, her hand darting towards his pocket again, a hurt look on her face as she tried in vain to prize his hand away.

'Rosa, that's a wonderful name, and how old are you?'

'Let me have it,' she protested.

'Tell me, then you can.'

'I'm eight,' she shouted.

Vladimir's hand dropped unconsciously to his side, his eyes suddenly taking on a distant expression as he felt Rosa's greedy hand grabbing the chocolate bar from his jacket pocket. He was far away for an instant in the place where the heavenly chorus of screaming young girls and boys filled his ears and every fibre of his body was alight with a surge of pleasure unlike anything he had ever known before the war had started. The sound of Rosa tearing the wrapping from the chocolate bar jolted him back and he found himself looking at her munching happily away, the pulsating in his groin beginning to fade. He checked his watch before returning his gaze to his prize.

'Now why don't you come with me, your mama and papa are waiting for you, and we've got lots of little girls just like you that you can play with.'

'Lots?'

'Yes, lots and lots.'

'Can I bring my teddy?'

'Of course you can, what's his name?'

'Tomas.'

'Hello Tomas,' Vladimir replied, reaching out to stroke the teddy clasped in Rosa's arm. She placed her ear to Tomas's mouth, listening.

'Tomas wants to know if my mama and papa will be coming with us?'

'Of course they are, now why don't you come downstairs with me, deal?'

'Deal.'

Waiting patiently for Rosa to get out of bed, Vladimir took her tiny hand in his, smiling down at her.

'Where are we going?' Rosa asked.

'To a very special place.'

'How special?'

'The most special place in the whole wide world,' Vladimir replied, leading her by her hand from the bedroom, Tomas hanging from her other hand down by her side. The dark landing outside leading to the stairs suddenly felt eerie to Rosa and at the top of the stairs she involuntarily froze as she looked down into the silent darkness, Vladimir immediately feeling her arm pulling. He looked down at her and smiled.

'Everything's alright,' he assured her.

'Where are my mama and papa?' Rosa replied, her tone apprehensive again.

'They're downstairs waiting for you, just like I told you,' Vladimir persisted with a hint of irritability, his patience beginning to wear thin.

'But why can't I hear them?' she protested, panic rising in her voice as she tried to pull away. Vladimir's grip tightened on her hand, making her cry out in pain. He had been in this situation many times before. The brighter children like Rosa were always more difficult to fool and sometimes he had to drop the pretence and adopt a different approach. Before Rosa knew what was happening, she was being dragged screaming down the stairs by her arm, Vladimir's grip on her hand like a vice. Halfway down the flight Tomas slipped from her other hand, and she glanced back to see him sat on one of the steps, looking down at her in a silent goodbye, just like Henrietta.

At the bottom of the stairs an acrid smell coming from the kitchen assaulted her senses. It was like the smell she and Henrietta always joked about when they talked about how their papas made the toilet smell first thing in the morning before they went off to work, but this was overpowering. Then Rosa was being dragged over the threshold into the kitchen and it was there, witnessing that sight, that she was propelled into a world beyond her comprehension. Then, her screams of protest abruptly stopped, and she began hyperventilating as she saw two trails of blood mixed with brown excrement on the floor joining at the open door leading outside. Powerless to break free from her captor's grip, Rosa found herself sliding along the cold stone floor, desperately trying with no avail to avoid the faeces and blood which she felt, still warm and sticky beneath her bare feet as she was dragged over the doorstep into the chill of the black night.

The cold air instantly numbed Rosa's senses, quickening the dreamlike state of shock that had already taken hold by the time Vladimir handed her to a waiting soldier who lifted her, limp like a rag doll into the back of the truck. Mercifully for Rosa she was too far gone to even notice the corpses of her mama and papa lying opposite her in an untidy heap, staring at her wide eyed. Neither was she aware of the soldiers sat either side of her, their greedy eyes filled with sordid thoughts as they touched her face and hair, laughing as they discussed what was to become of her.

ONE - BOSNIA 1992

Marko had never left his homestead, born and raised in a rural part of Bosnia on the border with neighbouring Croatia. He was a farm boy, his family going back generations to way before the second world war. They lived a simple life and he had grown up on the same family farm that had been his fathers and grandfather's childhood home before him. Even the bed that he slept in and the kitchen table that he ate at were originals, as old as the family name.

He liked the peace and tranquillity of the farm, the golden hayfields that they lived off, and loved watching the bright orange sunsets, the most glorious often occurring in the autumn months.

By temperament a quiet boy with a kind smile and warm brown eyes, his tall slender build hid a formidable strength, built up from years of working the land with his father. His body was all sinew with not an ounce of puppy fat, unlike the boys he went to school with, most of whom he was sure wouldn't be able to run for the bus in a few years without having a heart attack. Looking at himself in the long mirror he couldn't help but admire his own physique.

His grandfather he had been told had been an excellent amateur boxer in the days before gloves were introduced to the sport and legend had it was the only man in the region involved in this form of bareknuckle entertainment who could boast a straight nose. There was no denying that the old black and white family photographs portrayed a rather stern faced man with a mischievous glint in his eyes and remarkably unblemished facial features.

Marko had never met his grandpa, having long ago been told that he had died fighting in the war, although the true ghastly details of his final days had been kept from him.

Filip had passed the highly effective jab and hook combinations which he had learned from his papa onto his own son. Even at a very early age Marko was a true natural, inheriting his grandfather's lightning quick thinking in the ring that Filip seemed to have missed, already struggling to keep ahead of his own son's punches by the time he was just ten.

When the time came two years later to be introduced to the customary junior amateur boxing contests, Filip feared that the pressure of the environment of the ring with the noise of the crowds might come as a shock to his rather reserved son used to the quiet of the farm, but to his relief Marko took to the spotlight like a duck to water, lavishing the adrenaline rush in the ring. In his very first bout the referee, a work colleagues of his father's watched in awe as Marko knocked out his opponent with the first punch, a lightning swipe to the jaw with his left as he distracted with his right. Over the next two years Marko remained undefeated in his age group, managing with considerable ease to match his grandfather's prowess of avoiding the traditional boxer's broken nose. Such was his talent and rate of physical development that by the age of fourteen he was as tall as his father and was afforded the unprecedented honour of being allowed to fight opponents up to three years his senior. Very soon the very mention of his name was sending waves of dread surging through his older opponents, some as old as seventeen, who one by one were subjected to humiliating defeat in the ring.

Despite all the adulation and respect that came with his reputation, outside the ring Marko shied away from the spotlight, preferring to blend unseen into the background in public as he always had, resisting any urge to change from the conservative, quiet schoolboy into the cocksure, loud mouthed bighead that some of his schoolmates had become of late, none of whom had any achievements to even shout about. As a somewhat awkward contradiction of his fearless reputation in the ring, Marko came across as a quietly spoken, at times overly introvert and even vulnerable individual.

When the end of each school day came and most of his classmates went home to humdrum houses or drab apartments in the nearby noisy town filled with ill tempered, miserable faced people all hurrying about, Marko came home to the open space of the fields and the calming birdsong that never failed to sooth away the often stressful days in the classroom packed with mostly annoying, loud, pretentious and even taking into account their young age, overly insular colleagues.

Whilst he could never be accused of being workshy with his daily chores on the farm when he got home from class and also on the weekends, Marko hit the age of fifteen like most people his age with no clear idea about what he wanted to do as a profession or trade when he left school the following year. This lack of forethought was of course partly due to his parents never speaking to him on the subject, silently hoping he would stay on the farm and take over when they became too old to continue, like his own father had done. His mama Ana, a tall blond beauty with strong cheekbones and penetrating ice blue eyes, prayed that he would still be around when they needed taking care of, determined not to end up in one of those desolate, dank nursing homes that spelled a sure and certain speedy demise to the door of one's own maker. The farm was still turning over enough to keep the wolf from the door and so because his parents never talked about him getting a weekend job to help with the finances, Marko had no notion of money and more importantly the need of it to make one's way in the world.

Filip was a tall stocky giant of a man with a rugged face from years working outdoors all year round, but whilst he looked and moved in a way that indicated he was as strong as an ox, sometimes Marko would observe him when he wasn't looking, noticing him wince and grumble from the aches and pains that were beginning to catch up with him from too many harsh winters working outdoors. His mother too, he had noted of late, had begun to age more quickly, her once elegant upright posture giving way to slightly hunched shoulders and more laboured, less graceful movements. Ana and Filip had decided to keep her recent diagnosis of the onset of rheumatoid arthritis a secret from Marko and his sister Karla just under two years his senior. At the age of seventeen she was the exact vision of her mother at that age, a real head turner and she felt very fortunate to have a brother whose reputation preceded him to keep the local vultures at bay. Karla was very much the home bird like her mother too, but she was in no hurry to find a suiter, quietly confident of her striking beauty and happy to bide her time with her honour intact until the right man came along.

Partly because he had grown up with a sister, Marko didn't look at girls the same way that most of his school friends did, who by their age had little else on their mind other than being the first amongst their piers to shed the stigma of virginity.

He was without any doubt attracted to girls and had felt the stirring in his loins like all the other boys in his class, but he didn't fantasize about what they looked like under their clothes or feel the irrepressible urge to take himself in hand as soon as he got home from school every day. If anything, Marko's extracurricular interest lay in what existed outside of Bosnia. His parents had never taken them away on vacation, only local excursions, and at the age of fifteen he found himself restless to discover the rest of Europe, his curiosity initially aroused by his favourite geography teacher who would excitedly describe with almost cartoon like animated movements the landscapes and cultures of foreign lands accompanied by frequent slide projector sessions, the huge images and colours of great cities and spectacular landscapes bringing his words to vivid life on the screen.

These presentations not only fuelled Marko's desire to travel, but also gave meaning and perspective to the history lessons which for the entire year had been centred around the first and second world wars and their effects on Europe and its people.

By the time it came to the lessons on Hitler's rise to power and the almost effortless way that the Nazis had carved their way across Europe, devouring everything in their path, Marko was thoroughly enthralled, by this time desperate to learn what had happened in Yugoslavia. To his amazement however, their rather dry mouthed and constantly tired looking teacher made no mention of their homeland. For most of the class who were more interested in what they were having for supper when they got home than what had happened on their continent fifty years ago, this omission passed almost unnoticed, but for Marko this was something he could not let go of.

Enquiring at home, Marko experienced an unnerving reaction he had never witnessed before in his father. The mere mention of the subject froze Filip in mid motion as he bailed hay in the barn, his eyes instantly darkening, turning distant, as if being struck out of the blue by a traumatic memory that he had fought so hard and for so long to suppress. Then, seeing Marko stood in front of him with a nervous expression, he forced a sad smile, putting down his pitchfork and approaching, placing a reassuring hand on his son's shoulder.

'Your grandfather, and many like him, died fighting to keep this land our own, and he would never have wanted you to waste your youth thinking about what went on during that time,' Filip finally said in a slow and measured tone.

'But I want to know, it's important,' Marko protested.

'All you need to know is that we are free because of the sacrifice that your grandfather's generation made for us,' came his father's reply, this time his voice a little strained.

'Why did grandma never talk about grandpa?'

That question brought the same distant expression back to Filip's face and Marko immediately knew he had overstepped the mark. This time his father did not reply, his mind far away.

'I'm sorry, I didn't mean to.'

'It's alright,' Filip replied calmly, Marko breathing a sigh of relief. Then Filip was back in the present again, smiling at him. When he spoke again it was in his customary reassuring tone, but there was also a hint of warning in his voice.

'As you grow older Marko, you will learn that somethings that happen in this world are best left locked away, out of sight.'

'You mean forgotten?' Marko pressed nervously.

'No, not forgotten, just kept out of sight in the dark, never spoken of,' Filip replied with a familiar tone of finality that Marko knew meant no more questions.

'I understand,' Marko lied.

Filip knew that his son didn't understand, but that didn't bother him. What was of grave concern however was that he knew his son was with one hundred percent certainty, going to learn the true meaning of those very words, and moreover, it would happen very soon.

The very next day, Marko, the conversation with his father only serving to strengthen his resolve to discover the truth, found himself in the school library hunting for any mention of events in Yugoslavia during the war. He found an assortment of books on the second world war which all contained mention of Yugoslavia in the contents pages, but Marko was dumbfounded to find that in every one of the books he had selected, the chapters covering his homeland had been carefully removed. Taking the books to the counter, Marko reported the wilful sabotage to the familiar middle aged frumpy librarian with large round spectacles. Noticing the title of the top book in his arms, she made a not altogether successful attempt at feigning annoyance, sighing and cursing whoever those damn pupils were who were always vandalizing her precious books. Then, almost snatching the books from a somewhat stunned Marko's grasp, she placed them behind the desk and ushered him away, waiting for him to leave before placing them in the returns pile to be placed back in their rightful places on the shelves later.

This setback did not deter Marko however, and after school that day he decided to visit the much larger library in centre of town which he hadn't been to in such a long time. He knew that his parents would be expecting him home straight after school to help on the farm, but such was his desire to pursue what was by now spiralling into an obsession, he persuaded himself that he would be able to make up a plausible excuse for being late.

Sitting on a different school bus headed for the centre of town after lessons that day, Marko thought about those missing pages and how they had been removed with precision and care. Surely an unruly thieving pupil would simply have torn them out quickly to avoid detection, and anyway, why choose the sections on Yugoslavia. Something hadn't been right about the expression on the librarian's face when he had reported the obscenity and she had registered the subject matter. It was as if her reaction was rehearsed, like an actress on television. He had thought about asking one of the librarians at the town library for help in locating the relevant volumes when he arrived, but he worried that this might raise a red flag of some kind again, but for reasons that he couldn't yet fathom.

He edged forward seat by seat towards the front of the bus as pupils got off along the way so he would hear the driver he had spoken to, to shout when he arrived at his stop. By the time the bus stopped opposite the grand old town hall, it was mostly empty and as the door opened and the noise of the bustling town poured in, Marko felt a sense of trepidation, like a fly about to drown in the bottom of a glass as it fills with water. By sheer force of will his made his thighs act, standing up and crossing the empty aisle to step down onto the pavement packed with people hurrying about. The various jarring array of sounds around him seemed to amplify, closing in like snarling wolves about to pounce, and he had to close his eyes for a moment to regain his composure, preparing himself by imagining he was in the ring waiting for the ding of the first bell. He felt himself knocked off balance and opened his eyes, for a moment thinking he really was back in the ring. He caught the backward glance of a passing stocky male pedestrian with an annoyed expression and for a moment Marko's adrenaline raced as he half expected a confrontation, but his would be assailant kept walking, disappearing into the crowd. This random encounter, whilst most unfortunate considering Marko's already nervous state of mind, had at least gotten his pulse racing and he was now highly alert in boxing ring mode and ready to take on whatever challenge came next. Quickly scanning the street to get his bearings, he recognized the memorable features of the library a hundred yards away on a corner, having passed it on one of the rare outings to town with his father a few years back. The building stuck out from the adjoining structures in an odd, uncomfortable way, its exuberant architectural columns supporting ornate, intricately detailed arches at odds with the more traditional appearance of the surrounding shops and offices. The library even outshone what pretty much everyone in the town considered to be the most important local landmark, the foundation and pillar of the utmost prominence, the town hall stood on the other side of the street. It was as if the library's architect was making a rebellious statement, a blatant challenge to the complacency of the old traditional society, who's representatives sat at the seat of power, hidden inside their fortress, inaccessible to the population of the town, confident that the imposing, uninviting and somewhat oppressive structure would always be enough to stop the masses from questioning their authority. In comparison, the library, with its elaborate and somewhat delicate looking arches, provided an open, welcoming façade.

Stood at the entrance admiring the structure before him, Marko reflected on the architectural style of the library. It was highly appropriate he pondered, that a building containing all those books and harbouring all that knowledge, should present itself as inviting to those who were curious enough to want to learn, and so, with a hearty smile and a spring in his step, he entered.

The first thing that greeted Marko inside was the silence, not in itself surprising for a library, except that its intensity made him realize just how much the noise of the street had affected him. The quietness, away from the bustle outside, washed over Marko like a warm, soothing summer evening breeze back home on the farm, and he stood there for a long moment, closing his eyes as he soaked up the tranquillity of this new found sanctuary.

A deep voice roused him from his oasis. He opened his eyes, turning his head towards a tall broad shouldered man dressed in a dark suit with his back to him, stood speaking to a middle-aged wiry lady with greying permed hair sat behind a counter. He spoke in an authoritative yet rather hushed tone, the words barely audible as if he didn't want anyone else to hear. The librarian stared back at him as she listened silently, looking somewhat perplexed. Reaching into his inside jacket pocket, he handed over a neatly folded document which she opened with a sense of urgency, her eyes narrowing as she read. Then she nodded submissively to her expectant visitor, refolding the letter hastily and handing it back. Without another word or any other form of acknowledgement he pocketed the letter and turned on his heel, catching a transfixed Marko off guard. Locked in the suited man's stone-cold menacing gaze, Marko realized by his appearance and demeanour that this was obviously someone of considerable power and influence. They both stood frozen to the spot for a moment, before the stranger began marching straight towards him, his step surprisingly quick for a man of his bulk. Marko involuntarily stepped to the side as he approached, those piercing eyes seeming to bore into him, reading his every thought. The man kept Marko in his roving gaze as he passed uncomfortably close on his way to the exit, Marko not daring to turn and watch him leave. Low urgent murmurs drew his attention back to the counter, the librarian hurriedly issuing instructions that Marko couldn't quite make out to a young, slender assistant on the near side of the counter, who then almost ran down one of the numerous tall, long book aisles, disappearing from view.

It was at this moment that Marko was struck by a notion well beyond his unworldly years, his mind forming a logical link between events at the school library and his present location. Despite the urgency of the situation, he still managed, although be it with considerable difficulty, to resist the overwhelming urge to sprint in the same direction as the young assistant, instead walking as casually and inconspicuously as possible so as not to attract the attention of the librarian who had settled back to her duties behind the counter, her expression that of someone carrying the weight of the world on their shoulders.

As soon as he was out of sight of the counter, Marko half marched, half ran, locating the section marked European History after a frantic search across the end of the aisles. Consciously slowing his pace and breathing as he approached, Marko turned into the aisle to see the young assistant hastily loading her arm with books. He stood there for a moment, unsure of what to do, too late to avoid drawing her attention. She glanced at him, wide eyed with shock, like a deer caught in the headlights, before returning to her task, frenetically searching the shelves to pile further books onto her already straining arm.

'Here, let me help you,' Marko offered, drawing nearer, trying to see the titles of the books.

'No I'm fine, really,' she replied in a panicked tone, turning her body away to keep her selection secret and not wanting to make eye contact.

'But you'll drop them,' Marko persisted.

'I said I'm fine,' she almost shouted in a frightened tone that sounded more like a warning as she pulled out another book, this time carefully covering the title on the spine as she did so and flipping the book upside down to hide the cover, before abruptly hurrying away, cradling her heavy load close to her chest like a mother guarding her baby.

Alone in the aisle Marko inspected the areas where she had been busy, two chest high sections of the old wooden shelving covering both world wars, now partly empty. The assorted books pertaining to the many countries involved in those two conflicts were all there, all except Yugoslavia. Partly out of frustration but mostly out of his youthful impulsiveness, Marko decided the time had come to confront the librarian behind the counter head on as to the reason why the books he wanted had just been removed.

'The books you require are all out I'm afraid,' came the immediate dismissive reply from the librarian when he asked, not even looking up.

'But I saw her, the woman you were talking to right here. She took the books,' Marko challenged. The librarian sighed, looking up and fixing him with a cold stare, her pained expression reminding him of the maths teacher at school just before one of his many outbursts when pushed to the end of his tether with an unruly pupil.

'You must be mistaken young man,' came the curt but slightly nervous reply, her gaze faltering momentarily.

'But she was right here,' Marko persisted, his voice louder than he intended and attracting attention from a few of the other patrons as he scanned the area in search of the assistant.

'I'm going to have to ask you to leave now,' came the librarian's sharp response, her worried eyes following his as she picked up on the curious glances he was getting.

'Not until you explain why I can't have them,' he continued unthwarted, his somewhat commanding tone surprising himself as well as his host. With that she jumped to her feet with considerable speed, alarming Marko despite her small frame, her eyes looking as if they might burst out of her sockets at any moment.

'Go, now.' Marko had expected her to shout, but instead she spoke quietly in a low voice, her tone calm yet firm and authoritative. Marko hesitated.

'Please,' she begged, almost in a whisper, reaching out and touching his arm, her gaze now soft and maternal. In that moment Marko suddenly understood, and with an almost imperceptible nod he turned away to leave, the woman watching him for a moment before glancing around furtively, the other visitors now immersed again in their reading.

Arriving home over an hour late that afternoon Marko expected to receive a tongue lashing from his mother, but when he opened the ancient creaking door leading into the farmhouse through the kitchen, he found his mother sat at the kitchen table, staring at the wall, her face ghostly pale with eyes wide but blank, staring into the far distance, and she looked like she'd been crying. For a moment she did not seem to notice his presence, as if lost in a daze, but as he closed the door behind him, she startled, her head turning towards him. Bursting into tears she was up on her feet and rushing towards him before he had time to speak, flinging her arms around him and hugging him tighter than he had ever remembered.

'Mama, what's the matter?' Marko enquired as she sobbed on his shoulder.

'Oh my God, I thought something had happened to you,' she blubbered.

'Happened to me, what could have happened to me?' Marko replied, almost laughing, his dismissive reaction only serving to anger her. She stepped back from him, her teary face full of rage now.

'Don't you ever do that again, do you hear?' she shouted.

'Yes, but.'

'Promise me,' she pressed, this time more of a plea.

'I promise,' Marko replied instantly, realising but not understanding the distress that his seemingly innocent actions had caused. Then she was embracing him again.

'You're a good boy Marko,' she said softly in his ear, before kissing him on the cheek and releasing him from her arms.

'Things are changing Marko.'

'What things?'

'Things that it is best not to discuss.'

There was a finality in her tone more reminiscent of when he was a young boy protesting about some matter that would seem so trivial now, but on this occasion, it was the undercurrent of fear in her voice and the look of dread in her eyes that rang the alarm bell in his head, telling him it was time to stop asking questions.

'I'm sorry mama, I didn't mean to.'

'It's alright,' she interrupted, keen to bring an end to the conversation.

'Now quickly, there's bailing to do before supper, I'll distract your papa when he gets home to give you more time to catch up,' she commanded, her voice less strained, but the look of worry still lingering in her eyes.

Working up a sweat in the barn as he worked double quick to try and catch up, Marko thought about the events surrounding his new found curiosity, countless questions spinning around like a tornado in his head. His experiences at school with the history lessons and the strange incidents in the two libraries lent a new perspective to his discussions about his grandpa with his papa the previous evening, the conviction that everybody seemed to be wanting to cover up the events of the past, entrenching itself firmly in his mind. But why had his mama been so worried about him? What tragic event had she been envisioning in her mind that would force her into such a panic? As he powered away frantically with the pitchfork, his heart beating faster and faster, the notion suddenly came to him. Mama was worried about the present. She had foreseen that for some reason, another storm was coming, another conflict between men, a conflict that threatened the life of her beloved son. But what could her premonition be based on? What knowledge did she have of the past to prompt her to be fearful now? His rational mind kicking into gear in the same way that he would calculate his sequence of jabs and punches in the ring, Marko concluded that his mama knew things about events surrounding his grandfather's death during the war, perhaps savage, sordid things, the same things that his papa had been so keen not to talk about. Perhaps he hadn't died in the traditional heroic way always portrayed in the movies. Marko had already learnt about the Nazis and their malicious sadistic treatment of the Jews and other so called undesirables as they had rampaged virtually unopposed across Europe and as his imagination ran riot, the vision of his grandfather being captured and subjected to all manner of torture and humiliation before suffering an agonizing death formed in his fertile mind. Perhaps the children of all the other surrounding European countries were being deprived of the truth about the savage events in their own countries, just as Marko was in his.

His mind spun full circle, bringing him back to the question of his mama. Why now, decades after the end of the war, would she suddenly be fearful for his life? What event had triggered her panic? He stopped to take a breath, his heart racing fast like after a long workout on the punchbag, feeling the sweat running down between his shoulder blades. Looking up he saw the huge mountain of bailed hay and checking his watch he realized he had broken his record.

'Marko?' he heard his father call out, spinning round to see him stood by the door in his oily factory overalls, his eyes looking more tired than usual, his smile somewhat forced.

'Supper's ready.' He turned away then, instead of engaging Marko in the customary brief exchange on how each of their days had been, Marko instantly knowing something was worrying him. The train of thoughts in his mind still spinning, albeit it more slowly, he shouted out impulsively.

'Papa?'

Filip stopped in his tracks, frozen for a moment, Marko realizing all too well that his papa knew what he was going to ask. Then he turned slowly, as if having to will himself to do so, his expression strained. In the past when Marko was younger Filip would have pre-empted a difficult question with his usual fatherly smile and reassuring words, but today he just stood there waiting for Marko to speak.

'What's happening to our country?'

Filip didn't speak for a moment as he pondered his reply. Then, with a sad smile he sat on the familiar rest bench by the door where he had had so many meaningful conversations with his son over the years, enjoying the warm early evening summer breeze. He looked down and ran his hand over his favourite piece of grain in the oak, before looking up at Marko expectantly, silently beckoning him to join him, just like old times. Marko sat next to him, watching his father's face as he looked straight ahead, composing himself.

'Soon, very soon now, you will begin to see changes in the way people behave towards one another.' He paused, still not looking at Marko, almost as if he was afraid to.

'There is a history to our country that has remained quiet for many years, a dark stain that our people have tolerated ever since the war,' he continued, his voice laboured now.

'Is it something to do with what happened to grandpa?' Marko blurted out without thinking, his father visibly flinching at the question and looking down at the floor.

'Sorry papa, I didn't mean.'

'It's alright Marko, it's alright,' Filip interrupted in a reassuring tone, Marko looking down as he felt a firm hand on his knee. Filip was quiet for a long moment then, struggling for his next words.

He turned to look at his son, an expression in his eyes that Marko had never seen before. It was fear, genuine fear, but of what?

'Your sister is going to go away for a while, your mama and I have decided.'

'But why, I thought she wanted to stay living at home and continue with her job in town?' Marko asked.

'It won't be for very long, just until...' He trailed off, catching himself, but realizing it was too late now to avoid the inevitable.

'Until what,' Marko replied, his words reverberating like a deafening bell in Filip's head, Marko seeing his eyes glaze over for a moment before coming back into focus again.

'During the war, things happened that.' Filip stopped mid-sentence, hesitating, Marko's piercing eyes full of anticipation.

'Things happened that left open wounds when the war ended, wounds that have never healed.'

'You mean what the Nazis did,' Marko interjected, his tone of surety drawing a look of deep dread from Filip, but not for the reasons Marko thought.

'No, not just the Nazis,' he replied, his voice wavering.

'Who then?' Marko pressed, his tone a mixture of shock and confusion. Filip found himself torn at that moment, knowing his next reply could have profound effect on his son's perception of everyone he would meet from that point on in his life, especially those from ethnic origins other than his own. How was he supposed to explain to a fifteen year old boy that for decades a deep seated hatred had been simmering away under the surface of Bosnian society, a bitterness that had only been kept at bay because of the dictator government that had not permitted any talk of redressing the wrongs of the past. That dictatorship was now a thing of the past in what had been the former Yugoslavia, but whilst the nation had enthusiastically celebrated their country's emergence into the free world, this long-awaited political liberation also brought with it another freedom, that of the uninhibited desire to finally settle old scores. Filip had grown up under dictator rule, and whilst times were hard, there was at least peace between the ethnic groups that made up the country, albeit a peace that was forced upon the people by its rulers. By the turn of the last decade the unrelenting desire of the people had placed such pressure on the political framework, that the government finally gave in to the call for a referendum. Suddenly Yugoslavia was split into politically and militarily independent countries.

To young teenagers like Marko, this geographical fragmentation was of little interest, but to Filip it signalled the start of something that he feared more than anything. The feelings of hostility were barely palpable at first, certainly in Bosnia, but in Croatia, the long slender strip of land that separated Bosnia from the Adriatic Sea, the animosity gathered momentum quickly, like an unforeseen storm suddenly sweeping across the land. The catalyst that turned hostile words into actions came in the form of the military who silenced the newspapers to keep the outside world in the dark as to the savage campaign of atrocities they were about to embark upon. They had plenty of willing recruits in the form of civilian militia to bolster their numbers and like the sounding of a bell, the onslaught of ethnic cleansing had begun.

Like ripples in a pond, rumours began to spread across the border into Bosnia of strange goings on, of people being displaced from their homes, but few could comprehend the notion that what had started as the resettlement of the ethnic groups would quickly erupt into a relentless wave of brutality. With the Croatian media scattered to the four winds and any independent news reporter daring to try and alert the outside world considered fair game, the abominations taking place quickly gathered momentum unopposed. Even when the expression ethnic cleansing began seeping into the minds of neighbouring Bosnians, few were prepared to entertain the reports of the rape camps and the piles of civilian corpses rotting in the streets, and so, as it had been in Europe in the days immediately before Hitler's troops marched into Czechoslovakia, life continued as normal, with most of the population happily wrapped up in their blissful bubble of denial, ignoring the inevitable.

For a parent like Filip who knew what was coming, the agony of spending every waking moment worrying about what was to become of his son and daughter was starting to take its toll. There was some comfort in the knowledge that Karla at least would be safely tucked away with her aunt hundreds of miles away, but the certainty that the conflict would spread outwards inexorably in all directions in a wave of savagery brought home the realization that this measure was only buying time. If he told Karla the truth about why she was being sent away then it would only serve to sabotage his and her mother's efforts to save her, as like Ana, her stubbornness would compel her to stay by her mother's side. As for Marko, the dilemma was far more complex. Unlike his sister, he had yet to finish school, meaning there were no plausible arguments that they could put forward to fool him into leaving them, even for a short time. The fact that school would of course become a thing of the past as soon as civil order collapsed was of no use to Filip or Ana in their dilemma, as by this time all exits out of their country would be undoubtedly blocked, and the chance of persuading Marko to leave them, even if they could bring themselves to be honest about what was happening, was precisely zero. Such was the unpredictability about the speed with which the cleansing would begin, that Filip and Ana had deliberated the overwhelming temptation to send their daughter away immediately instead of allowing her to serve her notice at the lawyers office in town, but with the economy far from strong and this being her first job since leaving school, they were nervous about her leaving without a suitable reference to place her in good stead for the potentially prosperous employment she would find through her aunt's connections in the government, although in the light of the current situation the absurdity of that scenario existing in the former Yugoslavia was becoming clearer with each passing day. Fortunately, they both agreed on the way forward and united in their thinking, they were able to convince themselves that the remaining three weeks that remained of her notice period at the lawyers office would give her more than adequate time to leave before the borders were closed.

In amongst all of this careful planning, Filip and Ana had of course considered leaving everything behind and taking their children with them, but the momentary relief that that notion brought was quickly overshadowed by a stark reality of becoming a refugee in their own land, on the road and probably more vulnerable than at least having the security of four walls around them, although for how long they hadn't dared to speculate. And so, as every day passed, these two loving parents had to fight harder and harder to suppress their inner fears and keep up the pretence. Ana had forced herself to keep her meltdown that afternoon a secret from her husband even though she needed his shoulder to cry on more desperately at this moment than at any time in all the years they had been together, but to let slip about Marko's indiscretion after school would have brought out a side of Filip's personality that would only serve to heighten the already almost unbearable tension in the home brought about by the sordid secret they were keeping from their children.

'Papa?'

Hearing his son's voice again jolted Filip from his thoughts, and he looked at Marko gazing at him expectantly, instantly remembering the terrible question his son had asked moments before.

'Sometimes in this life Marko, it is hard to know who your real friends are,' he offered, already knowing that this would not be enough to quench his son's over zealous determination to get to the truth.

'But what has this got to do with..?'

'Sometimes in war, things get confused and twisted, bent out of shape,' Filip interrupted.

'What things?' Marko persisted.

At that moment Filip's expression changed. His eyes softened and he smiled at Marko in that same reassuring way that he always had when his son had been perturbed by something as a young boy and words of explanation had proved of little use. Marko recognized that look, one that he hadn't seen in a long while and as he gazed into Filip's eyes, he was suddenly hit by the notion that his father was silently pleading with him to stop asking questions, perhaps to protect him from the truth. 'It's alright Papa, it doesn't matter," Marko added hastily, not wanting to see his father in any more pain. Filip's whole being visibly changed as he heard those words, like a crushing weight had been lifted from his shoulders and he felt his eyes involuntarily begin to well up. Then Marko abruptly found himself in his father's embrace, Filip determined not to let his son see his tears.

'One day Marko, when you are much older, you will understand,' Filip said in a sub-conscious effort to unburden himself from the guilt that had been building up inside him for lying to his son.

'You're a good boy Marko, you always have been,' he quickly added to avoid Marko replying with another question. And with that, he released Marko from his embrace and was quickly on his feet, walking away so as not to let Marko see the redness in his eyes.

'Finish up here and come in for your supper,' he concluded, not looking back as he reached the open door, stepping outside.

The atmosphere around the dinner table in the kitchen that evening was noticeably different, at least to Marko. Glancing at his mother Ana he could tell that she was still upset from before, despite putting on a highly convincing brave face, and Karla and Filip were seemingly fooled at least, which was a relief to Marko. Filip as always asked the family to share their experiences of the day and as always Karla was the first to pipe up. She glanced a little warily at Marko, looking to her papa for the reassuring nod, before talking excitedly about her plans when she arrived at her aunt's, Filip and Ana's relief at her obvious enthusiasm palpable. As he watched his sister, it dawned on Marko how much she had become like her mama. It wasn't just that she looked exactly like Ana did in her wedding photo that stood proudly on the mantelpiece over the log fire, it was her mannerisms, even down to the way she flicked her long blond hair back when she spoke and chewed her lip when she was thinking about what to say next. What was odd to Marko however was that neither Karla nor Ana seemed in anyway sorrowful about their planned separation. Karla had always been inseparable from her mother as far back as Marko could remember, and it seemed strange that she seemed to have no regrets about leaving her mother's side, even if it was only for a short time. Marko realized in that moment that there was a hidden reason as to why his sister was going hundreds of miles away, and a stealthily quick glance at his father's strained expression cemented this conviction. They were sending Karla away because they were afraid of what was coming, the very same thing that his father could not bring himself to talk about.

The breakthrough in Marko's quest for the truth, came a few days later. The newspaper headlines that Marko always glanced at on the school bus driver's lap when he got on the bus to go home every weekday afternoon had up to that point provided no insight into what was on the horizon.

Waiting as always for the daily crush of rowdy students, Marko had filed on board with the last of the pupils, and as he did so his eye had been drawn to a photograph on the front page of the newspaper being read by the nameless middle aged rotund man sat behind the wheel who had been their driver for as long as Marko could remember. He wore a miserable and somewhat irritable expression, giving off a demeanour of unapproachability which had stood the test of time in going a long way to ward off any sly comments from his passengers. He did however notice Marko's momentary gaze out of the corner of his eye and as he pushed the lever to close the door in readiness to move off, he folded the newspaper and passed it across the aisle to his curious passenger without a word, a surprised Marko thanking him, receiving a kind nod and hint of a smile in reply.

As soon as Marko looked at the photograph in the headline, he knew that the face staring back at him belonged to someone with ill intent, with wide eyes full of rage like those of his opponents in the ring. But like the contenders he came up against, it wasn't just rage in those eyes, there was something else. It was the look of fear lurking beneath, trying to hide, but still perceptible to the trained eye. Marko would expect the general of any army to look steely and confident, but it was the look of fear at the back of those eyes that alarmed Marko more because as he knew from his numerous bouts in the ring, an opponent who could not control his fear would often make unpredictable, desperate ill judged moves, and whilst there was only so much damage a boxer in that mental condition could do in the ring, a general in that state of mind in command of an entire army was a completely different matter. There was no direct talk in the newspaper article of any intent on the part of the army that this man commanded, only the mention that operations to maintain the security of civilians in Croatia was underway. Marko thought this was a very odd statement, considering that there had been no news of Croatia being under any threat of war. His thoughts flitted back to the discussions with his father and the news of his sister going away, but the missing part of the jigsaw looming larger than ever in his mind was still faceless, ever more taunting, still refusing to reveal itself. To a boy now in his final year at school who was looking forward to spreading his wings and flying out into the big wide world like a soaring eagle, his never ceasing and intensifying curiosity about what was happening on the home front now felt like a relentless weight on his shoulders.

His desire to travel the world aroused by the history and geography lessons at school over the last few years, he had found himself taking books home about countries as far reaching as India and Africa. His bedtime reading would fuel vivid dreams about adventures in beautiful landscapes and ancient cities with grand old buildings.

To his parents it was beyond reason that their son would want to do anything else than carry on the family tradition and the idea of travelling outside of the region, let alone to another country was completely at odds with their thinking.

Less than a week later, everything in Bosnia suddenly changed, the final piece of Marko's jigsaw finally showing itself, thanks solely to the fact that the Bosnian press had yet to become suppressed by the military. The impending storm came to light in a flurry of newspaper articles and television news bulletins which left Marko wide eyed with fascination and dread at the same time. He wondered why the goings on in Croatia had not been reported much earlier when the troubles had first started, suddenly the obscure reason for the mention in that newspaper article a number of days earlier about the security of Croatian civilians, hitting home with Marko like a well timed haymaker in the ring.

As part of the former Yugoslavia, Bosnia's government and its politicians had long wanted independence from their neighbouring countries, but they had always believed that a democratic settlement would be reached regarding the areas of land under dispute, a dispute that had been going on for most of the twentieth century brought about by the first and second world wars.

Like all the other children from his region, Marko still went to school, life for the most part carrying on as normal. The pupils from mostly Croat and Serb backgrounds had at first seemed completely unaware of the resentment that had risen to the surface after Yugoslavia had split into separate republics a year earlier.

This all changed when refugee families fleeing from neighbouring Croatia had started arriving, displaced children swelling the class sizes at Marko's school. Swept along by the rising tide of media fuelled hatred, old friendships between pupils of opposing ethnic backgrounds began to fracture as they started taking sides, riled up by hostile talk from their parents about their neighbours of decades before, and playground fights were now commonplace, sparked by the smallest seemingly insignificant remark. There had been talk of segregation for Bosnia's schools, but the government realized that to do this would be an open admission that their control over society was openly failing.

Irrespective of recent events, Marko's farm boy background put him in a minority at school and as such he had always felt like an outsider, despite the fact that he did have a few close friends, but most of his fellow pupils lived in town and as the years rolled by Marko had grown to realize that he had nothing in common with them.

As the refugees continued to pour in, things began to change for Marko at school. His well known prowess in the boxing ring had kept the school bullies at bay throughout his time there, but as the sentiment of antagonism gained momentum and pupils began arriving from Croatia who having seen the unimaginable could now only think of suppression as the legitimate form of justice, he began to find himself being regarded as the prize beast on a safari that every hunter wanted to bring down. Within a few days the few friends he had at school had distanced themselves from him and he soon found himself completely alone.

That was when the bullying started. Marko had taken their verbal abuse, hoping they would run out of steam. He had never had to put his boxing skills to the test at school, but one fateful day when he was confronted by his enemies at the end of a narrow corridor, he finally snapped. A few moments later his assailants were all laid out on the floor. Marko had to be dragged off the ringleader by the sports teacher as he pummelled the boy's face to a bloody pulp, the injuries that he had inflicted on him so serious that the police had to be involved.

Charges were brought but Marko's father simply laughed at the police, telling them that they would all have done the same if any of them found themselves outnumbered three to one, and mocking them by adding that the only difference was that they would have needed their billy clubs to defend themselves.

When Marko returned to school after a month's suspension, the other boys dared not make eye contact with him. His former close friends now fearing retribution for not being there for him when he needed them, made themselves scarce whenever he appeared, and his three former assailants were so afraid that they stayed away from the school altogether, suffering the humiliation of having to be home taught.

He started to become despondent at school, frustrated with the teachers who seemed to be ignoring the catastrophe that was coming, more interested in filling pupil's heads with useless academic information that in the light of current events were unlikely to be of any use to his generation.

There was one good reason for coming to class however. She had arrived recently as a Serb refugee. Radica was different, like him, he could tell, even though he had not yet plucked up the courage to speak to her. She was beautiful, but not in the self-assured way that the other pretty girls were. She was somewhat understated in her appearance as if she didn't want to be noticed, but something in the way she was drew new friends like a magnet. There she was, sat at the front of class, her long golden hair bright in the afternoon sun streaming through the windows. He didn't need to see her face, he had memorized her striking features, those eyes, emerald green, alert and piercing often entered his dreams.

School would be finished soon, not just for the summer break, it would be gone forever, a smoking ruin in a barren landscape and with it, all the innocence of being a child that the school had nurtured within its walls for generations would vanish without a trace. He worried about Radica, knowing her beauty would inevitably attract the depraved attentions of the Croat soldiers. Marko had heard about what they were doing to Serb girls and women. It made him ashamed to be a Croat, and he prayed that if the time came for an introduction, she wouldn't shun him.

'Marko,' someone called, the voice far away but familiar. Then he heard his name again, this time louder and angry. He felt the hard chalk strike his forehead, punctuated by spontaneous laughter from the class. He looked up, his austere middle aged greying mathematics teacher burning through him with her eyes, the other pupils all turned towards him. His eyes found Radica's and she quickly turned away, her fellow pupils on either side smiling at him knowingly. He cast a few of the boys a menacing glare, their laughter abruptly silenced.

Waiting for the bus home outside the school gates later on, Marko found himself surrounded by the hundreds of familiar pupils of all ages making the usual deafening din. As the buses began to leave, the drivers suffering the twice daily torment of their passengers, Marko found Radica in the crowd and he wondered if this would be the day when he would finally get to talk to her.

As the doors to his bus hissed open, Marko edged forward at the back, watching Radica say goodbye to her friends and get on with her little brother Johan. He waited for the rush of passengers, before getting on board, taking his usual seat just behind the driver, away from the rowdy pupils at the back. He began to read the driver's newspaper as the bus began its laborious trek. Marko's eyes were drawn to a photograph on the frontpage picturing distinctively helmeted UN soldiers talking with civilians in a village. As he read the article, he saw the mention of British soldiers and his eyes lit up. Perhaps at last they were intervening to avert catastrophe.

'My little brother wants your jacket,' came the deep growl of one of the older boys at the back of the bus, loud and annoying. Marko turned to see Johan crying out as Radica tried to shield him from a fat oversized bully.

'Get off him,' she yelled.

'Don't make me hurt you too,' retorted the bully.

Marko recognized him as one of the new refugees from his year who had arrived only a few days before.

'Leave them alone.' Marko's voice, commanding and deep, stopped the bully in his tracks. Spinning around he came face to face with Marko, regarding him with a contempt that indicated he was clearly unfamiliar with Marko's reputation. Neither did the bully notice that his cluster of friends who Marko recognized from old who stood behind him, had all backed away.

'Stay out of this,' boomed the bully.

'Or what?' Marko taunted, waiting for his moment.

'You must be a Croat to talk so tough,' the bully retorted, evidently not smart enough to read the worried faces of his comrades as he looked around.

'What if I am?' Marko replied, involuntarily feeling his fists tightening down by his side.

'You won't be so tough when the Serb army arrives,' the bully sneered.

'The British soldiers will put a stop to that,' came Marko's matter of fact reply, happy to engage in an argument before moving onto the inevitable next step in the dispute.

The bully laughed out loud.

'The British are just here to watch, everyone knows that. They won't be able to help you when the Serbs come to rape your moth…'

The swift punch to the bully's nose ended his sentence prematurely. He stumbled backwards and went down in the aisle between his colleagues, blood pouring from his broken nose. Marko kept his fists raised, ready for more, but the look of shock and resignation in the bully's watering eyes as he clutched his bloody nose that Marko was so used to seeing from his bouts in the ring, told him that the bully did at least have the primitive instinct to register when he was outmatched. As it was evident to Marko that the bully wasn't for getting back up and that his foolish band of followers weren't for helping him out, Marko guided a wide-eyed Radica and Johan towards the front of the bus, sitting down with them.

'Thank you Marko,' Radica finally said softly, a hint of shame in her voice.

'You'll be alright now,' Marko replied comfortingly.

'You do know, don't you?' Radica asked hesitantly.

'Know what?'

'That we are Serbs.'

'Of course I do,' Marko confirmed with a kind smile.

'But doesn't it matter?' Radica replied, surprised at his response.

'Not to me.'

They exchanged warm smiles, both feeling a strange new sensation, like magnetism.

'There's talk of people being taken away here in Bosnia as well now,' Radica said.

Marko took the golden opportunity to take hold of her hand, his whole body tingling with excitement as he felt the rush of attraction. He searched her face as she looked away, blushing, but leaving her hand in his.

'Don't worry, we'll stick together,' he replied as reassuringly as he could, knowing all too well how difficult that would soon become. She smiled at him then, her emerald eyes lighting up and he found himself gazing into them, before she looked away again blushing.

They sat in silence for the rest of Radica's journey, both looking out of the window but not seeing, lost in their secret world as they savoured the sensations rolling like waves through their bodies and minds, their hands remaining entwined, pulses racing, fingers gently moving together, caressing, searching each other. Johan had settled with his superhero comic book, oblivious.

Marko knew which stop was Radica's and when it came his heart sank. As the doors opened halfway along the main street in her village of fifty or so dwellings, she waited for as long as possible before pulling her hand away. Standing to leave with Johan who was already hurrying to the exit, she turned to Marko, transfixing him with her green eyes.

'See you tomorrow then?' she said. Marko gazed back, his eyes melting into hers.

'Yes, tomorrow.'

With that, she turned and was gone, the doors hissing shut. She looked up at him as the bus passed, her expression giving him the reassurance he longed for.

As the bus carried on out of Radica's village and further out into the farming community, Marko tried to continue with his newspaper to distract himself, but it was useless. All he could think of was her, those eyes, the long blond flowing hair and the electricity that passed between them when they touched. His entire being felt energized like never before, his body primed for anything, his mind razor sharp. He could feel the bully's presence at the back of the bus, he knew he was there without even turning around and he had to fight the urge to go back there and beat him to a pulp. My god, what had Radica done to him?

When his stop came, he turned to the bully and his friends huddled at the back, their loud voices ugly. As the bully spotted him, they all fell silent. Marko locked eyes with his victim, waiting for him to falter. After a few moments the bully looked away and Marko smiled before handing the newspaper back to the driver, who nodded at him with one of those fatherly well done my boy smiles, before he stepped down onto the road, the doors closing behind him.

Marko enjoyed the daily walk across the field to his home, the hay moving in gentle waves around him as the early evening breeze began to pick up. The farmhouse on the far side sat in perfect isolation, detached from the harsh reality of the unfolding world around it. The chimney was smoking as usual at this time of the year. Marko drifted back to thoughts of Radica as he strode through the field, feeling the soft tips of the hay on his fingertips.

As he neared the solid windowless wooden front door he hoped that the mood around the dinner table would be less dismal and subdued than in recent weeks. Entering the kitchen he was met with the rich smell of a stew cooking on the stove. Ana turned, his face raising a beaming smile as she approached, dressed in the same apron she had worn for years. She kissed Marko on the cheek, then handed him a large spoon before gesturing towards the stove.

'I'm sure it's fine mama,' Marko protested.

'I know, but I always like to have your seal of approval.'

Marko dipped the spoon into the simmering stew and blew on it before taking a sip, Ana searching his face. He nodded, handing back the spoon.

'It's perfect, as always,' he replied, smiling as he saw her face light up.

'Good, now go and call your father in from the barn.'

Marko made his way across the yard to the steep roofed wooden barn, looking a little worse for wear these past few years. One of the huge double doors was wide open and he stopped, hearing Filip talking to himself. Marko had at first found this amusing, but now his father's ranting had become erratic and angry, like someone engaged in a violent argument with an imaginary person.

Seeing Filip like this made Marko cautious about interrupting him, fearing that look in his eyes of fury and frustration. Marko watched his father for a moment, cursing away to himself as he worked on the ancient tractor.

He knocked on the door. For a moment his father didn't seem to hear. Then he abruptly stopped what he was doing and looked up, his spanner clenched tightly in his hand as he turned to see the silhouette of Marko stood in the doorway.

The expression on his face was something Marko had never seen before and it unsettled him. His father had a look of wide eyed fear, as if he was expecting to see the devil himself instead. For a moment his expression was frozen, the spanner held up as if he was readying himself for a fight. Then abruptly he snapped out of his trance, looking down to see the spanner in his hand. He placed it down on the workbench quickly, forcing a fatherly smile to hide the shame of his son seeing him like this. He wiped his oily hands on a clean rag and approached.

'Marko, how was your day, have you plucked up the courage to speak to that girl you keep talking about, what was her name?'

'Radica,' Marko said, the mere mention of her name threatening to set his mind adrift again.

'Radica, ah yes, that's right. Well?' Filip replied enthusiastically, suddenly resentful that with the country about to disintegrate into anarchy, the wonderful emotional journey for his son with his first relationship would likely be severed before it had time to flourish.

'I saved her brother from one of the new Serb bullies.' Marko exclaimed proudly.

'Good, and did you loosen his teeth for him?' his papa asked cheerfully.

'I broke his nose instead.'

'That's my boy,' Filip laughed, slapping Marko on the shoulder. Filip began to walk away towards the house, but realizing that Marko was not following, he stopped and turned to see his son glued to the spot.

'Come on, your supper will get cold.'

'Papa?' Filip's expression changed as he recognized his son's look.

'She's a Serb,' Marko confessed.

Filip approached with a warm smile, placing a hand on Marko's shoulder.

'Let's not worry about these things tonight, it's your birthday.'

Marko looked at his father, that familiar reassuring look making everything all right like it had always done as far back as he could remember.

'Come on, they're waiting for you.' With his arm around Marko's shoulder, he led him back to the farmhouse.

After a special dinner of Marko's favourite beef pasticada, Ana produced a small but beautifully decorated birthday cake complete with a painstakingly constructed marzipan boxer figurine and placed it on the table in front of Marko. She leaned forward to light the fifteen candles with a long match, managing the last one just before the match burned out and as she did so, Marko couldn't help but notice that her hand was trembling. The tiny flames flickered ever so slightly from the gentle breeze coming through the open window looking out over the fields to the country lane beyond.

Karla, who had changed into her prettiest frock for the occasion, smiled at him expectantly as he gazed into the candles, his mind far away, walking hand in hand with a certain young lady.

'Well Marko, aren't you going to make a wish?' Karla asked teasingly, all too aware from discussions with her mother, that her younger brother was in love for the first time.

Her words jolted Marko from his fantasy and he looked up, his family gazing at him with knowing smiles, exchanged mischievous looks of understanding. Marko closed his eyes, thinking, but it was not thoughts of Radica that came to him at that moment, and instantly Ana and Filip recognized his conflicted expression, exchanging glances as an oblivious Karla looked on.

Marko suddenly opened his eyes, almost catching his parents off guard, before he inhaled deeply into his strong well developed lungs, and with one blow extinguishing all the candles with ease, to the applause of his small but enthusiastic audience.

Ana immediately began slicing the cake and handing out the portions on the small-patterned plates that Marko remembered since he was a small child.

'Already fifteen. Soon he will be leaving his poor mama,' Ana protested half jokingly, cutting the cake neatly.

'It won't be for a while yet mama. I have to finish school first and then we have to wait for...' Marko's voice trailed off as he caught himself, Filip casting him an cautionary glance.

'Please Marko, don't leave me alone with your mother,' he immediately interjected in a pseudo pleading tone, drawing a scowling glare from Ana.

Karla smiled at her brother adoringly.

'Every boy must spread his wings,' she proclaimed, turning to Ana. 'But don't worry mama, I will stay with you.'

'You see husband, somebody around hear still appreciates me,' Ana exclaimed proudly.

'How can you say such things?' Filip laughed defensively, getting up to approach his wife. She pushed him away as he tried to embrace her, much to the amusement of Marko and Karla.

'Get away from me you old fool,' she protested.

'Oh, I see, I'm a fool now am I. Perhaps I should have married your best friend instead?' Filip countered indignantly.

'She never would have had you and you know it,' Ana replied with a scoff.

'She always used to say to me, if it doesn't work out with Ana, then I will be waiting,' Filip persisted.

'Liar,' Ana laughed indignantly, slapping Filip with her kitchen towel, before crossing the room to turn the old radio on. Loud Croatian folk music filled the room. She turned and held her arms out to her son.

'Marko, dance with your mama.'

'Oh mama,' Marko protested.

'Please, just one dance,' she pleaded with a smile.

'Go on Marko, dance,' Karla urged, giving him a gentle shove. Marko looked to Filip for support who held his hands up in submission.

'You'd better listen to your sister,' Filip laughed.

With a sigh, Marko reluctantly got to his feet and approached his mama, placing his right hand around her waist as she placed her left hand on his shoulder. As they began to dance, Karla and Filip started to clap in rhythm to the music.

Outside in the quiet lane on the other side of the hayfield across from the farmhouse, four figures marched along, silhouetted against the early evening sun, their heavy boots crunching on the gravel road. They stopped together in unison as they heard, music drifting across the field. Their uniforms were grimy and worn from the past months of savage fighting and that morning they had removed the Serb military insignia badges from their jackets in preparation for crossing the border into Bosnia, taking the opportunity to give their Kalashnikov assault rifles a much-needed full strip down.

Vladimir still had those expressionless ebony eyes with his boxer's nose and a cleanly shaven head. What was most menacing about him at that moment was his grin, completely at odds with his cold eyes, like a permanent frozen fixture. It was as if his face had been created from two people chosen completely at random.

After his recent atrocities in Croatia, Vladimir was by now utterly fearless in his pursuit of fresh game, always tracking a potentially hostile area with a few of his most trusted soldiers, his troops waiting safely hidden away for word from their general. He knew that as long as he was seen by his men as being the first to place himself in danger, then his command would never be challenged.

Vladimir had been promoted to general after his predecessor had been found one morning with his throat cut from ear to ear, his eyes still frozen wide open. As there had been widespread dissent amongst the troops about the then general's habit of sending them into battle but never being there fighting with them himself, the army knew that the murderer could have been one of any number of soldiers and had immediately given up trying to identify the perpetrator.

After a couple of weeks went by with no signs of any investigation, Vladimir knew he had so far, gotten away with it. He had planned the murder methodically and was certain that he had made it back to his quarters unseen but had since found himself increasingly haunted by the notion that some of his fellow sergeants might suspect him. He was after all, different from them in so many ways. They were what he thought of as traditional career sergeants, recruited into the army straight from school, moving through the ranks slowly and predictably as they served their time. By now they were enjoying a generous salary for doing nothing more than telling the mass of ordinary soldiers with no inclination or prospects of promotion, what to do, day in, day out, and had never until this point been involved in any actual combat. When the mobilization had started in Croatia, his fellow sergeants had greeted the prospect of having to engage the Croat military with dread. Whilst they had never spoken out at the time, Vladimir knew that none of them had any enthusiasm for placing themselves and their soldiers at risk for the sake of what was in their minds a mere squabble over what land belonged to which ethnic group. Worst of all for Vladimir, was that their Serb general in command of their entire battalion, had little appetite for embarking on a crusade to fight the Croat army to reclaim land in Croatia or beyond, his lack of enthusiasm evident in his lacklustre demeanour. He did of course follow orders from the Serb high command, and quickly had his battalion on the move.

Vladimir's fellow sergeants were all too aware that he had a unpredictable vindictive streak, demonstrating vehement abusiveness towards any soldier on parade that attracted his attention for the wrong reason, relishing humiliating them in front of their comrades and making them the target of ridicule, so much to the point that over a dozen of his flock had taken their own lives during his time as sergeant. His long standing general however had never reprimanded him for contributing to the demise of troops under his command, something that the other sergeants had always disagreed with, although they were too apprehensive of Vladimir to challenge his behaviour directly or via their general.

Very soon, Vladimir's frustration at the lack of sadistic vigour with which his general was commanding the battalion began to show in his increasingly erratic demeanour, his deep resentment and contempt for his general becoming clear to his comrade sergeants without him even speaking a word against him. Vladimir knew that all he had to do was wait for his moment to come, to take command.

In the event, he didn't have to wait very long. Only a few months into the campaign in Croatia, the Serb battalion suffered prolonged weeks of heavy casualties, and the general found himself beginning to fall out of favour with high command and his troops who were becoming increasingly demoralized. Vladimir knew his golden opportunity had come to win favour with the soldiers. Knowing that he was far better respected by the troops than any of his counterparts, he decided to rally the battalion to launch a daring counter assault on a key Croat army stronghold, confident that the sentiment of the soldiers would quell resistance from any of the other sergeants. To set the ultimate example to his troops and cement their eternal loyalty and respect, he led the assault from the front, placing himself directly in the firing line, unlike his counterparts. The offensive proved to be a great success, routing the Croat position and sending them fleeing with surprisingly few Serb casualties and Vladimir immediately found himself summoned to high command to receive his recognition.

He considered at this juncture that perhaps his long considered risky plan of action might not be necessary after all, that if he kept up his momentum on the battlefield, then he may find himself sat behind the general's desk regardless, but that glorious notion in his mind quickly evaporated. He knew all too well that soon his masterful military manoeuvre would be forgotten by high command, and so he decided to make his move, confident that if he acted quickly, he would stand a very good chance of being appointed his worthless general's successor.

A few days later the general was dead and high command saw no alternative. Vladimir's reckless gamble had paid off, but to quell any risk of being informed upon by any of his fellow sergeants as a candidate for assassin, Vladimir had beaten one of them to death with his bare hands in front of his troops on the first day of his promotion, for apparent insubordination, as a challenge to any rivals. When not one of the other sergeants there dared to intervene to save their unfortunate colleague, Vladimir knew his secret would be forever safe.

Overnight the entire basis of the way the Serb battalion operated under their new general would change beyond all recognition. Vladimir took great pleasure in rewriting the rulebook for his own ends, tearing out any of the pages covering the Geneva Convention. From now on there would be no Croatian troops taken prisoner, and as for the Croat civilians, Vladimir had an array of orders for his troops that would make the atrocities carried out in the former Yugoslavia under the doctrine of the Nazis seem like a tea party on a warm summer afternoon.

Vladimir knew that despite his sergeants being terrified of him, they would not willingly subscribe to his way of thinking, that his blatant disregard for the rules of engagement would go completely against their principles, so he simply relieved them of their duty and replaced them with a handful of soldiers who having fought directly alongside him in the last offensive, had demonstrated a level of fearlessness and savagery that would make them suitable to carry out the inhumane, barbaric orders that he now had in mind.

Very soon he had made the newspapers, the press naming him Vlad the butcher. He had smiled to himself when he first read it, flattered, especially considering that his drunken wife beating and raping father had in fact been a butcher, but at the same time he was enraged that they did not mention his father's profession. He would make them pay for the insult, but first there was a war to be won, a war to rid Croatia of all Croats and reclaim this land for the Serbs.

Vladimir had grown up listening to the screams of mercy from his mother every night in her bedroom when her father would return from work to rape and beat her. He had never understood why the sound of her pleading voice never upset him and despite hearing her screaming out his name for help, he never did. It wasn't out of any fear of his own father that he did nothing. The truth was that he felt no instinct to do so and instead he would simply go on playing with his toys.

The only occasion when his mind had registered any alarm regarding his mother was when he was thirteen. He had come home from school to find that his mother wasn't in the kitchen preparing supper. Then he felt the familiar gentle breeze on his face, coming from an open door leading out to the fields behind the farmhouse.

When he saw her hanging from the apple tree, his alarm of not knowing where she had gone was over. He knew she was dead, her wide eyes bulging as her body hung limp, the rope around her neck drawn tight under her chin. He just sat down on the ground, munching on a few apples and stared at her lifeless form until his father returned. His reaction was one of anger, cursing the corpse of his wife as if she were still alive, livid that she was not alive for him to rape and beat, and also because there was no one to prepare the meat he had brought home for supper.

After they had eaten, his father placed an arm around his shoulder and explained that the time had come for him to experience for himself what women were good for. Without even thinking to cut his wife down from the tree, he drove his son in the old beaten-up pickup truck towards town under the cover of darkness. Vladimir asked his father where they were going, but he would not answer.

They parked up on a quiet residential street, dimmed the lights and sat there in silence. When his father spotted the small slender figure of the young teenage girl in the rear-view mirror approaching on her own along the pavement, he waited for her to pass, sizing up her petit figure and long blond hair.

'This one,' he grunted in approval. Starting the engine, the headlights still dimmed, he drew the truck alongside her, winding the window down.

'Excuse me young lady,' he called out softly in a tone Vladimir had never heard before. She stopped, looking up at him in the truck, her innocent smile sealing her fate, Vladimir sat out of site in the passenger seat. 'I was wondering if you could help me, I'm lost you see,' he continued. Her attention was drawn to a small map that he had begun unfolding. She came closer as he held it out of the window towards her. 'Please could you tell me where we are on this map.'

The girl came closer, reaching out her hand, her finger finding the street. Then, with a quick glance up and down the street, Vladimir's father grabbed her outstretched arm and with astonishing speed, lifted her, dragging her through the open window and into the truck before she even had time to scream.

Pushing her towards a stunned Vladimir, he raced away down the street, his headlights dimmed, winding his window up as she began screaming.

'Shut her up Vladimir,' he barked angrily as he tried to concentrate on the road. Vladimir instinctively placed his hand over her mouth and held her in a bear like grip as she struggled. That moment had stayed with him always, the soft feel of her lips on his palm muffling her scream and that sweet smell of young innocent female flesh.

By the time they arrived back at the farmhouse, the girl had stopped screaming and had gone into shock, her wide eyes staring blankly into space.

Vladimir already knew what was coming next and as his imagination ran riot, a sudden new sensation ran through his body, he was becoming erect for the first time. She offered them no resistance as they led her into the house and into his father's bedroom. It wasn't until his father began to tear the young girl's clothes off that she began to resist again, pleading just like his mother had for all those years.

Vladimir felt his manhood throbbing as he watched his father undo the belt on his trousers and force himself on the girl as she pleaded. She screamed out in agony as he forced himself into her, raping her with brutal force as she begged him to stop, over and over. He grunted loudly as he climaxed, clambering off her exhausted body, the sheets red from her bleeding.

He turned to Vladimir.

'Now you,' he ordered. Vladimir looked at the girl, her silent eyes begging him not to.

'Do it,' his father shouted.

Then an evil grin spread across his face as his son quickly unfastened his trousers and pounced on her helpless form. Within moments he was inside her, savouring this new sensation and her pleas for mercy echoing rhythmically in his head.

Much later that evening after they had both raped her for the second time and the girl's strength and will to fight was all used up, they took her outside into the fields in the darkness. Vladimir's father made no secret to the girl of what was coming next, laughing at her pathetic whimpers when she saw the gun.

Forcing her down onto her knees with a single shove, he handed his pistol to his hesitant son. Vladimir knew what needed to be done, but in a way he was thankful that she was staring down at the ground so he could not see her terrified eyes, her hands held together as she murmured a prayer. When he pulled the trigger, it was without any conscious thought or remorse. He was simply finishing a job, like when he rinsed the soap off his father's truck every Sunday after washing it.

When the drink finally caught up with his father some years later, his face yellow with jaundice, a teary Vladimir sat with him as he lay on the bed, the same bed that they had raped the young girl on years before and where his father had raped his mother hundreds of times.

Vladimir finally asked him a question that had been on his mind for many years since he was a young boy.

'Papa, why did you do all those things to mama?'

His father had smiled sadly, drawing him nearer.

'Because I found out,' he replied with a mischievous grin.

'Found out what?' Vladimir replied, enthralled.

'That she was a Croat,' his father replied casually.

'But I don't understand?'

'You will do, very soon.'

'But..?'

'Hush now Vladimir, I need to rest,' his father cut in, closing his eyes. Vladimir sat with him then for what seemed like an eternity, listening to his father's breathing becoming shallower and shallower until as the evening sun shining through the window cast an orange glow   over his papa's face, he breathed out for the last time.

Those final words haunted Vladimir for a long time, all the way up until he had been recruited into the army just after the dictator leader Tito's death in 1980, when age old ethnic tensions held in check by his government began to slowly simmer away.

Like so many young men of his generation, he saw it as their duty and privilege to take action to right the wrongs of the past and the army became the fertile breeding ground for their anger.

His sexual brutality was what had first gained Vladimir his reputation in the army and he found himself being encouraged by his superiors, not disciplined for his behaviour towards Croat girls and women.

By the time he made sergeant in the early nineties, many of his fellow soldiers had already adopted his sexual barbarity and he knew that all he now needed to do was become general so he could command that they do his bidding, whether they wanted to or not.

No more a than a month after being made general, the soldiers from Vlad The Butcher's battalion were not just acting like he was, most of them were doing so willingly and he would watch with pride when the mass chorus of Croat girl's screams worked the soldiers up into a frenzy at the makeshift rape camps that would be created to cater for the latest influx of young orphan girls and also a few boys. Vladimir knew then that he had accomplished something quite incredible. He had altered the minds of his soldiers to his way of thinking. They were fighters by day and rapists by night.

'Recognize that music?' he heard someone say, breaking him from his thoughts, finding himself back in the country lane, the familiar music drifting across the field from the farmhouse. He detected the presence of Juraj stood next to him, his nostrils assaulted by his comrade's distinct body odour that always permeated from his pores after a long hot day.

His second in command was shorter and slimmer than himself, giving the impression of feebleness, a falsehood that many a soldier had learnt to their detriment, finding themselves bruised and battered by Juraj's lightning fists at the very first sign of insubordination. He had a long weasel face, his shaven head looking out of place against his intellectual looking features. Vladimir had often thought that all he needed was a pair of round-rimmed spectacles and dressed in a suit he would easily pass for a lawyer, although he would need to take a much needed shower first.

'They're playing Croat music,' Juraj snarled.

'And on our land, without our permission,' Vladimir replied in a tone sounding far more menacing by the complete lack of emotion in his delivery, as if he had recited this dialogue many times already, so much so that the words had lost all meaning.

'We should teach them a lesson,' his compatriot urged.

Vladimir looked around at the two corporals, hand picked for this particular evening's entertainment on virgin soil, for their seemingly limitless appetite for sheer depravity. The lowering sun behind them had thrown their faces into silhouette but Vladimir didn't need to see the hungry expression in their eyes, he already knew what they were thinking. He turned back to Juraj whose eyes were wide with anticipation, waiting patiently for his master's signal like an obedient dog.

In the farmhouse Ana and Marko were dancing much faster now to the quickening rhythm of the music as Karla and Filip cheered them along, everyone blissfully oblivious to what was about to happen.

Vladimir and the others were already halfway across the field when they broke from a steady jog into a full on charge, the two corporals in front forming the arrowhead, closing the last distance to the farmhouse with alarming speed.

In the farmhouse kitchen, time seemed to stand still as the door flew open with a loud crash and they all turned in unison with shocked faces to see the two corporals burst in, weapons raised. Filip was on his feet instantly, pulling young Karla behind him, Marko shielding Ana as one of the corporals charged past them and smashed the radio with the butt of his rifle. Then the thud of more bootsteps drew their attention away from the two corporals and back to the door as Juraj entered the kitchen with Vladimir immediately behind, closing the door gently behind him after a cursory glance back outside, his calm measured manner and emotionless stonelike expression striking an elevated level of terror into his captives far above that of the violent behaviour of the two corporals a few moments before. It was Filip that attracted Vladimir's attention first, his captive's eyes involuntarily locking onto his for an instant, before quickly looking away.

Vladimir silently took in the room, enjoying making his audience wait for a long agonizing moment before speaking. He enjoyed feeling the tension rise, sensing the terror in the confinement of a room where there was no escape. He always looked for something in a Croat's house to give him a decent opener, something to make the experience personal to him, so he would remember every family he murdered. There were no ornaments in the kitchen of any note, no pictures on the wall depicting a specific landscape to remember this family by. There was however something that he had never seen before in all the Croat houses he had visited, something exceptional, something he would always be able to recollect with fondness when he partook in celebrations for Serb children in years to come.

'What have we here, a birthday cake,' Vladimir declared sarcastically, yet with a hint of childish excitement. His eyes moved fleetingly over Marko before picking out Karla cowering behind Filip.

'Hello young lady, is it your birthday?' he teased, that terrible grin surfacing once more in readiness for the familiar ritual that was about to begin.

'Leave her alone,' came a loud voice off to his left. For a moment he was too shocked to register the indignance of the interruption. Before Filip could say anything to placate their executioner, Vladimir's grin evaporated and his head had spun round like a doll, his cold ebony eyes locking onto Marko, but to his utter astonishment, this mere farmer's boy held his gaze, seemingly unafraid, unfaltering. For an instant Vladimir felt his mind slipping away from him, hypnotized by those eyes that seemed to be dissecting his thoughts like a pathologist cutting open a corpses skull to examine the brain inside. With considerable mental effort Vladimir reeled away, snapping the mental grip that Marko had on him.

'What did you say boy?' he said, his usually low booming voice raised a few octaves, as if he had something stuck in his throat, enough for Juraj and the two corporals to cast him a concerned glance.

'It's my birthday,' Marko confirmed in a tone that could not be mistaken for anything other than a warning, as he made the most of his enemy's momentary loss of command over the situation. Vladimir straightened himself, his grin reappearing as suddenly as it had vanished.

'What is your name, boy?' Vladimir asked in his more familiar commanding tone, careful not to lock eyes again with his opponent again. Detecting his reticence at making eye contact for the second time, Marko decided to say nothing and just stare back blankly as a taunt, hoping Vladimir would fall under his spell again, but his interrogator had been here many times with Croat soldiers who had tried the silent treatment before finding themselves being subjected to all manner of degradation and torture. It wasn't that Vladimir didn't enjoy mutilating his subjects, getting people to talk was simply a means to an end, so as far as he was concerned, the less effort it took, the better. He paused for a moment, taking his time like he always did at the beginning of his interrogations.

'I said, what is your name?' he repeated, this time, slowly and quietly. That patient calmness in his voice threw Marko, more menacing that any shout and he realized with a shudder that the game was about to change.

'Marko,' he replied with as much confidence as he could muster.

'You obviously don't know who I am, Marko?' Vladimir replied in a regretful tone, like that of a priest giving a dying man his last rights. Marko's eyes narrowed at the remark, his mind frantically trying to recall all the faces he had seen in the media recently, but this man's identity was lost on him. The truth was that Marko had seen this savage monster before, although the photo of Vlad The Butcher has been taken at a distance for the photographer's sake and bore no obvious resemblance to the man standing in front of him.

Then Vladimir turned to look at Filip, whose frozen expression and eyes filled with mortal dread, signalling that at least he was in no doubt as to his tormentor's identity.

'I can see that your papa recognizes me,' Vladimir said with a majestic air, his expressionless eyes just for an instant showing an almost imperceptible flash of contentment. Turning back to Marko, his whole being seemed to loom larger over the boy who he knew would very soon come to regret addressing him so disrespectfully, the picture of how the scene would unfold already forming in his barbaric mind. Yet Vladimir, with all his savage intimidating prowess still found himself dumbfounded that this teenage farm boy was able to hold his gaze with those penetrating eyes, reading him, sizing him up, goading him with a knowledge and wisdom way beyond his years.

'I am General Vladimir Lubenski of the Serb army,' he continued, having to tear his eyes from Marko's gaze again, those words by now floating effortlessly off his tongue after being recited so many times to his captives over the last months and signalling the commencement of the familiar ritual. Vladimir waited for a moment as always, taking the time to savour the sound of his own name spoken out loud, although his announcement did nothing to heighten the tension in the room since his hosts were already in no doubt as to his intentions. Juraj had always thought that this somewhat redundant part of the ceremony was like watching a horror movie played backwards, where the victim would scream first before the monster would appear, and he promised himself that one day he would pluck up the courage to mention this to his master.

'Could I have a slice of your birthday cake, Marko?' he continued, careful to avert his eyes. Marko pondered the question carefully, his lightning quick mind working the angles in exactly the same way that he always did in the ring. If he said yes, then it would indicate that he was now begging for mercy from his captor, but if he said no, then he might endanger his family further. Best to keep his opponent guessing to buy more time.

Vladimir raised his hand to his ear, tilting his head towards Marko off to his side.

'You see Juraj, ignorant,' Vladimir proclaimed, shaking his head regretfully.

'Let's teach them some manners,' Juraj urged hastily, partly because he was getting tired of waiting for the kill, but mostly because he was late for his customary evening liaison with his vodka bottle.

Vladimir stepped forward and as if he was an invited guest at Marko's birthday, casually picking up a plate with a slice of cake on, seemingly unworried by the long knife laying on the table within easy reach for anyone of his captives who dared to make a lunge for it. Picking up a fork gingerly, he stepped back away from the table and delved into the cake, loading a large portion on the end of his fork, savouring the taste for a long moment like a judge in a baking competition, tilting his head this way and that as he contemplated his decision. Then he took another mouthful, turning to look at Karla, fixing her with his menacing eyes, chuckling quietly to himself as he continued to eat, enjoying watching her visibly squirm.

'Did you make this cake young lady?' Vladimir asked with a phoney air of courtesy as he swallowed down his last mouthful, cake stuck between his teeth as he grinned.

Karla was silent for a moment, terrified that whatever she said, her tormentor would take it as an insult in some way.

'Yes,' she stammered, flinching as she spoke.

'It tastes very sweet,' Vladimir replied heartily.

'Thank you,' Karla's replied impulsively, relieved that her reply had met with her captor's approval, until a split second later the empty plate slipped from Vladimir's hand, smashing on the stone floor as he stood there with a well rehearsed expression of shock.

'My god, a Croat with manners, I can hardly believe it,' he exclaimed, as if to himself. Then his mannequin smile suddenly resurfaced and he began examining Karla, this time with greedy eyes, moving over her body, imagining what she looked like under those clothes. He enjoyed this part of the preamble more than anything, watching his victims try to visibly shrink away as they recognized that look, realizing his intentions and knowing what was about to happen with a loathing inevitable certainty. Marko, Filip and Ana knew what was about to happen too, each one of them calculating their next move independent of each other.

Juraj had to fight to suppress an audible sigh, relieved that finally the moment had come. Glancing at the two corporals to read their expressions to check that they were poised and ready, he turned his attention back to their captives.

Vladimir paused for one last moment before delivering the punch line.

'I wonder if you and your mother taste as good?' Vladimir finally proposed, his toothy grin growing wider than ever as he watched Karla and Ana squirm with repulsion.

'Come forward,' he teased, holding out a beckoning hand to Karla, Filip instinctively blocking her path, his eyes wide like a cornered fox. Vladimir let out a little chuckle, reflecting on how often he had witnessed the spectacle of fathers desperately trying to protect their daughters, terrified eyes betraying their foolish courage, their dreaded understanding of the inevitable. Vladimir's expression suddenly changed, his grin falling away to be replaced by an expressionless mouth more in fitting with his dead, emotionless ebony eyes.

'I said, come here,' he commanded flatly, almost with a sigh of weariness, like a school teacher tired of having to ask a recalcitrant pupil to behave. It was at this point that Vladimir often saw the familiar and wholly predictable changed in the father's eyes, that look of terror giving way to one of silent, futile, pleading, something that Vladimir had always found utterly contemptible and he would let the moment linger before his next move, giving the father in question plenty of time to get on his knees and beg in a final selfless plea for mercy. There had been a few who had denied him this pleasure over the last months, but it mattered not, the outcome was always the same regardless. He knew right away as Filip's eyes stayed sharply focussed on him like a caged animal, that this father was not for begging. Without any tell tail change of expression or posture, Vladimir had suddenly taken three steps towards his prey, evidently intending to move straight through Filip like a ghost. He hadn't expected the boy in the room standing out of his eyeline to the right to dare try anything so foolish as grab the large cake knife from the table, but that proved to be a costly misjudgement on his part and if it hadn't been for the lighting reflexes of Juraj things may have turned out completely differently. An instant later, Marko found himself crashing to the floor from the rifle butt to his temple, the world around him spinning like a fairground ride. Momentarily distracted by the commotion, Vladimir took his eyes off Filip, just long enough for his captive to launch himself forward.

The single loud crack that rang out a split second later seemed to freeze Filip in mid motion, halting him in his tracks, the bullet shattering a pottery vase on the mantelpiece behind him. It wasn't until Filip grimaced and his eyes narrowed, his face taking on a confused expression, that the realization struck home with the same unmistakeable certainty as the sound of that gunshot, but it was Ana's scream that punctuated the tragedy of the moment.

Juraj's Kalashnikov raised, Vladimir turned back to see Filip reaching forward to try and grab him for support as his knees started to buckle under his weight and the blood began dribbling from the corner of his mouth. Vladimir's textbook theatrical reaction was one of acute amusement for Juraj and the two corporals. He took a small teasing step back to avoid Filip's hands, feigning with convincing sincerity, a look of complete surprise.

'You've been shot,' Vladimir gasped, holding his hands up in submission. Filip's legs suddenly gave way under him and as he went down, he reached out to Vladimir who backed away in disgust.

'Keep your filthy Croat hands away from me,' Vladimir screamed in horror, like a damsel in distress. Then Filip was down on his knees in front of his captors, his breathing laboured as blood filled his lungs, displacing the last remaining air. The room had suddenly become dimmer and much quieter to him and he knew that this was the end. In his last moments, his vision faltering, he saw his beautiful wife and daughter huddled together on the floor, but he couldn't see Marko and he wondered where his son had gone to as he finally slid from consciousness like a wave rolling back down a beach into the sea on a receding tide.

Vladimir had seen the light go out of many a man's eyes, always recognizing that exact moment of passing between life and death as the pupils suddenly relaxed and froze. It always sent a slight shudder through him, an image flashing before him, seeing his own eyes turn blank for an instant before he would push it away, telling himself that it was not his time yet, but all too aware that like the many victims he had claimed during this conflict, death would one day come calling, abruptly and without warning. Marko, his vision still blurred and his head as heavy as a boulder had barely been able to make out what was happening as he lay a few yards away from his father, desperately trying to regain his senses, but he knew that Filip was dead from the unmistakeable whimpering sounds of his mama and sister out of sight off to his right.

'Pick him up,' he heard, a commanding tone, that voice familiar. Then he was being hoisted up under both arms, a strange feeling of weightlessness running through his limp body. He was aware of someone standing directly in front of him, the features still blurred and he fought try and bring that face into focus, his memory of Vladimir's stark features helping to fill in the gaps between what he could see and what he could remember.

For a long moment Vladimir stood there, silently observing Marko, searching his face, waiting for his victim to find his focus as the two corporals held him up, careful to avert their eyes away from their general's hypnotic gaze.

'Time for your birthday present Marko,' Vladimir exclaimed with relish as he saw his captive's eyes suddenly narrow and lock onto his own, laughing with amusement as Marko's half-conscious dreamy expression changed to one of pure hatred, the returning strength in his body surging through him like an electric current as the adrenaline kicked in, taking the two corporals by surprise who had to exert themselves to restrain him as he strained every muscle in his body to try and get to Vladimir, stood there unflinching and tantalisingly close. The two corporals now having gained full restraint over their prisoner, Vladimir glanced behind at Karla and Ana clinging to each other, trembling and wide eyed. Turning back to Marko, he leaned in that little bit closer. He knew all too well by the look in those eyes what Marko wanted to do to him right at that moment, and he had to resign himself, with some regret no less, that once he had finished amusing himself with the two women, he would have to kill this boy. It was a pity, as young men of this completely fearless character were hard to come by and he had hoped to enlist him in his army, an option that many a young man in his position had taken just to stay alive even after witnessing the rape of their sisters, mothers, and on occasion, even their young brothers. With Vladimir's acute intuition however, he knew that this boy stood in front of him could never be brought to heel. Sadly this Croat would have to die, but not before he was forced to suffer the soul destroying degradation that was about to be played out in front of his very eyes, as all the countless others had before him.

'You're going to have to choose Marko,' Vladimir almost whispered mischievously, grinning broadly as he saw the surprised look of horror in his subjects eyes focussing mournfully on his mama and sister, before returning to Vladimir, his eyes burning with seething hatred, but realizing with a crushing certainty that he was no longer able to freeze his captor with his gaze and distract him, even for a moment.

'Choose, Marko,' Vladimir hissed this time, his expression like that of a victorious chess player calling checkmate.

It took Vladimir a moment to register what happened next, as he suddenly felt the warm flecks of blood splatter his face, the corporal to Marko's left dropping like a stone. The corporal left holding a stunned Marko had no time to react as a split second later the second bullet passed straight through his neck, severing his jugular. Involuntarily releasing Marko, he wrapped both hands around his neck in a futile attempt to stem the bleeding, his captive finding himself free. For an instant, before neither Marko nor Vladimir had time to move, they locked eyes, both torn between diving for cover or killing each other there and then. Vladimir was quicker off the mark, Marko still dazed from the blow to his head and by the time his legs received the message from his brain, Vladimir was diving across the floor, scattering a terrified Karla and Ana like skittles, before grabbing a screaming Karla around the throat from behind, dragging her to her feet and placing his unholstered pistol to her temple.

Time seemed to slow down for Marko as he found himself in the boxing ring, his mind calculating the next move. Spinning to check on the location of Juraj he saw him lying motionless, a pool of blood quickly spreading outwards around his misshapen head. His attention back on Vladimir his plan of attack was abruptly cut short by the sound of the kitchen door flying open to his left. His instincts took over and without looking, he dropped to the floor for cover, glancing up to see three more soldiers burst in, two of them immediately training their rifles on Vladimir as the third quickly scanned the room, Marko included, casually stepping over the corpse of one Vladimir's corporals to crouch down and check the prone form of Filip for a pulse, sighing as he stood again to join the others. Their uniforms were almost indistinguishable from those of Vladimir and his men, the same green and with no markings or insignia. For a moment Marko feared that Ana, Karla and himself would still meet their maker in that kitchen, shot in cold blood to leave no trace behind of the murder of Vladimir. It was the voice of the man that spoke that changed everything for Marko, the glimmer that they might possibly survive their ordeal. Sergeant Stanton had handsome, square jawed features with sharp, piercing eyes, now somewhat older than his years from his recent traumatic experiences in neighbouring Croatia.

'Release her,' came his deep voice, the tone commanding, yet calm and measured, but it was the accent, not the tone that gave Marko reason to hope. It was undeniably English, just like the actors from the British sitcoms that had recently begun to find their way onto Bosnia's television screens. Marko focussed on the man behind that voice, his different, shorter, yet more sophisticated looking rifle levelled at Vladimir. Whilst he had no doubt that this man and his soldiers meant no harm to him and his mama and sister, he knew with one hundred percent certainty that the man holding Karla hostage with his pistol to her head would not hesitate to pull the trigger.

Karla screamed again as she felt the cold metal of the barrel pushed harder against her temple.

'Don't make me kill this bitch,' Vladimir replied in a tone like that of a card player confident of holding the winning hand, yet still a little unsure of his opponent.

'I said, release the girl,' came Stanton's steady reply, seemingly ignoring Vladimir's threat, his apparent unwillingness to negotiate leaving Marko ever more doubtful about Karla's fate. From his position on the floor he could see one of the idle Kalashnikovs laying just out of reach and he glanced back to the soldiers, their attention averted.

Vladimir, by this point knowing all too well that there was no escape, wanted to take one last look at his three comrades strewn on the floor, hoping that at least one of them was still alive, but he knew that to take his eyes off the man directly in front of him for an instant would be fatal. He tightened his grip around Karla's throat.

'I'll blow her head off,' he shouted, for once Marko registering a hint of panic in his voice, that tone ringing an alarm bell in his head, making him realize that he would have to do something fast.

'Let her go and you'll receive a fair trial, you have my word Lubenski,' Stanton replied as confidently as he could.

In his cold calculating mind Vladimir weighed up the situation. Yes, he had no doubt that he would be able to secure excellent legal representation in the Hague, but he also knew that with the same certainty that dawn would come tomorrow, it was irrelevant how good his lawyer was, he would be going down for the rest of his life no matter what, so in that moment he made his decision. He wanted to die a hero in his prime, not an incontinent frail old man in some clinical white prison cell.

Stood cornered in that room with his pistol pressed against his hostage's temple, he knew his choice was simple. It would have been so easy for him to spare the young woman in his grasp at that moment, to make a false move that would make his captor instinctively pull that trigger, and for a split second, an alternative ending flashed through his mind, the daughter rushing back into her mama's arms, but that would mean the boy would be able to stare down at his own corpse victorious having been spared his sister and that would go against everything he had fought for over these last months. His life's work he knew would unravel before his eyes in the tiniest fraction of a second when he pulled that trigger, so before that moment came, he wanted to ask himself a question that he had been avoiding for far too long. If he had been raised in a loving home, a place where his parents had had a loving relationship, one where he had not been desensitised by his mother's screams for help night after night as his father forced himself on her, would he have turned out the way he did? The truth was, he really didn't know the answer to that question, and anyway he conjectured as his finger tensed imperceptibly on the hairline trigger of his pistol, what did it matter now?

The sound that everyone heard was unmistakeably a gunshot, but it was not from Vladimir's pistol, it came from somewhere else in the room, shredding the tendons in his hand and severing three of his fingers, the pistol flying from his grasp.

Stanton spun with lightning speed to level his weapon at the source of the gunshot as Vladimir, staring in shocked disbelief at the bloody mutilated limb that had once been his hand, felt an intense pain shoot through his skull from the cold hard edge of a soldier's rifle butt crashing into his nose, crushing the cartilage before he then found himself dragged stunned and defenceless away from a paralysed Karla frozen to the spot. Thrust down onto the floor on his front he felt his arms being dragged behind his back, the sharp edge of the plastic tie strip cutting into his wrists as his hands were bound.

The other soldier and Stanton were stood with their weapons aimed at Marko on the other side of the room, the Kalashnikov in his trembling hands, a reunited Karla and Ana staring at him in wide eyed disbelief.

Stanton could tell Marko was in a state of shock, and with the boy's finger still on the trigger he also knew the Kalashnikov could go off again at any instant. He glanced at the soldier next to him, gesturing for him to lower his weapon before turning back to Marko. Approaching him slowly, his rifle lowered in submission he spoke slowly and reassuringly, just like how his father used to talk to him as a young child when he was upset. To an outsider his tone would have sounded annoyingly patronizing, but Stanton had seen many adolescent boys in this condition recently and those experiences had taught him well.

'It's alright, everything's alright now,' he said, keeping his eyes trained on Marko's, realizing that the boy was still dangerously frozen in that moment when he had pulled the trigger.

Marko didn't move, his eyes still fixed on the middle distance, looking straight through Stanton, still holding onto the Kalashnikov tightly.

'It's over now, you can give me the weapon,' he persisted gently. Then very slowly he reached out with one hand and placed it on the barrel of the Kalashnikov, lowering Marko's aim, but careful not to try and take the weapon.

'My name is Sergeant Stanton, from the British army. You're safe now.'

At hearing that name, Marko suddenly seemed to snap out of his trance, his eyes finding focus on Stanton. He looked down as he felt the cold metal in his hands and saw what he was holding with a look of revulsion, immediately taking his finger off the trigger.

Stanton placed his rifle on the floor and stepped forward to let Marko surrender the Kalashnikov, engaging the safety catch before stepping away.

The drama over, Ana released her embrace on her daughter and flung herself down over Filip's corpse, letting out a loud continuous wail like that of a wounded animal, as Karla and Marko rushed over to comfort her.

'I swear, I'm going to kill you boy,' came a loud booming voice. Marko turned to see a prone Vladimir, one side of his face pressed against the stone floor as his captor started binding what was left of his wounded hand.

'Shut it,' Marko heard the soldier shout, punctuating his response with a solid punch to the exposed side of Vladimir's jaw, knocking him half unconscious.

Stanton had stepped through an open doorway into the next room, out of earshot. He took out a radio device from his breast pocket and depressed the red button.

'This is Dog Tag Messenger, we have the suspect, request immediate evac, over,' he enunciated clearly into the radio. There was a long pause as he listened intently.

'Roger Dog Tag Messenger, we have you're coordinates. Helicopter is inbound, two minutes,' a distant voice finally crackled over the radio. Pocketing the device, Stanton stepped back into the kitchen.

'We have to go,' he announced to no one in particular.

Ana looked up from Filip's corpse, teary eyed.

'What are you talking about?' she asked, wiping her wet face with the back of her hand.

'It isn't safe here,' Stanton replied, matter of fact.

'But this is our home,' Ana pleaded.

'Not anymore, I'm sorry,' Stanton persisted regretfully.

'We're not leaving,' Ana countered indignantly, glancing at a nervous Marko and Karla for moral support.

'Listen, there are more Serb soldiers on the way. We have to get you out of here right now,' came Stanton's more authoritative response.

'Not without my husband,' Ana commanded. Stanton glanced round at the two soldiers. While he didn't need their approval for anything, he felt it was only right in the circumstances. A quick decisive nod from both of them told him what he needed to know and they stepped forward, helping Ana to her feet before picking Filip's body up in as dignified a manner as was possible given the urgency of the situation.

The dusk light was fading as they emerged from the farmhouse, Stanton leading with Vladimir in front still somewhat dazed, the cold hard end of a rifle barrel prodding him forward before a swift boot behind his knees dropped him to the ground. The two other soldiers carried the limp form of Filip, with Marko, Ana and Karla following behind. Lowering Filip's corpse to the ground the soldiers carefully scanned the treeline half a mile away across the fields for signs of any activity, visibly relieved as the low hum of the helicopter in the distance reached their ears.

Stanton hated this time of the evening just before darkness fell, when the gloomy dusk light made everything seem to blend into one sprawling mass where movement ahead could easily go undetected, the perfect time for an ambush. Without taking his eyes of the kneeling form of his captive, Stanton could tell from the pitch of the thudding rotors of the helicopter how long it would now take to reach them, knowing that these agonizing next few minutes were the most dangerous. He reached into his pocket in anticipation of the next communication, balancing the radio on his thigh as he crouched.

'We have visual on you Dog Tag Messenger,' came a voice over the radio, Stanton recognizing the distinctive accent belonging to one of the pilots. He glanced to his left as he was joined by one of the soldiers.

'Looks clear Serg,' the soldier confirmed. Stanton depressed the red button.

'No sign of any activity from the treeline,' he announced.

'Roger, making our final approach,' the radio voice crackled, Stanton letting out a sigh of relief as he repocketed the radio and pressed the barrel muzzle harder into Vladimir's back as a reminder not to try anything. Despite the jarring pain of the cold hard metal in his right kidney from Stanton's rifle, Vladimir forced himself not to flinch, keeping up the pretence of still being dazed from the soldier's punch to his jaw minutes ago.

Huddled together with Ana and Karla, Marko looked up transfixed as the huge mass of the twin engine Chinook came sweeping down next to the farmhouse, its front end rearing up at the last moment to bring it to a hovering standstill perilously low, a powerful tornado of dusty air enveloping them as it descended, the massive rear door already lowering directly in front of them to reveal the cavernous hold and the aircrew before touching the ground. Above the deafening whine of the engines, Stanton hauled Vladimir to his feet as the two soldiers ushered Ana, Karla and Marko up the ramp before picking up Filip's corpse and following on, quickly placing him down at the top the ramp to immediately turn back and assist Stanton and Vladimir about to start up the ramp.

Suddenly a rapid succession of sparks flew off the metal of the tail section directly above Stanton's head and he instinctively crouched for cover, the Chinook's starboard heavy machine gun positioned halfway down the fuselage bursting into action with a deafening chatter in the direction of the muzzle flashes lighting up the treeline. With Stanton momentarily distracted, Vladimir seized his chance, bolting for the cover of the field. Stanton was quick to react and determined not to let the prize that had eluded him for so long slip away, fired off a single shot, winging his prey in the right shoulder just as he made the cover of the tall hay. Feeling the searing hot burning sensation as the bullet clipped his shoulder blade, Vladimir instinctively dropped face first, vanishing from view. Stanton, keeping low, had already taken the first strides in the direction of the field when he felt the vibration in the air of bullets whizzing past within inches of his head, and in that moment his razor sharp mind was forced to make a swift calculation regarding his mortality.

'Serg, we have to go,' he heard someone shout over the din of the machine gun fire and the rotors. He turned to see the two soldiers part way down the ramp, laying out covering fire over his head.

'Serg,' the soldier on the left screamed at the top of his lungs, his panic evident.

Stanton scanned the field one last time, knowing his injured subject wouldn't have made it far. His legs were willing him to rush into that tall hay, but he knew with a morbid clarity that if he didn't get up that ramp in the next few seconds, his wife back home would be getting a knock on the door from a sombre faced luckless corporal in the morning. Then, without thinking, he found himself sprinting up that ramp as more bullets bounced off the metal structure around him, the Chinook's engines screaming as the rotors hauled its heavy bulk skywards and away with the ramp still raising, the side blazing machine gun not pausing for breath until they were well out of range.

Vladimir lay face down in the crumpled hay, motionless. As the sound of the Chinook faded, he turned his head and opened his eyes, slowly struggling to his feet. With the severe muscle cramp in his wounded shoulder starting to set in, he had forgotten about his aching bandaged stump of a hand.

A small platoon of dishevelled looking soldiers approached across the field, carving a deep channel as they trampled the crop. A young sergeant stepped forward, grimacing as he saw the bandaged remains of Vladimir's hand.

'General, your…' the sergeant began, silenced mid sentence by the angry glare that met him.

'Where are the others?' he enquired nervously, immediately realizing the stupidity of the question.   Vladimir glanced behind at the farmhouse regretfully.

'Take some men and get the bodies,' he said wearily, with a tone of resignation that he rarely permitted any of his sergeants to witness. He staggered past the sergeant in the direction of the treeline, the other soldiers recognizing the look of angry resentment on his face and not daring to make eye contact as their sergeant summoned them to the farmhouse. As he made his way across the field, Vladimir looked up at the sky in the direction that the Chinook had fled, his eyes filled with a vengeful fury. They had taken his best sergeant from him, someone who he had been able to count on to watch his back in Croatia. The truth was, he had never really felt close to Juraj on a personal level, but then he had never really liked anyone in that way. The notion of being one of the comrades so to speak, singing along together drunkenly every night with his men after too much Vodka as Juraj had always done, had always been an odd notion to him. Juraj, the other sergeants and the soldiers under his command had been up until that point, and always would be nothing more than a means to an end, dispensable pawns on a chessboard. He would have to choose Juraj's replacement very carefully. The men had looked up to him, both in his seniority as Vladimir's right-hand man and also as a comrade in arms, someone they felt was one of them and were happy to take orders from, someone they respected, even when on occasion he did go way over the top with a soldier that might rub him up the wrong way.

By the time he made it to the treeline, the platoon was close behind with the corpses of Juraj and the two corporals, and as they too disappeared into the gloom of the woodland, a calm tranquillity returned to the scene, the hay rolling like waves as a light evening breeze picked up, the farmhouse stood peaceful as it had done for generations. To the outside world it would have appeared that nothing had changed.

Huddled together by the ramp door inside the cold cavernous hold of the Chinook that shuddered noisily from the vibration of the twin engines overhead, Marko, Ana and Karla knelt over Filip's corpse, all lost in their own distinctive distant memories of happier times as a family.

'Marko' came a distant voice in his head. He thought at first it was his father calling out to him, like he always did when supper was ready. He felt the familiar touch of a heavy gentle hand on his shoulder and, still lost in his own world, he looked up expecting to see Filip stood over him. Instead he saw the face of Stanton, his helmet still tightly secured, instantly recognizable from his distinctive chiselled features and razor sharp eyes.

'Someone wants to see you up front,' Stanton shouted over the din of the engines. Ana and Karla looked up nervously as Marko stood.

'Don't worry, he'll be right back,' Stanton assured them with a reassuring smile.

Leading Marko from the aft section past the two side gunners strapped into their elaborate heavy machine perches, Stanton reached the cockpit, a mass of controls lighting up large panels seemingly suspended above a sea of Perspex glass all around them.

Two green glad pilots sat side by side donning huge shiny black helmets fitted with bug like night vision visors. Stanton gently tapped the left-hand co-pilot on the shoulder who glanced round before nodding to his pilot to take the controls. Turning back to them, his visor still down, his helmet reminded Marko of an ant's head seen under the microscope.

'This the boy?' The co-pilot asked loudly to make himself heard over the engine noise.

'This is him,' Stanton replied, Marko detecting a warm pride in his response.

'I heard you saved your mother and sister back there, sorry about your father,' the pilot offered.

Stanton smiled sadly at Marko, placing a comforting hand on his shoulder again.

'When we get back to base, we're going to get all of you airlifted to Britain,' Stanton announced, Marko's eyes lighting up.

'You're going have a new home, in our country,' added the co-pilot with a broad smile.

'You mean it?' Marko asked, looking to Stanton for reassurance.

'Least we can do. You're a hero, right Frank?' the co-pilot added, smiling at Stanton.

'Damn right he is,' Stanton replied, beaming a proud smile at Marko.

The co-pilot turned his attention back to the controls, his pilot acknowledging with a nod.

Looking past the pilots downwards through the Perspex, Marko could see the mass of the familiar lake that he remembered visiting often as a young boy, as it passed a few hundred feet below, the glass like water glimmering in the setting sun.

Suddenly the co-pilot slumped forward as a Perspex panel shattered below his feet, the right hand side of his upper back exploding outwards as the large calibre round ripped through his torso, narrowly missing Marko's head as it passed straight through the metal ceiling above. Down below to the left, not far from the edge of the lake, Marko saw a bright flash and then a speeding projectile visible by its tail flame accelerating at an incredible speed, straight for them. As the missile flew straight past the cockpit, Marko heard a deafening explosion behind him, the cockpit rocking violently to one side.

It was the high pitched screams of Ana and Karla that he would always remember most about that next moment. Spinning around, he could see that the mid section of the Chinook was all but gone, along with the mutilated corpses of the two side gunners. As the entire tail section of the Chinook came apart in a mass of twisted metal his gut instincts took over and he launched himself down the length of the fuselage towards Ana and Karla in a futile attempt to save them. They reached out to him in vain, an instant later vanishing along with Filip's body, trapped inside the tail section as it tumbled away. A split second later their screams were silenced as the aft fuel tanks exploded, engulfing them in flames. That moment seemed to last forever, frozen in Marko's mind, that image of their panic-stricken faces burning like the flames from the explosion into his retinas, refusing to fade.

Then everything was spinning and he felt himself being pulled violently by his arm. He turned to see Stanton dragging him away from the gaping hole in the severed fuselage, back towards the cockpit, struggling to stay on his feet as what was left of the Chinook, spun around uncontrollably, suspended by the front rotors like a fairground ride he remembered as a young child, the stricken craft losing height as the pilot desperately fought in vain with the controls to keep them airborne, the continuous alarm blaring.

Marko just had time to see the shiny surface of the water rushing up to meet them through the cockpit glass before he was thrown forward and knocked half conscious by the impact. He was vaguely aware of a suffocating, claustrophobic silence as they sank trapped inside the wreckage into the water. The world around him became dark and numbingly cold as the fuselage descended nose first into the depths. Then he was floating, weightless like a spaceman, vaguely aware of being dragged upwards as the fuselage dropped away. Looking down he saw the lifeless forms of the co-pilot and pilot strapped into their seats, the pilot's neck broken, bent at an impossible angle as they became smaller, disappearing into the darkness.

As he broke the surface of the water his ears were filled with the sound of splashing. Craning his head, he realized that Stanton was dragging him to the shore. After what seemed like an eternity in the freezing cold water that numbed his already impaired senses, they finally made landfall, Stanton dragging him up the muddy bank and laying him in the recovery position on his side.

'Marko are you alright,' he heard Stanton ask, a genuine tone of worry in his voice, parental even. Marko turned his head, seeing Stanton's concerned face come into focus. Marko nodded, still too dazed to speak, before he felt Stanton helping him to sit up.

Looking at Stanton it took a few moments for Marko to realize that something was very wrong. Stanton's face seemed to be getting paler by the moment, like the life was running out of him. Then he saw it, a jagged piece of metal protruding from Stanton's left side through the fabric, just above his waist, blood seeping through his uniform. He was about to say something, but Stanton had turned away from him. Marko watched as Stanton scanned the area, the sunset now rapidly giving way to darkness as he frantically scanned for signs of any activity. Grimacing from the first of the many inevitable stabbing pains deep in his side that he knew signalled the start of the internal bleeding process, Stanton reached into his fastened chest pocket and retrieved his radio, depressing the red button.

'This is Dog Tag Messenger, helicopter is down, I'm on the north side of the lake, you should have my coordinates,' he said quietly, his voice strained as he fought back the pain.

'Roger Dog Tag Messenger, we have your coordinates and are inbound. ETA five minutes,' crackled the radio voice. Placing the radio down, Stanton tried to get to his feet but only made it to a low squat before his legs gave way under him, Marko reaching forward to steady him as he went down.

'Marko you need to check over that ridge and make sure they're not closing in on us,' he suggested, breathing harder now, his discomfort becoming evidently more acute by the second.

'But what about you, you're hurt?'

'It's alright, I'll be fine here. Now go,' came Stanton's reply, doing his best to put on a brave face.

The pungent smell of burning aviation fuel grew stronger as Marko climbed the shallow ridge, its shape silhouetted by the glow from the hidden flames. Reaching the top his gaze was immediately drawn to the burning wreckage of the aft section of the Chinook, the knowledge that the charred corpses of his family were trapped inside that twisted metal wreckage like a macabre funeral pyre, hitting home with a morbid certainty.

His face ran with tears as the terrible realization hit him that they were all gone forever. He gazed helpless, his eyes stinging as the heat from the flames quickly dried his tears. Then suddenly, almost like a much needed distraction from the horrific sight he was witnessing, he remembered the sergeant.

As he hastily clambered back down the ridge Stanton was lying back on one elbow, placing a white field dressing pad on his wound to try and slow the mortal bleeding, grimacing with pain as crimson red blood quickly soaked through the gauze. In an instant Marko was kneeling beside him, panicking as he saw the extent of the bleeding.

'What can I do, tell me?' Marko shouted in frustration.

Taking Marko's hand, Stanton pressed it against the sticky blood-soaked pad.

'Keep the pressure on,' Stanton replied, his voice weaker now. As he pressed down, Stanton stifled an involuntary scream through gritted teeth, Marko instantly taking the pressure off.

'No, keep pushing down,' Stanton moaned, his pupils beginning to dilate. His coordination beginning to waver, he clumsily tore open another dressing, covering the first, but in an instant, it was saturated, the blood running between Stanton's fingers. Marko frantically reached for another dressing, but Stanton's hand stopped him.

'What are you doing?' Marko exclaimed incredulously.

'Leave it,' Stanton moaned almost dreamily, his face now ashen and his eyes half closed, moving his elbow to allow himself to lay fully down and rest his heavy head.

'No, let me…'

'It's alright,' Stanton protested, struggling to keep his eyes even slightly open. He reached out with one hand and grasped Marko's shoulder as hard as he could.

'You're a good boy Marko,' he said softly, a faint smile on his lips which Marko noticed were beginning to turn blue.

'But this is all my fault,' Marko replied sorrowfully.

'No, you must never think that you hear?' Stanton commanded, this time choking a little as Marko noticed blood spittle on his lips.

'You're going to make it to Britain,' Stanton gasped with a smile.

'And you're coming too, you have to,' Marko demanded, Stanton offering a sad sigh in response.

With his other blood-soaked hand, Stanton reached inside his jacket collar, searching, before he wrapped his hand around his two dog tags secured around his neck with a short flimsy chain. With a sharp downward tug, the tags came away in his hand and he held them out to Marko, the broken chain still attached.

'These are yours now, take them,' Stanton spluttered, the blood running from the corners of his mouth now.

Marko's eyes welled up as he took the bloody tags, wet and sticky in his hands, wanting to say something, but unable to form the words.

'They will keep you safe,' Stanton gurgled. Then, hearing the rhythmic throb of the helicopter approaching, he let out a final sigh of relief. Taking his last gurgling breath, his hand still on Marko's shoulder, he drew him nearer, whispering something into his ear, blood speckling Marko's face. Then, seeing Marko's nod of understanding, Stanton smiled one last time, the kind of smile just before falling into a deep sleep, and as he closed his eyes, Marko felt his hand slip from his shoulder.

Looking down at Stanton, that grin on his face, he could tell that the man who had saved him was at peace, already up in heaven. He thought of his own father who he knew was still far from heaven's gate, his final moments in this world he was certain having been filled with anguish. That line of thought led him to Vladimir, and he cursed himself for not having had to sense to put another bullet in that murderer when he'd had the chance, except of course it wouldn't have been that simple and he knew it. One day he would find that man and finish the job, would force him to look into his eyes one last time before he… He stopped, pulled himself back from that thought, realizing that in the last few hours he had changed into someone more than capable of taking another man's life.

The loud thwapping of the helicopter rotors snapped him out of his trance and he looked up, a much smaller single engine Lynx approaching low and at speed on its final approach, the pilot clearly not taking any chances.

He looked back down at Stanton, thought about what he had choked into his ear in his final moments, pondering the responsibility that had been placed on his shoulders. An overwhelming wave of guilt suddenly overwhelmed him, suffocating him, and he broke down into a flood of tears, the traumatic stream of events of the last few hours racing through his mind in a matter of moments. He wanted more than anything else at that moment to ask his father for forgiveness, not just for not being able to save him and his mama and sister, but also because he felt like he had just lost another father as well.

TWO

Darkness was falling fast like a suffocating shroud on the quaint sleepy village, its single narrow street already thrown into deep shadow, now the setting sun had finally disappeared behind the buildings.

Children there had suddenly stopped playing out after their supper, their parents now gravely serious about the once unthinkable rumours about the dangers to young girls especially that had spread like wildfire from nearby villages.

To the outside world however, unaware of the relentless tide of ethnic cleansing and all the depraved atrocities that it involved which had started as a mere ripple in a pond in Croatia a number of months before, this village like so many in that mostly rural area of Bosnia just over the border would have appeared as tranquil as the picture postcards had portrayed for generations, except for one thing.

A few nights before under the cover of darkness, the light from the moon obscured by heavy cloud, large blue crosses had been daubed with hasty tardiness on the old wooden doors of some of the houses. Some were on a few houses side by side, others seemingly at random on the odd door here and there. The crosses looked if anything like some ritualistic graffiti, but what was most odd was that already two days old, not one single occupant of the affected dwellings had made any attempt whatsoever to try and remove these crudely applied aberrations that defaced their front doors.

At a large kitchen table inside one of the tarnished dwellings, Radica sat with her family quietly eating a late supper. Her sister Vanessa, two years her elder, worked in one of the clothes shops in town. Unlike Radica, who had inherited her mother's looks, Vanessa bore more resemblance facially to her father, yet she was much more like her mother in demeanour and character, having had no desire to carry on her education after leaving school, happy to follow in her mother's footsteps as a homemaker, whenever the right young man chose to come forward.

Their stern faced father Miroslav had been home late from work that evening after a heated union meeting at the end of his shift at the steel fabrication factory, the subject of which he had adamantly refused to discuss with any of his family, even his wife Jannike. She was furious at him for not phoning to let her know he wouldn't be in at his usual time, an arrangement he had promised to adhere to for her own piece of mind, made ever more fragile by the frightening stories that had reached her ears via her Serb housewife neighbour in recent days, the Croat lady on the other side having suddenly abruptly stopped talking to her a week ago after years of friendship, without any explanation, although the reason was now abundantly clear.

Despite her drawn features that evening, Radica still reflected on how beautiful her mother still looked as she watched her eating her food tentatively, her appetite obviously lacking. Radica had noticed the sudden change in her mama's demeanour a week before. Her parents had had disagreements before over the years, and Radica always knew when because her mama would become withdrawn, inward, exactly as Radica did sometimes. But she'd never known her mama to stay away in her dark thoughts for more than a few days at most. Her mama had always talked to her when she was feeling down, ever since the age when Radica developed a keen sense of intuition, something that had strengthened their bond immensely over the last few years, but this time Radica was feeling shut out. She had never had to prod her mama to talk, Jannike always coming to her to open up, but on this occasion after it was evident that something had been on her mama's mind for some time, Radica had felt it necessary to make the first move, confident that this would do the trick. The reaction however was something she had never expected, a short tempered response that sounded like a clear warning not to pursue her line of enquiry.

The atmosphere at home had been different ever since, the last few days proving a considerable challenge as Radica tried her best to stay out of her mama's way, hoping that she would come round in her own good time.

When she had left for school two mornings ago with her little brother Johan, affronted by the blue graffiti on the front door as she opened it leave, her first thought was that it was the work of one of the local youths who lived further down the street, notorious for playing practical jokes, but as she walked with Johan towards the school bus stop on the edge of the village, seeing the same crude markings on a number of other dwellings, a cold feeling gripped her, a sense that this was not the work of some mere prankster, but something far more sinister.

At school that day she had hastily quizzed her friends, but whilst a few of them had witnessed the same markings in their streets, they didn't know the meaning or the reason.

Radica's consternation was further heightened when on arriving home late that afternoon, she saw that no attempt seemed to have been made to remove the unsightly graffiti, not from one single door. Her frustration getting the better of her, she had been unable to hold her tongue when she entered the kitchen with Johan to find her mama busying herself at the sink, the clatter of pots and pans much louder than usual.

Hearing the door open seemed to startle Jannike and she spun round, Radica catching her wide eyes, an undeniable expression of fear as if she was seeing the grim reaper, not her own daughter and son. An instant later she caught herself, managing to force an unconvincing smile, a glimmer of fear still in her eyes.

In that moment a strange realization struck Radica, a notion well beyond the innocence of her youthful mind. She could tell by that lingering look of dread in her mama's eyes, that she was silently begging her not to ask about the blue crosses on the doors in the village, not to make her have to lie to her own daughter about whatever it was that that had plagued her mind for almost a full week and was obviously connected to the symbol crudely daubed on their front door.

Miroslav returned home from work much earlier than usual that evening. As he opened the front door, Radica, who was stood helping Jannike prepare supper, turned, surprised to see him at this hour and looking out of breath as if he had been in some kind of a hurry. Jannike, on the other hand, simply glanced around and smiled at him, leaving Radica perplexed that her mama thought there was nothing out of the ordinary about his odd time of arrival.

The atmosphere around the table that evening gave Radica further cause for concern, as Miroslav and Jannike seemed distracted, eating their food hastily without even tasting it. They reminded her of the meal time habits of the mongrel stray dog they had rescued years ago. Rex as he had been named, had long since passed away, but Radica would never forget how he would wolf his food down with both ears tuned in to every tiny sound, looking up from his bowl wide eyed at the slightest noise to check that the coast was clear, before returning to his food.

A front door closed with a loud thud a few houses down and both her mama and papa looked up from their food, just like Rex would have done. They both sat there frozen for a moment, listening for any further sounds, then glanced at each other in silent acknowledgment, before continuing with their meals. This nervous ritual occurred a number of times over supper, as any kind of sound, even the familiar voice of a neighbour talking in the street, would instantly halt them in their tracks.

Radica had never been as relieved to be excused after finishing her food, happy for the first time in her life to be at the sink, doing the dishes. Anything was better than having to spend any more time sat at the kitchen table having to endure her parents on tender hooks.

After supper was done and the kitchen was all ship shape, Radica made the excuse that she wasn't feeling too well and asked if she could go up early to her bedroom. She had never imagined that the tedium of her monthly periods would serve any purpose other than to make one week in every four a teenage girl's nightmare, but that evening she was glad of those menstrual cycles, even if on this occasion it was a lie. Jannike simply smiled at her knowingly, understanding her vague explanation like only a mother could, and with that, Radica took her leave, the sanctuary of her room never more appealing as she closed the door behind her.

The next day Radica reluctantly took Johan to school with her as usual, her instincts telling her that she shouldn't be leaving her mama alone in the house, yet her conflicting rational logic suggesting that her own papa wouldn't have left for work earlier that morning if Jannike was in any kind of danger.

All through the day, Radica's mind played over and over, a vision of her returning home after school that day to find that her mama had scrubbed the symbol off their defaced front door.

When she and Johan stepped off the bus at the end of the day and they began to make their way along the street towards their house, her heart sank, as blanking out all the other dwellings, her young sharp eyes immediately picked out the door leading into her own home at the far end, the blue paint still there, completely untouched.

Reaching the front door, Radica discovered to her consternation as she turned the door handle, that it was locked. For a second her stomach leapt in her mouth, a premonition that something terrible may have happened to her mama racing through her mind, but then she heard the click of the turning key from the inside. Expecting to find her mama stood there she was surprised to find Miroslav, his tall frame almost filling the doorway. Looking over their heads as if he hadn't even noticed them stood there, he stuck his head out, glancing nervously up and down the street before quickly beckoning them inside in an ill tempered manner, immediately closing the door behind them and locking it again.

'Papa, what's wrong,' Radica enquired as she saw Jannike stood at the sink, not even turning to greet her children as she always did, even if they had been bad.

'Go and change, supper will be ready soon,' Miroslav snapped for the first time in as long as Radica could remember, even Johan registering his angry tone.

'Mama?' Radica called out instinctively across the kitchen, but Jannike still refused to turn around and look at her, her whole body seeming to tremble.

'Do as you're told,' her papa shouted, his whole being seeming to grow larger, towering over her and her terrified looking brother, who looked like he was about to cry.

'Come on Johan, up to your room,' Radica said, her voice wavering as she tried to comfort him, placing her hands on his shoulders and walking him out of the kitchen into the hallway, not daring to look back at Miroslav.

Jannike turned from the sink as soon as they were gone. Her face was wet from fresh tears, her hands shaking as she stepped forward to grab a kitchen chair and park herself down for fear of her legs giving way under her. Miroslav sat next to her, placing a comforting hand on her shoulder.

'What are we going to do,' Jannike asked with a distant terrified gaze, as if seeing some kind of horrifying scene unfolding in the middle distance.

'We have to stay,' Miroslav answered firmly.

'No, we must leave, tonight, or…' Jannike replied, trailing off.

'You know what will happen if we try to run.'

Jannike turned to her husband, taking his hands in hers.

'But they will be coming for us, very soon, and when they do, how will we protect our children?' she sobbed, searching his eyes for even the tiniest glimmer of hope.

'We will hide, in the cellar, like we discussed, and…'

'But we will be trapped down there if they find us,' Jannike protested.

'It's our only chance.'

'But we could distract them when they come, tell the children to run.'

'And then what will become of them, even if they do escape, out in the open.'

'At least they'll have a chance,' she begged.

'No, they won't,' Miroslav replied regretfully.

'But...'

'We are a family, we have to stick together, no matter what,' he interjected firmly.

'And die together, is that what you want?' Jannike replied, her voice an octave higher.

Miroslav was silent for a moment. He thought back to the father he had never met, remembering how his mother, now long gone, used to tell him stories as a young child about how brave his father had been in the war, fighting along with the other young men from the village, the very same village that he still lived in. She had always been proud to remind her son that his father had died a hero on the battlefield, but when he had enquired about where all the graves were where his father would have been buried with his fallen comrades, she explained that they had all been cremated and their ashes scattered in the same graveyard where so many soldiers from the first great war, Miroslav's grandfather included, had been laid to rest.

Like so many young children born at the end of the war and too young to remember the terrible hardships that their mothers had had to endure, Miroslav had grown up proud of his father's sacrifice for his country, until one day something happened, a discovery, an event that changed everything and still haunted him to this very day.

He had been twelve years old, playing out with his friends during the summer school holidays. He remembered that on that day, the sun was blisteringly hot like no other, and being at the age where planning and preparation wasn't something at the top of their lists of priorities, they had not thought to make sure that they took plenty of drinking water with them. Deciding to cycle many miles out of the village, much further than ever before, they found the ancient woodland that they had heard was haunted and that no one, not even the locals, had ever dared to enter.

Arriving down an overgrown dirt track that had evidently not been travelled for many years, they lay their bikes down in the shrub. Checking behind them to make sure no one had seen them, they stepped from the blaring heat of the midday sun into the eery quiet of the trees, disappearing into the much cooler gloom.

What young Miroslav noticed first was the complete lack of sound, other than their own footfalls in the undergrowth. There was no twitter of birds in the tall trees, warning of intruders, no scurrying of rodents fleeing as they made their way.

The customary boyish teasing by the group of any single explorer who showed any nervousness only served to push them deeper into the darkness.

Up ahead they suddenly saw, as one, sunlight shining directly down in a huge funnel, breaking the darkness, and whilst no one dared say, they were all relieved that there was an escape from the cold damp darkness that by now was making them more frightened than they had ever been in their lives.

Entering the bright open area and feeling the hot sun beating down, they saw that the ground was completely devoid of foliage, no trees, no flowers, no shrubs, nothing. Instead, a huge, circular, low mound of mossy earth stretched from one side of the clearing to the other.

Fascination getting the better of Miroslav and the others, they began swapping fanciful theories about what the earthy mound signified, all of them agreeing on one thing, that this was the mysterious source of the rumour that had spread around the school like wildfire.

It wasn't too long before they found themselves daring each other to go up to it, to touch it, walk on top of it, even try and find out what was inside.

Then they found themselves prodding the edges of the mound with large sticks from fallen tree branches, clambering up on top, then kneeling down in a circle and digging down frantically with their bare hands in a race to discover what was inside.

They were never the same after that day, the innocence of their childhood ripped from their very being. In an instant their whole perception of life, of the world around them changed. After they had been digging for almost an hour, they all suddenly stopped, frozen in mid motion as they saw the skull that was staring up at them, the mouth wide open in a silent scream, the skeletal remains still dressed in uniform, the frayed fabric discoloured but undeniably that of a soldier. But what would haunt them most about that sight was not so much this one fallen soldier, but the countless layers of skeletons receding deep into the darkness of this tomb.

Everyone except Miroslav looked up at each other, then around them at the huge mass grave that they were standing on, the sickening realization hitting them like a sledgehammer. Miroslav didn't register as his friends all jumped to their feet and ran, everyman for themselves, away into the darkness of the forest. He was still on his knees, still staring transfixed at the tangle of skeletal remains. He had seen something glinting just very slightly in the sun, instantly realizing what it was. He shuddered as the terrifying notion struck him, a terrible alternative reality that he had struggled with ever since his mama had told him about his father's war hero death. He had wanted to believe her so badly, believe that she was telling the truth, but in his darkest fears, he had always feared that it was a lie. Slowly, his hand trembling, he reached down and hooked a finger under the thin brass chain hanging loose around the neck of the fallen soldier, feeling the hollow eyes in that skull glaring at him accusingly. He lifted the chain, the two dog tags hanging down out of sight, coming into view, face down.

Taking a deep breath, Miroslav turned the tags over in his fingers and rubbed the grime away, praying that the inscription would be that of a fallen German or Russian soldier. He had been staring for a long time at the inscription before the tears came, dripping onto the skull still staring up at him.

Leaving the tags around his father's neck as a mark of respect, he covered the hole back over and made his way. His loyal friends were still waiting for him where they had parked their bikes, but when they questioned him about his late arrival, he just said that he had lost his bearings.

He thought long and hard over the coming days about telling them about the dog tags, but he knew it would only make them feel as he did and that was something that he wouldn't wish on his worst enemy.

Things were never the same between Miroslav and his band of brothers after that. If they had shared the trauma of the experience as young men and not boys, then perhaps with that more developed level of maturity, the event would have brought them even closer together, but they were too young to be able to put it behind them and seeing each other only served to remind them of that terrible day. They stayed friends in a manner of speaking, but the damage was done, and after their final year at school they drifted apart.

Miroslav never told his mama what he had found, although for many months afterwards he was filled with an anger, a sometimes almost overpowering urge to call her to account for lying to him, but as he got older he realized that she had simply been trying to protect him from the truth. Now there was another truth that he wanted so desperately to keep from his own children, a dark stain could never be removed from the map of the former Yugoslavia, a bloody smear so old that most men his age had put it to the back of their minds long ago, certain that it would stay buried forever. But now, decades later, the hatred, the anger that he had been so certain would just die away and decompose like the corpses in that mass grave, had resurfaced, simmering away like a bowl of hot water on the stove, threatening to boil over at any minute, with the hand needed to turn the heat down before it was too late, absent like a frightened schoolboy too scared to turn up for a fight after class.

'Miroslav?' Jannike's voice stirred him from his thoughts and he looked up to see her same anguished expression. He stared back at her, the irrepressible reality of the situation staring him in the face, like a sheer brick wall towering over him, blocking his path, impossible to climb.

'Tell the children to pack their things, we leave after dark,' he finally answered, understanding all too well that whilst they probably wouldn't get far, it was better than waiting to be cornered in their own home.

Lost in his thoughts, he didn't even hear Jannike thundering up the stairs, he was trying to work out the route that would give them the best chance. The old car parked out back was reliable enough, and he knew the lanes well, confident that he would be able to navigate the twists and turns in the pitch black, albeit slowly. He found himself picturing the route leading them deeper into Bosnia, away from the Croatian border. Suddenly he heard a motor engine and for an instant he was driving along in the darkness with his family. Then, abruptly, he felt his gut involuntarily tighten as the reality of that moment kicked in. The engine sound was far too heavy to be that of a car.

He sprang to his feet, racing for the window, and parting the net curtains just enough to looking out onto the street, the oblique angle affording him little latitude, but just enough to…

He felt his bowels loosen. Shouting for Jannike, barking the words without thinking, he ran for the back door, but as he began to turn the key, movement caught his eye through the small window just to the right and his heart sank as the finality sank in. He yelled for his family over and over as he flung the cellar door open. Spinning around he was confronted by a sight that immediately brought tears to his eyes. His children were stood there all wrapped up in their coats and boots, looking up at him, reminding him of the many days out in the car as a family that he had always cherished. Jannike was staring at him with a pleading look, her eyes flitting from him to the open cellar door, then to the back door. She didn't need to go and see, the ugly loud voices of soldiers out there reaching her ears. Their eyes met, a look of sad silent understanding between them.

Outside, emerging from the deep shadows of the street, the two green Croat Army trucks, their cabs adorned with the proud symbol of a sword with a crest encircling a castle, rumbled along, a third truck bringing up the rear, the complete lack of any markings matched with the abundance of thick mud all down the sides giving it the air of a vehicle that's purpose was perhaps for less conventional military activities.

Cowering in the darkness of the cellar, a wide-eyed Radica and her family listened in silence as the rumble of the trucks grew louder, reaching a deafening roar as if they were directly overhead, the floor boards above them vibrating. Then, mercifully, the rumble began to fade, the trucks reaching the far end of the village. Miroslav and Jannike's sighs of relief were clearly audible in the darkness, but short lived when moments later they heard the loud screech of heavy brakes. A silent panic began to fill the dark dank space, Vanessa's quiet sobs deafening in the close confinement, Radica pulling her close to try and comfort her.

By his sheer menacing physical presence, the tall broad-shouldered figured that jumped down from the cab of the front vehicle, was able to summon the presence of the dozens of unshaven hungry eyed soldiers leaping down from the back of the trucks without having to speak a single word. Aleksandar was in his late thirties, his brutish round shaped face emphasized by his shaven head, yet he had the eyes and smile of that of an excited child on Christmas morning. This odd contradiction in his looks gave him a somewhat unpredictable air, something that some of his soldiers had learnt to their mortal cost.

As he stood waiting for the soldiers to assemble, he thought back, reminding himself as he did on these special occasions of when it was in his life that his hatred of the Serbs had started in earnest.

It was his grandfather who had first set his mind in motion when he was a young boy, telling him about how the nasty, murderous Serbs had helped the Nazis round up Jewish Croats in their tens of thousands to be marched off to the extermination camps and how when time began to run out, the Croat militia had gladly agreed to help perform the mass executions, creating an improvised small hooked blade specially for the purpose, that could rip out a dozen throats per minute.

The day his grandfather lay on his death bed with his family, he had drawn eight year old Aleksandar close and whispered something into his ear. His parents had enquired some days later as to what his grandfather had said, but Aleksandar had refused to tell, it was his special little secret, his grandfather's talisman of sorts, and to this day he had kept silent.

Aleksandar knew that he needed a loyal dog to watch his back, someone dumb enough to think that he was his right hand man, yet subordinate enough never to try and interfere with his superior's tight control over his men.

Emil was a natural, a self declared convert going back many years, the perfect disciple to reinforce the will of Aleksandar's sadistic doctrine. He had been born with the same primitive urge in his genes, a behaviour that had first reared its ugly head when he was thirteen. Emil had begun to find himself looking at his big sister in a new way, a way that he couldn't comprehend at first. He started to notice the pert shape of her breasts under her thin T shirts that she wore, her nipples tantalisingly pronounced, and he was fascinated with the shape of her buttocks and desperately yearning to discover what the place between her legs looked like.

Then one day when their parents were out, he crept along the landing from his room when he heard the shower running, and watched her undetected, naked through the slightly ajar bathroom door that she had forgotten to close properly. He didn't remember busting into the bathroom and dragging her, terrified and screaming out of the shower and forcing her down onto the floor. His first recollection of that event was the sensation in his throbbing groin as he forced himself inside her, the power, the control he was able to exert, that thrill only heightened further as she screamed out in pain louder and louder, begging for him to stop.

After he climaxed and rolled onto his back, his senses were so blinded by the exhilaration of this new experience, that he didn't register his sister dragging herself up from the floor, sobbing as the blood between her legs began to congeal, staggering away in agony to her room, hastily grabbing whatever clothes were within reach before hurrying down the stairs.

By the time his parent arrived home, Emil had cleaned up the bloody patch on the bathroom floor, thankful for the cheap lino that his father had installed a few months before. When they asked him where his sister was, he shrugged innocently, explaining that she had gone out a number of hours ago, without so much as a word.

Emil knew his sister would never come home, that she wouldn't be able to face up to the shame of being in that house again and that worst of all, neither of her parents would believe her if she told them the sordid truth.

By the time nightfall came, Emil's parents were fearing the worst. Their daughter had never run away before. She was a happy girl with not a care in the world and she would never do anything untoward. After phoning the police, her father decided to go out looking for her. Emil had insisted on coming with him, but despite his thoroughly rehearsed pleas of anguish, his father still said no, instead making him stay with his mother in the hope that their daughter would return. Emil made repeated guiltless attempts to comfort his mother, but she was inconsolable, resorting to the vodka to steady her nerves.

The frantic search of the small town and surrounding roads that night proved to no avail. The next day the word went out in the small town and the search widened and intensified, but after a week, with not one sighting, Emil's parents, their will finally weakened, found themselves unable to hold onto hope any longer and could do nothing other than accept that they were unlikely to see their daughter again.

As for Emil, he spent the rest of his school years obsessed with fantasies of raping every pretty girl in his class, but he lacked the social confidence needed to lure any of them into his lair. He watched with growing frustration as his more intelligent friends charmed their way into girl's bedrooms and by the time he left school at sixteen, a mental block had cemented itself firmly in his mind, an inability to communicate on any verbal level with girls.

His anger built inside him to such a degree that his mind had no room for anything constructive, stunting his academic development, and when he left school with no qualifications, enlistment into the army was the only real choice he had, a view wholeheartedly endorsed by his parents. He settled into the regimented life of a corporal right away, his self esteem rocketing. His pent up sexual frustration from his latter school days had at last found the perfect outlet, and he quickly developed into a physically fit and mentally focussed fighting machine. He didn't have time to daydream about raping young girls anymore, and when he lay his head on the pillow every night, he was too exhausted from the day's physical training to dream about it either.

For years Emil lived in barracks with his fellow young soldiers, where they would go for months on end without leave. His mother had never gotten over the loss of their daughter and soon afterwards had slid inexorably into the dark abyss of drink. His father, on the face of it, had managed to maintain some assemblance of structure in his life at first, putting up with his wife's drunken rants and violent outbursts, mostly directed at him, but over time the change wore him down. After visiting his parents during his first stay of leave a few months into his new army life and seeing the saddening deterioration in their mental and physical states, Emil always found excuses to stay away. He convinced himself that his revulsion was solely based on the intolerable contrast between his regimented life in the army and what could only be described as the slovenly lifestyle of his parents. Yet buried deep in his subconscious lay the real reason why he couldn't bear to be in their company anymore, a notion that would haunt him only occasionally, if he had an idle moment here or there, a guilt that he would push away with his mind as soon as it surfaced from the murky depths of his past. He knew it was true, he was the reason why his parents had become what they were, mere tragic shadows of their former selves. Most times he would be able to force the guilt away with one small shove, but sometimes it just wouldn't budge, replaying over and over in his mind like a broken record, taunting him, until sleep was the only release.

When Croatia began its descent into darkness, Emil, totally by accident, found himself attracting the attention of Aleksandar, during one of their first attacks on Serb civilians.

To his day he remembered her, that young blond girl, no more than fifteen, being dragged from her pleading parents while the soldiers held them, making them watch as they tore her clothes off like wild animals and forced her down into the dirt. It wasn't the sight of the first soldier forcing himself on her that aroused him, it was her shrill screams for mercy.

At first the girl's helpless parents thought Emil was trying to help as he charged in and dragged the first soldier off her, breaking his nose and sending him packing before he found himself brawling with three others. Aleksandar was watching from a nearby truck, impressed at the speed with which Emil dispatched his three rivals, before unbuttoning his trousers in front of the girl's begging parents and dropping down onto her to claim his prize. There and then as he witnessed the spectacle, Aleksandar knew Emil was his man.

Aleksandar was brought back to the present by the ear piercing shout of Emil barking orders as he stepped forward from the second truck. With all the soldiers assembled, Aleksandar began his traditional ritual, holding a finger to his mouth to silence his audience before raising his Kalashnikov into the air to squeeze the trigger. A single shot rang out, echoing down the street.

Placing his other hand to his ear in a mock gesture, he listened in silence for a moment.

'You hear that Emil?' Aleksandar asked.

'I didn't hear anything general,' replied Emil, as if reading from a speech.

'That's the sound of fear, Serb fear,' Aleksandar replied, relishing the sound of his own voice and the instant reaction of his soldiers, their eyes lighting up, evil grins spreading across their faces.

'Emil, the music,' Aleksandar commanded loudly.

Emil climbed back up inside the cab of the lead truck, reaching for something. Suddenly the happy melody of Strauss's Blue Danube Waltz began blaring at deafening volume from two huge speakers mounted on the cab roof.

For a moment, the soldiers did not move, they were waiting for the command. Then Aleksandar raised his hands and began to conduct his imaginary orchestra, the signal to begin. The soldiers instantly dispersed, smashing down doors displaying the blue cross as Aleksandar continued conducting to the amusement of Emil, sat perched on the truck bonnet, watching the entertainment with glee.

Inside one of the dwellings spared the blue graffiti, two young children sitting with their parents at the dinner table, already restless from the sound of the activity outside, looked up again as they heard the loud music.

'Papa, I hear music,' the boy exclaimed excitedly.

His mama and papa, their faces grave, exchanged terse glances.

'It's nothing, now eat your food,' their mother replied reassuringly.

'Let's go and see,' the girl chuckled, ignoring her, but as she jumped down from her chair her father's arm shot out like lightning to grab her.

'But I want to look,' she protested, desperately trying to wriggle free, her father's grip tightening on her arm.

'Sit back down,' he commanded sternly.

'Stop it, you're hurting me,' she cried out, trying to prise his hand away, her objection only serving to infuriate him, and she suddenly found herself being picked up by his two enormous hands and parked back down on her chair.

'Eat your supper,' he shouted angrily, levelling a finger at her. She looked down at her food, sulking, her nervous brother obediently loading his fork with food, looking away. The father felt a hand on his arm, looking up to see his wife with a pleading look. She turned back to the children, touching them both gently on their shoulders.

'Don't worry, the music will stop soon.'

In the darkness of the cellar, Radica fought to calm Vanessa, who was by now on the verge of hysteria, her words becoming fragmented and incoherent. They heard the front door crash open upstairs, Radica having to place her hand over her sister's mouth to stop her from screaming as they all huddled together as one. Loud voices and heavy footsteps echoed above their heads before suddenly, everything went quiet. The deafening silence of that moment seemed to last forever before it was shattered like breaking glass by the thud of rapid footsteps descending the stairs, Radica almost suffocating Vanessa as she tried to muffle her screams.

From the other side of the door a deep voice boomed, taunted them.

'Come out, come out, wherever you are.'

Abruptly the door flew open with a crash as wood splintered, shadowy figures rushing in with their rifles raised, barking orders in their ugly Croat tongue.

Outside, the mass of panic stricken Serb villagers were being herded together like cattle by the soldiers, the blaring music providing a macabre commentary to the unfolding scene.

As Aleksandar stepped forward to inspect the catch, Emil, still sat on the cab cradling his pistol, found his attention drawn to a certain young girl appearing from a doorway with her family. He had had the pleasure of many young girls over the past months, but this one was strikingly beautiful, unlike her older sister, although she too would be of use to the soldiers. Jumping down from the cab he rushed forward and grabbed Radica firmly by the arm.

'Get off me you pig,' she screamed, spitting in his face.

Miroslav rushed forward but froze in mid step, as Emil raised his pistol, waving it at him playfully.

'Naughty, naughty.'

Then Emil lowered his weapon, smiling reassuringly at Miroslav. For that brief instant, a faintest expression of hope glimmered in Miroslav's eyes, before Emil's expression suddenly hardened again and swiftly raising his pistol, he shot Miroslav squarely in the forehead. Radica's mind was momentarily frozen by the sound of the gunshot before she realized, her whole body convulsing against Emil's hold as she screamed like a banshee, a wailing Jannike and Vanessa dropping to their knees to cradle Miroslav's corpse, Johan just stood there staring, far too young to be able to comprehend what was happening.

Radica tried to swing her fist at Emil, but it was caught mid motion by Aleksandar. She spun her head, their eyes locking as he smiled at her greedily.

'She's a fighter this one, and beautiful too,' he concluded to Emil. 'No one touches her but me, understand?' he commanded, Emil nodding reluctantly, more than a little resentful of Aleksandar's claim over his valuable find.

Dragged away with her sister, kicking and screaming as Jannike cowered protectively over Johan with the other captives, Radica and her sister were hauled up by their arms into the back of the third unmarked truck by two soldiers stood just inside, a group of other teenage girls cowering together in the darkness. At once Radica hurled herself at the opening but was thrown back by the soldiers who laughed with amusement.

Figures had begun to appear at the windows of some of the unmarked houses, pulling back net curtains to witness the spectacle. A door opened and an old woman emerged, evidently unafraid, followed by her nervous looking husband. Her eyes full of hatred, she marched with surprising sprightliness towards the cowering Serbs grouped together inside the cordon of troops. Pushing without any hesitation through the loose perimeter, she began spitting repeatedly at the Serb prisoners, immediately drawing cheers of applause from the soldiers.

'Hang the Serbs from the willow trees,' she shouted, over and over. Her boldness appeared to prompt more Croats to emerge from their homes, yelling vehement words of hatred at the captives as Aleksandar stood with Emil, delighted to see Croat civilians of all ages turning on people who for decades they had regarded as close neighbours. As the spectacle unfolded before his eyes, Aleksandar couldn't help but marvel at how easy it had been to rile up the populace and unravel in a just matter of months the many years of harmony that had existed between the Croats and Serbs, albeit superficial. Faster than he could ever have dreamed was possible, the thin veneer of civility had been peeled back to reveal the festering wounds of the past that had never fully healed and had now finally erupted, the poisonous puss seeping into the minds of the very people who had for almost half a century, kept their hatred buried.

The old woman's husband, visibly appalled by her behaviour, decided finally the time had come to drag her back indoors, but as stepped forward to intervened, Emil appeared, blocking his path.

'Leave her old man, she is Croat, she has the right,' Emil pronounced, placing a firm hand on the old man's shoulder. Then Emil took hold of the manic ranting old woman by the arm. Turning her head, she saw Emil smiling at her proudly, his pistol held out to her, gesturing for her to take it. She stared at the weapon for a moment, a conflicted expression on her face.

'Go ahead, take it,' Emil invited.

She looked past Emil at her husband stood helpless, his pleading eyes silently begging for her not to do it, Emil's eyes following hers.

'Don't look at him, look at me,' Emil commanded, the old woman evidently torn, her eyes fleeting between Emil and her husband.

'I said, look at me,' Emil pressed, his tone more insistent.

Her eyes fixed on his, drawn by the irrefutable authority in his voice, she looked at the gun within reach. Emil noticed her expression suddenly change at that moment, a glint of almost childish spitefulness. Her gaze shifted from the gun to the huddled captives, then to her husband. He was weeping, the tears running slowly down his cheeks as he shook his head slowly in a final plea for her to stop. Her eyes narrowed for a moment as she pondered, the conflicting emotions spinning around in her mind. Then, as if the very devil himself had taken possession of her, a grin, emotionless like a plastic doll, spread across her mouth, and breaking free from her husband's gaze, she took the pistol from a delighted Emil and turned back to the crowd. It felt heavy in her hand as under the supervision of her tutor she raised it slowly to take aim, the soldiers joking with each other as the terrified captives began jostling for position behind each other to the sound of the music still blaring out, reminding Emil of the game of musical chairs he used to play as a young boy.

'Go ahead, take your pick,' Emil encouraged, stood to the side of her. The prisoners at the front of the crowd were panicking now, some trying to burrow their way into the huddled mass behind them, packed tightly together to keep themselves safe. A young woman tried to run, only to find herself in the grip of a soldier guarding the cordon and thrown back, sprawling face down in the dirt, much to the loud amusement of the soldiers, drawing the attention of the old woman, her aim shifting. On her knees, looking up, the young woman found herself staring straight into the eyes of her executioner. She raised her hands together in prayer, holding the old woman's gaze, pleading, praying in a garbled jumble of words, the soldiers falling silent in hungry anticipation.

As if on cue, the reverberating music ended abruptly, leaving in its wake a deafening silence and with it an intensity in the cold night air that washed over the scene like a crushing wave as all eyes were on the old woman. In the gravity of the moment she hesitated, Emil quick to notice her faltering grin.

'Shoot her,' Emil ordered firmly but calmly in her ear, but she didn't seem to hear him, her finger still lingering gingerly on the trigger.

'Do it,' he shouted at the top of his voice.

The old woman jumped as the pistol went off with a deafening crack that echoed down the street. It took her a moment to realize what had just happened, her eyes finally focussing on her victim laying face up, staring wide eyed, the other prisoners now all cowering on their knees in a tight huddle, some pleading with the soldiers looking down at them, unable to refrain from their vulgar, mocking taunts.

Aleksandar appeared alongside Emil as he carefully took the pistol from the old woman's grasp, completely unaware of him doing so as she just stood there stone still on that same spot, staring down at the dead woman.

Aleksandar regarded the captives cowering inside the cordon in the same way that a scientist would examine a disease under the microscope. He didn't see real people, just Serbs. They were all one and the same, molecules of a virus that had been allowed to spread unchallenged over the decades throughout the former Yugoslavia, evolving, thriving, multiplying to the point where there was a certainty of never becoming threatened. The Serbs had stolen from the Croats, not just their land, but the lives of the very people themselves during the last war, collaborating with the Nazis in exchange for vast swathes of Croat property, The Reich granting them legal entitlement to territory that was not theirs to give.

Aleksandar's soldiers were all looking at him now, eagerly awaiting his final command, their index fingers subconsciously caressing the cold steel of their Kalashnikov triggers. After what seemed to them like an eternity, they began exchanging quizzical glances, curious as to why he had not already issued the order. Becoming suddenly aware of their disrespectful restlessness out of the corner of his eye as he kept focussed on Aleksandar for the final nod, Emil let slip a swift menacing stare, the soldiers immediately back to attention. As far as he was concerned, they would wait for as long as it took. A few moments later Aleksandar, turned to Emil and nodded before backing away, to watch from the side lines as Emil and the soldiers herded their pleading, screaming flock towards the brick frontage of one of the houses, kicking and dragging those who refused to get off their knees in prayer.

Inside the unmarked truck, Vanessa was huddled together with Radica and the other girls. She was rocking back and forth now, her hands pressed over her ears, her eyes tightly shut, quietly mumbling incoherent words. Most of the others were hunched crying, listening wide eyed to the screams outside. A few were far away somewhere else, their eyes blank, their broken minds blocking out the terror of what was happening.

Leaving Vanessa to be comforted by one of the others, Radica moved forward in the darkness, crouching on her own at the rear of the truck, peering through the narrow slit between the tarpaulin curtains, the two soldier captors now stood guard just outside not wanting to miss the final spectacle. She searched the throng of people, some back down on their knees pleading, others turned away to the wall so they wouldn't have to see the soldiers lined up, their Kalashnikov's raised. Then, she saw them. Jannike was facing away, holding Johan close, arms wrapped tightly around him, pressing his head into her chest in a futile attempt to shield him. That image, that moment as she saw Aleksandar stood to the side, his hand raised, holding it there teasingly for an eternity, before dropping his arm, would stay with her forever. The chattering sound of the Kalashnikovs was deafening, drowning out the final screams of the prisoners as they went down. Fighting her instincts to look away, Radica forced herself to look directly at her mama, her face mercifully turned away with Johan's still hidden as she fell to the ground on top of his body, a haphazard pattern of bullet marks in the blood splattered wall where she had been stood a second before.

In the crushing silence as the echo of the Kalashnikovs died away, Radica felt the air being sucked from her lungs as she fought for breath, a sudden panic setting in as the knowledge that they were gone pressed down on her. She turned away then, looking into the darkness of the truck, the shadowy form of her sister and the other girls all blending into one.

'Get rid of the bodies.' The familiar voice of Aleksandar outside jolted her, the confined space of the truck in which she found herself a prisoner starting to contract around her as the crushing gravity of her predicament sunk in. There was no chance of escape, she was smart enough to know that, and anyway, she would never leave her sister behind. Over the sound of activity outside she heard heavy bootsteps approaching. She retreated into the depths of the truck to join the others, kneeling in front of her sister to shield her as she saw one of the heavy flaps at the back of the truck part, a huge form clambering inside. Radica was unable to stop herself covering her face with her hands as the figure approached. The thud of the boots stopped directly in front of her, the acrid body odour of her tormentor filling her nostrils in the confined space as she felt his warm breath on her hands.

'Let me see you child,' she heard, the voice calm, but failing in its desired reassuring effect.

'Don't touch me,' Radica blurted.

'Nobody's going to hurt you,' came the reply, sounding almost offended. Then she felt two giant hands touching hers and she knew she was powerless to stop them. As her hands were gently peeled away from her face, she saw Aleksandar crouched directly in front of her, a concerned fatherly expression on his face that would have easily passed as genuine if she hadn't known better.

'That wasn't so hard now was it,' he continued. 'You mustn't worry, we're going to take good care of you and your friends.'

Radica couldn't help but notice the less than cursory glance he gave to Radica's sister and the others, clear validation to even an unworldly girl like her that he was lying about his intentions. She heard more bootsteps and looked past Aleksandar to see Emil clambering inside.

'The men are restless Aleksandar,' he proclaimed, addressing his superior by name and not rank when they were in private. 'When do we get to enjoy our catch?' he demanded, casting his greedy eyes over the girls, his mere words enough to bring forth a fresh wave of tearful anguish from them.

Despite the urge to throttle his sergeant at that very moment for undoing his carefully chosen words of reassurance, Aleksandar stayed right where he was, taking a deep breath, realizing now the pointlessness of keeping up the charade designed to keep this new batch of girls calm.

'These are going to the Englishman,' Aleksandar said coldly, as if discussing a cargo of vegetables.

'After we are done with them?' Emil challenged, a predictable response Aleksandar thought, and one that deserved an answer that would leave his subordinate in no doubt that his general was still very much in charge.

'No Emil, they are to remain unspoilt, do you understand?' Aleksandar commanded in a condescending tone, speaking slowly as if instructing a youngster.

Emil took a moment to answer, his way of letting his general know he didn't appreciate being spoke to like a child.

'Yes, general,' he finally replied with a hint of sarcasm. With that Aleksandar sprung to his feet with alarming speed, standing nose to nose with an alarmed Emil, who realized that he had pushed his luck a little too far with the manner of his response.

'I will personally execute anyone who lays a hand on any of these girls, including you sergeant, do I make myself clear?' Aleksandar hissed.

Emil wasn't about to cower in front of his superior, meeting his gaze square on, but he knew without any doubt that Aleksandar meant exactly what he said.

'Yes general, crystal clear,' he replied in as respectful a tone as he could summon.

Emil stepped aside to let Aleksandar pass. Hearing him jump down from the truck he turned back to the girls, looking down at them, paying particular attention to the one closest to him, so easily within reach, yet forbidden for him to touch. She was staring up at him, fixing him with a defiant expression, taunting him even. It was as if she already knew that this mere sergeant stood towering over her wouldn't so much as dare to touch a hair on her head, or any of the other girls.

It would have been so easy for him to overpower her at that moment, he knew it, the other girls way too far gone to be of any hinderance while he forced himself onto her. She knew it too he was certain, but he could tell by the goading look in her eyes that she knew he wouldn't.

THREE

Captain O'Neil sat behind his standard issue metal army desk in his less than comfortable padded chair, staring into space. Everything around him in his prefabricated office, the walls, the ceiling, the floor, even the metal grille on the window, was the same dismal shade of grey. The sparseness of his immediate surroundings was ineffectual right at that moment because he was far away, his mind journeying along the dark corridors of his past, pausing at some of the doors only momentarily without stepping inside, stopping for longer at others, unable to resist the compulsion to step inside, but always careful to leave the door open behind him in case he found what he saw too intense.

Lately he had found himself drifting from the present far more often. He hadn't made any sincere attempts to pull himself up as to the why, preferring instead to numb out the accusing voices in his head with his favourite anaesthetic. He poured another large measure of whisky without looking, long ago having stopped trying to moderate his nightly intake. He threw the measure down in one, too far gone to even register the taste, or the gentle burning sensation as it ran down his gullet. Even before he put the glass down, he knew it wouldn't be long before he needed another, and he cursed himself for being so weak, something that he had always prided himself in not being.

Raised in a traditional military family in Lincolnshire with a strict but fair father in the engineering corps and a mother who like many army wives, thought it unwise to love their children too much, for fear that they might grow up too wanting of affection and too sensitive to withstand the harsh rigours of officer training at Sandhurst, the unthinkable prospect of having the only son amongst peers not to graduate, far too much to bear.

Despite seeing more than his fair share of carnage in Northern Island during his first luckless tour after graduation, O'Neil had still been certified by his highly respected long standing army psychiatrist as being mentally fit, appearing to have come through that hell without so much as a trace of the traditional post traumatic symptoms that were often seen in officers who had experienced far less on the streets of Belfast. What O'Neil hadn't been made aware of by his commanding officer was that the medical report had gone on to note that his apparent complete lack of trauma was extremely rare for soldiers serving in Northern Ireland, a characteristic at that time considered an invaluable asset for any soldier and something which was certainly not lost on his superior.

In September 1992, three months into his third tour, having reach the rank of lieutenant in record time, he had returned to the underground impenetrable barrack fortress late one dismal grey afternoon after his regular patrol, up to that point a day he remembered for the complete lack of any paramilitary activity worth mentioning in his report more than anything else. As soon as he had put his foot in the door and handed in his firearm, he had found himself being summoned to report to his commanding officer. Sat behind his desk, his usually composed superior was unable to contain his anger, as he explained to O'Neil that he had received a direct order from the Ministry of Defence no less, that his lieutenant was to be relieved of duty in Belfast with immediate effect and was to return to England forthwith.

No explanation had been given in the faxed document, simply an instruction to be followed. O'Neil of course knew the real reason for his commanding officer's rage. It wasn't the manner of the communication or its abruptness, or even the fact that no one from the ministry had even had to respect to telephone his superior on a secured line to thank him for his anticipated cooperation. It was because he was losing the best lieutenant he had ever had under him, someone he knew was irreplaceable.

O'Neil's squad were sorry to see him go, their trepidation about who was going to command them next all too apparent in their faces as they said goodbye in the mess hall only an hour later. Truth be told, none of them had ever really liked him. He was too mechanical for their liking, emotionless, tireless, never interested in sharing a joke, but he had kept them alive out on the streets, the casualty rate under his leadership lower than it had been under any other lieutenant, and they knew all too well that his replacement was highly unlikely to be able to keep them even half as safe.

Within a few days of arriving home to barracks in Colchester, forty miles East of London, he was losing his mind. He'd had the option of returning to his parent's home in leafy Surrey where they'd moved to in the last few years after his father had retired from duty, but the thought of the endless questions from his mother about why he had been sent packing from Northern Ireland, questions that his commanding officer had been unable to answer, would only serve to heighten his restlessness. He felt like a long distance runner in a marathon way out in front with victory certain, only to find himself suddenly disqualified by the umpire and left having to watch the other runners pass him by as he stood helpless on the side lines.

He wasn't on duty at the barracks, so had contemplated spending a day out on civvy street to try and clear his head, but he knew this would be a problem. If his time in Belfast had taught him anything, it was that the people that the British army were there to serve, to keep safe from harm, were for the most part unworthy of the sacrifices made on their behalf. If there was one experience that had stayed with him during his time over there, it had been the day a bomb disposal engineer had abruptly met his maker. O'Neil and his squad had been called out to clear a street after a report of a car bomb. With the entire terrace street cleared of its residents, a cordon had been made at both ends.

Despite being covered head to toe in blast armour, the explosion had reduced the luckless engineer to what could only be described as a large shapeless slab of smouldering meat, the smell of burnt flesh reaching the nostrils of locals stood watching with morbid fascination. As O'Neil scanned the faces of the civilians, young and old, children and tots, searching for any signs of a gun that may have been sneaked into the crowd to take out a luckless distracted soldier, he saw them, their eyes burning with hatred, their mouths curled up at the corners in silent sneers at the sight of the smoking corpse a hundred yards away. They were waiting for something else to happen and O'Neil knew it. When the medical team arrived not long after, those same eyes lit up like an excited child's on Christmas morning. An almost audible cheer went out when what was left of the engineer was removed, elation in those members in the crowd as the still smouldering remains were shovelled up by two medics and placed in the open body bag, the ultimate joyful indignation for those civilians living in the street who would shovel up after the rag and bone man's horse that still made its weekly round.

That day changed everything for O'Neil, his whole perception of why he had joined the army and being in Northern Ireland to keep the peace, falling away like the huge sandcastles he used to build as a young child on the beach that the gentle waves would always wash away on the next tide. Without realizing it, the emotive part of his mind had detached, tucking itself away firmly out of sight.

He had never been a particularly sentimental man, any such tendencies never having had the chance to develop as a child during his rather austere upbringing, yet what he saw that day shut down a lot of circuits in his brain. His men saw the change in him right away. They had all witnessed the horror of that event, seen how some of the bystanders had silently revelled in the victory of that engineer's mutilation, their eyes unable to hide their vengeful glee. Back at the barracks there had been tears from some, big strapping men holding it all inside until they finally got to the privacy of a toilet cubicle.

Nobody who had been out on that patrol had any appetite in the mess hall that evening, except for O'Neil. He always made it a point to eat with his men, his officers following suit purely out of politeness, but when he entered the room that evening, the look on his face made their blood run cold. His whole expression was a complete blank, there was no sorrow, no anger, no emotion of any kind. More shocking was that when he sat down with them, his tray loaded with a full plate of hot food, he made no mention of that tragic day's events. He had always made some mention about each day, albeit all matter of fact, a simple clarification about some procedural matter or other, but that evening he just sat down with them and tucked right into his favourite plate of egg, ham and chips, seemingly oblivious to his men sat waiting for him to offer some much needed philosophical words of wisdom to help them come to terms with what they had seen that day.

One by one the soldiers got up to leave, some out of dismay at seeing their lieutenant carrying on as if nothing had happened, some simply because they found themselves unable to summon the will to eat, their appetites absent. In the end only the officers remained, sat in silence with him out of courtesy. They knew why he hadn't said anything to his men to comfort them, it wasn't the army way, to encourage soldiers to express their feelings. They were fighting machines, not human beings, and to allow them to indulge their emotions in front of their superiors would only make them weak and cloud their judgement out on the streets.

The perceived wisdom of the approach that O'Neil and his officers took in these kinds of circumstances was they all knew, completely flawed, but it was the doctrine they had all subconsciously signed up to at Sandhurst, an ideology that had stood unchallenged for an eternity and one that the men left sat around the table that evening would never be allowed to change.

O'Neil decided it would be best for the civilians of Colchester if he stayed inside the barrack walls. He knew there was no rational to tar them with the same brush as the people he had seen that tragic day in Belfast, but he knew that in his mind the only way to compartmentalise that event was to draw a line between army and civilian. On the train journey to the barracks, he kept seeing those same faces, their blood thirsty eyes punctuated by evil grins, but they weren't merely images that had flashed through his mind during his last hours in Belfast, these faces he was hallucinating were being worn by people that he was passing on route to the barracks. He kept his eyes closed for most of the way, pushing those faces from the past from his mind as he tried to concentrate on figuring out why he had been relieved of his post.

Unsure of how long it would be before he would be summoned by the illusory ministry that had so abruptly cut short his time in Northern Ireland, O'Neil made sure to quickly develop a regimented routine in barracks. On his first morning he rose at five in the morning as he had done for the last six years and breakfasted in the mess hall, exchanging pleasantries with fellow personnel to at least try and give himself some kind of reference point. After working out in the gym for an hour he showered, then grabbed a book from the library and sat out in a quiet corner of the parade ground to read, finding comfort in the sound of sergeants barking orders at officer cadets undergoing drill. The weather certainly wasn't warm, but it had been a long time since he had spent any personal time outside in the open, away from the windowless confines of the underground bunker quarters of his previous home, and he was thankful for the fresh air and the feel of the cool gentle breeze on his face.

In the evening when the squaddies were off duty and indulging themselves in the barrack bar and other amenities, O'Neil would sit out in that courtyard, relishing the open space that for the first time in years posed no threat, no snipers lurking in the shadows, no car bombs tucked away under abandoned stolen vehicles waiting for a luckless soldier to pass. Tucked away inside the barrack walls, he felt safe and secure. Outside those walls, even though far from the troubles of Belfast, he knew he would find himself looking into the eyes of those same people from that day, searching for suspicious movement in dark doorways, constantly checking over his shoulder.

Four days later he got a knock on his quarters door mid morning to find a young corporal stood out in the corridor at a respectful distance holding out an envelope. Even though he hadn't donned his uniform since arriving, O'Neil was impressed that this messenger still made a point of saluting him after handing over the item, before turning on his heel and marching away. Finally, his big day had arrived, yet O'Neil felt conflicting feelings as he opened the envelope and took out the crisp white folded letter. He felt he had adjusted surprisingly well during to his brief respite from active duty inside the security of the barracks and before even opening the letter, he knew whatever it was he was about to read, it would mean his imminent departure back out into the real world with all its uncertainties and dangers, lurking unseen.

The instructions in the letter were succinct and to the point. He was to report to a one Mr. A Sanderson at Whitehall the following morning at ten o'clock, no explanation as to why, not even a clarification as to who this Sanderson was, or in what official capacity he was acting.

The letter wasn't even signed by anyone of authority, merely a clerk no less by the name of Lowry, a slight that met O'Neil with significant disdain, having become accustomed to receiving instructions only from a superior, as was the army tradition. The final irrefutable insult in the letter however came in the form of an explicit remark regarding dress code, stating that it would be most appreciated if he attended the appointment in non-military attire, meaning a plain suit and tie. Civilians went to meetings in suits, army lieutenants wore their uniforms adorned with their medals to distinguish them as individuals who had made sacrifices on behalf of their country, above and beyond.

The rage inside him, the indignity of the manner of his summons quickly faded however as he thought the situation through, consoling himself that to be sought out by Whitehall was an honour in itself and that the purpose of the meeting would likely be to garner the expertise he had accumulated from his considerable experience in Northern Ireland, although at that moment he was unable to deduce exactly what the purpose would be.

He took the train early the next morning, his barely controllable phobia of the outside world mercifully numbed by the clone like suited commuters, their business attire barely distinguishable from his own, stood around him waiting on the platform, an audible groan rippling through the crowd as a monotone voice announced a delay on the screeching loudspeaker.

Still somewhat uneasy when he boarded the train which was thankfully only half full at this early stage of its route, O'Neil found an aisle seat near the door, the by now natural instinct to always be close to a means of escape in any enclosed space guiding him. He found himself unable to keep his eyes from automatically wandering, scanning the faces in the carriage around him for any familiar signs of danger, but there was none, no one watching him out of the corner of their eye, or looking away with their hand subconsciously wandering into their inside jacket pocket to reach for a weapon. Instead, most people were absorbed in their morning newspapers, while others simply looked out of the windows, their expressions a mixture of loathsome dread at the thought of yet another boring day at the office, or blank, thinking of where they would rather be as the world passed by outside.

As the train pulled into Liverpool Street, O'Neil, by now dreading the inevitable rugby scrum of commuters at the station, waited for the throng of passengers already out of their seats to disembark and hurry away. Stepping out onto the quiet platform, he made a point of controlling his step, walking not marching towards the ticket barrier to enter the huge concourse filled with hurrying commuters deftly avoiding each other as they crisscrossed in all directions.

He had already decided that he would steer well clear of the tube, partly because of the human carnage caused by the terrorist nail bomb years before, but mostly because he knew he wouldn't be able to cope with the claustrophobia of a packed carriage. Instead, he weaved his way through the scurrying crowd, narrowly avoiding a few collisions, breathing a huge sigh of relief when he finally reached the main exit, emerging into the noisy traffic to hail a passing cab.

Thankfully for O'Neil the cab driver was happy to just drive and not talk unless spoken to, enclosed in his cab with its glass screen separating him from his passenger, listening with the odd chuckle to the familiar gentle Irish accent of Terry Wogan on the radio which instantly reminded O'Neil of his former life, but for a good reason, the soothing Southern Irish drawl of Britain's favourite morning DJ always providing welcome relief from the troubles.

Arriving in plenty of time, O'Neil was escorted along the ancient corridors of Whitehall by a young fresh faced male clerk summoned by the security desk. They passed what seemed like endless doors, the clerk not speaking, until he stopped abruptly and with a fake politeness asked O'Neil to wait, gesturing to a long wooden bench adorned with a rather thin cushion covering on the seat. With that the clerk marched briskly away.

Taking a seat, O'Neil felt his mind drifting, trying to conjecture again without any success, why he had been sent for.

'They're ready for you now sir.' It took a moment for O'Neil to register the voice and when he looked up, he saw a tall wiry bespectacled man in his mid forties, smiling down at him.

'My name is Lowry,' he added with a hint of pride as O'Neil stood, straightening his jacket, careful to resist any urge he might have felt since waking that morning to give this individual a piece of his mind if he was to have the misfortune of meeting him in person. Instead, he settled for simply pretending that there was no one stood in front of him, something that wasn't lost on Lowry, his smile faltering, but in a way that indicated he was used to being treated condescendingly on occasion. The unpleasantries concluded, Lowry turned away and knocked quietly on the door to the right of the bench, pausing until he heard a grunt of invitation from within before opening the door and stepping aside, nodding with a forced courtesy at O'Neil stood waiting.

Stepping inside, the first thing that struck O'Neil was the repugnant cigar smoke hanging in the air, rising upwards like a fog from the four old men in the gloom sat in their ancient blood red leather studded armchairs like stuffed dead animals.

'Thank you, Lowry, that will be all,' came a mutter from the faceless figure sat on the far left, and with that O'Neil heard the door close behind him. In the long moment that followed he found himself stood there in silence. None of the four spoke or even got up to greet him. They simply stared up at him from their seats, nursing their crystal whisky glasses in one hand and cigars in the other, observing him, taking him in, reading him. He knew that they were sizing him up but it didn't bother him in the least. As a young man in officer training at Sandhurst he had found himself stood on parade, every inch of his uniform being scrutinized by his then sergeant for the slightest imperfection.

'Sit,' the same man on the left finally said in a clearer, gravelly voice, as if he was commanding a dog.

O'Neil knew that this pompous old bugger wasn't going to formally introduce himself or any of his entourage, but it didn't matter, O'Neil knew he was Sanderson. If the tone of the remark was designed to intimidate him, it didn't work, as without even glancing in the old man's direction, he took his seat in the only other matching chair positioned conspicuously opposite them, looking straight ahead at the dark oak panelled wall behind his hosts adorned with a few original paintings that whilst rather obscure were undoubtably of considerable value.

O'Neil could see that Sanderson was dressed in an expensive black pinstripe, his manicured white hair and gold round rimmed spectacles giving him an almost scholarly air. He would have put him somewhere in his sixties by his wrinkled tanned leather complexion, but his steel grey eyes belonged a much younger man, and whilst he looked fairly slim, he was unusually broad across the shoulders, giving the impression of someone who had not sat drinking whisky and smoking cigars his entire life.

His three suited colleagues on the other hand who looked facially ancient, all had rotund physiques and tired eyes, giving the impression that they could easily drop dead at any moment. It was plain as day to O'Neil which of the four was in charge of the meeting, his notion quickly clarified as without even introducing himself, his host began rambling on about the unfolding situation in Bosnia, announcing what a terrible travesty all that ethnic cleansing was in the light of what went on during the second world war, his comments meeting with nods and grunts of agreement from his three colleagues. By the highly familiar tone with which they addressed each other, O'Neil was certain that they were all old chums going way back, probably all the way to Eaton or Harrow.

O'Neil knew that he hadn't been summoned just to listen to the vague mumblings of a bunch of old men and quickly found himself wondering when they were going to get to the point.

His rant finally over, Sanderson started exchanging detailed notes about O'Neil's army career with his esteemed colleagues completely from memory, all in the third person, trading remarks about which facets of his experience may be of some use. It was as if O'Neil wasn't in the room, some of their comments marred with condescending slurs and criticisms and he knew they were testing him to see if he was submissive and obedient enough to do whatever bidding they had in mind.

The debate over and all four of them finally satisfied that O'Neil was their man, Sanderson turned back to him.

'I'm sure I don't need to remind you that you're very being here today falls under the official secrets act that you signed a number of years ago,' he said condescendingly. O'Neil had been expecting that opening line and made a point of looking a little bored as if he had heard that remark too many times to remember. Sanderson noted his expression, and whilst it irritated him, he made a point of not showing it.

'What we need, O'Neil,' he continued in his best public schoolboy superior tone, making a point of not to addressing his subject respectfully by his rank. 'What we, require, is someone who can toe the line out in that retched country.'

He paused then, confident that O'Neil would find himself unable to resist asking exactly what he meant, but O'Neil had been here before with arrogant pricks like this at some of his father's supper parties when home on leave from Sandhurst, and he was well practised at making them work for his attention.

O'Neil simply looked at him expectantly, letting slip just the hint of a condescending smile, Sanderson glancing at his three colleagues as they all exchanged quizzical looks,

their ring leader realizing that this dog sat before him was not going to be quite so easy to train.

'The situation out there isn't quite working out as we wanted.' He paused only briefly this time, knowing O'Neil wasn't going to be drawn, no matter what.

'What we need is someone who can help open a more meaningful dialogue between the British contingent out there and the warring factions.'

'And why would we want to do that?' O'Neil's question came as a surprise, interrupting Sanderson's step.

'Well, I would have thought that was obvious, wouldn't you?' he replied, sharing a murmur of amusement with the others.

'Not to me it isn't.'

'Then let me enlighten you lieutenant. With the way things stand, our lads in the field are being asked to keep the peace and protect the civilian population from what amounts to a bunch of well armed thugs from opposite ends of the ethnic spectrum hellbent on wiping each other out.' He paused, sighing regretfully before taking a gulp of whisky.

'Now that wouldn't be so bad, if the rules of engagement were fair, but they're not. Our soldiers cannot engage the enemy unless fired upon, which effectively makes them a toothless tiger.'

'So what is it that you think I can achieve?'

'We want to offer these Croat and Serb savages something that will persuade them to slow down the slaughter of the civilians.'

'You mean a trade?'

'Think of it as an inducement.'

O'Neil didn't reply, he just sat there, poker faced. He knew what was coming next, the reason why he had been summoned dropping into place like a coin in a slot, but he wasn't going to say the dirty words for them, he wanted to hear this old wise wolf masquerading as an old city gent say it.

'So, what do you say lieutenant?' Sanderson finally added.

'Say to what exactly?'

'Arms in exchange for the lives of innocents.'

'A noble gesture,' O'Neil replied, trying his best to hide his sarcasm.

'We thought so,' Sanderson replied smugly.

'And what about our troops, do you think they'll be happy getting shot at with their own bullets?'

'The chances of that are very slim.'

'Maybe at the moment, but what if the rules of engagement change,' O'Neil challenged.

'No one in the UN is interested in escalating this conflict any further, trust me lieutenant.'

'Things can very easily take an unexpected turn of events in these situations.'

'This isn't Belfast, lieutenant, these Serb and Croat generals aren't some bloody tinpot terrorists.'

'Not to you maybe,' O'Neil protested.

'What do you mean by that,' Sanderson almost snarled.

'I read the papers, I know what's been going on over there, the ethnic cleansing, the mass rape.'

'Then surely you can understand how important it is what we're trying to do.'

'I understand that all too well, but let's not try and pretend that these people you want to negotiate with are anything more than cold blooded murderers citing a political cause, just like the paramilitaries in Northern Ireland.'

Sanderson didn't reply for a moment, he wanted to take the heat out of the discussion, to reintroduce the rational context.

'All your career lieutenant, you have put your neck on the line, day in, day out, to protect people who have always had a choice. They could have left Belfast of their own free will at any time.' His leather chair creaked as he leaned forward a little.

'These civilians have no choice, they're penned in like chickens in a coop, sure and certain that the fox is coming for them. And while they're waiting, the UN is doing nothing. Don't you see, this is our chance, your chance, to help secure safe passage out of Bosnia for as many of them as possible before it's too late.'

'Why me?' O'Neil asked after a long moment of reflection. 'Why not send one of our top diplomats?'

'Because these generals distrust government officials, they will only deal with their own…' Sanderson caught himself, about to say the word.

'They're own kind,' O'Neil added for him.

'If you like.'

'Then why not send one of our generals, a brigadier even.'

'They need someone they can relate to, someone still active in the field of battle, like they are now, not some top brass old fart who hasn't left his desk in years.'

'And what's in it for me.'

'Well, apart from being recognized as the saviour of Bosnia, you'll go down in history as the youngest brigadier the army has ever had.'

'And what if I don't want to be a brigadier?'

'Then I'm sure we can find some other suitable distinguished position for you, perhaps in the government.'

O'Neil wanted to make them sweat before his next words, if only for a minute. He knew all too well that the four men in this room were powerful beyond the realms of any perceived reality, that their decisions and actions were beyond rebuke, even from the prime minister himself. Although he had enjoyed the mild satisfaction of refusing to roll over like an obedient dog every step of the way, he was all too aware of the harsh reality of his predicament. These old men were his new masters and even before he arrived for that meeting, the decision as to whether he would accept their proposal had already been made for him.

On the way back to his barracks so he could pack, O'Neil had plenty of time to try and decipher the truth about what his new masters were really about. The notion of saving innocent civilians from slaughter seemed genuine enough. The supply of arms in exchange of course was part of a much longer game, as the whole of the former Yugoslavia, of which Croatia and Bosnia was only a part, would succumb to the tide of ethnic cleansing, and the supply of arms to fuel that conflict would go on for many years to come.

O'Neil didn't entirely buy the safety catch explanation from Sanderson about there being little risk of their own soldiers having British weapons used against them. The UN's position on engagement had been designed to show the Croat and the Serb military that they were being watched, that was all. The thinking was that this deployment of UN troops on their home ground would frustrate the ability of both sides to carry out their ethnic cleansing and hence force them into a ceasefire where the argument could be settled by political means.

Sadly, the Geneva Convention which formed the ethical backbone of the UN, was by now being largely ignored by the Croat and Serb forces who were speeding up, not slowing down their systematic genocide. This toxic mix of circumstances in O'Neil's mind, made it increasingly   likely that the UN troops would begin to find themselves under fire and suffering considerable casualties. O'Neil conjectured with certainty that it wouldn't be long before the situation became too dangerous and the UN troops were pulled out, leaving the civilians to face extermination. In the light of all the facts and projections, O'Neil comforted himself with at least having two good reasons to do what he was told. Firstly, he had no choice, as to refuse would have meant the end of his army career, but secondly, he felt that in principle the cause was actually worthy, even though the notion of saving civilians from slaughter failed to touch him on any emotive level, the sad realization that too many years on the hostile streets of Belfast had made him a soulless, cold machine.

There was one nagging question, a doubt that wouldn't leave him. Not since the second world was had any government's military arm anywhere in the world given a damn about civilians caught up in warfare, not in Korea, not in Vietnam. Even the Falklands had been a publicity stunt for a prime minister to avoid defeat at the next general election. Arms manufacturers were only interested in one thing, money.

He knew that Sanderson must have ulterior motives for passing up millions of pounds of revenue from selling arms to the Croats and the Serbs, to instead settle for getting refugees in exchange. It was beyond the realms of possibility that Sanderson had suddenly, well into his autumn years, developed a conscience after a lifetime in Whitehall. He was the kind of capitalist with not so much as a glimmer of care for the plight of innocent people.

By the time O'Neil got off the train back in Colchester, he was sure beyond any doubt that the humanitarian trade that Sanderson had outlined was merely a smoke screen. He was sure the arms were being supplied to the Croat and Serb armies at market value, like all the arms deals Sanderson had ever made. It would have been more honest for Sanderson and his three cronies to have met O'Neil in a board room at one of the armament factories that they were undoubtably major stakeholders in.

He wondered or more accurately, he feared what would become of him after all this was over. After all, people with this kind of power could arrange without any difficulty for him to fall victim to some random fatal accident at any time, and he knew that Sanderson wouldn't lose any sleep over making that decision.

He was trapped, that was for sure, and he would have to obey orders to the letter like a good little soldier. He suddenly felt like that young naive trainee officer at Sandhurst again, suffering the indignation of having to demonstrate loyal subservience to his sergeant, except this time, his superior wouldn't just yell down his ear if he got something wrong.

He had arrived at that meeting a lieutenant and had left a captain in exchange for his cooperation, not because they wanted to promote him, but because he was going to replace another man of that rank, and as Sanderson had explained, it really wouldn't do to put a lieutenant in a captain's job, not at all. No details about the captain he was replacing had been given, simply that it was time for a change of leadership at the base, which O'Neil took to mean they were sacking the man in charge for not towing the line, to quote Sanderson's words.

Sanderson of course hadn't given him any files on the two generals he was to meet, after all as far as the Ministry of Defence was concerned, the notion of entering into discussions with armies clearly at odds with the will of the British forces was unthinkable.

He was simply told the dates and times when he would meet them. They would confirm with him what merchandise they required, and he would relay that information using one of the oldest and still most reliable forms of secure communication, Morse code, where it would wind its way to Sanderson. When a shipment of arms arrived, refugees would be transported in exchange to the base where he was stationed, for safe passage out of Bosnia.

The UN of course could never learn of the true nature of the arrangement, O'Neil was sure of that. Undoubtably, they would discover through the wire that Serb and Croat generals had visited the base with their white flags held high, but any reservations that the UN might have about local interference with the official mandate by the British army would quickly be allayed when they began to receive word of refugees arriving safely.

O'Neil had never met the captain he was replacing, arriving at the army base near the border with Croatia to find his predecessor already gone. It was highly irregular for there not to be a face to face meeting in these kinds of circumstances, and he could only conjecture that the man he had hoped to meet had either been too embarrassed or ashamed of being relieved from his post to face his successor.

He had already met with the Croat and Serb individuals by the end of his first week behind his new desk, arriving on two consecutive days and both late at night under the cover of darkness with the appropriate level of security. The atmosphere in his office, meeting those two generals who he knew all too well were already responsible for the murder of tens of thousands of civilians, was surreal to say the very least, reminding him of what it would have been like to have to sit down over coffee with the heads of the rival paramilitary groups in Northern Ireland.

So why then, had O'Neil no anger towards these two murderess individuals, the blood still visible under their fingernails. Instead, he found himself treating them as he would generals on his own side, even trading salutes when they had been shown in.

The business side of the meetings had been brief as the generals had both sat in the same seat on the other side of his desk, conveying the necessary details without delay, but then instead of both parties standing to signal the end of each meeting, O'Neil had found himself happy to exchange a few pleasantries, even share an anecdote or two, before his guests were shown out, exchanging salutes again as they went, neither general aware that O'Neil was doing trades with both sides.

O'Neil had found himself unable to summon any guilt or remorse after those meetings. The conspiracy which he was now a central part of was a betrayal of everything he had trained for at Sandhurst, yet he felt no shame. His mind was functioning, but he felt numb and dead inside, like an empty shell. He knew it wasn't post traumatic stress, the symptoms were all wrong. There was no depression, no suicidal visions, no rage, no tears, just a feeling of not wanting to be around himself. It would take him years to finally realize that way back in Northern Ireland, his mind had shut down his emotional response circuits to protect him from psychological damage.

He had started with the drinking the night the first refugees had arrived. As he stood outside in the cold in the moonlight, he had watched the unmarked green army truck come to a halt in the compound and seen the shivering, weary faced refugees being helped down from the rear tailgate by his soldiers waiting with blankets to put around them, before they had been led to a huge army accommodation tent.

It took a moment for O'Neil to register as he picked out the faces in the pale moonlight, and at first, he thought he must be seeing things, but stepping closer his initial observation was confirmed. In the throng of people, young children were being held by their parents, a few older sons helping them, but there were no daughters in tow, instead a group of teenage girls appearing together as the last people to get down from the truck.

The girl's faces weren't filled with exhausted relief like the others, instead they had a haunted look, huddling close together, wide eyed with fear and shrinking away as the soldiers tried to place blankets around them. They watched the families disappear inside the tent, murmuring to each other in brief debate, before following, casting worried glances at the soldiers as they went inside. One of them caught his eye, a beautiful blond who wouldn't look out of place on a catwalk, but it wasn't her elegance that he remembered, it was the look in her eyes. She was silently accusing him, her expression a mixture of fear and anger, a look he would never forget.

O'Neil downed another whisky without even realizing to try and push away that girl's face and the many others that had followed in her steps, cursing himself, not just for having not put an end to the whole sordid racket that night, but worse, for also indulging himself.

A tapping sound suddenly jolted O'Neil from his thoughts, and he found himself back in his metal prison staring down at the empty whisky glass. Looking up he realized someone was knocking on the steel door outside. Hurriedly placing the glass and half empty whisky bottle in his deep desk drawer, he sat up in his chair.

'Enter, he called out in as sober a fashion as he could muster.

A young corporal entered, and by his sombre expression O'Neil knew, having to fight not to let his intoxicated condition get the better of him. He had been powerless to stop the mission to arrest Vladimir and so had taken the only option. Sanderson had replied to his coded communication within an hour, agreeing with O'Neil that the situation was a dire one. If Vladimir was taken into custody, he would undoubtably bring Sanderson's house crashing down. He told O'Neil to sit tight and let him arrange the necessary from Whitehall. There were British and American mercenaries all over the region that could be called upon to deal with matters like these.

O'Neil hadn't made Sanderson aware of his concern about one of his sergeants for mortal fear of retribution. Right from his first meeting with Stanton, alarm bells had rung in his head. There was nothing concrete for O'Neil to go on, but his instincts told him that something was off, that Stanton somehow had wind of what was going on, and was just waiting for the moment to make his move.

O'Neil had surmised the plan of action that Sanderson was going to implement that evening to contain the situation, which would allow O'Neil to kill two birds with one stone and keep the secret safe. He was certain that Stanton wouldn't have confided in anyone else at the base, he was too long in the tooth to make that mistake, although there was no real knowing of who he may have communicated his concerns to back in Britain, but that was something O'Neil couldn't do anything about.

He had of course been kept informed of events as they unfolded and had been relieved to learn that Vladimir had escaped, but it was too late to call off the mercenary dogs, an order that only Sanderson could give. At hearing the news from the command unit, O'Neil had thought of calling off the ambush, but he suddenly caught himself, thinking the situation through. With Vladimir still at large, Sanderson would be able to continue business as usual, having no qualms about being responsible for the deaths of a few soldiers, happy to put it down to collateral damage.

'What is it corporal,' O'Neil asked, trying not to let slip a grin.

'They found the downed helicopter sir and…'

'Any survivors,' O'Neil interrupted.

'Just one sir.' O'Neil's expression froze as his blood ran cold.

'A teenage boy sir,' the corporal added before O'Neil had time to ask.

'Damn it,' O'Neil exclaimed in a rehearsed phoney expression of open anger, masking his elation that the shooting down of the helicopter had gone to plan and that Stanton, the thorn in his side of recent months was out of the way.

'They found him with sergeant Stanton sir, said he tried to save him, but…'

'Alright corporal, you can go,' O'Neil cut in with an over exaggerated sigh, putting his head in his hands for good measure, allowing him to hide his relief. Hearing the steel door thud close as the corporal left, O'Neil sat back in his chair and took a deep breath, before retrieving his liquid solace and pouring another measure. At least this one, he said to himself as he lifted the glass, was in celebration. The glass emptied in an instant, he thought through his next moves. He would wait until the morning to contact Sanderson with the good news. The matter of Vladimir's escape was not one of any urgency, and anyway, it was late, and he was tired, the news of Stanton's death taking a huge weight of his shoulders, and with it, a wave of weariness hit him as he felt his whole being unknot and relax.

He would have to decide what to do about the survivor, the boy, as there was a risk, albeit a very small one that Stanton may have imparted information to him. But it could wait until morning when he had a clear head and anyway, his special guest would be arriving very soon.

An exhausted Marko was already dead to the world on a cot bed in one of the huge refugee tents, stirring not in the slightest at the sounds of the others milling around, when the familiar unmarked army truck from Radica's village screeched to a halt in a fenced off unlit area on the other side of the compound well out of sight from the refugee area.

Two British soldiers quickly appeared and dropped the tailgate as faint muffled cries from inside the truck drifted out, almost swept away by the cold night breeze. Moments later the tarpaulin parted and one by one, gagged and with their hands tied behind their backs, Radica and the girls were dragged out by their captors.

The passenger cab door opened with a loud yawn and the shadowy figure of Aleksandar jumped down, walking to the rear of the truck, his catch by now kneeling in the dirt at gunpoint. As he appeared, the two British soldiers seemed to visibly step back, the girls cowering, all except Radica, who looked up at the towering figure stood over her and fixed him with her vengeful gaze.

Aleksandar locked eyes with her for a moment, before slipping her a sly smile. Whatever notions of revenge this girl was harbouring, she would never have the chance to act them out. There was no escape from the life that she would soon find herself living and he had a fairly good inkling that she knew what her new existence would entail.

Inside O'Neil's office, Aleksandar took a seat.

'Did you like the girls I brought you on my last visit captain?' Aleksandar enquired, nursing his whisky, relaxing opposite his host sat behind his desk.

'First rate as usual,' O'Neil replied, leaving his measure untouched for now.

'Good, then I'm sure you will like these ones.'

'And which one would you recommend?' O'Neil enquired greedily.

'Oh, you won't be able to miss her.'

'Really?'

'Just look for the one who doesn't look away,' Aleksandar instructed. 'She's fearless, I tell you.'

'Sounds like she needs to be tamed,' O'Neil replied in kind.

'Then you'll need all your strength my friend, I can assure you. But as I always say, the more they fight, the bigger the prize.'

'I'll drink to that,' O'Neil replied, clinking glasses with Aleksandar before they both downed their measures in one. His guest's expression suddenly became more thoughtful for a moment, O'Neil a little too hazy from the drink to notice.

'Captain, you know this war won't last forever.'

'If only Aleksandar,' O'Neil chuckled.

'Have you thought about the future?'

O'Neil looked up to see Aleksandar fixing him with his gaze.

'You mean, after we all go home?'

'Wherever home will be,' Aleksandar replied wryly.

'Quite,' O'Neil agreed.

'There is so much more we can do together once this is over.'

'I've already given that some serious thought,' O'Neil announced, smiling as Aleksandar's eyes lit up with anticipation.

FOUR

Marko didn't feel the searing heat from the flames as he walked towards the burning wreckage, nor did his clothes catch fire. He felt calm and relaxed because he knew he had been to this place before.

'Karla, mama, where are you?' he called out.

He couldn't see them in the flames, but he knew they would emerge as he remembered them, beautiful and unscathed.

'Marko.' That voice, he recognized it, but it was not from the flames, it was coming from behind.

He spun round, his face contorted with horror as the burning forms of Ana and Karla approached with their arms held out pleadingly. Marko instinctively backed away, but they followed him. Not looking where he was going, he stumbled over something solid, falling backwards.

By the time he felt the strange searing sensation it was too late, his clothes erupting into flames, instantly engulfing him as he lay helpless in the burning wreckage, becoming one with in the twisted red hot metal labyrinth, as Karla and Ana had been before.

Looking up through the flames he saw Ana and Karla stood over him, and he could see they were no longer charred, burning forms, but completely untouched and perfect.

'Help me,' Marko screamed, reaching out in writhing agony through the flames, but they were already turned and walking hand in hand away into the distance.

Marko awoke from his nightmare with a gasp, sitting bolt upright in the darkness of the tent, the only sound a few snoring refugees. The entrance was open slightly, flapping slowly in the night breeze, a faint light from outside.

Marko blindly felt his way carefully towards the opening, bumping into the odd occupied cot to be met with grunts of compliant.

Slipping quietly outside unseen into the cold night air, he hid in the darkness, the only illumination, the floodlights shining their bright cold artic white glare outwards from the perimeter onto the open ground surrounding the base. Looking around, he saw that the compound was lifeless and eerily quiet, other than a few sentries on patrol at the perimeter gate, in quiet conversation.

Then he heard what sounded like muffled anguished voices coming from somewhere in the distance. Following that sound, Marko quietly crept towards a high wire fence, those fearful voices coming from somewhere on the other side, not a sentry in sight. He looked up, the obstacle at least eight feet high, a challenge, but one he could overcome. Gripping the metal wire, he began to climb, barely able to find any footholds in the gaps, the mesh buckling a little under his weight. Halfway up, a deep male voice from the other side of the fence froze him in his tracks. Despite the cover of darkness, he would be easy to spot if a sentry happened to appear. He listened intently for a moment, bracing himself for the inevitable, but that deep voice had fallen silent. Seizing what might be his last chance, Marko quickly climbed the remaining distance and vaulted over the top, swiftly clambering down the other side, jumping the last few feet so his landing wouldn't make any sound.

He crouched in the darkness, listening again to try and get his bearings. The voices were still muffled, and he realized they were coming from inside a building somewhere. This part of the compound he saw, was laid out with what looked like neatly placed metal shipping containers side by side.

Creeping forward up against one of the containers, Marko peered round the end of the structure. In the darkness, he was just able to make out the forms of two sentries stood outside one of the containers, talking in hushed tones, their rifles hung loosely over their shoulders.

Marko was sure that those distressed voices were coming from inside that huge metal structure, and he realized they were female. Suddenly one of the sentries banged his rifle butt angrily against the metal cabin, the voices falling silent.

'Quiet,' one of the sentries said loudly, just short of a shout, sharing a laugh with his comrade.

Marko thought he could hear one of the prisoners inside the container start up again, but then he realized the sound was coming from somewhere else. Off to his left the last container had its double doors slightly ajar, illuminated by a soft glow from inside, the solitary female muffled cries drifting out.

Waiting for his moment when both the sentry's backs were turned, Marko darted across the no man's land separating him from the row of containers and slipped in between the narrow gap between the first two structures.

Feeling his way, he was able to move unseen along the rear side of the row until he reached the final one, slowly making his way along the side towards the open front.

The sentries were a better distance away now, the container out of their immediate line of vision. From his position, partially hidden between the two containers and with one last glance in the direction of the two sentries, Marko sneaked through the narrow opening to disappear inside.

The sight that met his eyes, illuminated by a small portable lamp, instantly filled him with that familiar rush of adrenaline from the boxing ring and without thinking he was in motion, racing forward and reaching down to grab the uniformed assailant who was pinning his struggling victim's arms down, the soldier's face obscured by his bulk. Hauling him sideways, Marko delivered a solid punch to his jaw, rolling him dazed off his victim.

When he saw the girl lying there with a cloth gag in her mouth, he was frozen in a moment of disbelief.

'Radica?' he exclaimed, instantly realizing that he may have alerted the two sentries.

Radica could only stare up in wide eyed shock at Marko as he helped her to her feet, seeing that she was mercifully still fully dressed and unviolated.

Then she looked down, suddenly remembering the man who had subjected her to that terrible ordeal. Her eyes filling with rage, she unleashed a frenzy of kicks into her prone assailant's ribs who still half unconscious, let out muffled grunts of protest in reply.

'Come on, we have to go,' Marko interjected, dragging her away towards the door. She turned, fixing him with a look of determination.

'Not without my sister and the others,' she demanded, Marko instantly realizing where the other girls were.

'They're being guarded, there's no way to get to them.'

'I'm not leaving them,' Radica persisted.

'Listen to me, we can get help and then come back for them,' Marko offered, all too aware that every second they wasted reduced their chance of escape.

'No, I can't leave her,' she replied in a pleading tone, but knowing he was right.

'It's our only chance.'

Radica felt her stubborn will to resist fall away at that moment, submitting to Marko as he led her to the entrance, able to see through the gap between the doors. The sentries were nowhere to be seen, and his heart stopped for a moment as his mind raced with the terrible notion of them creeping up out of Marko's limited line of sight. He listened for the sound of movement, then turned back to Radica, knowing she wouldn't take no for an answer when he told her.

'I can't see the guards, but they could be anywhere,' he said quietly.

'We have to get them out.'

'But they'll be locked in.'

'We have to try,' she replied, her stubborn wilfulness returning. Marko knew in that moment he had no choice.

'Alright, but keep your head down, and whatever happens, don't let go of my hand,' he instructed quietly, leading Radica out into the darkness.

A few moments later, a prone O'Neil began to stir, letting out a moan as he felt the pain kick in. Forcing himself to roll over onto his side, he let out a stifled scream of agony as the sharp edges of his cracked ribs grated together.

Marko and Radica had almost reached the container housing the others when a loud deep shout off to their left raised the alarm, followed by a torch beam that picked them out, their faces like startled deer in a car's headlights.

They were running then, Radica holding on tight to Marko's hand as he made for the nearest perimeter fence behind the row of containers, the angry shouts of the sentries seeming only a few feet behind. Marko and Radica disappeared between two of the containers, racing along the length of the vessels towering above them on either side. Reaching the fence, Marko could tell by the sound of the sentry's voices that they were very close now, realising there was only time for one of them to escape.

'Give me your foot, I'll help you up,' he said.

'What about you?' she replied.

'I'll hold them back.'

'No, we go together.'

'There's no time to argue,' Marko insisted, Radica registering the panicked pleading in his tone. Placing her right foot in Marko's hands and keeping her leg straight, she felt him lift her against the fence, his arms thrusting her upwards as she hung on, the momentum propelling her climb to the top. Then she was over the other side and clambering down, jumping the last few feet. As she turned to Marko trapped on the other side, she saw a torch beam illuminating the narrow alleyway between two containers behind him.

'I'll wait for you,' she promised, and with that she was sprinting away, past the reach of the perimeter lights and into the darkness. With Radica safely out of reach, Marko turned back, one of the sentries blinding him with his torchlight.

'Don't move,' he commanded, a little out of breath, his rifle trained as he stepped to within spitting range, just how Marko wanted it.

In that instant the possible outcomes of Marko's predicament tumbled over on his mind. Regardless of whether his captor would really shoot him if he didn't obey, he knew that he couldn't escape now unless…

'You found them?' came the other sentry's shout.

Marko seized on the momentary distraction as the young corporal, not quite experienced enough to know never to take his eye of the target, even for an instant, allowed his attention to be distracted by his comrade.

Lunging forward, Marko parried the rifle to the side with his left arm, the surprised corporal spinning his head back round to face Marko as a fist crunched into his nose, before the second punch to his gut bent him double, dropping him to his knees as he fought to catch his breath. Marko was already scaling the fence with frenzied speed, jumping almost from the top to break his fall with a roll, before sprinting away, the adrenaline carrying him faster than he could ever remember.

The second sentry appeared from between the containers, his torchlight picking out his comrade on his knees still fighting for air.

'Over here sir,' he called out, O'Neil joining him a few moments later, staggering in evident pain.

He instinctively looked through the fence, searching for signs of any movement.

'Give me your weapon corporal,' he ordered, the rifle in his hands in an instant.

Wincing as he straightened himself to take aim, O'Neil fired wildly out into the far reaches beyond the fence in a desperate attempt to hit the escapees that he couldn't even see, sending his corporals ducking for cover as sparks erupted from the wire fence clipped by stray bullets.

Already clear of the reach of the perimeter lights, Marko was spurred on by the repetitive crackle of the gunshots. Abruptly the firing stopped, but he kept running.

Suddenly he felt the familiar sensation from his early childhood of branches scratching his face and flung his arms up to protect his eyes. He pushed forward into the trees, not content to stop at the edge of what he hoped would be a dense woodland.

Stopping for breath when he felt sure he was deep enough in the dense foliage, Marko crouched down, listening for any sounds of pursuit, but all he heard was a deafening eery silence.

Then he heard a branch snap off to his left, too loud to be a small animal, and he just prayed it was her.

'Hey,' he ventured, almost a whisper, listening for a response.

'It's me, Marko,' he added, his voice a little louder this time. His words were met again by total silence, and he feared he had stumbled across more soldiers. He could tell it was just one person, but that didn't mean it was…

'Marko, where are you,' came Radica's soft voice.

'Over here,' he replied. The sound of crunching foliage underfoot grew louder, and then quickened, moments later Marko feeling Radica fling her arms around him, the warmth of her body pressing against his as he embraced her. He felt wetness on the side of his face, realizing she was crying.

'What are we going to do?' she sobbed.

'We have to get as far away from here as possible,'

'But what about my sister and the others,' she persisted, a fresh flood of tears, flowing down her cheeks.

'We'll get help, I promise,' he said, knowing all too well that this was a commitment he was in no position to make.

'You promise?' she replied, a tide of guilt rising in Marko's stomach.

'Yes, I promise, now come on,' he lied, leading her by the hand further into the darkness of the woods, unsure of what or who they would encounter.

Radica felt like they had been fighting their way through the low branches of the trees for hours when she finally let go of Marko's hand and collapsed to the ground, exhausted and shivering from the cold.

'Please Marko, I have to stop, just for a minute,' she pleaded. He leaned down, placing a reassuring hand on her shoulder.

'Come on, we have to keep going,' he said, hauling her to her feet with both hands, leading her on.

Having spent so many hours in the woods, their eyes had become accustomed to the darkness, the black canopy of the trees around them taking on form. Looking up, Marko could see the faint murmurings of grey in the night sky, a signal that dawn wasn't far away.

Returning his gaze to the path ahead, Marko suddenly froze, Radica too exhausted to register any alarm.

Up ahead, in contrast to the irregular shapes of the trees, he could just make out the manmade form of a peaked roof.

'Radica, look,' he exclaimed, careful to keep his voice down, in case someone might be home.

'What is it,' she replied, as if about to fall asleep on her feet, her eyes too heavy to make out the possible sanctuary just up ahead.

'Come on, we might be able to rest here,' he encouraged.

Drawing closer, keeping Radica safely behind him, Marko deduced that the unlit dwelling was either abandoned or its inhabitants were asleep, but as they reached it, he saw the front door was strangled with creeping ivy, the tendrils trying to force their way inside around the frame. He gingerly tried the handle, then pushed gently. The door, although caught stubbornly against the frame from the damp, was evidently unlocked, and with a firm shove it gave way. He waited for a moment with the door barely ajar, listening for the sounds of any disturbance from inside, then pushed it open.

The settled darkness of the room was disturbed as the silhouette of Marko appeared. In the gloom he could see it was completely unfurnished, the sparse walls punctuated by a few small windows. Ushering Radica inside, he closed the door firmly behind them, hoping in vain to find a bolt of some description to secure it with, deciding he would sleep upright with his back against it.

They were both too tired for their bodies to feel the uncomfortable bare wooden floor beneath them as they sat, huddled together to keep warm. It was there in that cold lifeless room as their bodies warmed each other that they both felt that wondrous sensation again, a heaven that neither of them could have put into words. In that moment Radica forgot the horrors of the night as she felt the warmth of Marko's body. They huddled there, feeling themselves melting into each other for what seemed like a blissful eternity. Neither of them spoke, not wanting to break the spell which they hoped would last forever.

An owl hooted outside in the darkness, startling Radica, cruelly jolting her back to the present, thoughts of her sister and the others flooding over her again in a suffocating wave. Feeling her shudder, Marko stirred from his trance.

'How are we going to save them Marko?' she asked quietly, looking down at the floor.

'We'll get help tomorrow when we reach the nearest village.'

Radica looked at him then and he could see another burning question in her eyes.

'What happened to your family?' she enquired.

Marko didn't answer for a moment, the guilt rising up in his empty belly as he tried to think of what to say.

'I'm sorry, I didn't mean to.'

'It's alright,' he replied, knowing by the look in her eyes that her family was also gone.

'You would have liked my mother,' she said, fighting back new tears.

'Was she as beautiful as you?' Marko ventured, drawing a sad smile.

'Even more so,' she replied, her voice cracking.

'I find that hard to believe,' he replied.

'Stop it,' she protested, leaning into him again for warmth.

Marko reached into his trouser pocket and removed sergeant Stanton's dog tags, still attached to the broken chain.

'What are those,' she enquired, as he opened his hand to look at them, the engraving etched with dried blood.

'They belonged to the man who saved my life. He gave them to me, just before he died,' he replied solemnly.

'But who was he?'

'A British soldier.'

'British?' she exclaimed.

'He told me that his dog tags would keep me safe.'

'Do you believe that?'

Marko slipped one of the tags from the chain, turning to her. Taking one of her hands in his, he placed the tag in her palm, gently closing her fingers around it.

'For luck,' he said, pulling her close to him to ward of the cold, returning the second tag on its chain back to the safety of his pocket.

'Get some rest, I'll keep watch,' he said.

'What's going to happen to us?' Radica asked, her head on his shoulder.

'Everything will be alright, go to sleep,' he replied reassuringly. Looking down at Radica as she closed her eyes, he stroked her blond hair, listening to her slow breathing as she drifted away.

FIVE

Radica had no idea what time it was when she awoke to find Marko gone, but she knew it was morning by the daylight filtering in through the grimy windows. Quickly getting to her feet, she peered with difficulty through a filthy pane, but he was nowhere to be seen.

Opening the door, she stepped outside into the cold damp misty morning air. Through the rising mist she could just pick him out in the distance, crouching as he gathered wild mushrooms.

She was about to call him when the sight of something made her freeze. Behind Marko, thirty feet away, a tall figure stood stone still, his camouflaged uniform blending in almost perfectly with the trees, the long barrel of his rifle trained on an unsuspecting Marko. She caught sight of another figure a little further away, this time ahead of Marko, crouched in the dense foliage.

Marko heard a twig snap behind him and not thinking clearly from lack of sleep, he stood and turned, expecting to find Radica.

Radica could tell by the soldier's unwavering focus on their target, that they hadn't noticed her yet. Helpless to act, she knew that she would regret her next decision for the rest of her life, but there was no alternative, knowing what would happen to her if she didn't run.

She had tried to push from her mind the rumours about what soldiers were doing to teenage girls, but in her heart, she knew they were true. Her conscience was anchoring her feet to the ground, and she had to fight her every muscle as she slowly backed up around the side of the house out of sight.

Every moment she stayed would make her chance of escape slimmer and she knew she mustn't look back. A few moments later she had vanished silently into the mist.

Marko dared not glance in the direction of the dwelling, even for an instant. He could only pray that Radica was not still asleep inside and that she had seen and run. He stood perfectly still, hoping that the soldier would take his time, giving Radica a better chance of escape. His mind raced with visions of more soldiers creeping up on the house, of finding Radica and then…

He forced those terrible thoughts from his mind, focussing on the figure slowly approaching. The soldier came within six feet, the barrel of his Kalashnikov aimed squarely at his captive's chest. Marko sized up his opponent, his cold expressionless eyes giving him the look of someone who had killed too many people to care.

The insignia on his jacket was Croat, which was something at least, but this soldier looked like someone accustomed to killing indiscriminately for the sheer thrill of it. Heavily clad in his uniform and boots, Marko knew he could outrun his captor using the trees as cover if he could just get a few yards and miss a bullet in the back.

He had heard the reports of young men being taken from their families and recruited under pain of death for desertion. Would this soldier really shoot him when they could give him a rifle instead? The answer, he realized as he stared into that soldier's lifeless eyes, was yes.

Spinning around he ran, only to find himself knocked to the ground by a blow to the chest. Looking up he saw the second soldier stood over him, his rifle butt raised and ready for another strike, his piercing eyes looking like they were about to pop out of his head.

'Look what we've found Brago,' he announced, not taking his eyes of Marko.

Brago stepped forward, his weapon lowered, fixing Marko in his gaze again.

'Who else is with you?' he asked, his voice as emotionless as his eyes.

'No one,' Marko replied as convincingly as he could.

Brago pondered the reply for a moment, then looked at Lex, putting on his familiar pantomime face.

'No one you say?' Brago exclaimed, as if performing to a theatre audience. At this, Lex seemed to instinctively step back as if anticipating Brago's next move, Marko reading his body language, realizing that he had underestimated his captor.

'You're absolutely sure?' Brago pressed.

'I swear,' Marko offered, trying not to beg.

'Don't lie to me,' Brago roared at the top of his voice as he raised the butt of his rifle.

'Brago,' Lex shouted fearfully, his raging counterpart stopping in mid motion. 'He told us he wants everyone alive, remember?"

Brago hesitated for a moment, fighting the urge to kill this lying boy. Then, with a sneer, he shouldered his weapon and leaning down, grabbed Marko by the arm, his grip like a vice.

'If you try anything, I'll kill you, understand?' he warned, extracting an obedient nod from Marko, before heaving him up with a formidable strength, to march him away, Lex bringing up the rear.

It wasn't until early afternoon that the truck rolled into the Croat army camp. Marko had been given plenty of time on route to think about his situation and plan his next move. His mind constantly drifted back to his family, and he had to consciously drag his thoughts away from them to keep his mind focussed on the present. There would be time enough for him to meander through the brightly lit corridors of his childhood when he was finally safe, but right now he had to stay sharp, or he wouldn't be around long enough to enjoy those memories, or to find the girl who had stolen his tender heart with such ease. Jagged images stabbed at his mind, vividly playing out the terrible thoughts of what might be happening to her.

As the hours rolled by, sat in the darkness in the back of that truck with other young men that they must have captured along the way before they found him, Marko's mind started to settle, allowing him to   think more objectively, to rationalise what he thought might lay in store for him, and to plan with the same analytical skill he used to size up opponents in a fight. He knew Radica was smart and strong willed, and something deep down, a gut instinct, told him that she would find her way to safety.

Looking around at the sombre faces of his companions, almost indistinguishable in the gloom, the only light pushing through the narrow gap between the joins of the two tarpaulin curtains at the rear, his previous intolerable notion of being recruited as a soldier became more real than ever, and he knew that he would need to escape soon, or he would find himself bonded into slavery with a rifle in his hand. There was however, a more pressing matter that he would need to take care of at the earliest opportunity.

Brago, sat at the rear of the truck guarding his prisoners, had not taken his eyes of Marko since they had set off. Even without looking, Marko could feel those lifeless eyes burning into him. He knew his captor had taken a real shine to him, and that he would be wanting to give him a good beating as soon as they arrived, wherever they were going.

The truck rolled in past the guarded gate and entered the camp arrayed with tents, metal cabins and crates of supplies. It wasn't as orderly as the British camp, and the soldiers weren't clean shaven either, sat around, looking bored and dangerously restless.

Hearing the screech of brakes, Marko felt the truck come to a stop and knew his moment had finally arrived.

As the tarp curtains at the back of the truck parted, the prisoners squinted as the afternoon light poured in. Marko waited for all the others to get down from the truck before moving. Brago stood eagerly waiting for his last prisoner to disembark. Marko already knew what was coming, which suited his plan just fine as he wanted a big audience for maximum effect.

He deliberately avoided eye contact with Brago to give him the impression that he was afraid and made sure his captor had plenty of time to make his move as he passed him, getting ready to jump down. He didn't need to wait long to feel the familiar hard edge of the rifle butt in his back, shoving him forward out of the truck to land face down in the dirt, making his fall as dramatic as possible to draw the attention of the idle soldiers.

Marko waited for the sound of Brago's boots landing behind him before he started getting to his feet, another blow to his back sending him back to the dirt, this time drawing a roar of laughter from Brago's comrades, distracting him just long enough for Marko to get to his feet and back away a few yards.

'Why don't you show your friends how tough you are, without your gun,' Marko challenged at the top of his voice, over the din of the soldiers.

A crushing silence fell as Brago spun his head, somewhat surprised to see Marko stood further away. As he fixed him with his glare however, he wasn't met with a customary look of apprehension this time, but instead, a smug taunting grin, for all to see.

Their audience waited, stone still, anticipating Brago's next move, and he could feel all their eyes on him. Without taking his eyes off Marko, he held his Kalashnikov out to his side expectantly like a prima donna, one of the soldiers rushing forward to take it. Then, pushing his shoulders back to puff out his large chest out like a cock getting ready to fight, he let out a deafening roar before charging forward like a bull as his comrades cheered him on.

Marko's timing was impeccable. He sidestepped Brago at the last moment, knowing that with his considerable bulk, his opponent wouldn't be able to stop in time. As a dumbfounded Brago raced past him, he stuck his leg out, clipping Brago's shins to send him sprawling face first into the dirt.

The crowd fell quiet again, all eyes this time on Marko as he stepped away again from Brago who dragged himself to his feet, wiping the dirt from his eyes to fix on his opponent's position again.

Marko, as the ultimate sign of disrespect, had his back turned to his captor as if the duel was already over, his hearing acute enough to hear him coming.

Faint murmurs began drifting from the crowd, Brago glancing around, catching a glimpse of some of his comrades smirking at him.

Turning his attention back to Marko, he advanced again with his fists raised but this time he didn't charge, instead approaching slowly to get within striking range.

Marko turned around, a mock expression of surprise that Brago had come back for more, drawing laughs from some of the soldiers evidently amused by his comical antics. He stood perfectly still with his hands down by his side as Brago came within range, as if his opponent meant him no harm, goading him to make his next false move, presenting him with an unguarded face that he couldn't miss, already knowing which kind of punch Brago would try for.

As Marko had anticipated, Brago jabbed straight outwards, but Marko was one step ahead. Darting to the side, Brago's punch sailed past his head and before his opponent could follow up with his other fist, he was met with a solid counter jab that connected perfectly with his nose, blood pouring down his face in torrents as he staggered backwards, Marko stepping in to deliver a swift succession of stomach punches to drop Brago to his knees, bent double.

The audience could only watch in awe as Marko stood over his helpless conquest, the dirt soaking up the pool of blood as he strained to get his breath back.

To bring the dule to a decisive conclusion, Marko raised Brago's head, ready to deliver the knockout punch.

'Stop,' came a deep, commanding shout.

Marko turned to see a tall stocky uniformed figure approaching at a march from the direction of a number of rusting metal shipping containers, an open door leading out from the end structure.

Even before he got close enough to make out the rank of general embroidered into his jacket shoulder lapel, Marko could tell this was a man of superior rank by the way the soldiers backed away in reverent silence. Marko backed away from a disgraced Brago who struggled to his feet, his bloody face and dirt encrusted uniform plain for his superior to see. Despite his predicament, he still stood to attention, this gesture making his dire appearance appear even more ridiculous.

Aleksandar stopped directly in front of Brago, looking him up and down with utter contempt, before fixing him with his gaze, his eyes burning straight through the sergeant stood before him.

'What the hell is going on here?' he barked, right in Brago's face.

'Sir, I was just…'

A hard slap across his bloody face silenced him mid sentence.

'This is an army camp, not a playground,' he yelled at the top of his voice, his roaming glare sweeping the camp, the soldiers not daring to meet his gaze.

Aleksandar turned back, this time fixing his attention on Marko, taking him in for a moment.

'You're quite the fighter aren't you boy,' he announced. Despite the hint of warmth in his expression, Marko was unable to find any words of response.

'Come with me,' Aleksandar invited, Brago's face unable to conceal his bitter disappointment as his general, to whom he had been a faithful dog, placed a reassuring hand on Marko's shoulder and led him away, without even a backward glance at his sergeant.

Reaching the open doored container Marko noticed that this unit had been modified, the impossibly heavy double doors replaced with a welded bulkhead and a smaller entrance. There were narrow windows cut into the side walls protected by heavy steel blast mesh grills.

Aleksandar ushered Marko inside, before following him in and pulling the door closed behind him with a heavy thud.

Inside, the container was surprisingly airy with the daylight shining through the windows, picking out an array of different scaled maps on the walls. A large old heavy wooden desk sat at the far end, a red studded leather armchair parked behind it, a matching one opposite, treasures acquired during a raid on a wealthy Serb businessman's home in Croatia months previously.

Aleksandar had insisted on making these items a permanent fixture for his office, not out of any particular attraction to them, but because they reminded him of that glorious afternoon, the look in that overfed thieving landowner's eyes as he was forced to watch his screaming sixteen year old daughter being raped by

Aleksandar's men over that very same desk. It had taken hours to get her filthy Serb blood out of the heavily grained wood and sometimes when he was sat behind it, he was sure he could still detect its odour, lingering.

The leather creaked as he eased himself into his chair, gesturing for Marko to come forward, his guest somewhat hesitant.

'What is your name?' Aleksandar asked.

Marko hesitated.

'What's the matter, are you deaf boy?'

'Marko,' came the reply.

'Marko,' Aleksandar repeated slowly to himself.

'Sit down,' Aleksandar commanded, waiting patiently for his nervous guest to oblige.

Opening a drawer and reaching inside, Aleksandar retrieved two large crystal glasses and a half empty bottle of whisky. Pouring generous measures, he pushed a glass across the desk towards his guest, lifting his own.

Marko stared down at the golden liquid, surprised by its pungent scent.

'What's wrong boy, don't you like whisky?' Aleksandar enquired.

'I've only ever had beer,' he replied shamefully.

'Beer,' Aleksandar exclaimed with a chuckle. 'You can't drink beer boy.'

'Why not.'

'Because you my boy are a natural, a fighter, strong and tough, tough enough to beat my sergeant in a brawl.' He let the comment sink in for a moment.

'You must learn to drink a fighter's drink.' He gestured for Marko to lift his glass, smiling as his guest did so.

'Let's drink a toast,' Aleksandar exclaimed proudly.

'To what?' Marko replied quietly.

'To slaughtering the enemy, of course.'

At this, Marko's eyes darkened, his intuitive host picking up on his change of expression.

'You don't think that what we are doing is right?' Aleksandar enquired.

'I don't understand why it has to be this way,' Marko protested.

Aleksandar looked him straight in the eye for a long moment, his expression a conciliatory one, before placing his glass down and sitting back in his chair.

'Long before you were born, Yugoslavia as it was then, was ravaged by war. Our people, the Croatian people, were hunted down by the Nazis.'

He leaned forward in his seat, placing his elbows on the desk, his hands curling up into fists, Marko instinctively pushing himself back into his seat as Aleksandar's whole expression darkened like a sudden black stormy cloud, his eyes brooding.

'But the Nazis didn't do this with their own hands, they didn't need to.' He looked Marko directly in the eye and for a moment, there was a flicker of deep sadness before it was swept away by a look of sheer rage.

'Serb militias formed overnight, eager to do the Nazi's evil work for them.' He looked away then for a moment, as if lacking the will to continue.

'They recruited young Serb men, thirsty for the blood of us Croats, rounding up hundreds of thousands of our Croat men and...' He stopped abruptly, hesitating.

'Not only men, but women, and children.' He drifted then for a long moment, journeying back in time. When he spoke again, it was as if from far away.

'Some of the women and children they raped and slaughtered. Most were herded into crowded cattle trains and sent to the concentration camps.'

Marko so desperately wanted to speak, to ask questions, but he knew that by the sad distant look in Aleksandar's eyes, it would be unwise to stir him from his thoughts.

'It was the land,' he suddenly said, abstractly, as if more to himself. He looked up at Marko again then.

'Land that they had long claimed us Croats had stolen from them generations before.' His eyes had regained their fury now.

'And in return for their savagery, the Nazis colluded with the corrupt Serb lawyers to make sure they were given title to what they claimed was theirs, and vast swathes of land that what was not.

'And was it true?' Marko impulsively blurted, regretting those words as soon as he spoke, Aleksandar's eyes flashing with a spark of anger before he caught himself.

'It was lies, all lies, made up by the Serbs because we had more than they did, because we had worked much harder than them so that we could own more land.' He toyed with his glass for a moment.

'When the war ended, those of our people who had managed to flee into the mountains returned and tried to legally take back what had been stolen from us and to bring those Serbs responsible for the slaughter to justice, but Yugoslavia's newly elected dictator crushed them with brutal force.' His wrapped his hand around the glass, gripping it tight, as if trying to strangle the life out of a living thing, and Marko feared it might shatter.

'For four generations we were forced to live side by side with those murderous thieving Serbs, until finally Yugoslavia's dictatorship government came to an end. A vengeful grin took over his face, his eyes widening.

'And now, we are taking back what is rightfully ours.' He picked up his glass again.

'Now, drink,' he commanded.

'What if I was a Serb?' Marko challenged nervously. Aleksandar's hand stopped in mid motion, the glass inches from his lips. Marko held his breath as Aleksandar stared at him, pondering his words, before his expression suddenly softened, an almost fatherly smile spreading across his face.

'Because you're not,' he replied reassuringly.

'But how do you know?' Marko tested further.

'Your jawline, your nose, the way you hold yourself with pride, and most importantly, the way you fight. You're a Croat through and through.'

He gestured for Marko to pick up his glass.

'Drink,' he commanded again, this time his tone a little more forthright.

Waiting for Marko to lift his glass to his lips, he tipped his own back, downing the measure in one.

Marko mimicked, almost gagging, his host laughing with amusement, refilling his guest's glass as soon as he put it down, wiping his mouth with the back of his hand.

'Again,' he commanded, the second whisky making Marko's head spin.

Aleksandar knew he didn't need to enquire about Marko's parents. He had lost track of the number of solitary children his soldiers had picked up on their travels, the story always being the same. Anyway, he didn't want to give Marko any reason to think about family, he needed to encourage him to let go of his past and concentrate on the great future that he had in store for him.

'You're lucky my soldiers found you when they did, if the Serbs had gotten hold of you then…' He trailed off, leaving the rest for Marko to imagine.

'Well, you're safe now,' he added, picking up the bottle again and pouring.

'So, let's drink to that,' he invited, lifting his glass, Marko following his lead. A knock on the steel door interrupted them.

'Yes,' Aleksandar barked angrily.

The door yawned opened and one of his younger fresh faced sergeants stepped inside, closing the door behind him, facing front at attention.

'You have a visitor general,' he announced, not daring to meet his superior's agitated glare.

'Who?' Aleksandar replied, his eyes narrowing with surprise.

'A British soldier.'

'I see, and what does he want?' he enquired, noticing Marko's expression change to one of worry.

'He says it's urgent, something to do with some escaped refugees,' the sergeant pressed, glancing at Marko. In that instant, Aleksandar's roving eye still on Marko, he knew.

'Two minutes,' he commanded, his sergeant turning on his heel to leave.

'Get up' came Aleksandar's command as soon as the door closed, already out of his seat. He kicked aside a small rug on the floor next to his desk to reveal a steel trapdoor. Heaving it open, Marko saw a small metal bunker, just big enough for one man.

'Quickly, get in.' Marko hastily dropped down inside, laying on his side on the cold metal floor with his knees pulled up to his chest, Aleksandar lowering the door to seal him in complete darkness, the claustrophobia of the cramped, cold box instantly pressing down on him.

Aleksandar was back behind his desk, the rug back in position just in time for the second knock at the door.

'Enter,' he called out, as he settled back into his seat again.

As the door opened, he suddenly realized the second whisky glass was sat on the other side of his desk. He went to reach for it, but it was too late, his sergeant already escorting a young pale faced corporal into the room.

With a nod, the sergeant turned on his heel to leave. The corporal approached, coming to a stop at a respectful distance.

Aleksandar looked up at him, relishing the nervous look on his guest's face who dared not make eye contact with the man whom everyone in the British army knew was one of the key architects of the genocide. He let the tense silence hang for a moment.

'How can I help you corporal,' he enquired in his deepest voice, the one he liked to use when interrogating captured enemy soldiers.

'Captain O'Neil sent me to enquire...' the corporal replied, hesitating mid sentence.

'To enquire about what?'

'A boy refugee escaped from our base last night and the captain thought he might possibly be here,' the corporal replied speedily, unable to suppress an audible sigh of relief at finally getting the words out.

'And how would I know if he had, we get lots of refugees here?'

'Captain O'Neil thinks he may have stolen some dog tags.'

Only inches below the corporal's boots, down in the darkness, Marko's hand instinctively reached inside his trouser pocket, gripping the hard metal of the tag.

'Really?' Aleksandar replied, genuinely intrigued.

'They belonged to one of our sergeants, by the name of Stanton. The boy was with him when he was found dead.'

'We search all our refugees when they arrive, so I can assure you that this missing boy of yours isn't here, but I'll be sure to let your captain know if by some miracle he turns up.'

'Thank you, general,' the corporal replied politely, finding the need to refer to this monster by his rank utterly distasteful.

With that, he stepped back, making ready to leave. As he turned, he noticed the second whisky glass on the table, his eyes lingering for a moment.

'Was there anything else corporal,' Aleksandar asked, his tone somewhat impatient. The corporal looked up.

'No, nothing,' the corporal relied hastily, turning to make for the door again.

At this moment a hideous notion struck Aleksandar from out of nowhere.

'Corporal?'

'Yes, general?'

'Are you sure no one else escaped, no other boys… or girls perhaps?'

'No general, absolutely sure,' the corporal replied truthfully, O'Neil having sworn the two corporals on guard duty at the time of the incident to complete secrecy about the girl. Aleksandar studied his face. He was an expert at spotting lies, certain by the look on his guest's face, that he was being truthful.

Down in the darkness, Marko's mind raced as he tried to figure out why the corporal would have lied, but whilst he couldn't come up with any notion as to the reason, his instinct told him he should keep Radica a secret.

'Thank you corporal,' he heard Aleksandar reply from above.

With a final nod, the corporal turned to go. Waiting for his guest to close the door behind him, Aleksandar got out of his chair and kicked the rug back to lift the trapdoor, Marko uncurling himself as Aleksandar reached down to help him up. Waiting for him to stand, he held his hand out expectantly, like a schoolteacher to a naughty pupil.

'The dog tags,' Aleksandar demanded, immediately noting Marko's hesitation. 'Give them to me.'

Marko removed the solitary tag on the chain from his pocket and placed it in Aleksandar's palm. He turned the tag over to examine the inscription.

'Why did this Sergeant Stanton give you this?'

'He said they were for luck.'

'Where's the other one?'

'I lost it when the chain broke,' Marko lied, holding Aleksandar's gaze. There was a moment then, a silent exchange of understanding that happens between a father and a son. Aleksandar couldn't be sure that Marko was being honest, but there was no reason to link the other tag to any of the girls he had supplied to O'Neil.

By the expression on Marko's face, Aleksandar knew that the tag was of great importance to him. Offering it back, Marko took it out of his hand instantly, hiding it away in his pocket again, safely back in his possession.

He looked up at Aleksandar with enquiring eyes.

'Why am I here?' he asked.

'Why?' Aleksandar replied, surprised.

'Why me, I mean?' Marko felt Aleksandar's firm hand on his shoulder again.

'Because you remind me of what I was like at your age.'

'You?' Marko replied, taken back.

'We are very much the same, you and I.'

'But how?'

'In time you will come to understand, but for now we must concentrate on your future. You are a born leader Marko, but you have much to learn.'

<u>SIX</u>

Radica had been walking for so long that she had lost all track of time. Thoroughly exhausted and dehydrated, her aching legs threatening to collapse beneath her at any moment, she was driven on by the primeval panic that comes with the fear of imminent death, clambering through endless miles of dense woodland, desperate for signs of habitation, a safe place to rest.

She was cold and filthy, her face and limbs scratched bloody by the endless miles of dense foliage that she had fought through. Every tiny sound made her stop and take cover, terrified of running into soldiers, not just Croat, but Serb as well, who she knew would probably rape and kill her with the same savagery that she'd suffer at the hands of her enemy.

She stumbled over a hidden tree in the undergrowth, cursing. Dragging herself to her feet, she looked up through the canopy of the trees. The cloudy sky had darkened and at first, she thought it was about to rain, but then a stark reality gripped her. It wasn't the onset of rain that was upon her, it was nightfall, realizing that her eyes had become so accustomed to her surroundings from being out there so long that she hadn't realized it was getting dark.

A fresh urgency compelled her legs into motion again as she felt herself shiver, knowing all too well that she would die from exposure in the night if she didn't find shelter very soon.

Hearing a strange whistling, she froze in mid motion. It sounded like the wind in the trees as she listened. Then her heart started thumping in her chest. It was music, drifting through the undergrowth. She cautioned herself, realizing it could be a trap, like sirens leading young sailors to their deaths that she had read about as a young child.

Keeping low and moving as quietly as possible, she followed the sound directly in front of her, desperately praying that this would be her sanctuary.

A flickering orange light, barely visible through the dense foliage, halted her in her tracks again. She heard muted male voices above the music on a radio, a traditional folk tune.

Creeping forward, trying not to tread on any branches, fearing that the sound of just one of them snapping would give her away, Radica came within a hundred feet. She could make out the faces of men, women and children in a clearing, huddled around a fire, warming themselves against the night chill that had fallen suddenly. The shapes of small dwellings just beyond stood like crouching giants.

A group of the men were stood guard, facing outwards in a circle, rifles aimed into the woods, eyes scanning the trees, ready to react, and she was terrified that they might shoot at the slightest sign of movement or sound as she emerged.

'Please, don't shoot,' one of the younger guards heard Radica call out from the darkness of the trees, instantly training his weapon on the source of the voice. He could tell whoever was out there was a young female, but he knew it could be a trick.

As the radio went dead, the women around the fire hastily gathered their children to them, their men reaching for their weapons down by their sides.

'Show yourself,' the guard commanded, keeping his voice as low as possible. His fellow sentries stayed where they were, holding their positions around the perimeter, all too aware that soldiers often used young damsels in distress as bait to throw their kill off guard.

The guard stared into the darkness, listening for movement, but all was quiet.

'Show yourself, or I'll shoot,' he repeated, a nervous edge to his voice this time.

The sound of undergrowth being trampled reached his ears, his aim homing in.

Radica's form emerged from the trees, the guard keeping his weapon trained, even after registering that the voice he had heard from the darkness matched the person coming towards him.

'Lower your weapon Zanus,' he heard a familiar voice call out from behind, an older woman passing his shoulder to approach Radica and take her by the arm, supporting her as she led her towards the group by the fire, the warmth of the flames sending a heavenly wave of warmth through her as she reached it.

Another middle aged woman approached, Radica catching a glimpse of her kind motherly smile as she carefully draped a blanket around her shoulders, Radica's two saviours helping her down onto an empty makeshift wooden bench, a space vacated by one of the young men a minute earlier when the commotion had started. A young girl sat next to her, looking up with innocent, enquiring eyes, searching this new visitor's face, but Radica's expression was blank, her exhausted mind and body already shutting down now that she had finally reached safety.

She felt something warm in her hands and looked down to see a bowl of steaming stew with a wooden spoon, her constricted stomach, that she had had to force into submission for the last twenty four hours, screaming out from deep inside her as the rich aroma reached her nostrils.

Her mind too far gone to engage her inhibitions, Radica wolfed the stew down like a starved animal as her audience looked on with expressions of pity, the sight of someone eating like this no surprise to them, having seen it many times before with solitary luckless refugees they had taken in. They had seen worse in their time, girls, and boys appearing half naked, shamefully trying to conceal their blood encrusted orifices that had been so savagely violated. Radica's appearance when she had emerged from the darkness, coupled with the way she walked seemingly unencumbered, had given them all hope that she had not fallen victim along the way, but it wasn't until the mothers sat around watching her after she had finished her stew and gulped down a large mug of water, saw the look in her eyes, that they were sure, the tell tale traumatic distant expression mercifully absent.

With Radica's stomach full and her thirst quenched, the overwhelming tide of sleepiness was fast to take her, and she was only vaguely aware of being helped up from her seat and taken to one of the dwellings where she was laid down on an old worn couch lit by the glow from logs burning in a small fireplace, asleep before her head hit the pillow.

It was an hour or so later when the families around the campfire retired to bed with their protesting children, the cordon of perimeter guards still in place, the men due to relieve them in a few hours accompanying wives and mothers indoors to get a few hours of sleep.

Radica was completely dead to the world when the young couple arrived home. The partner in the bedroom, the woman came through to check on Radica, the dirt on her face baked dry by the heat from the fire, the logs now almost burnt down. The woman noticed something glinting on the stone floor in the orange glow, directly below the couch. Bending down she picked up the dog tag, turning it over in her hand, the engrained inscription still darkened with traces of blood, making it easier to read in the dim light.

'Leave her be,' she heard her partner suggest from the doorway behind her. She turned, the tag in her hand catching his eye.

'Wait, is that?' he enquired, approaching to take it from her, his suspicion confirmed.

'Why would she have this?' he asked, more to himself than his partner. 'It's British.'

'Is that good, or bad?' she replied nervously.

A sudden burst of gunfire outside stirred Radica from her deep slumber, her eyes opening dreamily for a split second, before the alarm bell rang in her head. A second volley rang out, Radica already on her feet, her panicked hosts racing for the nearest exit on the other side of the room. Flinging the door open, they performed a frenzied dance, cut down by the hail of bullets that greeted them, Radica narrowly avoiding the stray rounds that peppered the wall around her as she dropped for cover.

Sprinting out into the hallway she saw another door dead ahead. She knew that if she hesitated, she would die. Radica burst out into the night like a greyhound, running blindly as deafening gunfire and screaming reverberated in her eardrums. Every instant she thought would be her last, waiting for the tearing sensation of bullets as they ripped through her flesh and shattered bones.

The pain, when it did come, was familiar and merciful, the sharp snagging of branches on her face, and she threw her arms up to shield her eyes, realizing she had reached the trees that encircled the small settlement.

She kept running as fast as she could into the darkness of the forest, the gunshots and screams following her as a warning not to slow down.

It seemed like an eternity before the haunting shrill pleas for mercy, punctuated by single gunshots in response, faded into nothingness, leaving a deafening silence in their wake.

In that moment as she fought to get her breath in the darkness, the calamity of what had just occurred, combining with the horrific events leading up, brought an overwhelming wave of grief crashing down on her and she had to bite down on the filthy cloth sleeve of her arm to stifle the animal like wail of anguish that rose up from deep inside, tears stinging the countless scratches on her face as they poured down.

Time seemed to recede into the abstract as her mind tumbled over and over, childhood family memories surging in an unstoppable deluge. Then, from the depths of her thoughts an instinct guided her hand, feeling for an object she had not yet consciously recalled, and it was only when she realized it was not there that the image of the dog tag materialized, the loss of the only trace of Marko propelling her back into the crushing danger presented by the present, once more out in the open darkness, the numbing cold already having worked its way into her bones again. Glancing quickly around, listening for any movement from the black void all around her, she then forced herself onwards, feeling her way blindly further into the darkness.

By the time dawn came, Radica was so cold that she had lost all sensation in her limbs, having to consciously force her legs to move, one trembling step after another.

The trees had begun to take on form again, and she thought at first that her eyes had become reaccustomed to the darkness. It wasn't until she heard the chorus of birds in the trees, giving her cause to look up, that she saw the black sky had given way to a murky grey.

A sound that she instantly recognized as something mechanical prompted her to drop for cover in the undergrowth. It was the deep hum of a vehicle off to her left, getting louder. Her eyes searched for movement between the trees, trying to identify if the approaching object was civilian or military.

Then she saw it, the rusted brown cab of an old farm wagon, and before she knew it, her lifeless legs had miraculously awoken and were carrying her as she stumbled frantically through the foliage towards the invisible road that she knew must be there. The treeline parting before of her, she saw the dirt track directly ahead. With the last of her strength, she dragged herself, staggering, out into the middle of the track without looking.

With an ear splitting screech of brakes, the wagon skidded to a halt only a few feet from her stricken body as she collapsed to the ground, her legs giving way from under her. The engine still running, both cab doors swung open simultaneously, two men dressed in shabby farm clothes jumping down, the younger brandishing a double barrel shotgun.

Radica looked up to see the looks of sheer relief on their faces.

'Christ, I thought I'd killed you,' the older craggy faced man exclaimed, Radica surmising that they were father and son.

'What are you?' he asked suspiciously, his son scanning the trees with his shotgun raised for signs of any pursuit, all too aware that this girl could be a ruse for an ambush.

Her traumatized mind already slipping from her grasp, Radica could only stare up at the old man, his question well beyond the realms of her comprehension.

'Tell me your name?' the father prompted, urgency in his tone now.

'Radica,' she replied in a slur, his eyes lighting up.

'Then you are Serb, yes?' he hastily replied, his expression full of hope.

'Yes,' Radica confirmed dreamily, her eyelids getting heavier with each passing moment. She felt herself being lifted from the ground then, aware of the embrace of someone carrying her. The sounds of the cab doors slamming and the revving of the engine as the van sped away registered only as indeterminable noises in her mind, before she slipped from consciousness, her head on the son's shoulder.

Only seventeen, the son's face was that of someone much older, the experiences of the last months having left a tragic legacy imprinted in his features, his eyes having witnessed atrocities that would remain embedded in his mind forever, lurking in the back of his subconscious, those countless horrific images always threatening to resurface at any moment.

For most adolescent boys of his age, the sensation of a beautiful teenage girl resting against them would arouse feelings of excitement from deep within, but for this young man, the ability to feel any such emotions after seeing so much rape and butchery enacted upon innocent civilians was long gone, never to return. Instead, his focus was on the woodland on either side of the road, his shotgun pointed out of the open window, whilst his father kept his eyes on the road for signs of any vehicles up ahead. For him, having most of his years behind him and with his boy's mother having passed away a few years before, he was afraid, not for himself, but for his son. He had aged with the comforting notion of dying in peace with his family by his bedside, his last thoughts of the fulfilling life they would continue to lead after he was gone. When his wife had died well before her time after a short battle with lung cancer, the bond between father and son had changed, a fear of losing one another and being left alone taking hold. The onset of the conflict had heightened that morbid loathing, images of what might happen to his son after his own death, haunting his dreams more intensely with each passing day.

But for now, he knew, he must concentrate on the present, and his arrangement with the general that had granted him and his son sanctuary.

He spotted the familiar landmark up ahead, a tall tree with a split trunk halfway up, the branches reaching out in opposite directions like deformed elongated fingers, as if belonging to two hands melded together trying desperately to pull apart, symbolic, he had often thought, of the struggle between two peoples who only a short time ago, had still been living peacefully together.

Without slowing down, he turned the steering wheel hard to the right, veering the truck off the lane, vanishing into the thick undergrowth.

Jolted from her deep sleep by the sudden jolt of the manoeuvre, Radica was hit by a wave of panic, back in that Croat army truck with her sister and the other girls. Crying out, she felt a hand on her shoulder and lashed out at the son trying to rouse her from her nightmare, suddenly realizing where she was.

'I'm sorry, I thought,' she began.

'Everything's alright now, you're safe,' the son replied reassuringly, her outburst no surprise to him after all the things he had seen.

Glancing at the boy's father concentrating on his driving as he hauled the wheel left and right to navigate the axle breaking potholes, she thought he seemed far away in a world of his own, a frozen expression of sad resignation on his face, the look of someone who had long since come to terms with whatever fate awaited him.

'Where are we going,' she enquired as she looked out of the windows to see a dark narrow dirt track completely enclosed by a canopy of trees.

'Somewhere you can rest, at least for now,' the father replied without taking his eyes off the road, his expression relaxing as the cab suddenly grew brighter inside. Following his gaze, Radica saw that directly ahead the suffocating blanket of trees gave way to a clearing, a small number of humble dwellings passing them by as they drove on.

It was the sight that met her eyes a moment later that froze her rigid in her seat. On the far side of the clearing, soldiers, unmistakeable in their green uniforms, were unloading wooden crates from a curtain sided truck, and in that instant the true motives of this man and his son struck her.

'Don't worry, they won't hurt you,' the son pre-empted intuitively, immediately picking up on the terrified expression in her eyes. She looked at him, searching his face for the truth.

'They're Serb,' he emphasized pleadingly, meeting her gaze. 'I swear,' he persisted. Something about the son's voice convinced her he was being sincere in that moment and her eyes suddenly softened, bringing a smile of relief to his face as the truck came to a halt outside a larger dwelling close to the soldiers, its chimney billowing smoke.

'Come on, let's get you inside so you can get warm,' the father added, with a comforting fatherly smile that immediately made her think of her own.

With that, both cab doors swung open, father and son jumping down, Radica seeing the son stood with his hand held out expectantly, waiting for his passenger to disembark. He noticed that same flash of doubt in her eyes again for a moment, Radica unable to suppress a returning fleeting notion, her instincts telling her to run again, despite understanding all too well the futility of doing so.

Her eyes darted between the son, the soldiers and the house, the son reading her thoughts.

'It's cold out here,' he protested, appealing to her sympathies to lure her from the cab, his request seeming to have no effect for a moment as her gaze kept shifting.

'Please, trust us,' she heard the father interject, looking around to see him stood looking up at her from the other side of the truck, having made a point of stepping back from the open door, so she wouldn't feel trapped. It was the pleading look in his eyes that made up her mind, an expression of genuine fear for her safety, as if she was his own daughter, silently begging her not to run, and in that moment she knew that the rumours that had swept over the border with Croatia about what was happening to girls like her, were all true.

The son's face was one of tremendous relief as she finally reached out to take his hand, jumping down from the truck.

Radica and her escort stopped short as his father walked up to the house, knocking on the ancient heavy wooden door. After a moment it opened with a yawn, a tall young soldier instantly recognizing his visitor. He cast Radica only a passing glance, seeming indifferent to her presence, something of a reassurance. After a brief exchange of greeting with the father, he beckoned them inside.

Crossing the threshold, Radica's senses were instantly awakened by the rich aroma of coffee and cooked bacon, a blazing log fire throwing an orange glow over the group of soldiers sat eating hungrily at a large circular wooden table, as an old lady busied herself at the stove.

The father approached the throng and murmured something into the ear of a soldier sat with his back to them, the son touching her arm reassuringly as he noticed her look of concern, offering a comforting smile to calm her.

His messenger stepping back, the soldier slowly got to his feet. Vladimir's eyes involuntarily lit up as he turned and saw the bedraggled beauty stood before him, and for a moment he was back at home, sitting with his young daughter in front of the fire, letting her win yet another round of poker. Abruptly he found himself back in the kitchen, marvelling at how this girl stood in front of him could possibly bear such a close resemblance to his own flesh and blood.

'Who is this beautiful creature you have found?' Vladimir asked the father, his gaze fixed on Radica, as if under a magical spell of enchantment. The other soldiers turned their heads to see, exchanging glances of bemusement, never having heard their general address any female with such adoration.

Vladimir found himself moving forward as if his legs had taken on a mind of their own, but he stopped abruptly as she immediately backed away, her anxious reflex filling him with a self loathing he had fought so hard to suppress for so long, this girl's frightened expression mirroring his own daughters exactly when...

'Don't be afraid young lady, no one's going to hurt you,' he said quietly, pushing the memory back down into the dark depths of his mind from where it had come. He held out a black leather gloved hand towards her, Radica instantly realizing by the lack of movement in the lifeless fingers that it was false.

'You're with the general now, you're safe.'

'We have to save them,' Radica blurted out, the notion surfacing so quickly she had spoken before she could suppress it.

'Save them, who?' he replied with a feigned empathy.

Radica hesitated, unsure of this stranger's true motives.

'Tell me, maybe I can help,' he teased.

'There were other girls with me.'

Those words were sweet music to Vladimir's ears, and he instinctively glanced away for an instant to hide his greedy eyes.

'Then, we must save them,' he announced as he turned back to her, fixing her in his gaze with a forced expression of concern.

'When?' Radica countered hastily.

'You must rest first,' he replied, his plan already unravelling in his head.

'No, we must go now,' she insisted.

Vladimir stepped closer, smiling reassuringly as he placed his real hand on Radica's shoulder.

'We must wait until dark, so we will be invisible, yes?'

Vladimir looked deep into her eyes.

'Your friends will be safe very soon, trust me. Now come, you must be starving.'

Radica gave the father and son a weary silent nod of thanks as they turned to leave, Vladimir leading her to the table, gesturing to one luckless soldier who obediently stood, taking his plate of food as he gave up his seat, Radica collapsing down into the wooden chair. A soldier next to her offered a welcoming smile as the old woman placed a plate of bacon, fried eggs and bread down on the table with a knife and fork before her, Radica instantly delving in like a starved animal, shovelling the food down like it was her last meal, oblivious to the quiet amusement of the soldiers sat around her, Vladimir watching her with unabated fascination as he sipped his steaming coffee, his mind drifting back again to happier days, long gone.

The relief of finally finding a secure resting place, combined with the hearty breakfast, found Radica struggling to keep awake at the table and soon after finishing her meal the old woman was showing her upstairs to a small room, the merciful sight of the small bed by the far wall the last thing she remembered, the old sturdy woman supporting her as she staggered towards it, Radica asleep before she had even lain down. Drawing the old floral patterned curtains to shut out the daylight, the old woman looked down at her new guest, just one of many who had passed thorough. It was at moments like these that she hated herself, not just because of what she had become part of to stay alive, but because she was a coward, too afraid to tell this girl and all the others that had passed before her, the terrible truth about what their futures held.

An all too familiar burst of riotous laughter downstairs in the kitchen roused her from her thoughts, and with one last regretful parting glance at this young woman sleeping so soundly, she turned and left the room, closing the door quietly behind her.

The afternoon cloud cast an oppressive gloom over the British army base, the rumble of trucks and shouting soldiers filling the air as they dismantled the equipment and structures, packing the numerous shipping containers.

Inside his command module, O'Neil was busy at his desk, completing his final report. He looked up irritably as he heard a knock at the door.

'Come,' he barked. A young corporal entered, taking a few steps forward before standing to attention.

'You have a visitor sir,' he announced. O'Neil checked his watch and sighed as he remembered his appointment, realizing he had lost all track of time.

'Show him in,' he replied.

A moment later Vladimir entered, the corporal turning on his heel and marching out, closing the metal door behind him.

O'Neil could not help but notice Vladimir's lifeless black gloved prosthetic limb as he approached and took a seat opposite.

'What the hell happened to your hand?' O'Neil enquired boldly.

'A long story,' Vladimir replied regretfully. He took a moment as he settled into his seat. 'It's such a disappointment that our arrangement here has come to an end so soon,' he continued, eager to get down to business.

'Well, you know what they say, nothing good lasts forever,' O'Neil replied, pathos in his tone, trying to lighten the mood as he reached into a draw to produce an old bottle of single malt whisky and two glasses, Vladimir breaking a grin as he recognized the label.

'My favourite, you remembered,' he exclaimed, his expression back to his usual self, O'Neil relieved as he poured the measures and slid one across the desk.

'Cheers,' O'Neil announced, the two of them clinking glasses before downing their drinks in one.

'Thank you for your prompt payment, as always,' O'Neil proffered.

'You're most welcome, and when will the girls be delivered to my contact?'

'In three days,' O'Neil confirmed, refilling Vladimir's glass.

'Good, very good,' Vladimir replied.

Both downing their drinks, Vladimir sat back in his chair, his expression sad for a moment.

'I'm going to miss you captain, it's been a real pleasure doing business. You are a true, how do you British say, gentleman.'

'The feeling's mutual general,' O'Neil replied, toying with his glass for a moment. 'Perhaps we will meet again in London someday.'

'Oh, I think you can be sure of that,' Vladimir countered heartily.

'I look forward to it,' O'Neil replied with a smile, reaching for the whisky bottle again.

Radica was awakened by the early morning light filtering through the thin curtains, instantly aware with a sickening dread that night had passed her by, and with it the chance to find her sister and the other girls.

Jumping out of bed she raced for the door, flinging it open and bolting down the stairs into the kitchen, deserted apart from the familiar old lady looking round from her customary position at the sink, just in time to see Radica heave the heavy wooden door open and disappear outside.

Vladimir was stood in full battle dress with his Kalashnikov slung over his shoulder, his back to Radica, deep in discussion with one of his sergeants, numerous soldiers climbing into the back of a dozen army trucks.

'General?' he heard from behind him, the voice instantly recognizable. With a final word to his sergeant he turned to see Radica approaching.

'Good morning young lady, did you sleep well?' he enquired cheerfully.

'I know where the girls are, we have to go now,' she blurted, panic in her voice.

'I see, and where exactly are these friends of yours,' Vladimir countered.

'At the British base, not far from here,' she replied, those words instantly sending Vladimir's mind racing. O'Neil's incompetence at letting one of the girls escape posed a serious security threat to their operation. He knew what he needed to do to neutralize the dilemma, but as he looked into this girl's pleading eyes, the face that reminded him so much of the most precious person in his life who he had lost so tragically, he knew it was course of action he could never bring himself to take.

'I'm so sorry young lady, the British have gone home,' he answered.

'No, I was there,' Radica replied, tears welling up in her eyes. Vladimir placed his real hand on her shoulder reassuringly.

'But my soldiers passed the base yesterday on their manoeuvres, it was deserted, I swear,' Vladimir lied, Radica breaking down into a flood of tears.

In that moment, without thinking, he had embraced her, that same wonderful protective fatherly pride surging through him, just like when he used to hug his own daughter when she was upset.

'You have to help me find them,' Radica sobbed.

'When I return later, we will look for them, alright?'

'You promise?' she persisted, her face still buried in his chest.

'Yes, I promise,' Vladimir lied.

It was late afternoon when the Croat army truck rolled slowly into the charred ruins of the small settlement, the corpses lain strewn around, their bodies contorted, frozen in the moment of death, young children still locked in the embrace of their mothers, staring up wide eyed in terror at their executioners long gone.

Some of the women and older girls were naked from the waist down, legs still apart, their bloody mutilated genitalia the legend of the sordid sexual amusement of the soldiers, gaping bullet holes in their heads, the traditional calling card.

Marko could only stare open mouthed from the cab of the truck, his face ashen. To Aleksandar sat next to him beside the driver, the sight was one that failed to induce any emotional reaction, this scene being one he had seen many times, not just perpetrated by the enemy, but by soldiers under his command.

Suddenly Marko's door was open, and he jumped down from the moving vehicle.

'Marko, what the hell are you doing?' Aleksandar shouted, the driver jamming on the brakes, the soldiers sat in the darkness in the back of the truck stirring, suddenly alert and ready for action, moving towards the rear to disembark.

Jumping down from the cab, Aleksandar was immediately flanked by his soldiers, scanning the area for signs of movement, they, too, unperturbed by the ghastly sight before them.

Marko was kneeling on the ground cradling the corpse of a stricken woman just outside a doorway. He was stroking her long blond hair, her facial features all but obliterated by the bullets that had shattered her jaw and cheekbones. Hearing the familiar footfall of Aleksandar approaching from behind, he hastily picked up the dog tag lying on the ground next to her and pocketed it.

'Marko?' he heard Aleksandar say. He slowly turned his head, looking up teary eyed at his new guardian stood over him.

Vanessa and the other girls had been in darkness for so long that they had lost all track of time. All they knew was that they had been on the move inside the freight container since feeling it being lifted onto a truck and driven away that fateful night.

Before leaving they had been provided with a sizeable supply of food and water and realized that wherever they were being taken, it was a considerable distance away.

In the countless hours of darkness as the container rocked on the trailer over the bumpy roads, they had come to recognise each other by their individual voices which served as the only form of comfort.

When the truck finally came to a permanent halt, they thought perhaps that they had reached their destination, fresh murmurs of speculation circulating among them regarding their fate.

For what seemed like an eternity, nothing happened, no voices, no noises from outside to enlighten them as to where they were. Then, without warning, the truck started up again and they were back on the move, this time only for a matter of minutes, before coming to another abrupt halt.

The mechanical whirring sound they heard coming from outside was not one that any of them recognized, and it wasn't until they heard the heavy metal clang that reverberated deafeningly inside the container, coming from above their heads, followed by a sudden jolt as they felt themselves being hoisted upwards again, that they finally realized.

For the first few hours the vast container ship sliced through the calm sea with ease. When the storm warning came through, the captain weighed up his options. If he kept his course and the storm was as bad as predicted, then they might lose some containers on the top level. If he took a detour to avoid the storm then it would cost time and money, something that the shipping company wouldn't be happy about, and anyway, from his experience these storms were often not as severe as the broadcasts warned.

An hour later he realized his error, but by that time it was too late. He would just have to wait it out and hope. From high up on the bridge he scanned the vast floodlit cargo deck, looking for signs of any unstable containers as the fifty foot waves crashed over them, completely unaware of the cargo in the container perched precariously on the top level on the starboard side.

The girls huddled close together, their involuntary screams echoing inside the metal prison as the container rocked violently from side to side. As another huge wave crashed into the side of the container and they felt it lift on one side, some of the girls turned hysterical, before mercifully the container banged back down on all four corners again, but their relief was short lived as the next wave lifted them higher, the container taking longer to drop back down into position.

When their prison tilted up higher yet again, Vanessa knew this was the moment. She placed her hands over her ears to drown out the deafening screams and tried to think about her family and recollect as many happy memories as she could as the container lifted past the point of no return, throwing them all violently to one side.

The impact of the container plummeting into the sea mercifully knocked some of the girls unconscious. Ice cold water began to force its way inside through the narrow gap between the double metal doors and the bulkhead at one end, those unfortunate not to have been knocked out from the impact like Vanessa, impulsively banging against the doors in a futile attempt to escape.

The container filled with alarming speed, the weight of water quickly dragging their floating prison down below the waves and into the dark depths.

Vanessa, sensing their inexorable descent, closed her eyes, keeping her hands over her ears to shut out the screams. As the icy water rose to her neck inside the metal coffin, her body completely numbed, she instinctively took a last futile deep breath.

She kept her eyes closed as the water rose above her head, hoping she would pass out from the cold, but eventually, failing to lose consciousness, the involuntarily impulse to open her mouth and breathe overwhelmed her, the salt water filling her lungs.

In her last moments as she slipped away, Vanessa felt a strange presence in front of her and she opened her eyes, the apparition of Radica reaching out to her, smiling reassuringly like she always did in times of trouble.

SEVEN - ITALY 2002

The low evening sun sparkled in Radica's emerald eyes as she stared distantly out to sea. This was her favourite time of the day, listening to the sound of the waves rolling gently up and down the beach, the feel of the warm summer breeze flowing through her hair.

When she had first arrived ten years ago, another sound had drowned out the waves, the constant rhythmic thud day and night of artillery bombardment that haunted her from across the Adriatic Sea.

She had never found out what had happened to her sister and the other girls. After a few months of travelling with Vladimir as his girl soldier in search of them, witnessing with her own eyes the aftermath of atrocities carried out by Croat soldiers on the civilian population, Radica was still desperately clinging to hope, but knew, deep in her heart, that she would never find them alive.

The ambitious notion that her sister may have somehow escaped and managed to slip out of Bosnia had come to her during those early days of searching, but she knew that Vanessa was not a fighter like her, and she would never have been able to summon the courage to try and escape. Instead, she would have opted to willingly submit to remaining a captive to her tormentors in the vain hope that they would eventually show mercy and let her go, something that Radica knew with a morbid certainty would never have happened. She could only pray that

Vanessa's suffering would have at least been short before the final release of death.

If by some miracle Vanessa had avoided falling victim to the depraved appetites of the soldiers before being disposed of like garbage with the other girls, she could be halfway across the world by now.

Radica had done everything she could to find her sister, even after the war had come to an end three years ago, Vladimir hiring private investigators and seeking the cooperation of his many personal contacts, but after a while the realization that Vanessa had almost certainly died back in war torn Bosnia, an unidentifiable corpse buried in some mass grave never to be found, became a forgone tragic conclusion in Radica's mind.

When Vladimir had taken Radica in, she had quickly come to trust him as her new father figure, developing a close fondness for him. She had never been allowed to accompany him on his offensive manoeuvres with the other soldiers, always accepting his explanation that it was much too dangerous, although he had trained her to use and maintain an assortment of firearms.

Living in the old lady's house with Vladimir and a few other soldiers, Radica had felt safe, sharing in their stories around the kitchen table at the end of each day, where they talked about the increasingly horrific acts of the Croat army and ordinary Croat people against Serb civilians. Her traumatized mind fractured by the horrific recent events she had endured, Vladimir was easily able cast his spell of indoctrination upon her, Radica swiftly developing a seething hatred of all Croats. Even her affectionate memories of Marko began distorting in her dreams, the recurring vision of standing over him with a gun to his head always ending abruptly, just before she pulled the trigger.

A few months into their search for Vanessa, Vladimir could sense that Radica's hopes of finding her sister alive were diminishing, and he decided the time had come. His secret objective to turn his little protégé into an efficient little soldier for his future use had proved a success, but with it had come a relentless desire within her to accompany him and his soldiers on their offensives, impatient to claim her first Croat. He couldn't risk his secret asset in waiting coming to any harm and moreover, he wouldn't be able to live with himself if he betrayed the memory of his own daughter's tragic death by placing Radica in unnecessary danger.

That fateful conversation between them was one that he dreaded, but it was inevitable. Radica's reaction had been predictable, pleading to let her stay with him and learn his ways, but he insisted that the conflict was becoming more and more savage by the day, and he feared that he would not be able to guarantee her safety if the Croat army's intensifying campaign in the area developed more momentum, swift to remind her of what happened to pretty young girls who found themselves in the firing line.

He had to admire his protégé for her determination in resisting, exclaiming that she would be more than capable of taking care of herself with her trusted Kalashnikov by her side, if the Croats tried to take her.

It was Vladimir's trump card, the one he had been keeping in reserve, that finally won her over, an errand of mercy that he was certain would tug on her heart strings and keep her safe, far away from the battleground for the next few years, until the time came to set in motion his master plan when the enemy was finally defeated once and for all, and this country, his country, was cleansed of every Croat man, woman and child.

His supposition proved to be well judged, Radica's eyes lighting up as soon as he started to tell her about the role he wanted her to play with the large coastal property he had purchased across the Adriatic sea, big enough to house scores of displaced Serb women and girls, just like her, a refuge where traumatized souls could be sent to convalesce. He knew that she would be unable to resist the notion of helping others who had been subjected to ordeals far worse than her own, and that this would in some subconscious way, help her relinquish herself of the guilt of having left her sister and the others behind.

Her departure had been difficult for them both, Vladimir for the first time since the loss of his daughter, having to fight back the tears as he embraced her tightly that night, thankful that the darkness hid his teary eyes from the soldiers on guard duty. As the truck disappeared into the night, he couldn't help but think of the moment, less than a year ago, when he had held his dying daughter in his arms, powerless to save her. Visions of the armed escort coming under attack on route and Radica being savaged by Croat soldiers filled his thoughts until the early hours when finally, after a large quantity of whisky, he had succumbed to a fitful sleep.

Radica had arrived at the old rustic beachfront house a few days later. The Italian staff of three ladies, a kind faced lady in her mid forties and her two twin daughters in their early twenties, were already there preparing the rooms and supplies for the first arrivals.

Their reaction to this petit girl of sixteen appearing on the doorstep that evening had always stayed with her. The mother, her brown eyes lighting up as she opened the door to see Radica, greeted her with a respectful formality, immediately reaching forward to take her luggage and beckon her inside. Quickly introducing herself as Alina in almost perfect English, she shouted towards the wide staircase for her daughters to come down.

Hurried footsteps from upstairs announced their arrival, coming down the stairs and standing next to their mother who introduced them as Erika and Sophia. They were staring at Radica with a mix of fascination and confusion, silently transfixed by the vision of this young girl who had been placed in charge of an orphanage.

Sophia whispered something in Italian at her mother who immediately replied in a low voice, drawing a shocked gasp from her daughters.

'Please excuse my daughters, they cannot believe someone as young as you would want to run an orphanage, but I told them that you yourself are an orphan,' Alina explained apologetically.

Radica smiled warmly at the daughters, to then find herself being embraced by Sophia. Alina shouted at her daughter, offering Radica a look of apology, but when she saw that Radica was hugging Alina back, an expression of relief spread across her face.

That evening Radica ate with her new family out on the veranda. Over the dull repetitive thuds of far away artillery across the narrow Adriatic Sea in Bosnia, Alina talked about the preparations they had made in anticipation of the new arrivals, and by the end of the meal Radica was feeling invigorated, so much so that she found herself unable to sleep when night came.

After Alina and her daughters had gone to bed, she stayed on the veranda, staring out to sea, the waves now silky black against the moonlight, listening to the artillery as flashes of light from the explosions illuminated the shape of the mountains across the water. As her mind began to drift and her consciousness slipped away, Radica was sure she could hear the voices of her family amongst the sound of the waves rolling on the sand.

In her dream she was still awake, staring at the black waves flickering in the moonlight. Then she heard it, a muffled moan at first, not one voice, but many, coming from the black expanse of the sea, reaching out to her in anguish, calling her name over and over from beneath the black prison of the waves. Their cries became louder and clearer, as if rising to the surface, then abruptly, they fell silent.

Then she he heard a single voice, one that she instantly recognized, her blood running cold. A sound accompanied that voice, a frantic splashing in the water, Radica desperately scanning the waves, feeling her heart pounding in her chest as she saw her, bobbing up and down in the waves, arms desperately flailing.

Sprinting down the beach towards the ocean before she had time to think, Radica dived into the waves, her adrenaline so high that she didn't register the freezing cold of the water, her sole focus on reaching her beloved sister, but as she powered through the waves, Vanessa seemed to be getting further away. Straining every muscle to reach her sister, Radica was seized by the realization that she was now dangerously far from the shore.

Vanessa's head suddenly disappeared under the waves. Swimming towards the spot where her sister had vanished, Radica took a deep breath, diving down beneath the waves, desperately searching in the silent darkness. Breaking the surface to gasp for air, she was about to dive back down again when she felt a tugging sensation on her legs.

Panic gripped her as she realized something was dragging her under. Reaching down to try and prise herself free, she felt a multitude of hands gripping her legs. Thrashing wildly in the darkness to keep her head above water, Radica just had time to glimpse the figure of Vanessa sitting on the veranda, her features just recognizable in the moonlight, staring dispassionately out to sea, not seeing her.

Her lungs already filling with water, Radica screamed out Vanessa's name over and over, but her sister did not hear her. Then, with one final scream, she felt the waves rise over her head.

Awaking with a start, crying out her sister's name, her eyes transfixed on the black rolling waves, it took a moment for Radica to register she was awake again.

Quiet footsteps behind drew her attention, Alina carefully draping a woollen blanket over Radica's narrow shoulders before taking a seat next to her.

'You were dreaming, yes?' Alina asked softly, Radica nodding in reply, a look of deep understanding in her older companion's eyes, just like her own…

'Why don't you come inside, your bed is all made up,' Alina suggested. 'You're going to need all your strength for tomorrow, when our first guest arrives,' she added, noting Radica's hesitancy.

'How old is she?' Radica asked abstractly.

'Nine,' came the solemn reply.

'Nine,' Radica repeated, staring back out to sea, visions of what that poor little girl must have gone through racing through her mind.

'What is her name,' she added.

'Nobody knows, she doesn't speak,' Alina replied, those words confounding Radica's worst fears.

'Now come inside, you must rest,' Alina insisted. Turning her head to look at Alina again, Radica recognized her own mother in that kind face and getting up, she followed Alina inside.

When the little girl arrived that afternoon, she was ghostly pale, her eyes devoid of all emotion, blankly staring into the middle distance as Radica knelt to greet her in the reception lobby. She wanted so desperately to hug this beautiful young girl, but Alina had already cautioned her, explaining that any intimate physical contact would send her into a fit of panicked screaming, the horrific legacy of her experiences at the hands of numerous soldiers.

Out on the veranda, careful to keep her guest shaded from the hot sun baking the wooden deck, Radica sat next to her on a bench, Alina bringing a small plate of freshly made potato salad to tempt their new guest with. After glancing briefly at the plate that Radica held out to her, she returned her gaze to the horizon, lost in her own world. Radica had to feed her like a baby, swallowing down spoonful after spoonful slowly, not even registering the taste, her mind elsewhere.

Afterwards, they stayed sat side by side yet still not touching, Radica having to fight back the tears as she observed this poor traumatized little girl, her expression never changing. Most heart breaking for Radica was the look in her eyes. Instead of being full of life and childish curiosity about everything she was seeing, her eyes were that of a much older person, someone who had experienced things so traumatic that they had shut down, become lifeless, not wanting to see anymore.

Even the gentle trickle flowing between the slats in the bench and the rapidly spreading wet patch soaking her loosely fitting cotton pants was not enough to stir her as she began to urinate without even realizing.

Calling for Alina to bring a bowl of warm water and some towels, Radica gently removed her pants, her patient still far away, but now humming an indistinct tune as her body rocked slowly back and forth, Radica speaking comforting quiet words as the tears poured down her face, a wave of guilt crashing down over her, aware that her actions were causing this little girl distress. The sight that met her eyes as she carefully peeled down the sodden underwear, stopped her in her tracks, an involuntary gasp escaping her lips as she saw, the girl's humming louder and more anguished now, the rocking faster. It wasn't the red rawness caused by urine burns that evoked the sheer revulsion that overcame Radica at that moment, but the torn and mutilated state of this small child's genitals.

The bowl of warm water quickly arriving, Alina stayed to help comfort her with soothing words as Radica carefully began to bath the wounds, terrified that this might cause more physical pain, but to her surprise, she didn't flinch or try and pull away, she remained in her catatonic state and her humming grew softer as her subconscious registered the once familiar sensation of warm water on a cotton flannel. Afterwards, applying a soothing skin cream, Alina helped Radica wrap a fresh towel around her midriff.

That experience had left an indelible impression on Radica as she stayed sat with her, and for the first time since her ordeal had begun back in Bosnia, she felt as though she had found true purpose from those experiences, her heart overflowing with affection for the traumatized child next to her that she feared may never speak, never even smile again. Enquiring with Alina she learnt that there would be a further eight orphans arriving before the end of the week, the prospect filling her with a growing enthusiasm, a vision of the villa full of scores of convalescing lost souls bringing a smile to her face, the first in a long while.

That night the same nightmare crept up on Radica. Bolting awake in the darkness of her bedroom, she felt herself seized by a crushing torment that she had fought so hard to suppress. She cried out in anguish as the guilt surged through her, the accusing faces of her family refusing to fade away.

Alina was in her room in an instant, embracing her as the tears flooded down her cheeks.

'Why couldn't I save them?' Radica wailed repeatedly as Alina tried to comfort her.

'Hush now,' Alina said softly in her ear.

'But they're gone, they're gone, they're gone,' Radica blurted, those words tumbling out, over and over.

The orphans that arrived over the next months were all unique in their own way, not just in their age from five all the way up to seventeen, but in their widely varying extent of trauma. Some showed immediate signs of progress, others were tragically destined to spend the rest of their lives locked inside the prisons of their horrific past, incapable of living a normal life out in society.

The first little girl to arrive had not been the only patient incapable of speech, and Radica was fascinated by the way that new guests cursed with that same affliction would tend to congregate, finding silent comfort in each other's presence.

Croats, always the Croats, were responsible for all of this, Vladimir would proclaim when he telephoned her from Bosnia's ever worsening battleground, and she believed him without hesitation.

By the time the war ground to a halt two and a half years later, Radica had taken in over two hundred girls and was so spiritually immersed in her mission of mercy that she had little time or interest in the news reports which in her mind were all lies, trying to turn the world against the Serb people, her people.

It was fortunate for Radica that it would not be until years after the war ended that the true scale of the atrocities against the victims she had dedicated her life to helping would be really known and published in the media. If she had been aware of the numbers as soon as the war had finally come to a close, then it may well have crushed her, sending her spiralling into a complete mental breakdown, the realization that her orphanage catered for a minuscule fraction of the tens of thousands of girls and women who had been systematically raped at the hands of soldiers on both sides, not just by the Croats as Vladimir vehemently proclaimed, but her own people as well.

When a permanent ceasefire was forged at the end of 1995, all contact with Vladimir had suddenly been lost, Radica fearing the worst. She would never have been able to comprehend of course, that her hero father figure, the saviour of so many girls, had in fact fled like all the generals on both sides to evade capture by the UN so they could avoid being tried in the Hague for war crimes.

The winter and following spring passed with no word from Vladimir, although Alina was able to convince Radica that he must still be alive and well, as the monies necessary to pay for the cost of running the villa were still arriving on time, without fail.

It was in May every year, when the hot temperatures arrived, that Radica returned to spending her afternoons on the sun drenched veranda with that first ever girl they had taken in, now a teenager. She had always remained her favourite, ten years on, Radica still ever hopeful that she would one day break free from the chains of her terrible past. She was certain in her heart that this child would eventually speak again, even if it took decades.

She had felt elation of late, as for the first time since arriving, her expression had started changing ever so slightly when she addressed her, a certain sign that she was not just hearing, but beginning to comprehend Radica's words.

It was the highlight of everyday for Radica to sit and read to her, like a mother to her child, the thrill of coaxing even the faintest hint of a smile from her patient, truly something to behold.

That fateful afternoon however, Radica could tell by her demeanour that she was tired, one of her bad days, so they just sat together on the bench in silence, Radica at least able to comfort her as she held her hand. Looking out to sea, the thunderous rhythm of the artillery over the water having long ceased leaving an eerie silence that still registered with Radica.

Western Europe had greeted the end of hostilities with a huge sigh of relief, but for Radica there was no such consolation. For her, the end of this sordid chapter in modern history served only to open a dark doorway in her mind, the violent destiny that lay beyond the threshold pulling her inexorably nearer with each passing day. Vladimir had always promised he would never stop looking for those two monstrous individuals, their faces burnt into Radica's memory, emerging from the dark murky depths of her subconscious that she had fought so hard to supress while the war was still raging, promising herself that one day...

'There's someone here to see you.' Looking up, Radica noticed that for the first time ever, Alina's expression was tainted with a hint of nervousness.

'Am I interrupting?' Instantly recognizing that voice, Radica stood, turning to see the broad figure of Vladimir stood in the doorway. For a moment she couldn't speak, the suddenness of his arrival with no communication beforehand leaving her stunned. It had been a long time, but he hadn't aged a bit she thought. If anything, he seemed to have gotten younger, his whole appearance clean cut and manicured, looking much more like a powerful businessman in his dark hand tailored suit.

'Don't you have anything to say to me, after all this time,' he teased with a warm smile.

'I'm sorry, I just wasn't expecting you, why didn't you call,' Radica replied as he stepped towards her, Alina taking her leave, glancing back with a worried expression as she went.

'I wanted to surprise you,' he countered. They embraced then, Radica feeling the familiar comfort of his fatherly warmth as he held her tight.

'Why did you stop calling me, I was worried something might have happened to you,' she complained.

'Happened, to me,' Vladimir replied with a scoff, holding her out at arm's length, taking her in.

'Look at you, all grown up, you're a woman now.'

'Thanks to you,' she replied gratefully, noticing his gaze shift to the young child sat on the bench behind her staring out to sea.

'And who is this lovely young lady?' he enquired.

Before Radica had time to caution him, Vladimir had crouched down in front of her, searching that blank expression. Then Rosa's lifeless eyes seemed to shift almost imperceptibly, the moment of curiosity as she searched his face suddenly giving way to panic as she realized, her mouth falling open in a silent scream, then forcing out an animal like wail of anguish.

Radica rushed in to try and comfort her, Alina arriving in moments. Vladimir could only stand back helpless and witness the spectacle.

'Forgive me, I had no idea,' Vladimir offered apologetically.

'It's not your fault, I should have stopped you,' Radica replied, stroking Rosa's face, the grotesque noises emanating from deep inside her beginning to subside.

'Let me take her,' Alina interjected, Radica looking up to let her lift Rosa from her seat, her charge burying her face in her chest so she wouldn't have to see anymore, before hurrying away with her. Vladimir watched them leave, waiting for a long moment to pass before turning back to Radica.

'How many is it now?' Vladimir asked, eager to draw Radica's attention away from the sordid incident.

'Over two hundred now, thanks to you,' Radica replied.

'It's the least I can do, after what you've all have been through,' Vladimir replied, forcing a smile, which he then quickly let fade as an invitation for Radica to speak.

'What's wrong,' she replied, quickly taking the bait, Vladimir pausing before he replied.

'There's something I need to discuss with you, perhaps somewhere more private?' he said gravely.

'Why, what is it?' Radica enquired, her eyes narrowing.

'Let's take a walk,' Vladimir insisted, glancing towards the beach. Radica led him down the sun bleached wooden steps onto the golden sand, where they walked side by side in silence until they were out of earshot from the villa.

'So peaceful here,' Vladimir commented as a preamble to the matter he needed to discuss with her.

Then he stopped, Radica turning to see him looking at her, a tragic look in his eyes.

'What is it Vladimir?' Radica asked demandingly, the countless possibilities churning over in her mind.

'I have some very important news for you, but…'

'But what?' Radica replied, searching his eyes.

'You've made a new life for yourself here, perhaps I should let you leave the past behind.'

'Tell me Vladimir,' Radica pressed.

He stood face to face with her, looking deep into her eyes.

'You've found them haven't you,' Radica said.

'Yes, but they are far away, it will be difficult to...'

'Tell me where they are,' she commanded, Vladimir seeing the fire in her eyes, his master plan now in motion.

EIGHT

It had been a long time since Marko had recognized the face that stared back at him in the mirror. His eyes had lost all resemblance of humanity, icy cold and expressionless.

Pulling on his black suit jacket over his muscular bulky frame, he looked away from his reflection, all too aware that his appearance had changed beyond all recognition. His youthful and outward adventurous expression had given way to that of a much older and streetwise executioner long ago, punctuated by his close cropped hair that accentuated his menacing demeanour.

He had often thought of late, how he had become like the men he once despised, like the sadistic Vladimir, haunting him from the grave in his dreams.

Today was one of his darker days, when the sense of self loathing wouldn't let go. He had never thought it possible when he had arrived with Aleksandar and Emil that he would so willingly have become one of them, not just in his deeds but in this thoughts. The simplistic black and white mentality of his youthfulness that had allowed him to see things with such moral clarity back in Bosnia had quickly blurred into the many shades of grey when presented with the high end materialistic trappings and status that his new surroundings had to offer.

He knew that things would have turned out differently if Radica had still been alive, that with her strong tenacious will, she would never have allowed him to drift blindly into the murky depths of the world that he now inhabited.

There had been lots of other girls since arriving in London a decade ago, but he had never allowed them to get close, his line of work incompatible with long term relationships, let alone marriage and children. With his honed good looks and impressive physique, combined with a million pound plus loft apartment overlooking the Thames, there had been no shortage of suiters. He knew all too well that his secretive line of work meant that he could never settle down, and after breaking the heart of his third girlfriend in the space of twelve months with the by now thoroughly rehearsed line, it's not you, it's me, Marko had decided that he needed to stop with the hurting, at least for the foreseeable future. He had never stopped thinking about Radica. The first cut was the deepest, he knew that now, often reflecting that none of his other romantic interests had aroused his senses in the same way she had.

Radica wasn't the only ghost from the past to visit him late at night when he sat out on his balcony watching the night lights of the city as he nursed a large whisky. Stanton would be turning in his grave if he knew the path that Marko had chosen, and his guilt ran deeper still because he was yet to make good on his promise that he had made as his saviour spoke his dying words. He had every intention of carrying out Stanton's request, but he had to pick the right time, or his very own existence would come crashing down around him and it would all have been for nothing. He was torn between honour and necessity, knowing that until he fulfilled his pledge, Stanton would never be able to rest in peace. Then perhaps, he would be able to find closure on the chain of events that had led him to this juncture in his life. He knew that the simple farm boy from back home was gone forever, never to be reclaimed, but if he could at least do the good deed Stanton had asked of him, he might perhaps be able to rid himself of the self hatred that had weighed so heavily on him since arriving in the capital.

He always made the time to compose himself before his evening started, staring out through the floor to ceiling wall of glass affording a panoramic view of the river and the city beyond. This was the time of the day when his work always began, as the sun set and night fell to hide the multitude of sins that could only be played out in the darkness.

From what his employer had told him, he knew that this evening would end in bloodshed. That hatred that had fuelled the atrocities between the Serbs and Croats back in Bosnia had found its way to London at the first signs of the conflict being forced to a close by NATO, when the smarter senior military figures like Aleksandar realized that the game of musical chairs would soon come to an end, and it was time to leave before the music stopped and he found himself left without a seat.

Marko had left Bosnia with him willingly, mostly because there was nothing left for him at home. Aleksandar had been right when he told him that he would never forget his first kill. It had happened unexpectedly, not long after arriving, when what Aleksandar thought would be a simple intimidation meeting with a local Turk hood, had gotten out of hand. Everything had happened so fast that Marko had fired the shots before he had time to think. He had reflected afterwards that if he had reacted a split second later, then it would have been him and Aleksandar laid out with bullet holes in their heads instead, that incident proving an invaluable lesson in survival. Aleksandar had been in no doubt that his protégé had saved his life that night, and soon afterwards had presented him with the deeds to the Thameside apartment and the keys to a new Mercedes S Class, not so much out of respect as he had made great pains to convey, but because he knew he wouldn't last long in London without Marko by his side.

For Marko, his first kill was a critical turning point for his psyche, propelling him inexorably into a new realm of existence where his capacity for emotional response would be numbed significantly. Fear was now a thing of the past, an inhibition that he had vanquished the moment he'd pulled that trigger. That primeval instinct to kill or be killed would serve him well in the months to come, as London's gangland was turned inside out by a new level of savagery never seen in the capital before.

There was of course a penalty to pay for becoming a cold blooded murderer, but the self loathing that Marko felt every morning when he awoke was not because of the lives he had taken, they were the enemy that needed to be eliminate, plain and simple. It was the loss of his emotional spectrum that would prove be his curse. He felt dead inside, devoid of all feeling, each day like the last, a robotic process without any highs or lows, his existence becoming nothing more than to serve his master in whatever way was required.

Marko would soon come to regard the Serb gangsters that Aleksandar hated with such a passion as being no different from himself and his own keeper. To him they were all thugs fighting over disputed territories, just like back in Bosnia, and when Marko was called upon to dish out a dose of brutality which on occasion would end in murder, he felt no satisfaction whatsoever. It was a job for which he was rewarded handsomely, nothing more.

Aleksandar had been quick to register the change in Marko and was gratified with the result, having achieved his objective of turning his bodyguard into a loyal minion who would never question his instructions.

There was one tiny glimmer of light however in the eternal darkness of Marko's existence. She would come to him in his dreams, emerging from the depths of his abys, her beautiful face and emerald eyes as clear as day. She never spoke, but he knew she was trying to convey something with her expression, telling him that she was still... He would always awake at that moment, and for an instant she would be stood at the end of his bed.

On the way out of his apartment, Marko picked up the dog tags on the chain and his car keys from a side table. Pocketing the keys, he draped the dog tags around his neck, carefully tucking them down inside his pristine white shirt with the top button undone, out of sight. He never went anywhere without his lucky charm, the only object with which he could relate to his past existence.

Taking the lift down to the basement adorned with a prestigious selection of high-end luxury sedans and sports cars,

Marko got into his Mercedes and started the engine, the huge engine growling reassuringly as it found its beat.

Night had fallen as he drove out from the city's business district adjacent to the Thames, northwest towards the leafy suburb of Hampstead, the traffic by this time of the evening having eased considerably.

Aleksandar's vast mansion sat in gated manicured grounds surrounded by high walls and patrolled day and night by armed guards. Turning off the quiet residential road into the driveway entrance, Marko stopped at the gatehouse, one of the familiar guards sat inside appearing from the doorway, his hidden pistol inside his jacket within easy reach. Despite recognizing Marko's car, the guard still insisted on shining his blinding torch in Marko's face, before checking that there was no one concealed in the back or the boot. Marko had long since grown tired of this monotonous and unnecessary procedure, but he knew it was a hindrance of his own making, as he had used this very trick on a driver for a rival gang, forcing him at gunpoint as he posed as a visitor, there to do business with his boss.

There was of course a personal reason why this guard tried to burn Marko's retinas out every time he visited. Like all the other guards in Aleksandar's employ, he despised and envied Marko, regarding him as a jumped up little weasel who had wriggled his way into becoming the boss's personal bodyguard. While this mere boy enjoyed all the trappings of a luxurious lifestyle, he and his comrades, real men who had fought alongside Aleksandar in Croatia and Bosnia, were living a frugal existence in cheap rented accommodation and driving old clapped out cars.

Aleksandar was all too aware of their resentment that his protégé attracted, although none of them had dared speak out. He wasn't worried in the slightest, knowing that despite the discord, their loyalty was secured. They knew all too well that they were trapped in their lives of subservience by the knowledge that the alternative to their humble existence was far worse. They were illegal immigrants, their residency in London only made possible by the influence that their keeper was able to exert on the authorities. Outside of his protective cordon, they would be detained and deported back to Bosnia, with the risk of arrest by the UN authorities or far worse, torture and death at the hands of Serb civilians, hungry for revenge.

Having performed his pointless procedure, the guard nodded to his comrade sat in the gatehouse. With a loud yawn, the eight foot solid sheet steel gate began rolling open. Marko knew at exactly what point there was enough room to drive through so he wouldn't have to wait for the gate to open fully. This was his opportunity to annoy the two discourteous guards and one that he never passed up. Ramming his foot down on the accelerator as soon as the gate had opened sufficiently, he raced past them, the tires squealing and the engine roaring, punctuating the insult by immediately slowing as he was over the threshold, slowing to a respectable crawl.

Eying the armed guards patrolling the grounds, their vague forms illuminated by the security spotlights positioned on high ornately designed masts, covering every inch of the extensive grounds, Marko proceeded up the long driveway to the magnificent white walled mansion, a guard stood either side of the reinforced solid wood double front door. Deliberately parking close to them directly outside as a sign of disrespect, Marko got out and approached the entrance. He knew that these two individuals disliked him with the same venom as the gatekeepers, but as he had already been cleared at the gate, they knew that they had no reason to detain him even for an instant. The only insult they could convey as he passed between them, opening the door to enter, was a refusal to acknowledge his presence, an affront that Marko was happy to return.

Closing the door behind him, Marko could instantly tell by the rowdy deep gravelly voices coming from the cavernous high ceilinged front lounge, that Aleksandar and Emil were on usual form, having indulged in their traditional pre-emptive ritual of downing a few single malt whiskies. Whilst he had never spoken out on the subject, their tiresome habit exasperated Marko to the extreme, as in their far less than sober state they would be relying on their little foot soldier's alertness to get them through the evening's as always of late, highly unpredictable proceedings unscathed.

'Marko my boy,' Aleksandar exclaimed heartily from the comfort of his ox blood red leather studded couch as he saw him enter, Emil looking round from the back of his matching couch opposite to exchange a more formal nod. Since arriving in London, Marko had witnessed the slow but inexorable physical decline in both Aleksandar and Emil, as their natural tendency to indulge in malt whisky and red meat had begun to catch up with them. Emil had come off worse, his once lean, muscular body having begun to sag, his angular facial bone structure now vanishing behind thickened flesh, matching with a rouged complexion from the drink. By comparison, Aleksandar had taken steps to offset the diminishing effects of his new lifestyle by working out daily in his home gym and the results showed in his appearance, but the uphill battle would only get worse with age.

Marko had never been close to Emil, although he genuinely cared about the health of his mentor figure but knew there were some subjects that could never be broached, physical fitness being one of them.

'So, I trust you're well rested and ready to do battle,' Aleksandar teased as he got to his feet with surprising speed considering how much he'd had to drink, Emil also standing, though markedly slower and with less purpose.

'Of course,' Marko confirmed.

'Then let's get this over with so we can celebrate. I have a beautiful young lady all ready for you for later Marko.'

'Thank you,' Marko replied with feigned appreciation.

'Wait, Marko, haven't you forgotten something,' Emil slurred jokingly, the drink well and truly having got the better of him on this occasion.

'It's in the car,' Marko countered.

'Oh but I have a new one, made especially just for you,' Emil chuckled, producing from the couch, hidden from Marko's view, a brand new crisp black chauffeurs cap. He approached, smirking as he came, and placed the cap on Marko's head, adjusting it just so. Emil would always insist on making him wear a cap when he drove them to meetings, a mocking joke that Marko had long ago stopped finding amusing. He knew that Emil had never really liked him, this upstart farm boy who Aleksandar evidently thought more highly of than himself, but Emil stopped short of fearing that the equilibrium of his business relationship with Aleksandar would ever be threatened by him, and so this ritual was simply meant as a subtle reminder to Marko of his place in the grand scheme of things. Aleksandar had never felt any need to intervene in this matter, as he knew it was a harmless way for Emil to vent his opinion, and behind Emil's condescending veneer, he knew that he had come to regard Marko with a modicum of respect, having seen him in action enough times to recognize him as a first rate bodyguard and assassin.

Aleksandar and Emil reclined in the back of the roomy Mercedes as Marko drove them to the West End. Aleksandar never talked during these trips, not when he was about to do battle with a Serb and Marko often pondered if his mind was recalling all the atrocities that he had seen back in Bosnia, those images flooding his hateful mind with the relentless motivation to rid London of all Serbs. Emil, the blunt instrument that he was, could nevertheless be surprisingly perceptive around Aleksandar when he needed to be, and he was always careful to refrain from attempting any conversation during these journeys.

Navigating the narrow multi coloured neon streets of Soho, Marko finally parked up at their destination, a generous vehicle space specifically reserved for their arrival, directly outside a building with a lewd brightly lit figure of a stripper above a black steel double door guarded by two gorilla sized doormen dressed all in black.

Checking the street ahead and also behind with the aid of his mirrors, Marko scanned the other parked cars and pedestrians for sings of danger. Many a gangster had met his end in exactly this kind of situation. Marko knew, because he had been party to an assassination just like this. Satisfied that there was no threat, he turned the ignition off and opened his door, emerging swiftly into the cold night air, his eyes still roving as he opened Aleksandar's door, standing directly in front of him to block the path of any would be shooter crossing the street from behind as he emerged holding a black briefcase.

Emil's chauffeur made a deliberate point of not opening his door as he had for Aleksandar. This gesture of contempt for Emil was one that Marko took advantage of occasionally as payback for his mockery, always ready to use the excuse if Emil challenged him, that his primary responsibility was Aleksandar, as key target for any rival gang, not Emil, that reasoning in itself an insult to Emil's status. Aleksandar cast Marko a sideways glance topped off with smile of amusement as Emil threw his door open and clambered clumsily out of the vehicle, slamming it behind him as a mark of protest.

Sizing up the two doormen as he brought up the rear, Marko noted there was nothing unusual about them, except that by the smaller than usual bulge in their jackets concealing the side arms in their shoulder holsters, it looked to Marko like they were packing the new compact Glocks instead of the customary larger Beretta's. This, he mused, was a largely irrelevant observation as both weapons performed with much the same efficiency, but Marko always obsessed about every detail in these situations, a discipline that he was convinced had kept him alive in these situations.

Making eye contact with the two doormen as he approached, a habit he always employed to check on any bodyguard's reaction, he noted that they didn't meet his gaze, a response which raised a red flag in his mind, a sign that they were confident they wouldn't be encountering him again as he left later on, except in a body bag. Registering the eminence of the much older Aleksandar and Emil, the doormen nodded briefly as a fake courtesy, pulling the double doors open for them to enter, pounding techno music pouring out onto the street as Marko followed directly behind, calculating their agility based on their posture and movement as he passed them, in case a confrontation ensued later.

Inside, the steel doors closing behind them, a third clone like bouncer led them through the large darkly lit club, even the more youthful Marko finding the blaring music an unwelcome distraction as he tried to memorise the layout. There were three stages, naked strippers, their slender forms illuminated by subtle spotlights, coiling themselves around chrome floor to ceiling poles like snakes. Suited punters sat around the edges, their greedy eyes soaking up the feasts on offer. Enclosed booths separated the stages, wealthier guests sat with semi naked girls draped over them. Marko knew from studying the plans that the steel door off to the left guarded by another doorman lead to the private rooms. Stood behind a long chrome edged bar to his right, Marko noted a tall lean male eying him as he passed, undoubtably a firearm placed within easy reach under the counter.

Arriving at a door at the far end of the club, their host knocked with a heavy fist. A small shutter slid back, two eyes peering out. With a loud clunk barely audible above the sound of the music, the door opened outwards, an older more experienced looking henchman with a flat boxer's nose, obviously the club owner's personal bodyguard, standing aside to usher them into a dark black walled and ceilinged corridor. Pulling the heavy door shut behind them as if it was as light as a feather, Marko was alerted to his superhuman strength, someone he would only be able to stop with a bullet to the head.

Leading them to a final door padded in black leather with chrome studding, their escort knocked firmly and waited. A few moments passed before the door opened outwards with a yawn, the second bulky bodyguard, almost indistinguishable in appearance from his counterpart, filling the doorway. Exchanging a nod with his doppelganger he stood aside, sizing up the three visitors as they stepped past him over the threshold into the dimly lit windowless inner sanctum.

The shadowy broad shouldered form of Stanislav was sat slouched in an old leather studded armchair behind a huge antique wooden desk at the back of the room, two matching facing armchairs positioned opposite. Cigar smoke hung in the light from a desk lamp that emphasized his sagging sweaty features. Reading a document on his desk, a duplicate placed next to it, he made a point of not looking up to acknowledge his guests, a familiar contemptuous tactic that Marko had witnessed many times before. Sizing him up, Marko would have put him at around fifty. From his flabby physique and smooth facial features, he didn't look ex-military, more like ex-merchant banker, but Marko knew from experience that sometimes it was the customers from more gentile backgrounds that proved to be the most savage.

A somewhat harmless looking English bulldog with a studded collar sat obediently on the floor next to Stanislav's desk for company, Marko somewhat surprised that their host hadn't opted instead for the more fashionable illegal pit bull breed revered in the gangster community.

Marko listened for the sound of the door closing behind him which didn't come, a sure and certain sign that reinforcements were lying in wait out in the club or behind the other black flush faced closed door at the back of the office, to the right of Stanislav's desk. He glanced behind, the first bodyguard now back in position at the door leading out into the club, Stanislav's second minder stood directly behind his boss, sizing Marko up. Satisfied that he had kept his guests waiting long enough to make his point, Stanislav looked up from his desk.

'Please gentlemen, sit,' he said in as courteous a tone as he could muster, unsuccessfully masking the utter contempt with which he regarded his visitors.

Aleksandar and Emil were accustomed to dealing with men like Stanislav, jumped up financiers from their homeland, who as soon as the war had started had been on the first plane out, having emptied their bank accounts before the military seized control of the financial institutions. While his two battle hardened visitors had fought knee deep in mud and blood, Stanislav had spent his time living a life of luxury, indulging in the many sordid trappings that London had to offer. To Aleksandar and Emil, the parasite sat on the other side of the desk had no right being part of the criminal underworld that they inhabited, and they fully intended to make him pay the ultimate price for interfering with the business empire that they had been building since their arrival. That could wait however, as on this occasion they had come to do legitimate business.

Stepping forward and taking their seats, Aleksandar and Emil were greeted with a low growl from the bulldog, Emil unable to resist a snide remark.

'Just goes to show that the old English expression is true,' he said with a sly grin, an annoyed Aleksandar casting him a cautionary glance.

'Oh yes, and which expression is that?' Branislav retorted.

'That dogs really do look like their owners,' Emil chuckled, only to be disappointed as Stanislav kept his composure, swallowing the insult with a forced smile.

'Let's get down to business, shall we,' Aleksandar interjected hastily before Emil could push his luck any further.

'Very well,' Branislav replied, picking up a gold plated pen and turning over the first three pages of both documents on the desk to find the signature leaves, Aleksandar carefully placing the briefcase on the desk and turning it towards his host. Branislav reached forward, releasing the two clasps and opened the case to find it packed with neatly bound wads of bank notes, his eyes lighting up like a child opening his biggest present on Christmas morning.

'Cash,' Stanislav said with a satisfied smile. 'Still the best currency, and the only one you can make disappear,' he added. Removing some of the numerous neatly bound wads to get down to the bottom of the case, he took one from the last batch, removing a single note at random and holding it under an ultraviolet handheld light that he retrieved from his desk drawer, Emil's annoyance evident in his expression. Mercifully however, he managed to refrain from making any remarks as Branislav removed each wad and fanned through them with the practiced efficiency of a croupier. Finally, satisfied that everything was in order, he closed the briefcase, signing the back pages of each of the two documents before offering them to Aleksandar who countersigned each, retaining one for himself to place safely in his drawer. Branislav sat back in his chair, his hands now resting on his lap out of sight, a movement that alerted Marko.

'Welcome to your new office,' Branislav exclaimed heartily. 'I will of course be taking my dog with me,' he continued.

'He's very loyal, I was hoping you would leave him here for me,' Aleksandar replied jokingly.

'I'm afraid he's not for sale,' Branislav shrugged.

'Well it's been a pleasure doing business with you,' Aleksandar concluded, smiling through gritted teeth as he stood with Emil.

'The pleasure, I can assure you, is all mine,' Branislav replied with a grin from his chair.

It was the almost imperceptible movement in Branislav's right shoulder as his hand reached forward for something under his desk that propelled Marko into action.

As the secret door to the side burst open, Marko already had his gun out, firing off a single shot to the assailant's head in case he was wearing a bullet proof vest, but his second shot to the bodyguard stood behind Stanislav was a fraction of a second too late, his opposite getting off a shot of as Marko's bullet severed his jugular, Marko taking a bullet to the chest, downing him. That moment provided Stanislav with his only the opportunity to flee and with surprising speed he was up and past his stunned hosts on the way to the door, his bulldog seeking refuge under the desk. Stanislav raced down the corridor towards the second door leading out into the club, his first bodyguard pushing it open in anticipation. His employer safely away, he charged headlong down the corridor towards the office, the loud music following him.

Stanislav's bodyguard, counting on only having to deal with the much slower Aleksandar and Emil, was more than a little surprised, as with the crack of the gunshot drowned out by the deafening music reverberating off the walls in that closely knit space, he felt the searing red hot pain and agonizing shattering of bone as a bullet passed through his left thigh, dropping him like as sack of potatoes, his weapon slipping from his grasp. Looking up as he desperately tried to reach for his pistol, he saw Marko struggling to his feet, his weapon still trained.

Still winded from the bullet lodged in his Kevlar vest, Marko staggered down the corridor in pursuit of Branislav.

The open steel door shielding him from the eyeline of the barman who he knew would be ready and waiting, Marko peered out into the treacherous darkness of the club. He had to assume that every henchman in the club would, at that very moment be converging on him, leaving him with only one option, Feeling the hard edges of the dog tags through the fabric of his shirt, Marko took a deep breath before racing out into the club, his pistol already trained on the exact position where the barman had been stood before and prayed still would be.

Marko had fired his first shot before his conscious had even had time to register his target. Falling backwards, both barrels of the barman's sawn off shotgun discharging into the ceiling with a thunderous report, which to Marko's utter relief was distinctly louder than the music, the sound causing the strippers draped around their chrome poles to freeze in mid motion like mannequins to join everyone else in the room looking in the direction of the bar. The quicker witted punters not yet too intoxicated, started the commotion that Marko had been counting on, instantly charging headlong for the front exit, impeding the advance of the hidden henchmen that Marko knew were by now, very close. To escalate the situation, he fired a volley of three shots into the display of liquor bottles hanging upside down on the mirrored bar wall, the spectacular display of shattering glass inciting a full panic.

Marko was just able to pick out the figures of two doormen closing in, by their exaggerated height and bulk as they knocked punters fleeing in the opposite direction aside like skittles.

If Stanislav had made it to the street, then he would be long gone by now. Marko knew his only chance of finding him was if he had sought refuge behind the guarded side door leading to the private rooms. Between the heads of the panicked throng, he glimpsed the guard still manning the door instead of making his way towards Marko, a sure sign that Stanislav was in there.

His black suit affording him a degree of camouflage amongst the similarly attired guests, Marko crouched low, charging headlong towards the that door. The first doorman appeared to his right, searching the crowd, Marko dropping him with a single shot before his assailant could pick him out. Off to his left, Marko saw a punter crash to the floor as the second doorman clipped him clumsily. He span on his heel, getting his fatal shot off a fraction before the doorman, whose own bullet narrowly missed. Out of the corner of his eye, Marko picked out Aleksandar and Emil in the crowd, suitcase still full of money in tow, safely making for the exit now the two doormen were taken care of.

He wasn't close enough yet to Stanislav's final guard, the risk of giving his position away with an over ambitious shot too great. There was only option, a tactic that he tried to avoid at all costs, but one that on this occasion he would have to employ. Keeping low, he raced forward, hidden among the last of the punters, grabbing a passing luckless fat drunken businessman. Before his victim knew what was happening, Marko had spun him round and using his considerable bulk as a shield, opened fire from his limited line of sight over his hostage's shoulder. The first shot narrowly missed the bodyguard's head, lodging in the steel door to his right. Instantly homing in on the source, the bodyguard was a fraction of a second too late on the trigger, Marko taking him down with a second bullet to the chest, his own shot straying wide of the mark.

Releasing the hold on his bewildered captive, Marko raced for the door. There was one other way out for Branislav on the other side, through a high window in a washroom at the far end of the long corridor dissecting the rooms. In his less than athletic condition however, Marko felt certain that his foe would rather wait it out in the hope that his loyal bodyguard and last line of defence was still alive.

At this late hour it was highly likely that there would have been punters in the private rooms when the shooting started, but they would probably have opted to stay put with the women pleasuring them than risk the mayhem of the club, although Marko could envision a number of them now climbing out half dressed through the washroom window into the narrow alley that led, after a few twists and turns, back out onto the streets of Soho.

The hallway on the other side of that door would be dimly lit Marko assumed, for the privacy of the customers coming and going, so any of the potentially vacant rooms on either side would provide Stanislav with ample opportunity to hide if he had thought better of trying to squeeze through the small washroom window. If he had registered the thud of the bullet lodging in the other side of the steel door, then perhaps he would already be frantically trying to make his escape.

The pounding music now playing to an almost deserted venue and with the arrival of the armed police imminent, Marko pulled the heavy door open, careful to stay clear of the line of fire in case Stanislav had concluded that he was now alone to fend for himself and thought it best to go on the offensive first. Waiting for a few seconds to pass, he tossed a beer bottle lying within easy reach on the floor into the corridor to provoke a reaction, but none came.

Peering around the doorframe into the shadowy corridor for an instant before moving clear of the firing line, Marko memorised the scene, a few open doors with frightened faces peeking out, darting out of sight as soon as they saw him, the doors slamming, followed by the click of locks. The washroom door at the far end on the left was closed. In that next moment Marko had to make his best calculation before his adversary slipped away from his grasp. Stanislav's face had definitely not been one of the half dozen he'd just seen, and with all the private rooms windowless, Marko knew he wouldn't risk getting cornered.

Charging like a bull, arms extended, his pistol held out with both hands, Marko's best hope was that Stanislav was still trying to compress his ungainly bulk though the small aperture high up on the washroom wall, but if he had given up, he would now be waiting on the other side of that door. Firing strategically spaced shots that splintered the flimsy wooden washroom door and the plasterboard partition wall to either side, Marko kicked the door open with his weapon trained, scanning the empty room, the window open, the crash of scattering bottles out in the alley, followed by the impromptu profanity of a rough sleeper being disturbed, confirmation that Stanislav was hopefully within reach.

Dropping down into the darkness of the alley after sliding deftly out through the small window, Marko was running for the neon lights ahead, jumping over the drunken vagrant slouched in his path. Concealing his weapon just before he emerged into the narrow street crammed with noisy inebriated revellers, Marko scanned the area, cursing with frustration as he failed to pick out his foe in the throng.

His instincts telling him to move in the direction of the nearest tube station, he spun, only to find himself directly in the path of a group of young rowdy women dressed as nurses, evidently out on a hen night, the lady in question wearing a red learner driver plate on her chest. Accosting this tall smartly dressed hunk she had discovered with a loud uninhibited suggestive remark, she grabbed Marko round his waist. Her language instantly changed to that of an enraged fishwife when he had no option but to manhandle her out of his way. Losing her drunken balance, she stumbled into a group of middle aged housewives with far less feminine physiques, staggering in the opposite direction. Marko's encounter with the learner driver hadn't raised voices loud enough to distract Stanislav who was lumbering along hidden in the crowd twenty yards ahead of his pursuer, but the cacophony of shouts and screams that ensued from the brawl that broke out between the two parties of female revellers caused a number of the crowd to look around, Stanislav among them. Instantly turning away again as he saw Marko, he knew it was too late. Knocking cursing people out of his way, Marko already gaining on him, Stanislav ran for the cover of a neon lit sex shop on a corner married with a brighter sign boasting a peep show downstairs.

Inside the dimly lit shop reverberating with German Techno music, Marko was confronted by a large crowd of Chinese tourists blocking his way, staring wide eyed at the wall to wall spot lit mirrored displays of videos, sex dolls and dildos of varying shapes and sizes.

Suddenly he felt himself thrown off balance from behind, just catching sight of Stanislav sending the tourists scattering as he ran for the flight of stairs with the bright neon words Peep Show above with an arrow pointing down. Unable to steady himself, Marko crashed unceremoniously into a display, dozens of videos raining down on his head as he hit the floor. Staggering to his feet, he instinctively reached for his gun, realizing it was missing. Scrambling around frantically on the floor amongst the sea of video cases illustrated with highly explicit imagery, his audience fascinated by this mindless shopper, he finally recovered his weapon, jumping to his feet with it in his hand, the tourists backing away in silent shock before instinctively parting like a wave in anticipation of his charge across the room towards the stairs.

Bounding down the steps, Marko found himself in a dark corridor, a long row of curtained booths along one wall. He cursed as he saw another staircase at the far end leading upwards. Racing past the line of booths, his weapon ready, he pulled the sea of curtains back just in case Stanislav had decided to take a gamble on his life, disturbed punters taking themselves in hand shouting a chorus of abuse as he went.

Up the stairs and back out on the street with his gun concealed, Marko searched wildly amongst the noisy crowd. A drunken high pitched female shout of protest alerted him from behind and he spun, catching the unmistakable lumbering bulk of Stanislav from behind, making for a busy road junction at the edge of Soho. Marko had already closed in considerably, weaving stealthily though the crowd, when Stanislav spun his head to check if he had still lost his pursuer, his eyes widening with shock when he picked out Marko only twenty feet behind. Charging forward in a last futile attempt to outrun his executioner, Stanislav reached the busy junction, running out blindly, a horn blaring as a black cab narrowly missed him, before a red London double decker bus travelling in the opposite direction hit him head on, taking him under the wheels and mangling his bulky form with a nauseating crunch of bones as the screeching brakes brought the vehicle to a stop, accompanied an instant later by the screams of shock from traumatized onlookers.

As he retreated seamlessly back into the crowd, Marko pondered with considerable disappointment that the evening hadn't turned out quite as he had envisioned, but then things couldn't always go exactly to plan, just as long as the job got done. After all, a dead man was a dead man, whichever way you looked at it.

Reclined comfortably in the rear of the chauffeur driven Jaguar, Radica savoured the luxury of her surroundings as she stared out at the grand old buildings of Piccadilly passing by, her emerald eyes glinting with anticipation in the bright early afternoon sunlight.

She had dyed her hair auburn and Alina, by now a seasoned accomplished hairdresser after taking care of so many new visitors back in Italy, had cut it to shoulder length, Radica satisfied that the desired effect had been achieved, so much in fact that she had experienced a double take when she had awoken bleary eyed the following morning and looked in the mirror, for an instant thinking someone else was in the room.

There was however one concern that was tugging at her, a fear that had begun to surface from deep within her mind the moment Vladimir had awakened her horrific past inside her mind on the beach that day, and on the plane, buckling up ready for take off, she felt strapped down in a seat on a rollercoaster that she would never be able to stop once she landed in London. It wasn't that she had any dread or doubts about her ability to carry out what she had come here to do, she was well prepared and knew in her heart that she wouldn't hesitate when the time came. It was the essential emotional discipline needed to control the rage that would be unleashed when it happened that she feared, to be able to carry out her work clinically, to finish the task efficiently and not succumb to the temptations of finally acting out the sadistic vengeful fantasies that had filled her young fertile mind immediately after her family had been murdered back in Bosnia. She had fought so hard to crush those graphic visions down into a manageable locked box deep inside and now, for all her self assurance, she was terrified that when her moment of redemption came, that lock would break under the immense pressure and the lid would burst open, sending her spiralling into a rampage of uncontrolled savagery that would sabotage her mission and bring about her own demise at the hands of the very monsters who had haunted her dreams for so long. Over the years Radica had managed to condition her expectations, to accept that she would never find them, always to be denied the opportunity to finally lay the ghosts of her family, their stricken faces from that day that still imprinted in her mind, to rest. Now, with this sudden unexpected turn of events, their same faces had changed to expressions of pleading expectation, and she knew that she must not fail them. Then and only then, would she see them smile again.

Vladimir had made all the arrangements down to the last detail, all she had to do was follow the plan to the letter and all would be well, he had assured her. There had been plenty of time to think on the drive from Heathrow airport. The older kind eyed chauffeur hand picked by her guardian and flown in for the occasion had not spoken other than to greet her in the arrivals lounge before taking her compact black suitcase. She felt comfortable in his presence as not once did he sneak a look in his rear view mirror to admire her beauty. Radica's thoughts were by now focussed on the events planned for that evening, the irrepressible realization that the outcome could never be certain, leading her to thoughts of her orphan family back across the ocean, especially her favourite who she worried for the most.

The driver turned off Piccadilly into the private courtyard entrance to the Ritz hotel, stopping outside the revolving doors of the front entrance. A doorman dressed in a grey long coat and top hat approached to open the rear door, Radica dressed to the nines emerging long stockinged legs first, her host having to fight to avert his gaze as the chauffeur got out and took her case from the boot, insisting on keeping hold of it as a much younger porter appearing from nowhere instinctively reached out to take it, surprised when he was denied custody of his guest's luggage and the not insignificant tip that usually accompanied such a courtesy at the most expensive hotel in London.

Accompanied by her chauffeur, Radica glided through one of the revolving doors into the opulence of the high ceilinged foyer, her carefully selected figure hugging designer business dress and matching jacket competing effortlessly with her fashion rivals sat around in comfortable armchairs nursing their drinks, some of whom jealous of her much younger age, threw her challenging stares which she cast aside with a contemptuous smirk as she passed on her way to the reception desk, her chauffeur cloaking her as he checked the passing faces, his right hand hovering over the concealed shoulder holster inside his jacket.

Looking up from her seat behind the counter, the beautiful young receptionist greeted her new guest with an appreciative smile as Radica addressed her in a polite and courteous manner, a rare quality in the clientele she was accustomed to dealing with. As they exchanged pleasantries, Radica suddenly heard the ugly harsh tongue from her childhood homeland slicing through the calm ambience from the other side of the foyer, her chauffeur instantly homing in on a tall overweight middle aged ogre in a black suit shouting obscenities in his native tongue at a luckless young porter struggling with a trolly bulging with overloaded suitcases.

Radica instinctively turned to see a duty manager rushing over to try and calm the ranting guest, only to also find himself on the receiving end of the tirade of abuse, the profanity lost on most of the shocked guests who fortunately didn't speak Croatian. The ugliness of the scene provoked a gut reaction within Radica and for an instant she was storming across the foyer, gun in hand, ready to silence this vile monster. Checking herself she turned back to the receptionist, her new acquaintance picking up on the last fading trace of her expression, the two sharing a moment of secret unspoken empathy.

The receptionist handing over the room key, Radica made her way to the elevator, her armed companion still by her side, checking the doors as they opened to find it empty. As Radica stepped forward, a young businessman who had just appeared tried to follow, but the chauffeur had already sensed his presence behind, turning on the threshold to obstruct him with silent shake of the head and his hand held out. For a moment, his kind eyes turned icy cold, a menacing stare emerging, the young man instinctively backing away. The threat resolved, he pressed the appropriate floor number, keeping his other eye on the businessman still stood in the foyer, the doors sliding closed.

He stepped out first when the doors opened on the fifth floor, checking up and down the long tastefully decorated hallway before nodding for Radica to follow, leading her to her designated room, seven doors down on the left. She instinctively passed him her key so he could go in first as a final precaution. With the door closed and locked behind them, he opened the built in wardrobe on the right hand wall opposite the bathroom door and entered a four digit code from memory on the console of a generous sized guest safe built into the wall. The lock clicked with a reassuring thud, and he pulled the small steel door open, retrieving a compact black briefcase no more than a foot in length with an overly robust combination lock. Taking it over to the writing desk nearer the large windows and carefully laying it down as if the contents were fragile, he lined up the combination sequence, the hidden internal catch clicking back. Opening the case, he stepped to one side for Radica to view the contents like a jeweller showing off a display of diamond rings.

Radica stared down into the case, her eyes darkening like a black cloud as visions of what she was going to do with the treasure at her fingertips flashed thought her mind. Looking up at her guardian stood next to her, she saw him smiling at her, but in that concerned worried way that her father had done just before…

'Thank you,' she said softly with a sad smile, almost wanting to hug him at that moment as he stood there. She thought she detected an almost imperceptible movement in his right arm, as though he was about to reach out to her, but then he simply nodded and turned, Radica watching him cross the room, offering a last brief good luck glance as he opened the door and left, closing it quietly behind him. Although Radica had only spent a couple of hours in his company, a feeling of loneliness gripped her for a moment, the isolation of her room quickly sinking in as she locked the door behind him, and she felt herself being drawn to the window, suddenly needing more than anything to have a view, any view of the outside world, to help settle her mind.

She stood there for a long moment gazing out, the elegant skyline of the West End's old lavish buildings giving way to the modern financial district of glass and steel high rises in the distance a few miles East along the Thames. On the far edge of that cityscape where the new age Eastern European flow of dirty money flowed back west along the Thames, bleeding seamlessly into the old establishment like a cancer, lay Shoreditch and Whitechapel, once the sweltering flesh pot of the East End during Victorian times, now fast becoming the new hot spot for foreign gangsters needing to launder their money in the overseas property development market.

The establishment that she would be frequenting in Shoreditch that evening, converted from a disused warehouse, flashed though her mind, having memorised the photos and floorplans before stepping onto her plane. She instinctively checked her Cartier watch, sighing with frustration. It was going to be a long five hours, but Vladimir had insisted she take the earlier flight, in case of possible unforeseen setbacks on route.

Turning away from the window, Radica poured herself a sparkling mineral water from the mini bar before sitting herself down at the desk. She reached forward and removed the brand new unused compact Glock 17 from its resting place inside the case, reassuringly solid and cold in her hand. She was well frequented with this particular model and had requested it specifically. With its shorter barrel it wasn't as accurate at a distance than the more popular Berettas, but that wasn't necessary for this occasion, it was considerably lighter, easy to conceal and most importantly, still boasted the high calibre unstoppable 45 calibre rounds of its much bulkier rivals.

Reacquainting herself with its feel as she wrapped her fingers and thumb around the contoured grip, she first checked the safety catch was engaged before depressing the magazine release, catching the reassuringly weighty fully loaded clip in her other hand. Placing the pistol down on the desk, she thumbed each bullet out from the breach end of the spring loaded magazine, checking each round carefully for signs of misaligned firing primers before pressing them back into the clip one by one. As a final precaution she pulled back the cocking breach, checking it was empty before depressing the trigger, listening for the distinctive sound of the hidden internal firing pin shooting forward. Finally confident that her weapon was not going to let her down and cost her life, she slid the clip back into the grip and repeated the action with the breach, the first round flying up into the open chamber before she released her grip, the breach flying forward again ready for firing.

Unzipping her locked suitcase on the bed and flipping the lid open, Radica lifted out her dress for the evening, a figure hugging sparkling sequined number that she had chosen for its seductive allure. As she held it up to herself in front of the tall wardrobe mirror she could picture him, utterly transfixed, unable to resist falling into her trap.

Vladimir had insisted that she have some recently taken photos for her trip to ensure that she would recognize them, after all it had been a while and appearances could change, but Radica had resisted, adamant that there was no need. She would know them when she saw them, their faces still imprinted clearly in her memory as if it had all happened yesterday. Perhaps once her job was done, they would finally stop creeping uninvited into her dreams to taunt her, but something was telling her that they would always be with her lurking in the shadows of her subconscious.

Marta had arrived a few weeks before Radica, crammed in the back of an inconspicuous white transit van with a dozen other girls. They had been locked inside their windowless prison since leaving that day, provided only with the sparsest assortment of old couch cushions scattered on the cold, hard steel floor, the dim utility ceiling light left on and the roof air vent above their heads mercifully open, but Marta knew from secretly examining a map a few days before that their supply of bottled water and already stale sandwiches would be barely enough to last them. Seeing that her more anxious colleagues had become quiet and withdrawn, she knew she needed to avoid causing further alarm, so had suggested an opportune moment early into their journey that it would be a good idea to ration their consumption, just as a precaution in case they got delayed for some reason.

Their brutish faced driver accustomed to wearing a forced smile, had assured his young impressionable passengers with limited success that their crude form of transport was the only way to get them out of Bosnia safely, the discomfort a small price to pay for the much better life that awaited them. His younger co-driver who looked like a weasel had mimicked his boss's smile, nodding silently but never speaking.

By the time they neared their destination after two days on the road with no washroom stops, the lidded toilet bucket secured by a clasp to the floor in the corner in plain sight of everyone was full to the brim. The last few luckless girls needing to relieve themselves had done their best to judge the abrupt turns and braking at junctions as the vehicle wound its way through the busy streets of the London, the by now stale nauseating stench of urine mixed with faeces making some of the girls retch as soon as the lid was lifted.

When the van came to its final resting place, the girls heard the engine die, the cab doors opening and slamming shut again, but they were still unsure if this was the end of their journey or just another service station stop so their drivers could switch positions behind the wheel. As they exchanged hopeful looks and murmurs another sound reached their ears, metal grating on concrete followed by a heavy bang that startled them. Loud talking began outside, the words spoken in English, the accent too thick for them to understand. The familiar voice of their driver answered in hushed tones as heavy footsteps approached the van. Hearing the unmistakeable sound of the rear doors being unlocked, the girls turned in unison, eyes wide with trepidation.

The sight that met them when the two doors were pulled open from the other side made them recoil like animals trapped a in cage. A dozen tall bulky figures stood in an impenetrable cordon blocking off any chance of escape. Their captives who were well accustomed to the stench that wafted out from the van didn't flinch as Marta had expected and she realized with horror that many girls had travelled this road before her.

For a moment the men didn't move, their greedy eyes pouring over the fresh meat like a butcher inspecting yet another delivery of freshly slaughtered carcasses. Then as if by telepathy they all sprang into action at once, some climbing into the van to ceremoniously drag the terrified wide eyed girls, most of them kicking and screaming, out into the dimly lit warehouse. Marta had already weighed up the odds and knew there was no point in resisting, far more sensible to let herself be taken without lashing out to minimalize the wrath of these monsters. The rest of the girls, despite putting up a determined struggle, were disembarked without injury, their captors resisting the urge to strike them as their prey lashed out, knowing they would face the much worse wrath of their own far more savage master if any of the girls suffered so much as a scratch.

He needed his new arrivals fit for purpose, the quality of his merchandize being of the utmost importance, after all, a girl with an ugly face was no use in his line of business. Of course he wasn't there in person to oversee his new delivery, he never had been, not since the first many months ago. The thought of lowering himself to be present and witness such ghastliness filled him with a revulsion that made him physically shudder whenever he thought about it. No, his place was high in his tower, hidden away from the filth and sweat of his highly lucrative empire, ensuring he remained immune to prosecution, shielded behind his respectable façade, should the house ever come crashing down. On this occasion however as sometimes occurred, he had taken an interest in a particular girl from the photos that had routinely been passed across his desk discreetly the day before delivery, summoning his contact to inspect her in person to see if she was as suitable for his purposes as her photo suggested.

By the time the last of the panicked girls had been dragged out of the van, Marta had picked out the smaller vans parked up neatly in a row against the far wall in the dimly lit warehouse, facing outwards for a speedy exit. Stood in a line, hands bound behind their backs, their captors took great pleasure in applying painful upward pressure under their arms to force them into a submissive silence.

Out of the gloom to their right, footsteps approached, not heavy like the booted figures holding them, but lighter, the tap of thin leather soles. As the figure's face materialized from the gloom, Marta dared to look up for a second, glimpsing the face of a middle aged man dressed in a dark suit. Unlike her ill kempt captors who reeked of stale sweat, he was cleanly shaven with manicured hair and smelled strongly of cologne, not like her poor long dead father had worn, but refined, expensive.

As he walked along the line of girls, the men behind them all too aware of their dispensability, were careful not to catch his eye. He lifted each slender chin with a black leather gloved hand, gazing at their solemn faces, holding them tightly by the jaw if they tried to turn their heads away, his grip making them wince.

Marta was stood at the end of the line, head down again like the others, but when she saw his immaculately shined black leather shoes finally appear in front of her, she raised her head voluntarily to avoid him touching her face. Meeting his gaze without hesitation, she saw his narrow lips curl in a faint smile, his steely eyes softening a touch as he admired her features. Then stepping back, he took the rest of her in, his roving eyes assessing the ample curves of her breasts and buttocks through her tightly fitting white t-shirt and jeans. For a terrible moment she feared he was going to insist on conducting a thorough physical examination, but satisfied that she was the right candidate, he simply nodded at the faceless figure stood behind her before abruptly turning on his heel and walking purposefully away, Marta and the other girls finding themselves being frogmarched towards the waiting vans as their revered visitor disappeared into the shadows.

<u>NINE</u>

Sanderson had already consumed a few customary whiskies in his dark dusty drawing room before he sank back into the reassuringly luxurious soft leather rear seat of his chauffeur driven Bentley.

He would be home late again tonight, a habit that his dutiful wife of forty years had become accustomed to. Christine had known for some time that he had other women in his life, and he had long since stopped trying to delude her with elaborations about the so called business meetings. She hadn't ever asked him to stop with the charade, she hadn't needed to. After that many years of marriage, they communicated just as effectively by the things they didn't say to each other, the disappointed yet understanding look in her eyes telling him there was no need to lie anymore.

Truth be told it didn't really bother her anymore. They were both on the wrong side of sixty and whilst they still slept in the same bed, Christine appreciative that her husband at least had the decency to wash the smell of his conquests away in the shower before getting in beside her, there had been no intimacy between them for many years. On their wedding anniversaries, when they would both, purely for appearances sake, get dressed up and dine out at an expensive restaurant, they would always talk not of any future plans together as would be fitting on these occasions. Instead Christine would reminisce about their two boys as she still referred to them, and Sanderson would sit opposite patiently pretending to listen. His wife would smile as she recounted some family holiday or other event when the twins were very young, her eyes glazing over, sparkling in the candlelight with the same vigorous youthfulness that had drawn him to her so many years ago. But then, as abruptly as a dark cloud, her smile would disappear, the forlorn look on her little boys faces staring out of the back window of the Daimler at her accusingly for not stopping daddy as he drove them away down the long gravel drive on the way to boarding school many years ago, returning to haunt her, the image as clear as yesterday, and the glimmer in her eyes would vanish.

Sanderson had always known that she resented him for taking her boys away from her, not just in the physical sense, but spiritually, the bond that only a mother can have with her children severed that day as they stepped into a new world with its dark corridors and stern faced teachers determined to turn these mere children who had yet to even reached puberty, into adults overnight, extricating them years before their time from the parental cocoons that had protected them since birth and forcing them out into the savage world of their new surroundings, populated by boys many years older than them, intent on exhorting the ghosts of their own much younger past in the very same institution, by bullying and sodomizing the very boys that they themselves had once been. And so the cycle would repeat itself, year after year with the fresh intake of pupils, suffering the humiliation and pain at the hands of their elders in return for the satisfaction of dishing out the same oppressive regime when the chance presented itself years later, a mantra that Sanderson had lived by even after leaving that same boarding school generations before, a built in instinct to view everyone as an enemy, not just in business, but in his personal life as well. He couldn't help but enjoy that same moment once a year in the restaurant, as Christine would look at him with that resentful expression that she was unable to supress after a few glasses of wine. He would resist the urge to smile, but it made no difference, she knew he was relishing the occasion, the torment she had suffered ever since that day.

They would sit in complete silence in the back of the Bentley on the way home, their absence from each other so complete that they may as well have been utter strangers. Opening the front door, Christine would make her way upstairs without so much as a word, determined not to let her husband see her cry. Closing the bedroom door behind her, she'd sit herself down on the bed and sob, not just because of what he had done to her those many years ago, but because of the kind of men he had made her dear boys into, cold and ruthless, just like their father. If she had only known that every year, to mark the day of their marriage, he had toasted himself for the upset he had caused her over a cigar and a large glass of brandy downstairs while she wept in the room directly above him, chuckling to himself like a mischievous little schoolboy, then it may have been enough to make her finally leave him.

As Sanderson stared out of the window on the way to his destination, looking at the passing night lights but not seeing, his mind drifted back to his late father. He had been high up in MI5, providing his only son with the automatic right of passage to Eton in 1948 at the age of eleven in the days when the school was at the height of elitism.

He was tall for his age and athletic, qualities that worked not entirely to his advantage. Being able to stand nose to nose with boys years his senior deflected any unwanted attention for the most part, but in turn made him the top prize of his year, singling him out for the affections of the hardcore bullies.

The oppression that the older boys dealt out on the newcomers was inscribed with an ancient regimented code that its victims had to follow and Sanderson adhered to this law just like all the others, suffering the humiliation in silence and never speaking of it, not even to a more intimate fellow pupil.

It was at the age of thirteen on a cold January morning battling on a rock hard rugby pitch that Sanderson's institutionalised existence took an unforeseen turn. Charging towards the goal line, ball tucked tightly into his chest, he collided with a much heavier opponent. The last thing he remembered about that day was the deafening crack of his skull crashing against his adversary's. He awoke in bed in a small private room the following morning, his brain throbbing with an intensity that made him fear it would explode, the school doctor whose judgement was severely impaired by his alcoholism, assuring him as he helped him sit up to take his aspirin, that he had merely suffered a concussion. Staring up at the red bulbous faced man leaning over him, an unprovoked premonition suddenly flashed before Sanderson's eyes, an almost incontrollable impulse to punch him in the face, but he put it down to the blinding pain in his head. It wasn't until he was up and about a few days later, the headaches having eased to a tolerable degree, that he realized that something was very wrong. The unbidden violent compulsion he had experienced with his school doctor took hold again without warning. On the way back to his dormitory early in the morning to get ready for class, he heard a familiar voice calling his name, turning to see his classmate Dawson dressed in his sports kit, a little out of breath, having returned from his obsessional solitary one mile run around the grounds. Dawson was quick to welcome his brave soldier back from the trenches as he put it in his usual jovial manner. The next thing Sanderson remembered was knocking a startled Dawson down with a haymaker before straddling his chest and following up with a rapid succession of punches that quickly left his victim's face covered in blood.

'Are you alright old chum?' Dawson asked, only half joking, trying to read the strange look in his comrade's eyes that made him instinctively step back.

Suddenly, like a black thundercloud giving way to a bright blue sky, Sanderson snapped out of his trance, seeing his worried faced friend stood before him unharmed.

'Still a bit under the weather eh. Maybe you should get back to the doctor,' Dawson suggested.

'No, I'm fine, still just a little groggy after the knock to the head,' Sanderson replied with a forced smile. 'I'll see you in class,' he concluded, quickly turning to walk away.

Finding the nearest washroom down the corridor, Sanderson locked himself inside one of the cubicles, sitting with his head in his hands, rubbing his aching temples.

'You can do this Sanderson, you can do this. It's all in your head, it's not real,' he whispered to himself over and over. He wanted to sit there all day, locked in his little room where he couldn't harm anybody, but Latin class would be starting very soon and he had to get changed into his uniform. Keeping his head down, still nervous of making eye contact with any passing pupils for fear of another episode, he hastily made his way to his dormitory for a fast wash and change, spurred on by the punishment that awaited any pupil who dared be even a second late for the much revered Mr. Pritchard's lessons, a firm advocate of the use of the cane for even the slightest infringement of class rules.

Arriving in the nick of time, his noisy fellow pupils already sat behind their desks barely had time to look enquiringly in his direction as he hurried to his seat, their master entering a moment later, his young scholars instantly falling silent. Pritchard was all too aware of Sanderson's incident on the pitch a few days before and true to form, in his usual cowardly cruel fashion, he decided to pick on the pupil he knew he could make a spectacle of with that lesson's Latin verbs, compounding the humiliating ritual by making his candidate stand for all the class to witness. Within moments of hesitantly getting to his feet, Sanderson found himself facing the familiar bark from his teacher, demanding the first conjugation for to run, in the present tense. His dull headache already beginning to intensify again, the image of Pritchard being carted off on a stretcher, his face beaten to a bloody pulp swept his vision before his tormentor had even finished asking the question.

'Sanderson are you deaf as well as stupid boy,' Pritchard growled with a sneer as Sanderson, his mind elsewhere, stood staring back with a blank expression, as if not comprehending the question, his less favourable classmates sniggering to each other quietly.

He felt his hands involuntarily tighten into fists down by his side, the muscles in his legs and arms primed, and in that moment he realized with a terrifying certainty that he was about to lose control and enact his violent premonition. Panicking, he bolted towards the door at the front of the class, his astonished classmates looking on as an enraged Pritchard moved to intercept his escape. Meeting Sanderson head on he was met with a look that made him impulsively recoil as he recognized not merely the indignant glare of an angry child, but the cold gaze of a fully grown man about to inflict serious harm upon him. To the utter disbelief of his class Pritchard stood aside, Sanderson flinging the door open to run away down the corridor.

The next thing Sanderson knew, he was standing in the place where he had sought refuge before, the ornate high glass ceilinged botanical greenhouse, yet he had no recollection of how he had got there. Looking around he saw he was alone, the gardener Sykes responsible for the vast array of flora currently elsewhere. His head still spinning from the ordeal in the classroom, he sat down on his favourite wooden bench, a small brass plaque screwed to the back rest inscribed with the name of the first caretaker of this tranquil glass sanctuary. Lowering his head into his hands, he began to sob.

'Well, well, well, if it isn't my favourite little plaything.'

Sanderson instantly recognized that voice, looking up to see the tall imposing figure of Richardson, three years his senior stood in the open doorway. He jumped to his feet to ready himself, but this time he didn't fight the inevitable barbaric premonition, instead letting it flow freely through his mind, feeling the adrenaline building into an unstoppable surge of energy.

'And look, he's been crying,' Richardson pressed as if to his usual accomplices who on this occasion were absent. Closing the glass door behind him, he approached slowly, that all too familiar wide sadistic grin spreading across his face.

'Make sure you spare some of those tears for me little boy, you know how I like to make you cry,' he sneered, beginning to unbuckle his trouser belt.

Sanderson didn't remember what happened next, his consciousness only returning when he was sprinting across the playing field, his mind in automation, leading him to one of the rear entrances of the school out of sight from any of the classroom windows, then down the corridor and up the wide stone stairwell to his dormitory to the row of white porcelain sinks on the far side, the reason still unclear. It was only when he caught his reflection in the mirror that he saw the blood splattered on his face, shirt and blazer. Suddenly aware of a discomfort in his hands he looked down, seeing his bruised and cut knuckles covered in blood.

Sykes had seen Sanderson racing across the playing field from the direction of the botanical house and had gone to investigate, finding Richardson unconscious, his face reduced to what could only be described as a bloody pulp, taking him back momentarily to the ghastly sights he had seen as a soldier on the beach during D Day. This time however he felt no instinctive compulsion to help the disfigured person lying at his feet. Despite being considerably disguised by his injuries, Richardson was still recognizable to Sykes. This quiet sanctuary, the place where he found himself able to push the horrific memories as deep into the recesses of his mind as was possible, was also one of Richardson's seldomly frequented lairs for forcing himself on his much younger quarry, hidden amongst the dense tropical foliage, his secret safe, or so he had always thought. Sykes had seen him leaving the glasshouse with a decidedly strong spring in his step on a hot June afternoon some months ago, followed not long after by one of the more diminutive new boys. It was the walk that alerted Sykes, instantly recognizing the unmistakeable staggered short steps inherent in the raped women and girls he had encountered in the French villages that the German soldiers had ravaged during their seemingly endless retreat Eastwards.

Unzipping his fly, Sykes took great pleasure as he urinated over Sanderson, careful to get as much of the on his face, Richardson's face flinching in his comatose state as the caustic cocktail ran into his open sores.

His decision to help Sanderson extricate himself from the mess he had placed himself in came to him immediately and it was only a matter of minutes later after he had called for an ambulance that he was stood in front of headmaster Evan's desk, making a full and formal statement, claiming that he had witnessed Richardson attempting to assault Sanderson that day, steering clear of an mention of past events, determined to keep the other boy's pride intact.

Sanderson was still in the dormitory trying to scrub the blood from his shirt and blazer when he was discovered by the two senior prefects sent to find him, who at that juncture were completely unaware of the reason for their errand. Brought head down before the ancient looking dusty faced Evans, he recognized Sykes stood to one side, regarding him with an expression not unlike his mother's, when as a young boy he would to get caught getting up to mischief. His mother would give him a talking to, whilst at the same time secretly encouraging him with her kind eyes. The prefects dismissed, Evans sat back in his chair, studying with more than a little fascination, the raw knuckled boy with the blood stained blazer and shirt who had put a pupil much his senior, the most notorious bully and sodomist he had ever had to endure at his school, in the hospital.

'Sykes here tells me that you and Richardson have had a rather serious contretemps in the botanic house,' Evans announced in his rasping gravelly voice, a result of a lifetime of cigar smoking. Sanderson was both surprised by the altogether conciliatory tone that his headmaster was taking and by the acute lack of accusation. He dared to look up from the floor at that moment, glancing at Sykes before turning his bewildered gaze to the figure sat on the other side of the enormous oak desk who he knew held his fate at the most prestigious school in the country, tightly in his hands.

'He also tells me that Richardson was the instigator of this unfortunate incident, is that correct?' he added, more out of formality than anything else, as he really didn't really care either way on this joyous occasion.

Sanderson's eyes shifted back to Sykes, instantly recognizing the message his saviour's expression silently conveyed. Sanderson nodded solemnly to his expectant master to be met with an almost congratulatory fatherly smile.

'Good, I'm glad that's all cleared up,' Evans replied, happy to put that the whole matter to bed.

'There is of course the matter of the incident with your Latin master,' he continued, Sanderson's appreciative gaze faltering.

'I'll be discussing this with him later today, but I'm sure we can take into account your recent misfortune on the rugby pitch,' he added promptly as he detected his subject's sudden change in demeanour.

'Now, how are you feeling right at this moment, any dizziness, nausea, blurred vision?'

'No sir,' Sanderson replied meekly.

'Excellent, then change your shirt and blazer and get to your next class.'

'Yes sir, thank you sir.' After a final appreciative glance in Sykes's direction, Sanderson turned, making for the door.

'Oh, and Sanderson,' he heard Evan's call out, Sanderson turning back at the door. 'Try to stay out of trouble for the rest of the day, will you?' he suggested in a sardonic tone, barely unable to suppress his fondness for the boy who had defied all the odds.

'Yes sir,' he replied, heaving the heavy oak door open to leave, closing it behind him as quietly as possible.

Out in the corridor about to climb the wide stone stairwell, he heard another voice calling his name, one he didn't recognize, turning to see Sykes approaching, realizing for the first time at that very moment that he had never heard him speak before.

'Good lad for giving that thug a good pummelling,' he said in a hushed tone, placing a congratulatory hand on Sanderson's shoulder. 'You rearranged his smug ugly face really good, put him in the hospital you did.'

'The hospital?' Sanderson replied, shocked.

'That's right. You won't need to worry about him no more,' Sykes continued, drawing an appreciative nod from Sanderson. 'You best go on now young master Sanderson,' he concluded with warm smile, turning away.

'Sykes,' Sanderson called out when Sykes was well into his stride. He stopped to turn.

'Thank you for, for…' Sanderson added, hesitating.

'You're most welcome, master Sanderson,' Sykes declared with a beaming grin, turning away again to disappear round the corner.

For any other pupil defying the authority of a Pritchard, the administration of the cane would be a foregone conclusion, yet amazingly to all the boys in Sanderson's year, the official line was that it was decided in consultation with the headmaster of the school not to press forward with the traditional punishment on the grounds that perhaps Pritchard had been somewhat over vigorous in his treatment of the pupil considering the obvious side effects of his recent injury. Pritchard's real reason for deferring from his request for the use of the cane was of course a mortal fear of his student.

Within hours of the incident, with Richardson missing from class and the bruises on Sanderson's knuckles attracting so much attention from his classmates having turned a deep blue, the rumours spreads like wildfire and by the end of the day despite refusing to comment on the speculation, he was being hailed a hero.

Richardson's parents, placing their own social standing above the interests of their son in the rumour rich circles in which they mixed, were determined that their son would not be labelled a coward, insistent that he return to school immediately after being discharged from hospital despite his pleading. His face still battered and bruised, he was forced to walk the corridors and suffer the humiliation of the barrage of sniggers and taunts. His once close band of loyal bully friends were swift to alienate him and join in with the daily ridicule that his less favourable classmates of old had been quick to seize upon.

Despite being egged on by his classmates, Sanderson resisted the temptation to seek out the now reclusive Richardson and dish out further retribution in front of an audience, but less than a week later, on a day when his headaches had returned with a vengeance, he found himself once again in the quiet sanctity of the botanical house, secluded from view on a newly installed bench. Hearing the door open he looked up, expecting to see Sykes's head above the foliage, but instead glimpsing his arch enemy. Still hidden, he stood, keeping low, to observe Richardson fling a rope with a noose tied at one end, over a steel roof beam above his head, securing the other end around the base of a pillar.

Sanderson was about to step forward to intervene when a voice in his head commanded him to stop and he found himself in a state of paralysis as he watched, still hidden from view as Richardson stepped up onto an upturned wooden box and place his head into the noose. Such was his haste to leave this horrible world behind that without any hesitation, he kicked the box away from under his feet, the taught rope under his weight tightening around his neck. He didn't struggle as the life drained out of him, relieved that the nightmare was finally over.

When Sanderson's mind finally released him from his debilitation he emerged from his hiding place. Richardson's pupils and retinas had blended into ghostly milky grey circles from the asphyxiation, but Sanderson was sure he was still looking down at him with a haunting vague hint of a smile.

Richardson wasn't the first pupil in the school's history to have taken his own life, but if it had been his intention to place a curse on the boy who had driven him to suicide, then Sanderson would soon discover that he had succeeded. The reaction amongst his classmates and the other years was slow to manifest itself, but not long after Richardson was in the ground, Sanderson found himself the outsider just as Richardson had been just before his death. Whilst no one dared say it to his face for fear of suffering a beating, hushed whispers began to circulate, even amongst his once close colleagues, rumours that Sanderson had privately hounded his victim to the point of no return.

He knew that there was no point in trying to set the record straight, a futile notion in the face of hundreds of silent accusers, and so he made no attempt to change the collective mindset, instead deciding that it was better to be disliked and revel in the fear that he had instilled in his hundreds of jurors than to be regarded as a normal person subject to acts of weakness.

In an attempt to control the violent will of the stranger living inside his head that continued to surface without warning and flood his consciousness with malicious instincts, Sanderson took to the boxing ring, cementing his reputation as an individual not to be trifled with and becoming the first fourteen year old in the history of Eaton to not only compete against pupils in the sixth form up to four years his senior, but to remain undefeated.

Such was the discomfort that by this time Sanderson's classmates felt in his company outside of the protective authority of the classroom, that headmaster Evans decided that it would be best if his star sportsman pupil be afforded his own sleeping quarters away from the communal dormitory environment, an arrangement that he lavished in, not only because he would now be spared the nervous silence that awaited him every time he went to bed and got up in the morning, but because he could stop worrying about the constant night terrors that would wake him with a shout, a source of much trepidation amongst his many bedfellows.

Away from the boisterous behaviour of dormitory life, and when he wasn't in the ring dismantling his next luckless opponent, Sanderson spent much of his spare time in his room, the tranquillity granted by the absence of other people helping greatly to calm his spasmodic violent impulses and channel his attention towards his studies.

By the time he graduated from Eaton's sixth form at the age of eighteen with flying colours, Sanderson had made a close friend of his alternative inner self, the first person to congratulate him when he opened the envelope containing his exam results. Following unquestioningly in the footsteps of a father that he rarely saw anymore, he went to Cambridge to study politics with his companion by his side, confident that with a change of scene he would be on his best behaviour amongst the fresh group of fellow contemporaries that awaited his acquaintance.

The university was a well known recruiting ground for MI5 and Parliament and he soon formed closed ranks with three of his fellow students, two of whom would join him in Whitehall to become his close political allies.

He often pondered in later years whether life in his new home would have been less complicated if he hadn't been so physically attractive, but instead fat and round faced like his colleague Smithson. It wasn't long before his athletic build and handsome looks combined with the aloof arrogant air afforded only to those who came from such high breeding, began to attract the attention of the female students.

His first was a blond from Chichester named Susan. She had earmarked him the moment she first saw him at class and a few days later after she approached him in the corridor after lectures in a direct manner much scorned upon by mothers at that time, he found himself upstairs in her room in the boarding house she shared with three other girls who were all out for the afternoon.

Sanderson had already surmised by her behaviour that he wasn't the first man she had asked up to her room, a conclusion confirmed when she wasted no time in getting her clothes off as soon as the door was shut. Sanderson, though brimming with a self confidence that made him sure he could deal with any challenge that life threw at him, found himself suddenly aware that in matters pertaining to the delicacies of intimacy with women, he had absolutely no knowledge. Lying back on the bed, her naked elegant body awaiting his attention, she looked up at him, his face a picture of bewilderment. Later that day he reflected from the privacy of his own room, that everything would have been alright if she had just kept her mouth shut.

'Oh dear, you've never done it before, have you,' she teased in a mocking tone, letting slip a giggle of amusement. Her smile faded as quickly as it had appeared when she saw his expression suddenly change, his nervous gentlemanly eyes widening with rage. Before she had time to react, he was on top of her, his hand pressed heavily over her mouth to stop her screaming. The intoxication that took hold of him then was more powerful than anything he had experienced before and without realizing what he was doing, he had opened his trousers and forced his way inside her. It wasn't the new physical sensation that flooded his mind with pleasure as he thrust deeper and deeper inside her, it was the sheer terror in her eyes matched with muffled screams, begging him to stop. Afterwards, as he straightened his trousers and shirt, looking down at Susan lying curled up in a ball, whimpering like a pathetic dog left out in the cold, he heard that familiar voice.

'I suppose you're expecting me to congratulate you,' he heard him say sardonically, much like his father used too when he had excelled in some manner or other.

By the time her housemates arrived home from lectures later that afternoon, Susan was already gone, her room empty, with not so much as a note on the bedside cabinet. She was never seen again in Cambridge and after a week or two of wild speculation, it was concluded by the wider college community that she had gotten herself into the family way, so to speak, and had decided to save herself the shame of being labelled a morally destitute slut.

She never went to the authorities, knowing that the police of 1953 England paid no attention to women crying rape, and after a few weeks passed without a knock on the door, Sanderson could finally breathe a sigh of relief. His close brush with the law should have been adequate to make him steer clear of any further involvement with the female fraternity, but very soon that voice came calling again, cajoling him at first, and when that didn't work, berating and accusing him of cowardice in the face of danger, too spineless to take a risk, have a little fun, even take it to the next level by introducing his closest colleague Williams to the sadistic pleasure that he knew in his heart he would not be able to resist revisiting, like an animal forever cursed with the craving once it has tasted blood for the first time.

He decided to set them both up in a foursome with Linda and Rachel, modern literature students who had seemed happy to engage in conversation in the pub on a few occasions. Whilst the girls had seen these amicable chance encounters as opportunities to flirt and nothing more, Sanderson had been examining them like flies under a microscope, clinically assessing their suitability, or more accurately, their vulnerability. They were slim and short, physical attributes that would make them easy to manhandle and overpower. They also liked plenty of drink, a lubricant that Sanderson could use to full advantage to achieve his aims.

He chose a Friday night, when most of the students in his collegiate lodgings would be out in the pub and the comings and goings wouldn't be noticed by any chance encounters out in the corridors. He had taken the precaution of reminding the girls that he would be waiting outside by the rear door round the back, eight o'clock sharp to sneak them in.

'Did anyone see you?' Sanderson enquired in a hushed joking tone when he met them at the entrance.

'Of course not,' an already tipsy Rachel replied with a giggle.

'And you didn't tell anyone where you were going?' he pressed.

'Not a soul, Scouts honour,' an equally tiddly Linda implored with a mock salute.

Whisking his guests briskly up the stairs and along the deserted corridor, he ushered them into his room and discreetly turned the key in the lock as he closed it behind him, Hank Williams on the record player and the presence of his cohort preparing cocktails at a makeshift bar on the small study table in a corner providing ample distraction for the girls.

Whilst facially attractive in his own way, Williams was not conventionally handsome like Sanderson, who was swift to use the disparity in their looks to guide his prey in the right direction. Whilst his cohort took care of the seemingly endless rounds of drinks, Sanderson piled on the charm, at first directing his compliments in equal measure between the two girls, before shifting his emphasis towards Linda, who he had earmarked days before as his choice, the desired effect of drawing her attention working like a charm while Williams took the opportunity to focus on flattering Rachel, all part of the plan they had discussed prior.

With Sanderson and Linda sat on the bed, their thighs already touching, and Williams cosying up with Rachel on the couch, it wasn't long before their prey, inhibitions falling further away with every drink, were both joining in a conversation that was leaning towards the suggestive, making hungry eyes at their prospective partners. Picking his moment, Sanderson piped up with his rehearsed suggestion.

'I know, why don't we take a little drive out into the country, see if we can find a nice pub somewhere. My car's big and roomy inside,' he teased, slipping Linda a cheeky wink.

'Really, how big?' she giggled suggestively.

'Enormous,' he replied slowly, placing a hand on her knee as he let the word linger on the end of his tongue, his delivery drawing laughs of anticipation from both girls as they exchanged acquiescent glances.

'Alright, but only if you wear your chauffeurs cap,' Linda mocked jokingly, guiding Sanderson's hand up her thigh a little.

It was well known that the local police turned a blind eye to the drink driving culture endemic in the student fraternity, quietly deferring to the unspoken authority of the institution that was the lifeblood of the town that just that year been awarded city status. Sanderson was surprised at how well he had acclimatized to the whisky over the last few months as he drove the Jaguar, a bright red gleaming weapon of charm that his father had awarded him for getting into Cambridge, out of the street lit suburbs and onto the dark country roads along a route carefully selected during his drive the previous week when he had found the perfect spot.

With Williams and Rachel fully preoccupied with each other in the back seat, Sanderson navigated the narrow hedge lined lanes with one hand on the wheel, his other sliding up between Linda's thighs in between gear changes, caressing the bare wanton flesh above her stocking line.

'So, where is this pub,' Linda enquired abstractly as if making some subconscious final protest before the inevitable.

'You don't really want another drink, do you?' came his reply, his hand shifting higher to brush her damp nether regions through the thin fabric of her underwear.

'I suppose not,' she said softly with a sigh, unable to suppress her arousal any longer.

In the headlights Sanderson spotted the distinctive bend in the lane up ahead distinguishable from the many he had already navigated on route by the enormous ancient oak tree set back off the verge. Slowing, he was forced to tear his hand away from its heavenly resting place as he negotiated the bend, then immediately swung the car off the lane, feeling the rough gravel track under the tyres as he dimmed the lights, the farm track leading him to the disused brick cattle barn he remembered, its roofline barely visible in the darkness. He parked up behind the building, out of sight from the lane.

The distractions of negotiating the numerous bends whilst molesting Linda's thigh had been enough to keep the dreaded voice at bay up until that point, but the moment he turned the ignition off, the noisy growl of the engine replaced by silence, his eternal companion was back, cajoling him.

He turned to Linda who was looking at him in a way that left no doubt in his mind as to what she was thinking, her yearnings heightened more now by the groans of Rachel and Williams on the back seat. Sanderson glanced behind, pleased to see that his cohort already had his conquests legs wrapped around his back, his bare buttocks pumping rhythmically.

Feeling a sensation in his groin, he turned back to Linda still gazing at him, and looking down he saw she had unbuttoned his trousers and was slowly caressing his erect manhood in her hand. The voice in his head was commanding him now with an irrefutable authority, a strength of will that he knew he was powerless to deny.

In the midst of her rapture, her eyes closed, Rachel took a few moments to register Linda's cry, at first confusing it with a remark borne of ecstasy, much like her own. Eyes wide open as if waking from a nightmare, she could make out Williams's head spun around above her in the darkness. It was the gargled choking pleas escaping from Linda's constricted throat that threw Rachel into a panic, her whole body involuntarily convulsing under the weight of Williams still pressing down on her, serving only to alert him to her protest. Gazing back down at her in the darkness, he hesitated.

'Please, don't,' he heard her whisper pleadingly, in a futile attempt to make a secret pact with the man that she knew was about to kill her.

Williams didn't move for a moment, and she prayed that he was deliberating her beg for mercy. She didn't have time to scream when he finally acted, his large hand moving unseen in the darkness, clamping over her mouth and nose, leaving his other hand making an indent in the leather upholstery next to her head as he propped himself up to apply the necessary pressure. In her frantic bid to stay alive she lashed out with her sharp nails to try and claw his face like a startled cat, but he was quick to respond, swiftly taking his smothering hand away, drawing his elbow back as he made a fist. Her shrill scream intended for her best friend to let her know that she was still with her was sadly to no avail, Linda already in the place she where she would very soon follow. The punch to her jaw that descended less than a second later, cutting off her cry, mercifully rendered her unconscious. Less than a minute later, her lungs denied of any further air, Williams rolled off his victim, shoving her limp legs to one side.

'Did you enjoy it?' he heard Sanderson ask, calm and dispassionate, as if they had just been to an unremarkable art exhibition together.

Williams looked up to see Sanderson facing straight ahead as if gazing at the star lit black sky outside, Linda hunched in the passenger seat leaning against the door, her head tilted back, staring straight up at the ceiling, her wide eyes rolled back in their sockets as if trying to catch a last glimpse of her friend.

'You can try and pretend all you like, but tomorrow when you wake up you won't be able to deny that you liked it.'

'How do you know?' Williams murmured.

'Because you and I are the same, don't you see?'

'I'm nothing like you,' Williams replied abhorrently.

That remark seemed to disturb Sanderson who turned his head, his smile just recognizable as his facial expression shifted in the darkness.

'Oh, but you are,' he countered, confident certainty in his voice. 'Now do your trousers up, we need to get rid of them.'

Hauling their conquests unceremoniously out of the car like carcasses, they discarded the corpses not yet even cold, behind the barn as arbitrarily as dropping litter in the street. Moments later without so much as a backward glance, Williams more so because he was in a state of trauma, they were back in the car and on their way, Williams silent in the passenger seat, the windows wound down a little to sweep away the scent of cheap perfume and sex as Sanderson sang along to the songs on the radio with a glibness that left Williams chilled to the bone.

In the privacy of his room, the walls closed in around Williams, the deafening silence pressing down on him like a crushing weight, his lungs having to fight for air as the sequence of events played over and over in his mind in a continuous loop that he was unable to shut out. The whisky to numb his senses served only to magnify the horror of what he had done, further fuelling his consumption, sending him spiralling downwards, until finally, the bottle empty, he was reduced to a whimpering, sobbing heap, curled up on the floor.

The loud banging on his door later that morning took a few moments to rouse him from his inebriated slumber. Forcing his eyes open, the sunlight filtering through the thin curtains made him flinch as the inevitable stabbing pain resulting from his excesses shot though his head. The loud banging continued and despite being far from fully cognisant, the terrifying notion still came to him.

'This is the police,' came a deep gruff voice from the other side of the door, Williams scrambling unsteadily to his feet, another bolt of pain cursing through his brain, the floor beneath his feet feeling like a stormy ship deck as he struggled to keep his balance.

'Open the door, or we'll be forced to break it down,' came the voice, much louder this time.

His mind completely incapable of coming up with a solution to the dilemma such as climbing out through the bedroom window, Williams staggered towards the door like a lamb to the slaughter. Turning the key in the lock he pulled it open hesitantly, dumbfounded as he stared out into an empty corridor. He peered tentatively out, turning his head, first left and then...

'Boo,' Sanderson shouted in his face, sending a fresh jolt of agony though his head as he stood there freshly shaved and well turned out, evidently not having lost a wink of sleep.

'Oh no, don't tell me, you tried to drink your sorrows away last night,' Sanderson teased, his cohort's hung over appearance plainly evident.

'Don't worry, it gets easier after your first time,' he followed up all matter of fact, as if describing his first driving lesson.

'Come on, get dressed, I know a great little back street place where they do a superb cooked breakfast,'

After sticking his fingers down his throat in the bathroom to make himself vomit and then drinking two large glasses of water on Sanderson's suggestion while his guest made himself comfortable in his room, Williams washed and shaved with trembling hands, narrowly avoiding cutting his face several times.

The fresh air of the drive to the less affluent district of the city helped brush the cobwebs away and by the time their hearty plates of bacon, sausages, black pudding, two fried eggs and toast was placed down in front of them in the busy cafe by the rotund wife of the flat nosed burly owner, Williams felt more than capable to tackle the assault on his digestive system that he had first feared would send him running for the nearest bathroom.

'So, how does it feel, now you've finally taken that big step?' Sanderson enquired enthusiastically, keeping his voice down, making sure he wouldn't be heard over the other patrons chatting at their tables as he tucked into his meal at their table in the far corner, away from the glare of the bright morning light streaming through the shop front window. Williams stopped in mid mouthful, staring directly at his partner in crime.

'Right now, I really don't know what I feel,' he replied quietly, chewing on his food as he spoke.

'It will come to you, I promise.'

'What will?'

Sanderson sat back in his chair, letting his food go down, pondering.

'Haven't you ever wondered why most people can never bring themselves to do what we've done?'

Williams didn't respond, he knew the answer no matter what it was, was bad.

'It's because they lack what it takes.'

'No, it's because they're good people,' Williams replied, barely able to supress the agitation in his tone.

'Good people,' Sanderson chuckled. 'Take a look around you, do you see one good person in this room?'

'So, what, now you're suggesting that every living being on this planet is a potential murderer?' Williams challenged.

Sanderson leaned forward in his chair, fixing Williams with his mesmerising gaze.

'What I'm saying is that every person is born with the primeval instinct to take life, but society blinds them to this desire by the misguided sense of morality that it brainwashes them with.'

'So what does that make us?'

'It makes us better than them.'

'How?'

'Because we have the conviction to define our own existence, free from the laws that bind our behaviour.'

'You make it sound like we're gods.'

'Perhaps we are old chum,' Sanderson replied with a broad smile.

'Or maybe we're just heading for damnation.'

'Trust me, that is not our destiny.'

'Then what is?'

'You will understand, very soon.'

'And what about Stiles and Baldwin, are you going to make them your disciples too?' Williams mocked.

'When the time is right yes, but for now let's make it our little secret, agreed?'

'And what about when they're found,' Sanderson challenged, leaning forward, his voice almost a whisper.

'What about it?'

'You know what I mean, the police.'

'Discretion will keep us safe from their clutches.'

'How can you be sure someone didn't see us?' he persisted.

'What's the matter, are you scared?' Sanderson taunted with a grin.

'Aren't you?'

'Not in the slightest.'

'Then you're madder than I thought.'

'Perhaps I am, at that,' Sanderson scoffed. 'Now come on, eat up, your food's getting cold,' he added, tucking back in.

The bodies were found later that day by the local farmer, making the national headlines in the Sunday morning's papers. For Sanderson, who relished the thought of his actions making the front page of all the major publications, reading the numerous articles filled him with a surge of exultation that he found it difficult to contain, wanting nothing more than to proclaim to the nation that he was the killer. Williams on the other hand, spent the day putting on a brave face on the cricket pitch as they battled the Oxford team, his lack of concentration leading to two dropped balls for which he received torrents of ridicule. Mercifully however for him, his team still triumphed, but by far fewer runs than their captain was happy with.

Sanderson was there to greet him at the end of play, to assure his doubtful accomplice that everything was in hand, that he just needed to hold his nerve and carry on as normal. The meeting was for his own benefit too, carefully assessing the condition of his patient, needing to be sure that he wouldn't in a moment of panic do anything foolish, like go to the police. He had already planned for the worst of course in the same meticulous way he had planned the murders, ready to act should the need unfortunately arise. He came away convinced enough that Williams could keep it together and ride out the storm, leaving his cohort with the logical suggestion that with each passing day the chances of the investigation leading the police to their door became less and less.

Religiously following the newspapers every morning, Williams's fears began to allay as over the next three weeks the murders became second, then third page news, soon the tone of the articles confirming that the investigation had obviously reached a dead end.

The repercussions for the reputation of the university were predictable, but the dean was swift to publicly state his opinion as absolute fact, assuring the female fraternity that these hideous crimes were perpetrated far from the university and therefore obviously committed by lower class uneducated thugs. This indisputable octave of authority steering any possible suspicions that may have existed amongst the female students away from their male counterparts played into the hands of the killers perfectly. It wasn't long before the murders were all but forgotten and university life was carefree and vibrant again, just as before.

Sanderson knew the voice in his head would come calling again soon, prodding him to do it all again, and when it did he would need to be ready to defy its command, his grasp on reality still solid enough for him to realise that if he didn't, the next murder would most likely prove his downfall in the hangman's noose. As if reading his thoughts, the voice remained elusive for some time, seemingly unwilling to emerge from the shadows of his mind to issue demands. When it did, taking him by surprise late one night just as he was about to drift off to sleep, he sat up and turned the beside light on.

'You've seen what I'm capable of,' Sanderson began, deciding it was time to take control.

'Very impressive yes, but I want more.'

'And I will give you what you need, but not now.'

'I decide, not you,' he heard the voice demand, already getting agitated.

'Would you rather I rush things and get caught, what use would I be to you then?'

'Then I would find someone else to do my bidding.'

'No, there is no one else, only me. If I die, you die.'

'You can't fool me, I don't need you.'

Sanderson got out of bed and walked into the small bathroom, retrieving a gleaming metal object parked in a mug on the sink.

'What are you doing,' the voice sneered.

'Proving that I'm right,' Sanderson replied, unfolding the cut-throat razor from its shiny handle.

'Wait,' the voice commanded in a fearful tone.

Sanderson lifted the blade to his throat.

'Stop.'

Pressing the cold metal to his skin he could feel the scalpel sharp blade almost breaking the surface.

'Please.'

'Please what?' Sanderson teased.

'Don't do it.'

'But why, you said you don't need me.'

'I do need you,' the voice begged.

'Prove it.'

'I'll do anything, just tell me.'

'Anything?'

'Just name it.'

'Alright, you have to promise to let me decide when from now on.'

The voice was silent for a moment.

'Promise me,' Sanderson boomed.

'I promise,' came the reply, meek and humble, Sanderson smiling like a conqueror as he withdrew the blade from his throat.

Sanderson never heard from the voice again, not even in apology, and the remainder of his time at Cambridge passed unchallenged by his alter ego. He still socialised with the opposite sex, but steered well clear of any intimacy, despite many would be suiters being drawn to his good looks and charismatic charm.

Such was his reputation amongst the female fraternity for rejecting their many advances, that disparaging rumours about his sexuality began circulating around the campus, dangerous for any man in a staunchly homophobic 1952 England when being convicted of homosexuality meant a long prison sentence.

He was swift to put the rumours to bed when word reached him, making a point of being seen with his tongue down the throat of one of the renowned collegiate sluts in a favourite pubs for students of both sexes, later taking her back to his and giving her a good seeing to, her loud shrieks resonating through the walls, leaving his male colleagues in no doubt that he was in fact just a regular bloke.

His choice of partner for such a public display of sexuality had been carefully thought through, knowing all too well that after being seen engaging with a woman of such low moral standing, no decent girl would touch him with a barge pole.

When he graduated three years later with first class honours, Sanderson was naturally welcomed with open arms by MI5, his father keen to keep the family tradition going. His three cohorts, Williams, Stiles and Baldwin all followed him into the civil service, but by comparison their paths were far less exciting, leading them down the somewhat pedestrian ancient wooden panelled corridors of Whitehall just like their own fathers.

It wouldn't be until much later that they would learn that Sanderson had chosen them as his close acquaintances way back at Cambridge for a specific reason, but by this time they would be trapped in a web of corruption, unable to escape, fuelled by an appetite for wealth way beyond their own capabilities, riches that only one man could provide, and in accepting this gift would become slaves to a ruthless paymaster who they had once considered their brother in arms, and now could only despise.

Quickly absorbed into the fascinating world of MI5, Sanderson realised that he was now spending more time with his father than when he had been growing up, although by the impersonal way his father addressed him at work, no one would have guessed they were related. Yet despite the formality, his father did confide in him, in private of course as to the true reason why MI5 ran in their family, a secret legacy that went all the way back to 1914 and the British government's decision to send troops to the slaughter fields of Flanders.

Sanderson's grandfather had joined the ranks of MI5 or what was then the SIS or Secret Intelligence Service, in 1909 when recruited from Cambridge University.

The Sanderson family had grown rich on the back of the devious manipulation of senior government ministers working in national defence. These puppets were paid handsomely to convince successive governments of the need to continually bolster Her Majesty's armed forces with new military hardware and to ensure that the manufacturing contracts were awarded to a cartel of companies of which the Sanderson family was the controlling majority shareholder. The First World War had made grandfather Sanderson wealthy beyond his wildest expectations, astounded that a conflict on such an enormous scale could have started over just one man being assassinated, no matter how prominent.

When Hitler came to power in 1933 and with Sanderson's father also by now on board, MI5 was swift to realize that another much wider conflict was imminent. The same corrupt ministers in Whitehall who had been sitting idle for fifteen years, aging in considerable comfort on their retainers were put back to work again. The scale of the conflict this time netted the cartel not millions of pounds, but billions.

The spanner in the works for the cartel came not with Germany's surrender in May 1945, but with the end of a technological race which MI5 had been privy to for some time. The first atomic bomb that devasted Hiroshima announced the ultimate weapon of mass destruction and rendered the use of conventional weapons in global scale conflicts obsolete.

With most National Defence expenditure now centred on keeping up with the Cold War nuclear arms race against the Communist Soviet Union, and with Britain reeling from the massive debt caused by the cost of the last war, the factories owned by grandfather's empire ground to a halt overnight.

An ally to the Sanderson cause came in the form of the newly formed CIA, an organisation created solely to keep the American military manufacturing complex in business, its first mission to capitalize on the growing frictions endemic between the democratic Western Nations and those under Communist rule.

Grandfather Sanderson died of a sudden heart attack in 1948 at age of sixty, leaving Sanderson's father in charge of an empire with what seemed at the time, a greatly diminished outlook.

The outbreak of war in 1950 between rival Communist backed and pro-Western forces in Korea had given the CIA their first major success, one which presenting their nations arms manufacturers with a three-year run of highly profitable armament orders. Britain's involvement, swift to come to the aid of its new best friend, was also sizeable, much to the relief of Sanderson's father, putting his factories back into full production. The conflict ending with both sides territorially back to exactly where they had started, the British government came under considerable criticism for wasting the lives of British soldiers for no objective gain.

For Sanderson himself, having come onto the board with his father just after the Korean war came to a close, the picture couldn't have looked bleaker.

In the early nineteen sixties, the CIA, having spent years stirring up trouble in Vietnam, hatched its master plan for a conflict that would drag on for over ten years, yet again purely for the benefit of the US arms manufacturers. Unfortunately for the Sanderson cartel, the British government, faced with the prospect of another debacle like Korea, declined to get involved. The cartel however, immediately spotting the potential problem with their rival manufacturers over the pond keeping up with the strenuous demands of a conflict that was accelerating at breakneck speed, were quick to offer the US government support, a move that secured numerous sub-contracts, perhaps not as lucrative as before, but lucrative enough.

By the time American involvement in Vietnam ended in defeat in the mid-seventies with a nation bitterly divided over the conflict, no US president for the foreseeable future was going to risk involving the nation in another conflict of this scale, and so the CIA's plans to find the next arena for warfare ground to a halt.

The following years were a barren wasteland for the cartel, Sanderson's father dying from cancer at the age of seventy one, leaving his only son in charge of a sailing ship drifting helplessly in a dead calm. The stagnation was interrupted only on occasion when Sanderson found himself reduced to fighting over scraps of business in Africa, arming governments slaughtering their own people in disputes over ethnic differences.

Then in 1989, salvation unexpectedly came knocking for Sanderson in a chain of events sparked by the collapse of the Iron Curtain and the fall of the Berlin wall. As the final decade of the twentieth century dawned, a door of opportunity had opened in the former Yugoslavia.

Sanderson had travelled overseas to offer his services, secretly meeting with high ranking military members of the newly formed rival Serb and Croat armies, each unaware of his complicity. He was successful in securing orders from both sides for a range of armaments from land mines to assault rifles, weaponry that he knew all too well would be used to kill UN troops.

It was on this trip that he had met the two opposing generals with whom he would form such a close bond. They had both ranted on about how the other side had forced them into an irreversible course of military action. It was whilst he was in their presence that he had heard them use that same expression spoken with a clinical coldness, ethnic cleansing.

A glorious picture had formed in Sanderson's fertile mind involving one of the by-products of the conflict. There would be multitudes of vulnerable orphans with nowhere to go, desperately reaching out to anyone who could secure them safe passage out of their war torn homeland.

'Sir,' came a voice, as if far away, stirring Sanderson from his thoughts. He looked up, his familiar middle aged driver Donaldson sat behind the wheel, cold steely eyes in the rear view mirror.

'We're here sir,' he confirmed in his customary respectful tone.

Sanderson glanced out of the rear door window, instantly recognizing the familiar leafy street of Victorian terraced houses sat back off the pavements by small yet immaculately kept front gardens.

'Of course,' he replied, at which Donaldson opened his door to get out, lifting a black leather attaché case with him from the passenger seat. He presented as an imposingly stocky brutish faced man dressed his tailored black suit, yet possessed a calm calculating mind, an attribute that Sanderson always insisted upon with any of his chauffeurs. Glancing up and down the street before opening Sanderson's door, he cloaked his employer as they walked up the short path to the distinctive dark blue wooden door, closed venetian blinds in the bay window to the right. Donaldson inserted a key and turned, pushing the door open for his employer to safely enter first, following behind before closing it behind them.

The hallway was traditionally narrow, emphasized by all the doors leading off being shut, secured by locks, top, middle and bottom, the only natural light from a locked skylight just visible at the top of the stairs.

Reaching the landing, Donaldson led the way. Sanderson had been here many times before and as they approached the rear bedroom door, the memories of previous visits already flooding back, the adrenaline surged through his veins. The three locks released, Donaldson pushed the heavy solid wooden door open, his bulk filling the doorway.

Marta was already on her feet in the gloom, back pressed up against the bricked up window, an old double bed the only furniture in the room. Donaldson reached for the light switch on the wall as he entered, the bare ceiling light bulb casting a harsh glow.

Her apprehension at being presented with the intimidating Donaldson faded by comparison when she saw the look in the much older man's eyes who entered the room behind him. His cold gaze was hypnotic, freezing her where she stood as he took her in for a moment, then nodded almost imperceptibly to his bodyguard. Marta's nervous eyes followed Donaldson's movements as he unclipped the attaché case, what was left of any colour in her face draining away when she saw what he was taking out. He stepped forward and placed the items neatly at the bottom of the bed, stepping back and staring at her expectantly, Sanderson marvelling at her expression of morbid dread.

'Put them on,' Donaldson commanded when she didn't move, his tone calm but authoritative. Marta hesitated for a moment before scurrying along the bed like a mouse and picking up the black lacy bra and panties, making for an open door leading to a tiny windowless bathroom.

'No, not in there. Here,' Sanderson demanded, his voice dry and gravelly, halting her in her tracks. She turned, fixed again by his glare.

'Please,' she begged, murmuring.

'No,' he replied, this time louder.

She looked at Donaldson then as if in a silent plea for help, only to be met with an impassive expression. Then, her body beginning to tremble, she stood in the middle of the room in front of her audience and stripped down to her underwear. Stood there so defenceless in her innocent plain white bra and blue cotton panties, Sanderson's pulse began to race as he saw in her the look of a pubescent younger teenager, exactly the vision that he had come to relish, and for a moment he thought of asking her to keep them on, but...

'And the rest,' Sanderson directed, his eyes widening with anticipation. Backing up to the bed, reaching down behind her to touch her new undergarments by some way of reassurance, Marta, much too afraid to turn her back on her captors, hastily slipped out of her bra, covering her breasts with her arms and with as much modesty as she could manage put on the lacy replacement, then turning side on to her visitors in a vain attempt to limit their view, she quickly slipped her panties down and pulled her new ones up. It made no difference to Sanderson that she was denying him a full view of her naked form, he would be seeing it in all its glory very soon.

Holding her head in shame, Marta could hear Sanderson's light footsteps on the worn carpet as he approached, his hand rough and dry on her soft skin as he lifted her head to look at her face, assailing her with the foul odour of cigars and whisky on his breath. He smiled then, stepping back, taking her by the arm to gently spin her like a ballerina awkwardly performing her first pirouette, relishing her slender back and firm shapely buttocks, before guiding her back round to face him again.

He glanced behind to Donaldson stood waiting, Marta seeing that same subtle nod again. It was at that moment as he turned and left, closing the door behind him, leaving her trapped in the room with the man with that evil gaze, that the panic she had been fighting so hard to suppress finally erupted, her first instinct to run for the bathroom door. Sanderson of course, having been in this room many times before, was one step ahead, moving with surprising speed for his age, blocking her path. She tried to push past him but he was too strong, throwing her backwards onto the bed so he could straddle her, pinning her down as his roaming hands tore her bra and panties off, exploring the delights of her breasts and vulva. He wanted her to scream out for mercy like the others had, but she was still struggling in silence. The hard slap across her face only served to stun her, so reaching back down behind him he forced two of his fingers inside her, drawing a wail of agony from her throat, that sound making his manhood throb with the intensity that he had been so longing for all evening. Then, turning her writhing over onto her front, he unbuckled his trousers, Marta screaming out in pain as he forced his way into her, thrusting hard and deep as her shrill cries brought him closer and closer to boiling point, until finally he shouted out in ecstasy, Marta feeling his repulsive hot seed flowing deep into her.

She lay there pinned down for what seemed to her like an eternity, an experience so unbearable that she wanted nothing more than to be allowed to die there and then, sobbing uncontrollably, her eyes tightly closed. Then she suddenly felt his weight lift and heard the door open and close again, followed by the inevitable sound of the locks turning.

Eventually, in considerable discomfort, she managed to get off the bed, placing her panties between her legs to stem the blood dripping down between her bruised thighs.

She stood bent over with pain in the shower, the water mercifully warm as she washed every inch of her body to try and clean the stench of her vile oppressor off, the basin beneath her feet running red from her open wound, but afterwards when she dried herself, she could still smell him on her skin.

TEN

Emil had been looking forward to this evening for a long time. This was his club and his alone, a place where he was in control, not Aleksandar.

He had bought the premises not long after they had arrived in London, his own little sanctuary converted from an old warehouse situated in the part of London he liked the best. It was far enough from the pretentious West End that Aleksandar loved so much, a gritty, up and coming neighbourhood on the North Eastern edge of the financial district. His was a club for fellow Croats and nobody else.

Unlike his partner who was rapidly succumbing to the superficial allure of gentrification that had begun to cloud the convictions stamped in his mind back in Bosnia, Emil was still holding on tight to his principle of absolute ethnic purity. To him, it wasn't enough that they hunted down all the Serbs that stood in the way of their business interests, Emil viewed all other ethnic groups endemic in London's multi-racial melting pot as vermin, including the indigenous Anglo Saxons.

He was proud of what he had created, a place where Croats still very much a minority in London, knew they would be welcome, safe from the ridicule of the lazy British opposed to the flood of the harder working Eastern European's who they blamed for taking their jobs in the manual labour market.

Over the last ten years, his club had become a beacon of hope for his fellow comrades and tonight, as part of a special ceremony, he was going to be honoured.

He had of course been discreet about his criminal activities, after all, he didn't want any of his fellow Croat's getting ideas and trying to muscle in on the empire he had fought so hard to build with Aleksandar. His loyal entourage of informants, young impressionable men working in the low paid trades, always came to him about any newly arrived Croat ex-military heavyweights who might pose a threat, a service for which they were rewarded with girls and cocaine, though neither ever at his club.

As the tally of murdered Croat rivals mounted up, conveniently for Emil, perceived as being carried out by Serbs and other hateful minorities, so did the indiscriminate mob reprisals, naturally under the countenance of the very man who the Croat community had come to see as their Godfather.

Emil knew that most of the men that joined his club were ex-soldiers who would never lose their appetite for sexual brutality against Serbs. Taking off their uniforms didn't cleanse them of their savage instincts and coming to London simply made them indiscriminate in their choice of victims, as faced with a lack of Serb candidates, they were swift to satisfy their insatiable cravings with any attainable girls or women, regardless of race or creed.

'Mr. Kovacevic, I'm sorry to disturb you.' Emil stirred from his drink induced trip down memory lane, suddenly aware again of the loud Croatian folk music being played by a band up on a stage at the far end of the packed dimly lit windowless vast room laid out with round tables draped with crimson red linens, the black walls and ceilings rendering the structure of the cavernous space almost indefinable. He looked up, a young drunken suited punter stood gripping the arm of a nervous looking girl no more than sixteen dressed in a one piece figure hugging black dress.

'Not at all, my friend,' he replied with a courteous smile. The girl sat next to Emil, also underage, looked away, not wanting to see, it was simpler that way.

'You are in need of some privacy, yes?' Emil deduced. He felt somewhat offended by the notion of a guest being absent for his speech, but business was business and for Emil that always came above everything else.

'Please, I would be most grateful Mr. Kovacevic.'

Emil beckoned him closer, talking into his ear, gesturing to a doorframe sized black suited doorman guarding a dark open doorway on the other side of the room.

'Thank you, you are most kind,' his paying guest replied, stepping back again.

'Not at all,' Emil replied with a wave of his hand, the girl being led away by the arm. The doorman stepped aside discreetly as he saw them coming, immediately moving back into position behind them as they vanished, the manoeuvre completely unnoticed by the hundreds of other couples, their perception already numbed by the abundance of Vodka being consumed.

Abruptly, the band fell silent, all eyes turning to the stage for the big moment, a tuxedoed host bounding up onto the spot lit platform, cordless microphone in hand.

'Ladies and gentlemen, citizens from our homeland, we welcome you to London,' he announced, joviality in his loud delivery.

Emil looked around the room at the cheering guests, soaking up the atmosphere. He knew which of the female partners in the audience were prostitutes, mostly from sight, the others distinguishable by the way they applauded half heartedly, unlike the few genuine Croatian ladies in the room, some of whom were shouting louder than their men.

'And now, I want to ask the owner of this establishment up onto the stage, Mr. Emil Kovacevic.'

Getting a little unsteadily to his feet from the alcohol amidst his rallying guests, Emil weaved his way between the sea of occupied tables, climbing the steps by the side of the stage, another vodka shot in hand provided by a waiting waitress. The host seemed to shrink in size with foreboding as the bulky form of his employer approached, almost snatching the microphone from his grasp as he held it out in surrender, before quickly making himself scarce stage right.

'It gives me great pleasure to see you all here tonight,' Emil roared, met with another louder round of applause.

'When I came to London, I instantly fell in love.' The band violinist, taking his queue, played a brief melancholy tune that was met with laughter from the crowd.

'But it wasn't the people that I fell in love with, it was this place in which you sit tonight. A place where I can be an honest Croatian, uncorrupted by the criminal British establishment,' he continued.

'And so, my friends, tonight we celebrate, and drink to our future,' Emil finished at the top of his voice, downing his vodka shot in unison with his raucous guests.

Over the din of the audience, the violinist began playing again, the crowd quickly dying down, the tune stirring a happy memory from Emil's childhood, a song from an early James Bond film his long departed father loved to watch whenever it came on the television.

'From Bosnia with love, I fly to you,' came a female tuneful voice from behind as the spotlight left him, Emil at first thinking it was the Vodka playing tricks on him.

'Much wiser since my goodbye to you.' Emil turned, smiling lustily as the spotlight picked out the elegant form of Radica in her figure hugging dress, approaching across the stage, microphone raised. He stood there hypnotised by her beauty as she draped a hand over his shoulder.

'I've travelled the world to learn, I must return from Bosnia with love.' She backed up a little as her hand slid down his chest to take hold of his tie, teasing him towards her.

'I've seen places, faces, and smiled for a moment, but oh, you haunted me so.' He reached out, trying to grab her round the waist to pull her closer, but she pushed him away playfully, surprising him with her strength.

'Still my tongue tied, young pride would not let my love for you show, in case you'd say no.'

'How can I say no?' Emil protested with a smile as he turned to the captivated crowd.

'To Bosnia I flew, but there and then, I suddenly knew you'd care again. My running around is through, I fly to you, from Bosnia with love', came Radica's final climatic verse, some of the more entranced men in the audience on their feet much to the jealous annoyance of their partners as the crowd burst into rapturous applause. The spotlight dimming, a mesmerised Emil watching helplessly as Radica slipped away into the shadows. For the briefest moment, he found himself gripped by an odd, unsettling sensation, but then it was gone, and as the band started up again, Emil turned away from the dark abyss into which Radica had vanished and came down from the stage to re-join the young girl waiting patiently at his table.

It was closing time at the club when the heavy steel door to Emil's office swung open with a bang, announcing his entrance. He stumbled in, reaching for the light switch on the wall in the darkness, cursing when the anticipated illumination was not forthcoming. Fumbling across the room, his memory and co-ordination considerably compromised by the higher than usual volume of celebratory vodka consumed, he bumped into the corner of his desk, letting out a grunt of discomfort, groping around before he finally found what he was looking for. The soft cream light of the reading lamp cast a spot lit glow on the desk, just enough for him to make out the small sink on the back wall. Propping himself up against the edge of the basin, he picked up a tiny plastic bottle next to the cold tap and unscrewed the lid, tipping two blue tablets out into his palm. He would need a double dose tonight he had decided, to get his stamina up for his girl of the evening, who right now was waiting downstairs for him in one of the private rooms. Running the tap, he popped the pills into his mouth before lowering the cupped palm of his other hand under the water, bending down to raise it to his mouth, swallowing the magic potion down.

Splashing water on his sweating face for good measure, he turned the tap off and straightened himself, catching his reflection in the mirror, taking just a split second too long to register the movement in the darkness directly behind him.

Propelled forward, his forehead shattered the mirror as it made contact. Then he was being spun around on his heels and thrust down into his old red leather studded desk chair, a searing pain shooting up into his head as a fist crunched into his nose, watering eyes blinding him as the blood poured forth in a torrent, Emil too stunned to resist the frantic hands that he could feel violating his body, searching for a weapon.

The probing fingers finally retreating, he looked up, his vision still distorted, desperately trying to make out the face of his assailant in the gloom. It took a moment to register her, still in her stage dress, the unmistakable business end of a pistol silencer aimed squarely between his eyes.

'You,' he gasped.

'From Bosnia with love, I fly to you,' Radica began to sing again.

'Who the hell are you?'

'Much wiser since my goodbye to you.'

'Stop,' Emil shouted.

'But I thought you liked my song,' Radica replied, feigning the look of a hurt young child, her expression suddenly changing to one that unnerved him, the way an old acquaintance smiles when seeing someone for the first time in years.

'You look different from when we last met. You've gotten fat,' she mocked.

Emil's drunken mind raced as he searched her face, completely at a loss.

'What's the matter Emil, are you having trouble joining the dots?'

'I, I don't remember you,' he almost stammered.

'Of course you don't, but then how could you, after all, there were so many of us back then.'

His eyes narrowed.

'Perhaps Aleksandar might remember me, I'm sure I'll get to ask him, very soon,' Radica taunted.

'Aleksandar, but how do…?'

'You came to our village and murdered my family,' she interrupted.

'You wanted me for yourself, but Aleksandar wouldn't let you. He said we were being saved for the Englishman.'

In a sudden instant of clarity, Emil felt his blood run cold.

'No, you were with the other girls in the…' He caught himself mid sentence.

'In the what?'

Emil's expression changed then, a cruel grin spreading across his face.

'You don't know,' he sneered.

'Tell me,' Radica commanded, her composure slipping.

In that moment, Emil knew the game was up, but he was pleased that at least he would get to go out at his club, drunk in his favourite chair and not stone cold sober having suffered hours of torture at the hands of some business rival. He knew that his executioner was a pro who wouldn't fall for any lies concocted to trick her into keeping him alive.

'No,' he replied defiantly.

He felt a long since familiar white hot burning sensation as a bullet tore through the flesh of his left thigh, passing straight out the other side into the chair, but he didn't cry out, biting down on the agonizing pain as he smiled up at Radica through gritted teeth.

'Tell me, are they still alive?' Radica pressed, the panic rising in her voice now, but he kept smiling silently, holding her in his gaze.

The second bullet shattered the femur in his other thigh, the jagged fragments of splintered bone lacerating surrounding muscle, this time Emil unable to suppress a stifled scream. He held his hand up in surrender, shaking his head. In that moment Radica thought that he was going to tell her what she needed to know.

'You're wasting your bullets,' he finally said, his jaw clenched. He slouched back in the chair, relieved to finally see a disappointed Radica levelling the pistol at his forehead, ready for the final farewell.

'Last chance Emil,' Radica offered, the tragic realization that her words were nothing more a pointless formality, taking hold.

Emil's expression unexpectedly softened in that moment and he smiled up at her sadly, like her father had on occasion in the days leading up to his death.

'A good man would tell you what you want to know', Emil said quietly. 'But I am not a good man, and so I will not.'

'But don't you want to meet your maker with a clean conscience,' Radica replied in a last futile attempt to appeal to his morality, one that he had never possessed.

Emil shook his head slowly, his gaze distant now.

'I have no maker. No god could be great enough to create a person as evil as me,' he concluded indignantly.

His focus came back to Radica then, the sad smile still lingering, waiting for her to pull the trigger. In his final moments, he heard a familiar comforting sound of old in the distance. It was the wonderful chorus of girl's screams, and for an instant as Radica pulled the trigger, he was back in his Bosnia rape camp, swimming in that eternal sea of sordid pleasures.

Gun in hand, Radica left Aleksandar's office at the end of the backstage corridor, closing it quietly behind her.

Emerging stage right, gun behind her back, she found the vast room deserted except for the familiar doorman by now sat down engrossed in a newspaper at the entrance to the private rooms as she had anticipated. Hearing her heels on the steps, the doorman clocked her out of the corner of his eye.

'So, you did stay and fuck him,' he laughed, continuing with his read.

'Maybe,' Radica replied coyly.

'Of course you did,' he sniggered.

'What's in there?' Radica enquired. He looked up, seeing Radica walking towards him, but by the time he saw the gun it was too late, the single round between his lungs paralysing him in the seat before she followed up with an almost casual head shot as she passed.

Once over the threshold to the private rooms, an oblique turn presented Radica with a narrow dark corridor that she remembered from her study of the building plans, lit only by dim miniature red strip lights directly above doors running down each side, gold embossed hotel style do not disturb cards hanging off some of the round handles. Hearing the muffled distressed moans of the girls seeping through the walls, Radica was spurred into action, slowly turning the first door handle adorned with an occupied card.

The sweating whale sized naked punter pinning his young prey down on her front barely had time to turn his head as he heard the door open, the bullet shearing the side of his head off, the bloody gore of his brains mercifully missing his victim, splashing across the wall next to the bed. Heaving his flabby bulk to one side, Radica turned the startled girl over, placing her finger to her own lips as she saw her wide terrified eyes.

'Get dressed and wait for me in the corridor, yes?' Radica offered quietly, the girl nodding silently.

Two minutes later, Radica, having completed her sweep of every room, having ended the lives of seven luckless guests, led the hastily dressed girls including Emil's quarry still waiting in trepidation for her employer, to the far end of the corridor where she knew there was a fire escape. Shooting off the heavy padlock obviously designed to stop the girls escaping, she ushered them out into the dark narrow alleyway, the hired people carrier she had arrived in parked in the adjoining backstreet.

O'Neil wasn't going to miss Emil, a loose cannon who had cost him many sleepless nights. Truth be told, it was a great relief that someone had finally taken him out, not that it hadn't crossed his mind to have someone do it himself many times.

Sanderson had kept his promise, with his considerable influence, pulling the right strings to ensure that O'Neil was fast tracked up through the ranks to Chief Inspector on his return from Bosnia, a lightning quick career progression, completely unprecedented in the London Metropolitan Police. Sanderson had done it purely out of self interest of course, needing a loyal subject placed right at the top of the constabulary to steer attention away from the trafficking, that in its tenth year was netting him over half a million a month.

O'Neil had known from the start that he was no more than a pawn in Sanderson's game, but it was a fair trade, his Swiss bank account swelling month by month whilst he continued to keep a modest lifestyle commensurate with his paygrade to avoid attracting attention. He did plan to spend his fortune of course, living out the rest of his life in the sun overseas somewhere when he retired, but he knew all too well that would never be possible as long his paymaster was still alive. It would mean that Sanderson's wife and the two sons would have to die as well, but that was something that he could arrange without two much difficulty, a head on car accident on a dark country lane perhaps. His gut instinct had been telling him to cut and run for a few months now. After all, he already had enough to retire in style, but he was trapped in a web of his own greed, like a gambler on a winning streak who knows he needs to leave the table while he's still ahead but can't bring himself to. And so, resigning himself to his rapacity, he had decided to ride the precarious rollercoaster of dirty money for another few years and in doing so, had also devised a devious way to capitalize on the relationship with his other partner in crime Aleksandar before finally bringing the curtain down on everyone with one last surprise performance before they would have the chance to beat him to it.

He'd had his share of women since Bosnia, and had been faithful to them all, his way of keeping himself on the straight and narrow, away from the temptations of pubescent flesh that the blond green eyed girl from Bosnia had awakened in him years ago. It had been ten years, but the sensation that had rippled through his body as he had felt her pubescent firm body under him in the darkness, the intoxicating smell of her innocence, was one that he had never been able to shake from his memory, a longing that the women in his life since had never come close to satisfying, even when he closed his eyes and pictured her during intercourse. There had been many times over the years when after indulging in too much whisky late at night after a bad day at work, he had almost succumbed to the temptation to borrow one of Aleksandar's under age girls for an hour to finally live out the remainder of that sequence of events he had been denied that night at the base, one he had fantasized about over and over, yet he had resisted, knowing that the uniqueness of that moment could never be mimicked by another girl.

The drive to Tilbury docks had seemed to take forever, despite the light traffic so early in the morning, the dawn light casting a dirty grey gloom over the ugly landscape of warehouses and factories. He knew he was still over the alcohol limit after yet another evening of overindulging alone at home in his apartment in the city, and Head of the Met or not, the last thing he wanted was to get collared. Taking the back roads to avoid all the known police hang outs, he arrived at the vast complex, passing the sign for the main gate as usual to turn off the access road much further on, pulling up at an electric wire mesh gate conveniently hidden from the main thoroughfare round a bend at the end of an old disused road.

Aleksandar had left the door unlocked, knowing who was coming, his mind elsewhere when it opened, unconsciously toying with his empty whisky glass as he sat slumped in the same old leather armchair behind the same old wooden desk he had enjoyed in Bosnia, their grandeur at odds just as before in the stark prefabricated dockside office with steel mesh windows.

'Little early for that isn't it?' Stirring from his thoughts he looked up, O'Neil dressed incognito in a dark overcoat, his guest instantly recognizing the morose look in his eyes and deciding to refrain from any further attempts at small talk. He pulled up a seat on the other side of the desk, making himself comfortable.

'I knew there was something wrong when I tried to call him at midnight,' Aleksandar said quietly, as if from far away.

'Where did you find him?'

'His office.'

'Any other bodies?'

'One of his bodyguards, and...'

O'Neil searched his expression, waiting patiently.

'Seven punters, all murdered in their rooms.'

'And the girls?'

'Gone.'

'Perhaps this gangster whoever he is, wanted them for himself.'

'Too risky, they'd be easily recognized in another club.'

A chilling notion was gripping Aleksandar, one that he doubted O'Neil would have yet fathomed. The kinds of girls that worked at his club were dispensable, hundreds of them died in London every year. This murder wasn't just about business.

'This is personal,' Aleksandar replied, a tone of certainty in his voice.

'Well maybe you should step up security while I see what forensics come up with.'

'And what about Scotland Yard, I assume they'll be wanting to speak with me?'

'Don't worry, you'll be kept out of the picture.'

'Thank you, yet another one I owe you. And talking of which.' Aleksandar opened a desk drawer, producing a thick brown envelope, sliding it across.

'Much obliged,' O'Neil replied, stuffing it inside his coat as he stood.

'Perhaps you should lay low at home for a while, at least until we have something.'

'I never let anything get in the way of business, you know that.'

'But you said this was personal.'

'And rest assured, I'll be ready for this assassin, whoever they are.'

Vladimir hated the tedium of air travel, the queues, the security checks, the business class seats that always gave him backache, the lousy refreshments, so he was already in a foul mood when he arrived at Heathrow that morning. He had made himself refrain from any whiskies on the plane, confident that otherwise he would have been arrested for assault when he disembarked.

Despite his sobriety, it was all he could do not to shout obscenities at the young jumped up over officious passport officer keeping him waiting, his sharp eyes flitting between the photo and Vladimir not just once, twice, but three times, scrutinizing his facial features. Vladimir snatched the passport back with a scowl as it was slid back across the counter without a word of acknowledgement, stomping off like a raging bull towards the arrivals exit.

Bosko and Jakov, ten years his junior, had flown out a few days earlier to ensure everything was arranged down to the last detail. Stood waiting in the crowd, dressed in customary black suits, white shirt, no tie, their huge frames towered over the assortment of onlookers at the arrivals gate. Bosko was first to spot him, almost knocking an older black capped chauffeur off his feet as he led the way, clumsily barging through the crowd to be met with disgruntled murmurs, Jakov knocking the chauffeurs cap off from behind as he passed, casting him a backwards menacing glare.

'Good flight boss?' Bosko enquired without thinking to read Vladimir's expression, reaching forward to take the wheeled suitcase.

'Do I look like I had a good flight?' Vladimir snapped loudly, people looking around.

'Sorry I didn't mean to...'

'Just get me to the hotel.'

'This way,' Bosko gestured, the two of them flanking their employer, escorting him outside to the short stay car park directly opposite.

Sinking into the luxurious leather rear seat of the new black BMW 7 Series, Vladimir let out a sigh of frustration as Bosko and Emil settled a brief argument over who got to drive.

Staring out at the vast expanse of the urban skyline looming into view as they made their way into London, Vladimir reflected with regret how long it had taken him to finally get to this juncture in his criminal career, and he relished the moment, very soon, when he would be stood pissing all over the dead body of the so called legendary Croat rival who had fled Bosnia before he had had the chance to put a bullet in his head.

It was his time now. He had taken a massive leap of faith to trust O'Neil this far, but he had always been a good judge of character, and O'Neil was just a mercenary after all, interested in one thing and one thing alone. There was no way of knowing if O'Neil was being honest about the percentage that Aleksandar had been paying him all these years, but it didn't matter, Vladimir was happy with the number O'Neil had accepted in exchange for toppling his rival and inheriting his empire, bodyguards and all. In less than a week he would be the new king of the castle, with the help of his unsuspecting loyal knight of course.

ELEVEN

Veronica as she was officially known in the service, sat observing a sleeping Radica from the comfort of an armchair in the gloom. She had half expected her muse to stir when she opened the door with the master key, but with the anticipated confrontation unforthcoming, she had been happy to take a seat for a while, weapon on her lap.

She was glad for a few moments of peace from the frantic schedule of her work. Her own daughter was long grown up and away in the US working for the CIA, disappointing her mother when she declined an open door into MI5 after graduating from Oxford. In truth, Veronica had predicted her decision and understood her choice, reminding herself at the time that she wouldn't have wanted to work in the shadow of her own mother either.

Sanderson had been her direct superior for over fifteen years, yet she knew absolutely nothing about him personally. It was a long standing and widely accepted culture that people in MI5 were highly secretive about their private lives, that was understandable, but at least she knew the names of the wives of the other directors and other little snippets of domestic information that would slip out after a few whiskies at the end of yet another long week. Sanderson however was a completely closed book, no family photos on his desk, nothing.

Sergeant Stanton had first sent a coded communication one month before his death. All it said was 'Believe Captain O'Neil is in some way involved with the Serb and Croat armies regarding the trafficking of female orphans, will need more time to obtain evidence, will report back.' She had followed standard protocol, taking it straight upstairs to Sanderson. It was the momentary shift in his expression that she remembered the most as she stood there watching him read the printout, his emotionless cold eyes involuntarily widening and his fixed smile faltering for just a second as he was caught off guard, before his composure returned to normal.

'Thank you, Veronica, leave this with me,' he had said without even looking up, his trademark lack of courtesy something she was well familiar with.

Veronica wasn't summoned to Sanderson's office to discuss the matter further over the next few weeks, even Stanton's demise going unmentioned, but when she was suddenly assigned to Captain O'Neil on his return from Bosnia shortly afterwards, she knew that the fallen sergeant had been onto something.

Posing as a top end recruitment consultant for the Met under the instructions of her boss, Veronica was provided with the rare opportunity to actually meet the very subject she would spend the next number of years spying on.

O'Neil wasn't the first British Army high ranker to turn bad. She had come across three in her career, but what disturbed her most about this candidate was his apparent emotionless predisposition, his fixed, somewhat stoic facial expression making him impossible to read, his military service file the only resource for her evaluation.

He had gone through the standard trauma in Belfast back in the eighties as a corporal, shot in the chest in eighty seven by a sniper, the surgeon stating in his report that in his experience, no one had ever survived that kind of injury before.

Mentally O'Neil was a blank, his annual psychiatric evaluation after his first year in Belfast noting that at no time during his tour had he demonstrated the traditional symptoms of trauma related stress following incidents that had left other soldiers in his platoon with severe psychological issues.

As lieutenant he was considered by both his subordinates and superiors to be an excellent leader, but while his men respected him, they also resented him for his scarcity of compassion, not just for his corporal's lives, but for those of the innocent civilians caught up in the carnage on the streets. While his soldiers would suffer the psychological torment from witnessing fellow comrades and civilians fall victim to bombs and bullets, some reduced to smoking slabs of flesh that had to be shovelled up into black bags, O'Neil would carry on as if nothing had happened.

Whilst Veronica was certain that O'Neil was more than capable for the role that Sanderson had in mind, she did have misgivings about his complete lack of for want of a better word, humanity, a characteristic that she feared would alienate him from his colleagues and draw unwanted attention, but Sanderson had brushed her concerns aside without explanation, effectively rubber stamping his approval.

True to form, O'Neil quickly attracted the same reputation with his new colleagues in the Met as he had in Belfast, a disdain that only intensified as The Iceman as they called him behind his back, climbed the career ladder at breakneck speed, quickly leaving his disgruntled contemporaries lagging way behind, making Detective Sergeant within a year and a half.

The autonomy afforded by his senior rank combined with the deliberately cultivated social isolation from his colleagues, provided O'Neil with the ideal conditions to develop his secret business dealings with Aleksandar undetected, until now, over eight years later, MI5's mass of evidence had reached critical mass.

They had been keeping an eye on Vladimir for some time, waiting for their moment, and Sanderson had been delighted when he had learnt that an assassin had been sent ahead to clear the way for the final piece of the jigsaw to fall perfectly into place.

Veronica wasn't prone to feelings of guilt in her profession, most of the people they were assigned to were criminals to the core, but something she couldn't put her finger on was telling her that when the time came, she would find it harder to tie off the loose end presently sleeping peacefully across the room from her.

Her grip instinctively tightened on her pistol as she heard Radica stirring, watching unseen as her subject slid out from under the sheets like a serpent, dressed in t-shirt and pyjama trousers, to approach the curtains, pulling them wide open, the bright morning light throwing her slender figure into silhouette.

'Stand perfectly still,' she heard a woman say with a calm authority, the accent Queen's English.

'Turn around very slowly.'

It was the cold steely eyes that first hit Radica when she saw her captor, the pistol levelled at her.

'I must say my dear that you are by far the most attractive assassin I've ever met,' Veronica complimented as she took in her quarry's beauty. 'And you sleep very soundly for a woman in your profession.'

Radica could only stand there like a mannequin, waiting for the next command.

'You can get dressed now. But you won't be needing this,' Veronica teased without taking her eyes off her prey, producing Radica's Glock concealed in her jacket pocket with her free hand.

Directly outside the entrance to the Ritz, a gleaming black Mercedes S Class with darkened windows waited. A tall expressionless chauffeur opened the nearside rear door as Veronica appeared from the entrance directly behind Radica, both escorted by a doorframe sized suit.

Locked in the back with Veronica, the Mercedes moved off to the end of the courtyard, joining the sluggish mid morning traffic.

'Where are we going?' Radica enquired, trying to keep her voice calm and confident.

'All things in good time my dear.'

Veronica opened a compartment in the rear of the driver's seat, removing a black silk bag.

'Put this on,' Veronica commanded softly, holding it out.

'No,' came Radica's indignant reply.

Veronica locked Radica in her cold gaze.

'Let me explain something to you, young lady. You are only alive at this moment because I have deemed it necessary,' she articulated with a clinical directness.

'But be in no doubt, I can manage perfectly well without you if need be. Now be a good girl.'

Reluctantly taking the silk bag, Radica slid it over her head.

'That's better, now make yourself comfortable,' she heard Veronica say.

In the darkness Radica's mind turned over and over, trying to fathom why in fact she was still alive, and not at that moment being dumped in the Thames weighed down with bricks. She knew her abduction must be somehow connected with Emil and Aleksandar, but whoever this woman was, she couldn't be working for them, otherwise she would be dead already.

Radica realized they must have arrived at their destination when the vehicle stopped yet again and she recognized the heavy mechanical sound of steel doors rolling back. She felt the car move forward again, the doors closing with a loud bang behind.

'You can take it off now,' the familiar voice confirmed as she heard the central locking disengaging and both rear doors opening.

Lifting the bag from her head, Veronica having already exited, she stepped out into a gloomy high ceilinged deserted warehouse, dim daylight forcing its way through the filthy high windows. Huge overhead gantry lights suddenly flickered on, flooding the room.

'Good morning young lady,' a soft gravelly voice called out, echoing quietly off the walls.

Radica stared silently at the man who had spoken. To her he looked ancient with his silver hair and a tanned face that reminded her of a shrivelled prune, his features accentuated by his wire rimmed spectacles, the bright lights reflected in the lenses. Sat behind a sparse metal desk, a black leather bound file before him, she couldn't help but think he looked completely out of place in his expensive pinstripe suit with red silk handkerchief tucked in the breast pocket. She was also instantly aware however, regardless of her opinion, that sat flanked by two enormous black suited bodyguards, he was a man who was accustomed to being taken seriously.

MI5 had been keeping track of Vladimir since the start of the Bosnian war, continuing to observe his involvement with the ethnic cleansing that had flared up again in neighbouring Kosovo and then Chechnya, paying close attention to the highly unequitable and subordinate relationship he had struggled to build with his Western European contacts, trafficking only a meagre portion of the multitude of orphans left defenceless on the streets.

O'Neil's arrangement with Aleksandar had netted Sanderson more than he could have possibly envisioned, often reflecting with an ironic smile how the sex trade had become as profitable and definitely more dependable than arms manufacturing. But now, after ten years, the flow of girls from Bosnia was beginning to slow.

Sanderson's lap dog had brokered no resistance when he had been instructed to make the necessary arrangements with Vladimir who had been waiting patiently in the wings for a decade, offering the Serb a deal far more lucrative than he could ever hope to achieve with his rip off Western European customers.

There was however an additional transition of power that Sanderson had sadly found himself unable to avoid any longer, one that filled him with a faint modicum of regret even. His loyal operative Veronica had done an excellent job of monitoring O'Neil's ten year run of keeping the Met off Aleksandar's trail and she had built a solid case. Sanderson had been meticulous in keeping her off his scent of course and was confident that any link between him and O'Neil had remained undetected all the way through the piece. He had succeeded in keeping Veronica's handcuffs away from O'Neil for as long as possible, but now, with more than enough evidence to make an arrest, he couldn't delay the inevitable any longer.

His decision to deal with O'Neil the old fashioned MI5 way had been met with much consternation and protest from Veronica, but his word was final, insisting that the press fall out for the Met and MI5 if O'Neil went to trial would be too catastrophic to contemplate. With O'Neil and Aleksandar six feet under, all the sordid secrets of Bosnia that had for all this time threatened to bring Sanderson down, would be erased from history forever and he could make a fresh start with the Serb.

'Please, take a seat,' Sanderson invited, gesturing to the matching metal chair on the other side of the desk, Radica immediately realizing by his tone that this wasn't a request. She glanced at Veronica stood to one side, receiving a prompt nod.

Sitting herself down, Radica suddenly found herself transfixed by this old man's ocean blue eyes that still burned with the energy of someone much younger. She felt as if he was staring straight into her soul, dissecting the dark reaches of her mind.

Finally, as if he was now in possession of her every thought, he broke into a mischievous adolescent smile.

'You've been a very naughty girl' he teased, a hint of menace in his humour.

'Tell me, why did you torture him first?' he enquired.

Radica didn't answer, but held his gaze.

'Was it personal I wonder, revenge for something he did to you,' he pressed, leaning forward, his elbows on the table, enjoying the torment.

'No matter,' he concluded with a shrug, sitting back in his chair.

'So, what should I do with you now, turn you over to the authorities?' he mused, that grin returning.

'Or maybe there is some kind of understanding we can come to?'

Radica found herself involuntarily glancing down at the black file on the desk between them.

'Good, I can see you're inquisitive,' he replied with a chuckle, with that, reaching forward as he kept his eyes on his prey, his bony wrinkled fingers opening the rigid black cover, letting slip a smile of satisfaction as he watched her expression change when she instantly recognized the face before her.

'Your next move was easy to anticipate,' he said, Radica staring down at a photograph of Aleksandar walking along a city street flanked by a young bodyguard.

'Tell me, what were you planning to do once you had murdered him,' he asked, Radica looking up at him, but keeping silent.

'Fly back home and carry on with your life at the orphanage, perhaps?' Sanderson continued with a teasing grin, Radica unable to suppress her surprise.

Sanderson turned the photograph over to reveal another image, studying Radica's gaze as she saw.

'This was taken here, in London, this morning.'

She stared dumbfounded at the photograph of Vladimir entering a high end hotel with his two henchmen, the name Savoy proudly engraved into the jutting stone facade above the entrance.

'He didn't tell you he was coming, did he. Why is that do you think?'

She looked up, the very same question in her eyes.

'You're being used.'

'What do you mean?'

'That would be telling now wouldn't it.'

'No, he would never do that to me?' Radica replied defiantly, yet a feeling of doubt was already beginning to form in her mind as she spoke.

'The fact is young lady, it really doesn't matter if you believe me or not, all that matters now is that you do exactly what we ask of you.'

O'Neil stepped out of the lift on the top floor of the Savoy hotel, approaching the door to the Royal Suite, the name embossed on the door in brass.

Knocking politely, O'Neil waited, hearing heavy footsteps approaching from the other side, imagining some gorilla sized bodyguard peering out through the peephole. With a click of the lock the heavy door was pulled open, Bosko's bulk blocking any view into the room. He glanced at a small photograph in his hand, his sluggish brain taking a few moments to match O'Neil's face with the image, before he stepped aside to let O'Neil enter the room, closing and locking the door behind him.

The penthouse lounge seemed to go on forever, adorned with a tastefully selected array of classical style furniture, daylight flooding in through the vast bank of tall windows overlooking the city. In stark contrast to the opulent surroundings, a large television sat on a cabinet was blaring out a re-run of Faulty Towers, the comical dialogue being accompanied by the deep, immediately annoying laughter of Jakov sunk into a cream leather couch.

'Jakov,' Bosko barked, his cohort looking round with an annoyed expression before reluctantly thumbing the remote, the screen turning black. He got up from the couch with the urgency of a sea lion basking in the sun, staring at O'Neil resentfully.

'Are you two related?' O'Neil asked mockingly.

'No, why?' Jakov replied defensively.

'Because you Slavs all look the same to me,' he retorted with a sneer, relishing the looks of anger that his comment provoked, safe in the knowledge that they wouldn't dare lay a hand on their boss's guest.

'All of us?' he heard a familiar voice ask, turning see Vladimir emerge from a bedroom doorway, noting that he didn't seem to have aged in the last ten years, if anything, looking sharper and fitter than when he had last seen him in Bosnia ten years ago. His host broke into a warm smile as he crossed the room.

'Well, there are some exceptions,' O'Neil replied jokingly as they stood face to face.

'I'm glad to hear it,' replied Vladimir. 'Come, sit,' he gestured to two large matching couches facing each other, a glass topped low table between them.

'How was your flight?' O'Neil enquired, Bosko and Jakov exchanging apprehensive glances.

'Uncomfortable,' Vladimir replied.

'Just as well it was a one way ticket,' O'Neil jested, drawing the hint of a smile.

Vladimir turned to Bosko and Jakov stood waiting attentively side by side.

'Jakov, the whisky,' he growled.

'It's only ten o'clock in the morning,' O'Neil resisted.

'No Chief Inspector, it's five o'clock in the evening, just not here in London,' Vladimir retorted with a smile as Jakov arrived with a bottle of single malt and two crystal glasses.

'So, finally you have made good on your threat,' O'Neil coaxed as Vladimir poured the measures, handing him a glass.

'You should know by now that we Serbs always keep our promises,' Vladimir replied, lifting his glass to O'Neil's before downing his measure in one, reaching for the bottle again.

'Are you pleased with the girl I sent?' he asked, refilling his glass as O'Neil nursed his still almost full measure.

'She's very, efficient. Where did you find her?'

'Oh, back in Bosnia a long time ago, she was just a child then.'

'Well, that's some woman she's grown up to be.'

'Yes, she's a real natural.'

For a reason he couldn't yet fathom, O'Neil had the uneasy feeling that there was something Vladimir wasn't telling him, but this was not the time to push his luck with his host, especially after meeting again for the first time in years.

TWELVE

It was after midnight when Aleksandar and Marko emerged from the recently acquired Soho strip club. A deluge of torrential rain with no sign of abating greeted them as they hurried along, having been unable to park directly outside because of overrunning roadworks. Their overcoats pulled up around their necks, the still busy neon lit street crammed with parked cars on either side, Marko's eyes darted left and right for signs of danger hidden among the crowd, relying on his peripheral vision, the pelting rain drowning out all sounds, his fingers wrapped tightly around the grip of his Glock concealed in his right hip pocket.

Crossing the street between parked cars, they approached Marko's Mercedes tightly squeezed between two other vehicles. A drunk hooded vagrant appeared out of nowhere, blocking their path to accost them for some change, Marko shoving him to one side to keep them on the move, ignoring the hail of abuse that followed.

Startled by a car horn behind, Marko spun to see a drunken reveller almost clipped by a passing vehicle as he staggered across the street. As he turned back, the Mercedes now only moments away, something else caught his eye.

A hooded faceless figure marching along on the other side suddenly left the pavement, crossing the street towards them. Marko alerted Aleksandar, shielding him as he pulled out his Glock, but as he raised the weapon, he saw a tiny flash of light, for a split second feeling the bullet glance off the side of his head before he fell unconscious, the round shattering the neon lit sex shop window behind him and puncturing an inflatable sex doll taking pride of place. Startled revellers scattered as the doll quickly deflated in an ungraceful curtain bow.

Aleksandar was already scrambling for cover along the sidewalk, darting between two parked cars, disappearing just as Radica rounded the end of a vehicle to find the prone bodyguard, blood running from his head wound.

Crouching low, she stalked like a cat along the row of cars towards Aleksandar's hiding place, training her weapon on the gaps between each vehicle. Squatted down, gun at the ready, Aleksandar desperately tried to listen for movement over the sound of the rain on the car rooves. Radica was only one vehicle from him when she heard the sudden wail of police sirens, alarmingly close. There was a moment of agonizing conflict then, her unstoppable desire for vengeance and her rational mind fighting for supremacy. Then, bolting across the street, she disappeared down a side alley, vanishing into the darkness an instant before flashing blue lights bouncing off the parked cars announced the arrival of police vehicles blocking the street at both ends, followed by the crescendo of slamming doors and raised voices as black clad, masked armed police stormed the area.

A flashlight beam picked out the hunched figure of Aleksandar who moments before had deftly dropped his and his boy's gun down the gutter drain grill, now cradling the limp form of Marko in his arms.

'Armed police, don't move,' he heard a deep voice bark above him. He looked up, blinded by the beam from the silhouetted black figure, rain running down his face.

O'Neil knew this was his only chance to satisfy a curiosity that had plagued him ever since that night back in Bosnia. With Aleksandar being held at Scotland Yard for a few hours at his specific request, he made the journey to the hospital, the notion of what he might find there turning over and over in his mind, tormenting him.

A uniformed constable had been placed on guard outside the door to Marko's room. It was just after one in the morning, and he was struggling to stay focussed, having taken the liberty of borrowing one of the hospital chairs. Hearing hard soled shoes tapping loudly on the vinyl floor in contrast to the constant soft squeak that the hospital staff made in their rubber soled pumps, he turned his head, jumping to his feet as he recognized the face of O'Neil approaching at a march.

'Long night constable?' O'Neil goaded.

'Sorry sir,' the constable replied as he went to reach for the door by way of apology, O'Neil beating him to it, stepping inside to close it behind him.

Marko was lying unconscious on the bed wired up to a slowly beeping heart monitor, his head bandaged, O'Neil observed his face for a long moment, the events of that night long ago flashing through his mind again.

He began searching the draws of the bedside cabinet, freezing as he heard Marko begin to stir. Waiting for him to slip back again he opened the third drawer down, removing a small hospital issue clear zip lock bag, able to make out car keys, a mobile phone, wallet… His heart jumped in his mouth as he caught a glimpse of polished metal, protruding just a fraction from beneath the wallet. He flipped the bag over, his blood running cold as the name inscribed on the brass tags stared back at him.

His first instinct was to reach for the spare pillow on the chair and smoother Marko, a moment later his rationale reminding him that he wouldn't get away with it.

He was just closing the cabinet drawer after placing the bag back, when he heard the door suddenly open behind him, spinning round to see a middle aged rotund nurse with a clipboard.

'I already told your constable, patient's not to be disturbed, even by you,' she pronounced as she recognized O'Neil from his press appearances, her loud voice rousing a semi-conscious groan from Marko.

'Yes, of course,' O'Neil replied, hurrying for the door for fear of Marko waking.

Radica was almost back at her hotel when she got the call, Vladimir explaining that Aleksandar's bodyguard was now a matter of extreme urgency, relaying to her the details of his current location. She didn't question how he knew, all that concerned her at that moment was eliminating the person that stood between her and the second man she had come to London to claim.

Twenty minutes later she was striding through the busy Accident and Emergency entrance of the hospital in her black hoodie, going completely unnoticed among the frantic maelstrom of late night drunken injuries.

Marko stirred, slowly opening his eyes, trying to focus as he scanned his environment, instantly realizing where he was as he touched his bandaged head, the vision of the faceless assassin that rushed back to him in that instant propelling him into action, tearing the adhesive electrode pads from his body, the heart monitor flatlining in a monotonous tone.

Pulling the sheets back to spin his legs off the bed, he tried to stand, his head still dizzy. Willing his legs into motion, he staggered across the room dressed in nothing but his open backed gown, at the door suddenly remembering his belongings and turned around, a frantic search of the bedside cabinet draws turning up the zip lock bag.

Leaving his room unchallenged, O'Neil having relieved the Constable from guard duty to go and fetch coffee, Marko turned a corner just in time to miss the shouting nurses running down the hallway in response to the alarm that his monitor had triggered on the control desk. Passing the elevator, he disappeared through the stairwell fire door, leaving it to close slowly behind him. A second later, the elevator door slid open, Radica hearing the commotion down the corridor as she stepped out, spinning round as the stairwell door banged shut behind her. Out in the stairwell she scanned the flights below, then raced upwards as she heard another door shut a few flights above her.

The corridor on the sixth floor seemingly deserted, she retrieved her weapon with silencer attached tucked into the small of her back, trying the doors on either side, only to find them locked, before halfway along, one gave way. Slowly pushing the door open, Radica had to hold her nose as a foul stench assailed her nostrils. Closing the door quietly behind her, Ruger raised, she scanned the dark room, just able to make out the source of the smell, bed pans lying on the floor next to a series of beds arranged in rows down either side, the occupants emitting an assorted chorus of snores. She began to make her way down the left side, catching the faces of ancient looking men.

The sudden sound of loud flatulence from the other side of the room distracted her for a moment.

'Nurse,' she heard the perpetrator call out, turning to see an arm reaching upwards to try and reach the assistance pull cord, just a few inches beyond his grasp.

It was the bed four down from him that caught her eye, and without finishing her initial sweep of the first row, she approached, weapon raised as she reached for the bedsheet pulled up over the occupant's head, the sound of deep slumber suspiciously amiss, in that exact same moment, a figure sliding out from one of the last unchecked beds on the other side of the room. Whipping the sheet back with one swift moment, Radica discovered another harmless geriatric on his side, wide eyed, staring into space.

The heavy blow across the back of her head from the empty metal bedpan sent her head spinning, as blinded, she hit the floor on her side, the gun slipping out of her hands, her arms flailing wildly for it in the darkness.

The unmistakeable feel of the silencer against her temple froze her in her tracks, and in that moment a torrent of happy memories of her childhood with her family came flooding forth. Then suddenly, the sensation of the cold metal was gone, the vivid images in her mind still present, and she was sure that she was already in heaven.

The sound of a door opening and closing somewhere off it the distance stirred her from her thoughts and she tried to move, a throbbing pain cursing through her brain as she tried to lift her head. Drawing her elbows in to push herself up off the floor, she finally staggered to her feet, the dark room still spinning, and made for the door.

Lazlo, one of Aleksandar's house guards, sent to collect Marko from the dark alleyway across the road from the hospital, had to fight hard not to laugh as his half naked ride appeared from the shadows and jumped into the back of the vehicle.

'Where to guvnor?' Lazlo asked in a half competent attempt at mimicking a London cab driver.

'Just get me home,' came Marko's irritated reply, Lazlo left in no doubt by his tone that he was in no mood for jokes.

'We've got the boss's house on full lock down, nothing to worry about,' Lazlo confirmed, dropping the cockney accent.

Nothing to worry about, with you and your gorillas in charge, that's a laugh, thought Marko.

'Boss says everything will be ready for tomorrow night.'

Lazlo was referring to the social function at Aleksandar's mansion, an event that he held a few times a year for his rich business associates so that he could keep up the pretence that he was one of London's legitimate elite businessmen, the irony being that these so called London's finest who attended his parties were actually just a criminal as their host, but of course bent lawyers and financiers were always thought of as so much more respectable than plain old fashioned gangsters.

Opening her hotel room door into darkness, Radica reached for the light switch as the door closed behind her, freezing as something out of place caught her attention on the other side of the room. Her head still groggy from the concussion, she reached behind her back for the gun that wasn't there.

'Aren't we the night owl,' she heard a familiar voice say from over by the window, a tall slender silhouette against the night sky. Turning on the light, she saw Veronica with her back turned, gazing out.

'I can't honestly say that you've filled me with much confidence so far,' Veronica commented, her gaze still on the view.

'I love London at night, do you know why?' she continued after a long pause.

'Because you're a vampire?' Radica suggested sarcastically.

'I've been called much worse I can assure you,' came the reply.

'It's because all the violent seedy ugliness that this city stands for is concealed by the darkness. By the way, I must say that the view from your room at this hour is particularly pleasant.'

'I'm glad you like it,' Radica replied flatly.

At that, Veronica turned to face her.

'There is a place, not far from here, where they put naughty girls like you, an inhospitable Victorian prison where the view is far less appealing, but let me assure you, if you fail in your duty then you will never get to see it.'

Removing an unsealed envelope from her inside jacket pocket, Veronica placed it on a small table by the window.

'You're running out of time my dear,' she said softly into Radica's ear as she passed, opening the door to leave. Radica crossed the room and picked up the envelope, pulling out a small gold embossed invitation card.

By the time Aleksandar got home to West Hampstead at four in the morning after facing the tedious formality of the interview at New Scotland Yard conducted by the same corrupt detective sergeant on O'Neil's payroll that he had met last time, he was in no mood for the phone call he received from Marko, begging him to cancel his social function. No, Aleksandar had insisted, the party would go ahead as planned. They very rarely argued, and the instant Aleksandar cut Marko's call off in a rage, he knew that he would be the one to apologize to his young protege.

After examining his head wound in the mirror, reflecting on how lucky he was to be alive, Marko found himself unable to sleep, not because he had come closer to death than ever before out on the street that night, but because he found himself unable to come to terms with his decision to let the assassin live at the hospital.

She was a girl for sure, and he had glimpsed the side of her face as he knelt over her with the gun to her head, but the notion that this could be the girl that he had lost so many years ago was unfathomable. That girl had died back in Bosnia, he knew that, yet in that moment he had been unable to pull the trigger.

Sat out on his balcony wrapped up in his duvet against the cold night chill, exhaustion finally took him as the sun began to rise and he slipped into unconsciousness, dreaming about Radica for the first time in a long while. It was a warm summer evening, the gentle breeze from the sea caressing Marko's face as he sat alone on a wooden bench on a golden beach looking out at the horizon, the waves rolling on the sand. Feeling the gentle touch of a hand on his own, he turned his head to see her sat beside him. She looked just like he remembered her from Bosnia, young and innocent, her emerald eyes melting into his. Radica hadn't seemed to notice the calming sounds of the breeze and waves giving way to the ugly drone of busy traffic behind them, but Marko did. Turning around to look, he was met by the landscape of a city looming up, instantly recognizing the landmarks of London. He felt the warmth of Radica's hand turn abruptly stone cold and he turned back to see someone else staring at him, a young woman with darker hair, her green eyes not warm and inviting, but ice cold.

'Soon, you will die,' she said quietly, letting go of his hand to stand and walk away without looking back, dissolving into nothingness like a ghost. Startling awake in the morning light, the heavy drone of traffic down below, Marko desperately tried to recollect the image of that face that he had been so captivated by only moments before, but she was gone.

Driving to West Hampstead that evening, aware that she was no longer in control of her destiny, the setbacks of the previous twelve hours having seriously dented her confidence, and with the added pressure of her new acquaintance dictating the agenda, Radica felt a sense of panic sinking in, as if she had swum way out of her depth, with the tide now against her, dragging her further from the shore.

She thought about the orphanage, the crushing realization that she may never see her girls again constantly haunting her, the fear of what would become of them, especially her favourite, almost too much to bear. The instinct to up and run had taken hold as soon as she had found herself alone again in her hotel room after her unwanted guest had left, but she knew with an undeniable certainty that whoever it was that her shadow was working for, they would find her wherever she tried to hide.

Pulling up to the floodlit security gate in her black Porsche 911 provided by Veronica especially for the occasion, she watched a guard step out of the gatehouse, shouldering a compact Ingram submachine gun. Lowering the electric window, she smiled, handing him the invitation to inspect.

Signalling his colleague in the gatehouse, the steel gate slowly slid open with a heavy yawn, Radica proceeding up the long gravel drive, noting the armed guards patrolling the floodlit grounds, the huge mansion calling her to her destiny. An assortment of luxury cars sat parked neatly out front, another guard stood waiting, guiding her to her parking space, tucking her in neatly between a Bentley and a Rolls Royce.

Opening her door, offering his hand to help her out, she accepted, flashing her dazzling eyes at him, her chaperone unable to resist admiring her elegant form from behind as she glided towards the guarded front door.

Marko hated the tedious pretence of these occasions, loathed having to mingle with black tuxedoed overfed business moguls with their glamorous partners often half their age cosying up with Aleksandar, hoping for a slice of his empire in exchange for whatever so called business services they could offer.

Sat upstairs in Aleksandar's private office, reviewing some prospective commercial property acquisitions that had been shortlisted, he checked his watch yet again, finally tearing himself away, the inevitable obligatory meet and greet charade downstairs beckoning.

Descending the wide sweeping staircase to the reception lobby, the stitched graze on the side of his head drew a few strange looks as he entered the huge high ceilinged main lounge. Aleksandar was already in full flow after an hour on the whisky, his loud booming voice echoing like a ship foghorn in the already crowded room.

Slowly making his way through the throng, Marko came upon him talking to a tall woman with her back to him, her open backed long black dress hugging her figure perfectly, her auburn hair tied up in a bun.

'Come and meet our lovely guest,' he called out as he noticed Marko. As soon as she turned around, fixing him with those emerald eyes, he knew, having to force an impassive expression to mask his surprise. Radica didn't seem to register in the slightest, and he realized that she was either a master at hiding her true emotions or truly didn't recognize him after all these years.

'This is Francesca, she's an art dealer.' Aleksandar announced. 'Perhaps you could show her the collection,' he suggested as he caught sight of a new arrival entering the room.

'Excuse me,' he said, offering Radica a courteous smile before marching away. Marko knew he had to act fast to get her alone, away from her primary target, where he would have time to think.

'Champagne?' he suggested, noting the empty glass in her hand. As if on cue, a tall white coated waiter sauntered by, Marko deftly lifting two glasses from his silver tray, handing her one.

Time to get down to business Radica thought.

'Weren't you going to show me Aleksandar's collection?' she asked, taking a sip.

'Yes, of course,' Marko replied, leading her across the room and out into the reception hallway to a door at the far end, opening it to beckon Radica inside. The collection was a priceless treasure trove of classic and contemporary works, all by dead artists. Their footsteps echoed on the oak floors as they began their tour, Marko stopping at a macabre hideous self portrait by Francis Bacon.

'I'm still trying to figure this one out,' Marko commented as Radica stood beside him, following his gaze as he looked up, admiring the work.

'Bacon's portraits always look so, tormented,' he added.

'Perhaps that's because he was tormented,' Radica replied, keeping her eyes on Marko as she reached up slowly with her free hand to remove a three inch metal pin concealed in her hair bun, hiding it in her palm as she lowering her hand again.

'I'd never thought about it that way, yes you're probably right.'

'Show me the Renoir,' she suggested, already having noted the painting further along the wall when they entered the room. As Marko turned away to lead her, she pushed the pin forward in her palm with her thumb, ready.

As if anticipating her next move, Marko suddenly stopped and turned to face her, halting her in her tracks, staring directly into her eyes.

'You know what's strange?' he announced.

'What?' Radica replied, trying not to sound taken aback.

'You haven't asked me how I got this,' he said, running a finger over his wound.

Radica's fingers tightened around the pin still hidden from view.

'Perhaps you did something to deserve it,' she replied coldly, calculating the exact position behind Marko's left ear.

'Why would you say that?' he replied, feigning surprise.

Radica knew it was now or never.

'Here you are,' she heard a familiar loud voice boom from the doorway, Aleksandar approaching as Radica's mind scrambled to try and recalculate the sequence of moves, instantly realizing it would be suicidal.

'Don't let him steal you away for too long young lady, or there's no telling where your evening will end,' he teased as he reached Marko's side.

'Sounds dangerous,' Radica goaded.

'Oh believe me, he is my dear,' Aleksandar's laugh bringing her blood to the boil.

'I'm not the one who's in danger,' Radica retorted involuntarily, regretting those words as soon as they left her mouth.

'Is that so?' Aleksandar chuckled.

In that instant Radica saw Marko's eyes shift almost imperceptibly from her face, downwards to her hand, and she knew that if she made a move now, it would be her last.

'I should be going,' she announced.

'So soon?' Aleksandar replied, sounding genuinely disappointed.

'I'll show you out,' Marko hastily interjected, taking her gently by the arm to guide her out of harm's way.

In the lady's room, Radica hid the pin in her bun again, taking deep breaths to try and regain her composure. She feared that her new female captor might finally put that bullet in her head if she returned to her hotel empty handed again, but this way she could at least try and buy herself more time. When she emerged, Marko was waiting with her long designer black leather coat over his arm.

'Have dinner with me, tomorrow,' he asked, as holding her coat open, she nervously turned her back to him to help her slide her arms into it.

'But you haven't even told me your name?' she replied.

Driving back to the hotel, Radica had to fight the impulse to speed away in the opposite direction and go into hiding in some quiet little village somewhere hundreds of miles away where Veronica might never find her, but she knew with a crushing certainty that her freedom would be short lived.

Opening her hotel room door, she was alarmed not to see the familiar silhouette of her would be executioner stood over by the window, instead, a small white envelope had been placed neatly on her pillow. Opening it with foreboding, she removed a handwritten note with the words, 'Good luck with your dinner date tomorrow my dear, let's hope it's not your last supper,' confirmation that her master had eyes and ears everywhere.

She lay back on the bed and thought about the bodyguard. If he had suspected she might be the assassin, then why had he let her escape, help her to even. She could only conjecture that he was the kind that preferred a lengthy hunt before the final kill. Whatever his motive, it was irrelevant as far as Radica was concerned. Tomorrow, he would die.

THIRTEEN

Marko had spent the day deciding when he would make his play. It was too risky to try over dinner, she might panic and run, leaving him unable to control her next move. He needed to get her alone and take her by surprise to stay in control, then he would be able to explain. The notion of her refusing to believe him despite everything he was going to say to her, was more terrifying than anything he had experienced, the thought of having to choose between her life or his filling him with a morbid dread.

Glancing up from his table in the classy, dimly lit Italian restaurant, the array of couples sat talking quietly over candlelight, he suddenly felt himself longing to be just like them.

Studying the reflection of his own candle flame in his glass of red wine that he had barely touched from the bottle on the table, rotating it this way and that, he thought of how when he had awoken that morning after a dreamless sleep, his first notion had been of her, a vision of pure beauty in her long black dress, her eyes more dazzling now than ever.

Neither of them was the innocent youngster of yesteryear anymore. They had evolved into strangers formed from their tragic pasts and Marko's journey from adolescence to adulthood had led him down a road that would likely end in death way before his time, he knew that.

Up until last night, Marko had been a man with nothing to live for but his work, but the very moment that he had laid eyes on her again, his heart pumping in his chest, that same unmistakeable surge of warmth rushing through his body like he had felt that night when they had escaped, his whole reason for being had suddenly changed, and now for the first time in years, he was on an errand of mercy to save someone's life instead of taking it.

He could only surmise that Radica had killed Emil out of vengeance for something that had occurred back then, and whilst he wouldn't be completely surprised to discover that Emil had indulged in the atrocities that he knew had occurred, he was certain that Aleksandar was innocent of any such savagery.

His notion of salvaging his relationship with her was marred by the fear that with everything she had been through back in Bosnia, Radica may have passed the point of no return, her trauma rendering her incapable of love, locking her in a singular cold unemotive world where she saw everything and everybody as a threat to her existence.

'Sorry I'm late.' Marko didn't register immediately, taking a moment to stir from his thoughts. Looking up he saw Radica hanging her long leather coat just a little too carefully over the back of the chair opposite, a sure sign to Marko that she was packing a weapon. Taking her seat in an off the shoulder black top and smart jeans, Marko marvelled at how alluring she looked with her hair down.

'I hope you like red wine?' Marko offered with a warm smile.

'Red is perfect, pour away,' Radica replied, taking a gulp as soon as Marko had filled her glass, savouring the rich taste. 'That's a good bottle,' she complimented, placing her glass down as she pondered her first move.

'So, Stephan, how did you meet Aleksandar?' she enquired, not quite making eye contact yet. Marko had planned to begin by throwing in a few vague clues early on.

'He rescued me when I was young.'

'Rescued you?'

'I was an orphan.'

'I'm sorry, what happened to your parents?' Enough for now Marko conjectured.

'It's a long story.'

'We have all night.'

'Another time perhaps.'

'You're being rather presumptuous, aren't you?' Radica smirked.

'Sorry, old habits.'

'I bet.'

'Anyway, so what's your story?'

'Mine's pretty simple really, I'm just here to make up for a lost childhood.'

'Why, didn't your parents take you to Buckingham Palace when you were young?' Marko retorted, studying her face to assess her reaction. He didn't want to get too sarcastic with his remarks, but he needed to gauge her self control so he could temper his approach accordingly. Radica's expression faltered a fraction, just enough for him to see a flash of venom in her eyes, bringing home the realization that she intended to spare him the same lack of mercy as that intended for Aleksandar.

The tension of that moment fortunately passed with the arrival of the tall waiter, handing them their menus before sauntering away. Neither of them were interested in eating, each for different reasons, their paths propelling them on as collision course that they were eager to bring to a head.

Averting eye contact by burying their gaze in their menus, each waited for the other to make the suggestion that would permit them the privacy they needed to conclude the evening's business. It was Radica that made the move, placing her menu down to reach forward to lift her wine glass from the middle of the table, leaving her other hand alongside within his reach. He looked up from his menu, looking into her eyes, trying not to become hypnotized by her gaze as he put down his own menu, sliding his own hand forward, the touch of their fingertips igniting that spark he had thought he would never experience again. Her sharp pupils seemed to soften in that moment, inviting him like a seductress, but not, he knew, to her bed.

'I don't think much of the menu,' he finally invited.

'Me neither.'

'My apartment has a great view down the Thames.'

'I'd love to see it,' Radica jumped in.

'Shall I get the bill?'

'Good idea, I'll just go and powder my nose.' Getting up from her seat to lift her coat from the chair, Radica headed towards the far side of the room with it carefully draped over her arm.

Marko knew the real reason why she had gone to the ladies, having already checked his own weapon concealed under his jacket in the small of his back, one bullet from the full magazine already chambered and ready, the safety off. He had been taught how to retrieve his gun safely from this position by Aleksandar when he had first come to London, mastering the art of avoiding the sensitive hair trigger.

In the lady's room, Radica locked the cubicle door and rechecked her replacement Glock that had arrived later that afternoon than she would have liked. She had left the silencer behind, knowing its added bulk would only be a hindrance at such close quarters. Chambering a bullet, she left the safety on, there would be time to slip it off when they got there.

Sat in his black Range Rover across the street, O'Neil thought it somewhat strange to see Marko and Radica emerge arm in arm, but brushed it aside, taking comfort in the knowledge that the target seemed to have fallen for her charms, like a lamb to the slaughter.

He watched as they parted, setting off in opposite directions towards their cars parked along the street not far apart. With Marko leading the way in his Mercedes, Radica followed directly behind in her Porsche, O'Neil pulling out into the traffic to follow a few cars behind, unaware of the tailing vehicle three cars behind him.

As Radica drove, she reflected on the how oddly natural and familiar it had felt when they had touched, and for an instant she found herself reminded of the boy from Bosnia who she had stopped thinking about a long time ago. She cast those thoughts aside, telling herself it was her memory playing tricks on her.

Arriving at the Thameside apartment block, both cars disappeared down a ramp into the underground car park, O'Neil pulling up opposite, the car behind him way back, keeping out of sight.

Marko had left the lounge ceiling light on low at his apartment, so when he pushed the door open Radica wouldn't be greeted by darkness, and panic. He showed her in, Radica careful not to take her eyes off him as she stepped in front, watching him close the door and turn the lock.

'You weren't kidding about the view, were you,' Radica complimented as he walked her towards the bank of floor to ceiling windows overlooking the night lights of the Thames.

'Would you like a drink?' Marko offered.

Radica turned to face him full on then, taking a step towards him, her mouth aligning tantalisingly with his.

'I have something much better in mind,' she teased, her green eyes burning with an intensity he had never seen before, drawing him to her. Their lips touched, a surge, more powerful than any adrenaline he had ever experienced flowing through his very being and he had to fight not to close his eyes in the ecstasy of that moment.

Then he saw her eyes suddenly change, the pupils almost imperceptibly contract, and in that instant, they were backing away from each, their guns out and levelled, the exact predicament that Marko had so wanted to avoid. He had been here before with seasoned bodyguards who could always be counted on to remain calm under pressure, but Radica was on a personal vendetta where she might squeeze the trigger impulsively without thinking.

'Radica, listen to me,' Marko said calmly.

'How do you know my name?' she replied, her wild eyes narrowing.

'I'm not who you think I am.'

'I don't care.'

'Why do you need to kill Aleksandar?'

'Because he murdered my family.'

'In Bosnia?'

'What does it matter?'

'Because I was there, with you.'

'No, you're lying?' Radica retorted, her finger tensing on the trigger.

'Wait,' Marko pleaded, slowly raising his free hand as he kept his weapon trained, eyes focussed on Radica, reaching up to feel his shirt collar.

'Stop,' Radica shouted. In that instant, Marko braced himself for the worst, loosening the three top buttons on his shirt, pulling it open to reveal the dog tags around his neck, feeling for the inscription on the surface of the top one to make sure it was turned outwards, breaking the chain around his neck with one quick yank, holding them up to her. Radica's face turned ashen as she saw the inscription, the gun shaking precariously in her trembling hand.

'No, you can't be.'

'We escaped from the British camp and found shelter in a cabin in the woods, remember?'

'No,' Radica insisted pointlessly, already knowing it to be true.

'I gave you one of these for good luck and the next morning I was captured, but you got away, and when I came looking for you, I found your tag in the hand of a dead blond girl with her face all blown away, and I thought...'

Radica didn't realize that she had lowered her weapon as she began to cry. Then she felt him take her in his warm embrace, sobbing in his arms for what seemed like an eternity.

As they sat together on the couch hand in hand, Radica told Marko about the day that Aleksandar and Emil had come to her village. Marko didn't want to believe, he had spent the last ten years with someone he had come to see as his father figure, yet as he listened, he found himself unable to refute the sincerity of Radica's story, having to fight to breathe as the crushing certainty took hold.

In the cruel twist of fate that followed, Radica asked Marko about what had happened to his own family. He found himself speaking about the events of that night for the very first time since it had happened. When he named the man with the childlike grin who had lost most of his hand, he saw Radica's expression turn to stone, her eyes involuntarily widening, her face frozen in shock, and in that moment he knew.

O'Neil was growing increasingly frustrated as he waited for what seemed like an eternity. He breathed a sigh of relief as the Porsche finally appeared at the top of the ramp, turning into the street to speed away from him. His moment of elation was short lived however, as the Mercedes appeared, turning at the top of the ramp, heading in his direction and he found himself cowering low in his seat to avoid being seen as Marko raced past.

It took him a moment to realize as his mind spun uncontrollably, then it hit him like a sledgehammer, and he felt the air being sucked from his lungs as the final piece of the puzzle that had eluded him for so many years fell into place.

Starting the engine, he screeched away, dialling Vladimir's mobile phone to warn him, cursing as it went straight to voicemail. He hastily dialled a second number.

In their penthouse suite, Bosko and Jakov assumed their usual positions, collapsed on the leather couch in front of the television, enthralled in a Dirty Harry movie, a noisy gun battle being played out.

Bosko grunted angrily as he heard a knock at the door, Jakov too enthralled to even notice as his partner got up. Looking through the peephole, Bosko unbuttoned his jacket, loosening his weapon in its holster before opening the door.

'What do you want?' he growled, looking the black suited figure of Marko up and down.

'He sent me,' Marko replied, his voice barely audible over the din of the prolonged gunfight on the television.

'Who did?' Bosko demanded, eyes narrowing, his shooting hand unconsciously moving a few inches nearer to his holster.

'The policeman. He wants me to give a message to your boss,' Marko replied, calculating his sequence of moves. Bosko beckoned him inside, closing the door, Jakov glancing around momentarily before turning back to the movie.

'Arms,' Bosko barked, gesturing with his hands, Marko obediently raising his limbs, taking the opportunity to scrutinize the room as his host patted him down, retrieving a white envelope from his inside jacket pocket.

'What's this?' Bosko asked, holding it up.

'The message,' Marko replied flatly, Bosko staring at it. 'Aren't you going to give it to him?' he questioned.

'Later, he's resting.'

'He said it was urgent, maybe you should read it.'

Bosko hesitated for a moment before tearing the envelope open, taking out a folded piece of white paper to open it out, his expression changing to one of confusion as he saw the blank sheet.

'Jakov,' Bosko yelled, his cry cut short by the jab to his Adam's apple as Marko reached for his assailant's holstered pistol with his other hand.

Jakov was on his feet with surprising speed as he reached for his weapon, but he was too slow for Marko, taking two bullets in the chest. Finishing a choking Bosko already on his knees with a single shot to the head, Marko was across the room in an instant.

As the bedroom door flew open, Vladimir, roused from his sleep by the gunshots, was already off the bed and going for his gun on the bedside drawer, but the two shots to his thighs brought him down before he could reach it. Down on his knees, he looked up to see Marko stood over him, the gun barrel against his forehead.

'Who the hell are you?' Vladimir demanded though gritted teeth. Marko didn't reply immediately, he wanted to savour this moment.

'I was just a boy when we met,' Marko finally said, his eyes burning with fury.

'Met, when?'

'Bosnia, you came to our house, it was my birthday.' Vladimir's eyes danced as he searched his memory. 'Time for your birthday present, Marko,' Marko mimicked. For a moment there was nothing from his captive, and then Vladimir's eyes suddenly widened as that fateful day came back to him.

'No, that's impossible, you were in the helicopter,' Vladimir exclaimed in disbelief.

'Yes, but I survived.'

'But, how did you find me?'

'A little girl told me.'

'Girl, what little…? Vladimir stopped short as a terrible notion struck him.

'Your special, little girl.'

'No,' Vladimir mumbled to himself as the betrayal hit home, the notion that his innocent minded protégé had gotten one step ahead of him, deceived him.

He looked straight into Marko's eyes then, grinning, the defiant expression of a dead man with nothing left to lose. He knew what was coming, and in those moments as he waited for oblivion, he was content that this mere jumped up farm boy would never have the satisfaction of seeing fear in his eyes.

Radica had agreed to wait for Marko, yet as she neared her destination, she felt herself buckling under the weight of an undeniable compulsion to make her move as soon as she arrived.

Parking up in the darkness at the end of the deserted private access road, Radica scaled the security gate and after a short march, careful to keep away from the gaze of the security cameras, found herself at the entrance to the unlit yard that Marko had described, the gate open, a black Bentley parked outside the cabin, a soft glow from inside the only illumination.

Stooping low in the darkness, she began to make her way towards the door of the cabin, her weapon ready. It was a dull thud that alerted her first, then she felt it, a searing pain in her left thigh as her leg went into spasm and gave way from under her. Collapsing to the ground she tried to level her gun in the direction of the sound of approaching footsteps, but was too slow, the kick connecting with her jaw, knocking her unconscious.

A foreboding dread seized Marko as he heard his mobile phone ring, compounded when he saw Aleksandar's number on the screen. Keeping his eyes on the road, he picked up the handset cradled in the central armrest, not daring to speak.

'I have the assassin,' he heard, those words resonating with a dizzying intensity in his head like a deafening church bell.

'Where,' Marko replied, desperately trying to keep his voice from cracking.

'Come to the docks.' The line went dead.

It normally took twenty minutes to drive to Tilbury from his apartment at this hour, Aleksandar knew that, and Marko was already halfway there. His compulsion to save Radica was commanding him to race straight there, but he knew he had resist. The remainder of the journey seemed to take forever, the nightmarish visions of the torture he would be commanded to subject her too her flashing through his mind.

Pulling into the yard, Marko parked up next to the Bentley and unsurprisingly, O'Neil's familiar Black Range Rover. Switching off the engine, he took a deep breath, trying to keep the rising tide of panic at bay. Through a metal grilled window, he could see Aleksandar sat in the darkness, his face just recognizable in the soft glow of the reading lamp.

As he opened the cabin door, he immediately picked out O'Neil stood at Aleksandar's shoulder in the gloom. Closing the door, he glanced right to see the form of Radica slumped semi-conscious, tied to a metal chair, wrists and ankles bound, her hair fallen over her face.

'Of course, it had to be a girl, didn't it,' Marko exclaimed with an ironic smile.

'She's no girl, she's a savage,' Aleksandar retorted angrily.

'Then we'd better find out who sent her,' Marko replied, knowing he needed to buy some time.

'She won't to tell us anything, she knows she's going to die,' came Aleksandar's reply, those words sending Marko's pulse racing with panic, knowing what the next command would be.

'She might be persuaded,' Marko replied, trying not to plead.

'Kill her,' Aleksandar barked.

Turning back to Radica, Marko unbuttoned his jacket, his holstered weapon strapped to his side. He crouched directly in front of Radica, hiding her face from view as he lifted her head. The touch of his hand stirring her, she slowly opened her eyes, in that moment recognizing him, her involuntary expression obscured from her captors. Glancing down at her leg wound, Marko was able to deduce that it wasn't life threatening.

Then he stood slowly, reaching for his weapon, but as he spun, raising his Glock, he heard the dull thuds of the silencer, two bullets hitting him in the chest, twirling him like a drunken dancer into the wall before he dropped to the floor motionless to the right of a wide eyed Radica. Before Aleksandar could react, he was staring dumbfounded down the barrel of O'Neil's Glock an inch from his forehead.

'All this time you were lying to me,' O'Neil snarled.

'What are you talking about?' Aleksandar offered.

'Your little boy from Bosnia, the one who escaped.'

'But what does that matter now, he's dead.' Aleksandar pleaded.

'You know what, you're right, it doesn't matter,' O'Neil agreed with a conciliatory smile, Aleksandar breathing a sigh of relief as O'Neil lowered his weapon a fraction. 'But I still have to kill you,' he concluded flatly.

'What?' Aleksandar exclaimed.

'It's time for you to step down.'

'Step down, for who?'

'The Serb.'

Aleksandar didn't get a chance to reply, the bullet exiting through the back of his head, spraying the wall behind him with the greyish red stew of his brains.

Turning to see Radica struggling furiously against her restraints, O'Neil approached, grinning like a Cheshire cat, his hostage glaring up at him, eyes wide with vengeful hatred, straining every muscle in her body to try and break free. He stood over her, chuckling to himself as she struggled in vain to get at him, the chair inching slowly forwards from her exertions.

'So, here we are again,' he finally said, placing his foot against a leg of the chair to halt its progress. 'Except this time, your boyfriend here won't be able to save you,' he mocked, glancing away at Marko's motionless form. 'I can't tell you how much I've been looking forward to this moment,' he gloated.

'Aren't you going to rape me first?' Radica piped up unexpectedly, freezing him in his tracks as she stared straight into his eyes defiantly. 'What's the matter, can't you do it anymore,' she goaded, smiling as his surprised expression changed to anger.

Radica found herself toppling backwards in her chair as O'Neil thrust his foot into her chest. She braced for the impact, craning her neck forward to protect the back of her head as she hit the floor. Placing his gun out of reach on the filing cabinet next to her, O'Neil frantically unfastened the buckles on the cargo straps restraining her hands and feet before descending on her like a bird of prey, straddling her as he went for her jeans belt.

Caught up in his frenzy, he didn't register the cold sensation against the back of his head for a few moments.

'Golden rule for any assassin, always make it a head shot,' he heard Marko say, turning his head to see him tapping the bullet proof vest concealed under his shirt. 'Up,' Marko commanded, O'Neil slowly getting to his feet, the barrel still pressed against the back of his head as Radica stared up in disbelief. Marko kicked the sides of O'Neil's ankles from behind, checking for a backup weapon.

'Over by the desk, move,' Marko instructed O'Neil feeling that cold metal prodding him forward, Aleksandar slumped back in his chair, greeting him with wide vacant eyes. 'Turn around.' As O'Neil obeyed, Marko stepped back at arm's length, his gun still trained.

'On your knees.' O'Neil resisted, testing his captor. 'Now,' came a shout from behind Marko, Radica approaching at a slow stagger, O'Neil's Glock in her hand. As he dropped to his knees, O'Neil knew this was the end, yet he didn't feel panicked. Instead, an almost tranquil calm had taken over, and in that moment of reconciliation only one question remained, whether to offer a final confession about her sister or to take it to the grave.

As Marko stood aside to let Radica take his place, O'Neil looked up, fixing her with an unfaltering gaze.

'Killing me won't change what happened to her,' he said in a tragic tone. Radica froze, her eyes narrowing.

'All these years, you've been searching, haven't you?'

'Tell me,' Radica half commanded, half begged, as she raised his weapon. He wanted to see her cry, just once before he died, so he kept silent, dragging the moment out. She stepped forward, pressing the barrel against his forehead, but still he kept his gaze steady. Then he saw it, her eyes welling up, and he knew it was time.

'They were meant to be on another ship,' he said.

'What ship?'

'But the truck broke down on the way to the port.'

'Where were they taken?'

'There was a storm,' O'Neil replied as if from far away, for a moment his gaze shifting away from her. Radica began to weep as she heard those words, bracing herself. 'When the ship finally docked, a number of the containers were missing.' Radica's face turned ashen as those words took hold like a vice.

'Their container was swept overboard,' he concluded, his gaze returning to his executioner. 'They drowned,' he taunted, a snide grin curling his mouth. She pressed the silencer harder against his forehead, her trigger finger tensing as he smiled up at her unflinchingly, willing her to squeeze just a tiny bit more.

'Radica, wait,' came Marko's voice from behind. She hesitated as Marko stepped forward, his gun trained on O'Neil.

"Trust me,' he begged, taking her other hand in his as he kept his eyes on O'Neil. She looked at him incredulously, then back at her captive, her eyes darting between the two of them. Then, fighting her every instinct to pull that trigger, she lowered the gun, a dumbfounded O'Neil watching Marko lead Radica, backing away towards the door with his weapon still trained, Radica stepping outside, quickly followed by Marko who quickly closed it behind him. When he heard the lock turn, O'Neil instantly surmised that they had decided to turn him over to his own establishment, but that feeling of relief at having been given stay of execution ended moments later when he heard the unmistakeable sound of a forklift motor starting up.

Looking out of the side window he was met by the blinding glare of the forklift's night beam and found himself thrown off balance as the cabin shifted, a series of muffled bangs sounding under his feet as the anchor chains snapped off their moorings, the jarring noise of metal scraping on concrete piercing his eardrums as the cabin began sliding along the ground.

In his panic, he picked up a small bronze sculpture on the desk and hurled it against the window, reaching through the shattered glass to wrestle with the metal grill, just able to make out Marko sat in the forklift as the cabin continued on its path. O'Neil suddenly felt his prison tilt upwards, fighting to stay on his feet as the structure balanced precariously for a moment before continuing its inexorable roll, sliding off the side of the dock and hurling him across the room as it turned on its side on the way down, crashing into the river, the impact almost knocking him unconscious.

The cabin surfaced partially, righting itself like a cork for a moment, before the weight of the water rushing in through the broken window began to roll the structure over, affording O'Neil a brief glimpse of Marko and Radica looking down at him from the edge of the dock, before the cabin's rotation took them from view.

The freezing cold water rose quicker than O'Neil had feared, the weight of the structure too great to stop the trapped air bubble needed to keep the cabin afloat from being pushed out through the broken window, his tomb sinking into the murky depths. The world around him receded into silence as he closed his eyes, forcing his mind back to that fateful training exercise in the Arctic over fifteen years before. They were marching fully laden with kit across the snow swept landscape when suddenly, the ice under their feet began to crack. As they scrambled for safety, O'Neil and two of his comrades crashed into the icy water, disappearing under the surface.

Dragged down towards their icy deaths as they struggled desperately to get their heavy backpacks off, O'Neil managed to free himself and swim upwards, only to find that the current had carried him away from the opening. Upside down against the ice, O'Neil took his bowie knife from his pocket and thrusts it upwards into the ice to stop himself drifting further, but he knew there was no time to try and get back to the hole. With his free hand, he punched the ice, over and over, all sensation in his fist completely numbed by the icy water that was turning red. With one last almighty punch that exhausted the very last of the air in his lungs, the ice finally gave way, and he squeezed his head through, gasping. It was in that instant as he felt the oxygen rushing into his lungs, that he realized something wasn't right. The sky was black, and the water was oily, its vile taste making him choke. Then, as he turned around, he saw the dockside above him, Marko and Radica nowhere to be seen.

He swam to the concrete wall towering out of the water, reaching out to grab a rusty steel ladder, praying that it held. An indescribable pain, greater than anything he had ever experienced in his life, shot up his arm as he gripped the metal, forcing a scream from his lungs.

Hauling himself up with his other hand he lay exhausted and freezing on the dockside. Even in the darkness he was sure he had broken almost every bone in his hand, sharp edged fractures poking through the surface of his swollen skin like a miniature mountain range, and he realized that in his trance, he had miraculously managed to punch the metal grill free from its housing.

Inside his apartment, Marko locked the door behind them and as he turned to embrace Radica, she beat him to it, kissing him passionately full on the mouth for what seemed like a glorious eternity. Leading her to the couch he sat her down, kneeling to examine her leg wound. The shallow channel of flesh that had been carried away along with the fabric of her jeans by the bullet had fortunately not left any muscle loss in his wake.

'You need to take these off, so I can bathe it, but you can change in my room if you like, my bath robe is on the back of the door,' Marko offered.

'It's alright, I'm fine right here,' Radica replied, staring into his eyes, eager to feel his hands on her.

As he slipped out of his jacket and went off into the kitchen to fetch the medical supplies, she took her boots and socks off, peeling her jeans down her long legs to drop them on the wooden floor. When Marko reappeared, the sight of her in a state of undress instantly sent a surge of arousal through him, and in that next moment he was kneeling back down in front of her, wanting nothing more than to touch her, to taste her.

'This is going to sting,' he warned, pressing the gauze doused in antiseptic onto the wound, Radica bravely stifling the pain, the touch of her firm skin through the material making him fear he was about to lose control. Then, removing the pad, Marko slowly wrapped a bandage around her high, the mere touch of his fingers on her soft flesh spiralling her desire. Finishing the dressing, he found himself gazing up into her emerald eyes, this time burning with a different king of fury, a passion, and it took him a moment to realize his hand had moved a few inches higher up her thigh. As he went to pull his hand away, Radica reached out with both hands to stop him, drawing his hand further up her thigh, until his fingers were brushing the hem of her panties.

She found herself laying back on the couch then, feeling the tender caress of his lips through that thin fabric, his hands reaching up to slip her panties down her legs, burying his mouth in the warmth of her womanhood. Radica's world span as waves of pleasure flowed through her body, growing in intensity. Then she was calling out Marko's name over and over as she felt her body rising from the couch. As the pleasure reached its crescendo, she screamed out his name, before collapsing back down again.

FOURTEEN

Radica and Marko were walking hand in hand, waist deep in a hayfield, the sun warm on their skin. They stopped and lay down, gazing up at the cloudless blue sky, the tall crop swaying above them gently in the breeze, a bird singing in a nearby tree.

'We don't have much time,' Radica suddenly said, turning her head to look at him.

'What do you mean?' Marko enquired, surprised, propping himself up on an elbow.

'They'll be coming for us soon.'

'Who will?' Marko replied as Radica stood, towering over him. From out of nowhere a gun appeared in her hand.

'Radica, what are you doing?' Marko protested, getting to his knees.

'I'm sorry Marko,' she choked, levelling the weapon at his head as the tears ran down her face.

Radica jolted awake, sitting bolt upright in the bed, the loud crack of the gunshot still echoing in her head. Marko stirred, looking up at her.

'What is it?' he asked, half asleep, his hand reaching out to touch her.

'Nothing, just a bad dream,' she replied, laying back down to pull the sheets back over her. She turned on her side, feeling his warm embrace from behind.

'What was it about?' he murmured.

'Nothing, go back to sleep.'

Within moments Marko's breathing had slowed again as he drifted back into a deep slumber. Radica stared at the wall, wide eyed, waiting until she was sure he was fast asleep before slipping slowly from his arms and sliding out of bed.

Donning his white cotton robe, she stepped out into the lounge. Through the wide expanse of windows, the sun was rising over London's skyline, and with it, the sure certainty that her captor would reappear before it set again. She sat on the couch, her mind drifting, lavishing in the wonder of the previous night when they had made love, before that memory was abruptly marred by the realization there was no way of avoiding the inevitable. There was no point in them running, but she at least wanted the chance to tell Marko the truth.

'Radica?' a voice called out from far away, stirring her from her trance. 'What are you doing up so early?' She looked up to see Marko, the morning light streaming in through the windows, realizing she must have been away for hours. In that instant she was gripped again by that same morbid certainty, Marko registering the look of sheer dread in her eyes that she now found herself unable to hide.

'What is it?' he asked, taking her hands in his as he sat next to her.

Radica took deep breath, preparing to speak. The intercom buzzed loudly, startling her, both of them looking up in the direction of the door before exchanging questioning glances, Marko getting up. At the door he pressed the button on the wall console. For a moment there was nothing, only a deafening silence.

'Good morning young lovers, I trust you slept well,' came a voice, distorted but still unmistakeable. They stared at each other in disbelief. 'Don't think about trying to escape, the building's surrounded.'

Radica jumped up and stared down through the windows at two armoured black police vans, their identification numbers painted in bold white on the rooves. She turned to Marko, shaking her head slowly.

'I'm coming up for a little chat before we take you in, so don't try anything stupid.'

The intercom went dead, just giving them time to dress frantically before there was a knock at the door. Marko opened it, O'Neil stood in the doorway dressed in a grey suit, jacket open, no holster, his wounded hand in a plaster cast. Astonished to see his uninvited guest not packing a visible weapon, Marko had to fight the compulsion to strangle him where he stood.

'Don't worry, you'll have plenty of time to think about me from the inside of a cell,' O'Neil commented smugly. Over Marko's shoulder O'Neil could see Radica staring at him from the lounge. 'Aren't you going to invite me in?' he said to Marko.

'You'd be a fool to step through that door,' Radica announced.

'Trust me my dear, I'm the only person keeping you both alive right now.'

Marko reluctantly stepped aside to let O'Neil pass before closing the door.

'Nice place you've got here,' O'Neil complimented, as he wandered through the lounge towards Radica, flanked by his host.

'Shame you won't be staying much longer,' he added, Radica glaring at him as he walked straight past her without so much as a glance, standing in front of the bank of windows, his back turned in a deliberate taunt. He looked down to the street below to see ten masked black uniformed armed police officers shouldering compact semi-automatic assault rifles, awaiting his command. Taking out a two way radio from his jacket, he pressed a button.

'I'm inside the apartment,' he confirmed, releasing the button.

'Awaiting your command,' came the reply. Staring out at the view, O'Neil waited for a long moment before beginning his victory speech.

'It's funny how things turn out, don't you think?' he conjectured, still gazing out, waiting a moment to see if he got a reply. 'Last night I was dead and you two were celebrating, and now here we are again, just the three of us.'

'Let's get this over with,' Radica interjected irritably.

'Oh no, I want to enjoy this moment, after all, I think I've earned it,' O'Neil retorted.

'You won't get away with this,' Radica shouted.

'But I will you see, now that I've tracked down the killers responsible for last night's murders at Tilbury docks, not to mention the three dead bodies at the Savoy and the massacre at the club.' He paused for a moment. 'And by the way, there's no need to worry about poor Vladimir, there are plenty more Serbs ready to take his place.'

'That's a very well thought out plan, but you're forgetting one thing,' he heard Radica say.

'Oh yes, and what's that?' O'Neil countered smugly. He waited for her answer, but there was none. As he turned, he saw Radica reach behind her back and produce her Glock, Marko stood out of reach.

'Radica don't. If you do this, we're both dead,' Marko yelled instinctively, moving towards her.

'Get back,' she shouted, turning the gun on him, her conviction freezing him in his tracks.

'Listen to your boyfriend,' O'Neil added hastily, raising his radio as Radica levelled the gun at him.

'You think you have it all figured out don't you,' Radica said, something in her delivery unsettling him. 'You have no idea who you're really working for,' she added with a knowing grin. O'Neil pondered that comment for an instant, calculating the odds. 'You can't keep me alive, so what have I got to lose,' she concluded, raising the gun higher to aim at his head.

'Radica, no,' Marko shouted as O'Neil depressed the radio button. He didn't have time to get his first word out, the back of his head exploding as the bullet exited and shattered the window behind him. His lifeless corpse tumbled backwards and dropped from view through the window aperture, a heavy thud following from below.

'What have you done?' Marko yelled. Radica tossed the weapon across the floor and marched over to him, surprising him with a passionate kiss.

'Whatever happens now, I want you to know that I never forgot you,' she offered sadly, dropping to her knees, raising her hands behind her head, Marko joining her in readiness for the invasion. Time seemed to stand still for them both as they looked into each other's eyes, before the sound of the apartment door crashing open brought them back to the harsh unforgiving reality of their fate.

Outside the apartment building, they were escorted handcuffed into the back of one of the armoured vans by four of their masked captors, the waiting sergeant slamming the two rear doors behind them and climbing up into the passenger seat of the cab.

Sat opposite each other on the metal benches running down either side, flanked by their silent faceless custodians, Marko searched Radica's face as the vehicle moved off, trying to get her attention, but she was far away, a blank look in her eyes that remained fixed for what seemed to Marko to last for hours on route.

Finally, the vehicle came to a halt, Radica stirring as she heard a familiar sound, the grating of heavy steel doors sliding open. Rumbling slowly forward before stopping, the engine fell silent.

Radica looked at Marko as they heard the cab door open, moments later, the double doors of the van pulled open by the sergeant, shouldering his weapon.

Shuffling forward to jump down from the vehicle into the familiar dark cavernous warehouse, they saw a shadowy figure sat behind a metal desk, Radica able to recognize the wiry frame and bespectacled weasel features of Sanderson in the gloom, impeccably turned out as usual in his pinstripe. The sergeant pushed them forward, forcing them down onto their knees in front of him.

'Thank you sergeant, that will be all.' Radica instantly recognized that voice, turning her head with Marko to see the tall slender figure of Veronica emerging from the shadows, a black suited chauffeur stood waiting by a Mercedes S Class.

With a silent nod, the sergeant returned to the truck as the rear doors were pulled shut from the inside. Stepping up into the cab, the vehicle backed out into the morning light, the steel doors rolling shut with a heavy bang again as the overhead gantry lights flickered on. Veronica, dressed in her usual business attire, stood next to Sanderson, the bulge of her holster just discernible under her fastened jacket.

'Nice to see you again young lady,' announced Sanderson, noting Marko's surprised reaction. 'And so glad you kept our little secret, you know how we hate loose ends,' he continued, nodding to Veronica who began unbuttoning her jacket.

'Please,' Radica begged as her executioner produced her Glock.

'Oh I'm afraid it's much too late for begging now my dear,' Sanderson chuckled.

'I'm begging you please, you don't understand,' Radica pleaded.

'There's nothing to understand,' Veronica replied coldly.

'I love him,' Radica shouted, her voice echoing off the walls. 'I've loved him from the first moment I saw him,' she exclaimed, this time looking directly at Marko. Their eyes met for what they were both sure would be the last time, in that moment both praying that they would be reunited again someday, somewhere beyond this world.

Veronica raised the pistol to Marko's head, but he kept his gaze locked on Radica's, wanting her to be the last thing he saw.

'I'm glad I found you Radica,' he said softly with a brave smile.

The gunshot sounded in Marko's head, but there was no pain or blinding white light, and to his astonishment, Radica was still gazing at him. As the second shot rang out, they both looked up to see Veronica holstering her weapon, stood next to Sanderson slumped back wide eyed in his chair, the left lens of his blood splattered spectacles shattered, a gaping bullet hole where his eye had once been.

'Quickly, we don't have much time,' Veronica announced, quickly helping them to their feet and leading them still cuffed to the Mercedes, the chauffeur slumped on the ground in a pool of blood.

Marko and Radica clambered into the back seat as the steel doors began to roll open, Veronica jumping into the driver's seat, the engine starting with a growl, the Mercedes speeding out between the doors with inches to spare on either side.

'Please, tell us what's happening?' Radica begged as Veronica turned onto the main road, accelerating away. She didn't reply as she scanned for any sign of pursuit, Marko grasping Radica's hand to calm her.

Suddenly the car lurched sideways as they turned left into another industrial area, the Mercedes bumping over uneven concrete as they sped into a deserted concourse surrounded by dilapidated buildings towards a parked black BMW 7 series, two gorilla sized black suited bodyguards stood waiting, the form of the driver just visible through the windshield.

Approaching to open the rear doors as soon as the Mercedes screeched to a halt, Marko and Radica were powerless to resist as they were pulled from the vehicle. Stepping out of the car, Veronica stood face to face with Radica.

'I'm afraid it's time to say goodbye my dear,' she said, glancing at Marko.

'No, we belong together,' Marko protested, his minder restraining him as Radica was dragged away screaming towards the BMW.

'Where are you taking her?' Marko implored as she was bundled into the back seat, the door closing behind her, getting one last look at her staring pleadingly out of window as the BMW sped away.

'Don't worry, she'll be perfectly safe,' Veronica finally answered once the car had disappeared.

'But who the hell are you?'

'Just think of me as your fairy godmother,' Veronica suggested.

'Well you've got a strange way of showing it,' Marko protested.

'You do deserve an explanation, I grant you. Let's take a little trip down memory lane,' Veronica suggested, nodding over his shoulder at the bodyguard who led the way, getting into the driver's seat of the Mercedes, Veronica gesturing for Marko to get into the back before joining him. On the move again, they were quickly back on the main road.

'Where are we going?' Marko enquired.

'To your mansion of course.'

'I don't live in a mansion,' Marko replied surprised, yet already surmising.

'You do now,' Veronica replied, recognizing the look on his face.

'That's right, Aleksandar left you everything.'

'I don't want it, I'm done.'

'But don't you see, you're the king of the castle now.'

'I'm no king, I'm just a farm boy from Bosnia.'

'We both know that you're far more than that, and with me as your queen, just think what we could accomplish.'

'What do you mean?'

'Together, we can bring his empire crashing down Marko.'

'What difference will that make, there will always be others.'

'But don't you see, Aleksandar and O'Neil were just a small part of the puzzle, a mere cog in the wheel of an ancient organization so powerful that nobody has ever been able to get to them, until now.'

'And what if I say no?'

'You won't, not when you discover what they're doing to them.'

'To who?'

'Thousands of them, just like Radica.' It took Marko a moment to process what Veronica was saying.

'Thousands,' he murmured to himself.

'That's right Marko, and together we can stop it all.'

'I want her back with me first,' he replied after a long moment.

"As soon as it's safe for her to return, you have my word.'

Veronica's expression abruptly changed then, and she looked away, suddenly quiet and subdued.

'Tell me what happened?' she asked, looking out of the window, but not seeing.

'Happened, when?'

She turned back to him then, Marko seeing a strange pleading in her eyes, and in that moment he suddenly realized who she really was.

'Please, I need to know what happened to him that day,' she begged.

As he recalled how her husband had saved him, Veronica's eyes began to darken with sadness and when he described how he had died, she turned away to look out of the window again, wiping her teary eyes with the back of her hand. When she finally turned back to him, he had already snapped the chain around his neck, holding out the dog tags in his cuffed hands as an offering.

'He told me to give these to you, when the time finally came.'

She slowly reached out and took them, clasping them tightly in her hand as the tears ran down her face. Then she looked up at him, her eyes filled with rage.

'Are you ready Marko?'

He didn't need to reply, she could see the answer in his eyes.